VICTORIA BLAKE

SKIN AND BLISTER

An Orion paperback

First published in Great Britain in 2006
by Orion
This paperback edition published in 2007
by Orion Books Ltd,
Orion House, 5 Upper Saint Martin's Lane,
London, WC2H 9EA

An Hachette Livre UK company

1   3   5   7   9   10   8   6   4   2

A CIP catalogue record for this book
is available from the British Library.

ISBN 978-0-7528-8181-2

Typeset by Deltatype Ltd, Birkenhead, Merseyside

Printed and bound in Great Britain by
Mackays of Chatham plc, Chatham, Kent

The Orion Publishing Group's policy is to use papers that
are natural, renewable and recyclable products and made
from wood grown in sustainable forests. The logging and
manufacturing processes are expected to conform to the
environmental regulations of the country of origin.

www.orionbooks.co.uk

For my sisters –

Deborah, a fellow member of the six finger club and
Letitia, who taught me the alphabet.

ACKNOWLEDGEMENTS

I would like to thank the following: Maureen for being my first reader and so much more; Richard, Rose, Keir and Faith for the company of fellow writers and listening to the early drafts; Teresa Chris for being an integral part of the process; at Orion – Kate Mills, Genevieve Pegg, Alison Tullet, and Gaby Young; the National Missing Person's Helpline; Clues Unlimited in Tucson, Arizona for the description of Frank as the fattest cat in London, a description I embraced with open arms. The following books were helpful: *Oxford* by Jan Morris, *Oxford Observed* by Peter Snow, *The Nemesis File* by Paul Bruce, and *Fifty Dead Men Walking* by Martin McGartland.

PROLOGUE

He holds the card carefully by its edges, staring intently at the image. The man in the picture is carrying a lamb on his shoulder and holding a shepherd's crook; a long blue robe descends to his sandal-covered feet. His gaze lingers over the man's face the longest – such a kind face, a man you could trust, could turn to in a crisis, perhaps, someone who would help you, might save you even. He imagines burying his face in the blue cloth of the robe. *Forgive me Father for I have ...* He feels the man's hand come down on his head. He sighs, puts his fingers to his eyes and is disgusted to feel tears. If only it were true; if only it wasn't the load of bollocks he knows it to be. He knows he is beyond salvation. This time they've got him; he's trapped.

All his childhood people have used God to frighten him, to try and control him; the Jesuits scaring the living daylights out of him and always in the name of God. Beating the devil out of him, they called it. Well, it didn't work. He gently taps his chest. He's still in here.

Just waiting his chance.

Above the picture of Christ are the words *Sincere Sympathy*. He smiles – he likes the idea of using something that is supposed to bring sympathy, that is supposed to be a tender thing, to frighten and confuse. Yes, he likes that. He opens the card and reads:

Lord, grant eternal rest to the soul of Thy faithful servant and comfort and console those who have been bereaved.

He looks back at the picture. No one ever talks about why the good shepherd is saving the lambs. Why not? Finding lost sheep is not the end of the story. No, the end of the story is blood running from the throat of an animal into the earth.

The end of the story is slaughter.

He picks up a pen and opens the card again.

The Holy sacrifice of the Mass will be offered for the repose of the soul of— His pen hovers over the space left to fill in the name of the dead. He remembers his mother receiving lots of these when his dad died. She'd kept them all bundled up in green elastic bands at the back of the drawer in the kitchen. A fat lot of good they'd done her. It was what had given him the idea. When he thinks of her he feels the pain start in his stomach. He waits for it to subside and then, in neat block capitals, he fills in the name.

CHAPTER ONE

It was freezing up here. Sam Falconer tugged the hood of her parka over her head and tightened the toggles, pulling it securely round her face, as something that could best be described as a sea-fret began to blow steadily towards her. Unfortunately, she wasn't anywhere near the sea; she was standing on top of Magdalen Tower in Oxford, looking out towards Headington Hill, which was shrouded in a grey cloud of drizzle.

To make matters even worse it was five fifty-five in the morning. The weather had been schizophrenic all week, warm spring sunshine one day followed by ground frost and hail a couple of days later, so when the alarm had woken her at five o'clock in her parents' house in Park Town, North Oxford, she had been clinging to the vain hope that it might be a lovely morning. But a glance out of the window showed a rainy and windswept garden. For a second she considered just going back to bed, but then she dismissed that thought because May Day was when both town and gown celebrated the onset of spring, and Sam, despite the fact that she now lived in London, had barely missed a year.

She wiped a drop of rainwater from the end of her nose and peered over the parapet of Magdalen Tower down to ground level. Off to the right stretched the High, jam-packed with people, some sitting on the shoulders of friends, many of them amiably drunk and many wearing hats decked with cherry blossom. Directly under the tower was Magdalen Bridge and then, off to the left, the roundabout on the Plain.

Traffic was building up on the three roads that ran up to the roundabout, but it would be a while before any cars would be driving into Oxford. This was people power, pedestrian power; this was the one morning of the year when you could walk down the middle of the High surrounded by twelve thousand others, safe in the knowledge that you wouldn't be knocked over by a bus. The celebration of spring took precedence over everything else.

The safety barriers were not stopping the usual idiots from jumping off the bridge. Sam watched as a young man and woman stepped off the parapet into mid-air. Magdalen Bridge was twenty-five feet high and there was probably about three feet of water in the river, which was filled with the usual things that drunken students liked to throw in there – supermarket trolleys, bicycles and traffic cones. Oxford undergraduates were supposed to be bright, but they never seemed to be able to work out the likely outcome of taking part in this May Day ritual. There'd be the usual broken ankles, legs and ribs. Last year thirty people had ended up in hospital. Security staff and paramedics were helping the couple who had just jumped out of the water, and the wail of an ambulance could be heard in the distance.

Sam stamped her feet and glanced at her watch just as the bells all over Oxford began to chime the hour. The first was greeted with a roar from the crowd below and then a loud countdown began. As the last chime rang out, the crowd fell completely silent and the choristers, grouped on top of Magdalen Tower, a couple of feet away from where Sam was standing, their surplices swirling round their knees in the gusting wind, began their first hymn to welcome in the spring.

Sam pulled the sheet of paper that she'd been handed before she climbed the tower from her pocket and looked at the first line of the first verse the choir were singing.

Te deum Patrem colimus – the cogs and wheels of her Latin turned slowly and ineffectively. She quickly sought refuge in the translation printed on the back. *Thee father God we praise*.

Well fine, Sam thought, but I'd be inclined to praise you a whole lot more if you could lift the fog and get the sun to shine a bit.

On all the previous occasions she'd come, Sam had been down there amongst the crowd, straining to hear the singing, but this year her brother Mark, an English don at St Barnabas's College, had somehow managed to wangle tickets for the tower. She looked across to where Mark was standing.

Brother and sister could not have looked more different if they'd tried. Sam was five foot one, petite, with blonde curly hair and blue eyes. Mark was six foot four, with black hair, greying slightly at the temples, brown eyes and a gangly body that always seemed to be on the verge of a complete break-down of coordination.

Nor were they at all similar in temperament. Mark was kinder, more forgiving and had less of a temper; he was also exceptionally clever and had been bookish from a young age. Sam, on the other hand, had always been more physical and a much more fiery personality. Her mother said that she'd come out of the womb fighting. Despite these differences, they had always been exceptionally close.

Next to Mark stood Brendan. His arms were folded and the rain was dripping from the brim of a green baseball hat, jammed onto his head at such an angle that his face was completely obscured. Sam hadn't met him before and had been surprised to find him waiting with Mark outside St Barnabas's that morning. Usually May Day was something that she and her brother did together and Mark hadn't told her he was bringing anyone else along.

During the short walk from St Barnabas's to Magdalen, Sam had tried to figure out if he was a friend or a boyfriend, but the conversation hadn't covered anything other than the terrible weather and the number of different May Days that Sam and Mark had attended. One thing, however, was immediately obvious: Brendan was exceptionally handsome. With his high cheekbones, dark brown eyes and long eyelashes, he looked as if he'd stepped straight out of an aftershave ad, and his tall, lean body only added to his attractiveness. If he was Mark's boyfriend he was much better looking than any of the previous ones.

At that moment Mark glanced at her and grinned. He looked up at the grey skies and then back at Sam and rolled his eyes. Sam smiled but then shivered uncontrollably as a cold drop of rain, which had somehow managed to find its way between her collar and her neck, trickled slowly down her spine.

Afterwards they all had brunch in the Quod Bar on the High, their three coats hanging on the stand behind them, dripping steadily onto the wooden floor. The bar had filled up rapidly with damp, hungry people and the windows were so steamed up it was impossible to see the crowds now streaming away from Magdalen Bridge and into Radcliffe Square, where some of the Morris dancers would soon be performing in front of the university church of St Mary's.

'Well, thanks for that, Mark,' Sam said. 'A truly chilling experience.'

She leaned forwards, shaking the rain out of her mop of blonde curls onto the floor.

Mark laughed and suddenly flung out long legs covered in black jeans, forcing a waiter to take immediate evasive action. 'You can always rely on me to give you the experience of a lifetime. Mind you, can you remember a single warm May Day morning from our childhood?'

Sam shook her head. 'It was always a question of whether there'd be any flowers to put in your hat or whether there'd be a small tornado of rain-sodden laburnum, cherry and wisteria blossom whizzing several hundred feet up, over the roofs of North Oxford.'

Mark turned to Brendan, who was tucking into a breakfast of toast, smoked salmon and scrambled eggs. 'Because we lived in St Cuthbert's, in the centre of town, all our friends used to congregate at home on May Day morning.'

'All *your* friends did,' Sam said, 'before skipping school and going out to get blind drunk.'

'You tagged along. We bought you shandy.'

Sam wrinkled her nose. 'Only once. After that I moved swiftly on to Guinness.'

Mark put his hand on Brendan's arm. 'I mean she was only ten!'

Brendan put down his knife and fork and brushed a fringe of fine light brown hair away from his eyes. 'What's the age gap between you?' he asked.

'Eight years,' Mark said.

'So you grew up pretty fast then,' Brendan said to Sam.

Sam glanced at Mark. One way and another they'd both had to do that, but she wasn't sure what Mark had told Brendan about their past. She decided that discretion was the better part of valour and simply smiled and nodded her head.

She picked up her knife and fork as a large plate of bacon and eggs was placed in front of her. 'Do you have brothers and sisters?' she asked Brendan.

'Just one – a sister. She lives in Oxford as well.'

Sam watched him tucking into his food.

He wiped his mouth with a napkin and grinned at her. 'Do I pass?'

Sam blushed and picked up her cup of coffee. The truth was she wasn't sure yet.

Later, when Mark had gone to settle the bill, Brendan placed his clasped hands on the table and leaned towards Sam. 'I know you weren't expecting me to be here. I hope you don't feel I muscled in.'

'No, no, of course not. Anyway, traditions are there to be broken, aren't they?'

'A brave statement from someone brought up in an Oxford college.'

Sam smiled.

'So your father was head of St Cuthbert's?'

'Peter's my stepfather.'

'What was that like?'

'Being the child of the head of an Oxford college is a bit like being a regimental goat. You get dressed up when royalty come but you're expected to present flowers not eat them.'

He laughed. 'What did your father do?'

'He was in the army.'

'What does he do now?'

'He's retired.'

'Does he live in Oxford?'

Sam had opened her mouth to reply but Mark came back to their table and instead of answering she looked up at her brother and said, 'Shall we go?'

He's a bit inquisitive, Sam thought, as she followed Brendan and Mark out of the restaurant and across the High, but maybe he was just nervous and trying too hard to make a good impression.

Despite the continuing drizzle, they stopped in Radcliffe Square to watch the Morris dancers. Sam had always loved them – their pristine white shirts and trousers, their hats filled with blossom. They were waving their handkerchiefs, ringing the bells attached to their calves and clashing their sticks. Of course, she thought, May Day is really all

7

about sex; it's about men being able to strut around like peacocks.

A clown wearing a coat made of a multi-coloured rags moved round the dancers, whacking them on the backsides with a pig's bladder attached to the end of a stick. Next to the accordion player a large green fertility bush stood and periodically a pint of beer would be handed through the foliage to the person inside.

The first time she'd come, Mark had hoisted her up on his shoulders so she could get a better view and she'd ended up fascinated by the young boys taking part in the dancing who weren't much older than she was. There were a couple here today, sweet and solemn, concentrating hard on the steps, while their more confidant elders shook their tail feathers, cracked jokes while trying not to crack each other's knuckles, and flirted with the women in the crowd.

People cheered enthusiastically as one dance ended. It was beginning to rain more heavily now and someone opened a large golfing umbrella over the head of the accordion player. The crowd, a mixture of students, tourists and locals, didn't seem that bothered by the rain. A couple standing nearby, huddled under one raincoat, gazed into each other's eyes and kissed long and deep. It was still only seven in the morning but the crowd reeked of alcohol, many of them would have been up all night, drinking to welcome in the dawn; the hangovers would start to bite much later in the day.

Standing with her back to All Souls, looking across the square, Sam wondered how it was that the Radcliffe Camera, that swaggering Falstaff of a building, could still manage to look so elegant even when shrouded in rain.

Mark touched her arm. 'Shall we get going?'

She nodded and followed Mark and Brendan across the cobbles along Brasenose Lane and into the Turl towards St Barnabas's College. Mark's rooms were on the top floor of front quad and consisted of one huge living room with windows looking down onto the High and then leading off that a bathroom and a small bedroom.

'Sorry,' Mark said, waving his hands in the air, 'I hadn't quite got round . . .'

Sam grinned at him, picked a shirt off the seat of a leather armchair and sat down. Brendan did the same with a pair of trousers and threw himself onto the sofa.

Books were a predominant feature of Mark's rooms. There were floor-to-ceiling wooden bookshelves on either side of the fireplace, and teetering piles next to Mark's desk and by the side of the sofa and the chair. The table in front of Sam was also covered, as was the side table next to Brendan. Finally, the cushions had been removed from the window seats and books were double-banked along there as well. Sam knew that there would be more piles in the bathroom and next to Mark's bed.

'Chaos is come again,' she said.

Mark ran his hand through his hair, picked up the shirt and trousers and threw them into his bedroom. 'Right,' he said, closing the bedroom door. 'That's better.' He took some books off the sofa and sat down next to Brendan. 'I tend to tidy up for tutorials but the trouble is I make a point of never having them on May Day. I used to, but they were a complete waste of time. Even if my students have got an essay they can be so drunk their lips won't move properly to read out the words.'

Sam laughed. 'You're not tough enough on them.'

'You're right. I don't like being tough on them at all. Mind you, I've got one at the moment I need to keep an eye on. It's a shame because he's very bright, but if he doesn't get his act together soon he's going to be in serious trouble. I've stuck my neck out as far as I can for him.'

'His students always adore him,' she said to Brendan. 'They're always falling in love with him.'

Mark frowned. 'Don't be silly. That's not true.'

'You love your subject and teach it with passion. You care about them as individuals. You're always worrying about how to get the best out of them.'

'Well, they start off having to do *Beowulf* and after that some of them can take a lot of talking round. They're required to cover so much, but if you can find the thing that really gets them going – that spark that ignites their hearts and their heads – it can be life changing for them. That's what I aim for.'

'He's a great teacher,' she said. 'I should know. I was his first pupil – he taught me how to read and write when I was four, bribing me with stationery when I got the alphabet right.'

'L M N always caused problems,' Mark said.

'Try saying it fast and it still does.'

Mark laughed, walked into his bedroom and came back holding a bottle of champagne. 'What do you think?'

Give me a break, it's quarter to eight in the morning, is what Sam thought. But at least her stomach was lined with a large breakfast and it *was* May Day and it looked as if Mark had a new man in his life.

'I think, yes,' she said.

After a protracted hunt to find enough glasses, Mark popped the cork and poured the champagne.

Sam picked up her glass and stood up. 'To the first day of spring.'

All three of them turned and toasted the windows now lashed by driving rain.

Vera Smith stopped and looked down at the puddle of lumpy sick, dribbling from the top step that led into St Barnabas's College, and grimaced as the sour smell drifted upwards and reached her nose. When the college went mixed she'd hoped that the girls might have a good effect on the boys, but it hadn't turned out that way; they seemed to revel in being just as badly behaved. She stepped carefully over the puddle and through the wooden gate into front quad. She paused for a second in front of the *No Visitors* sign – after forty years' service as a scout in this college, she had certainly earned the right to walk past that notice.

She tapped on the glass window of the lodge and the porter, Bill, who was on the phone, put his hand over the receiver and mouthed, 'I know – Bernie's got it.' Vera nodded and at that moment saw Bernie walking towards her with a bucket and brush. Her nephew was a tall lumbering lad with bright orange hair and freckles. He stopped next to her, and as he put down the bucket, bleach replaced the smell of vomit in Vera's nose.

'Morning, Aunty.'

'All right, Bernie, lad – make sure you don't let the water stand on the step. You know what they're like round here with their heads in the clouds. We don't want any broken legs.'

He grinned at her and picked up the bucket. 'Don't worry, I'll do it right.'

He probably would as well. He was here on work experience and seemed to be getting on OK. He kept himself clean and tidy and his heart was in the right place. He'd cheerfully clear up a puddle of sick, and not many would do that these days. She sighed. If he kept making himself useful around the place, he'd probably still be here in forty years' time. Maybe that wouldn't be such a bad thing, because the days when young lads from Blackbird Leys could expect to follow their dads into the Cowley Works were long gone.

She walked stiffly along two sides of front quad, towards the room where the cleaning equipment was kept. There was much more activity in the college than usual, probably because it was easier to get up for May Day celebrations than lectures. She changed into a three-quarter-length blue nylon work coat and, after a quick chat with some of the other scouts, headed towards her staircase.

Vera had managed to outlast four provosts and was by far the oldest serving employee of the college. People thought colleges were all about the undergraduates, but they weren't. They came and went in three years. Three years was no time, not in the history of a place like this. Neither was forty, mind. For Vera the college was its staff: the porters, the cooks and cleaners, the electrician, the carpenter and the gardener and all the people who served in the kitchens. The undergraduates were almost incidental.

A young man came crashing down a staircase out into the quad, spinning away from Vera at the last minute like a top that's bumped against a wall.

'Sorry, sorry,' he said and dashed towards hall in a whirlwind of flailing limbs.

Worried about missing breakfast, Vera thought. Young men and their stomachs were all the same.

She began slowly climbing the staircase. At the end of last term the domestic bursar had suggested she concentrate on cleaning the ground-floor rooms, but Vera wasn't having it. If she agreed, she thought, it would be a preamble to getting rid of her. She might try to do that anyway, she'd asked to see her after she finished work today, but Vera wouldn't give her the excuse that she was no longer up to the job. Never give them an excuse to get rid of you. And anyway, she knew the other scouts would complain about her not pulling her weight. Vera didn't believe in things being easy. She believed in hard work as the answer to practically everything. You got nothing in life from taking the easy way out. If she'd learned anything from forty years of cleaning up after people that was it.

She winced as she reached the top of the staircase and paused to get her breath back. Briefly the faces of all the young men who had lived in this room flashed through her mind. One in particular stood out. Stephan with the unpronounceable surname ending in x and z and w. He'd been the music scholar, a lovely boy. That summer the drama society had put on *Private Lives* by Noel Coward in the Provost's garden and he'd invited her. And she'd gone, despite the protests of her husband, saying that she was making a fool of herself and that it wasn't for the likes of them. Vera had insisted: 'He's invited me and it'd be rude not to go.' Anyway, she liked the old songs. She remembered him at the piano singing 'Mad dogs and Englishmen', with the rain beating down on his head. She still got Christmas cards from him and postcards from all over the world – Brazil, Ibiza, San Francisco. It was more than she got from her own sons. She wondered why she was thinking of Stephan and then realised that the boy who was in this room now, Adrian Hunter, reminded her a bit of Stephan. He was blond, too, and always nice to her.

There was no bin outside the door but Vera still knocked; it was only polite – sometimes they forgot to put it outside if they didn't want to be disturbed and she didn't like to barge in on them unannounced and Adrian was a wild one. She put her key in the lock, turned it and pushed. The door didn't move. She pushed harder. It opened an inch. She stopped, puzzled. Behind her the door of the other room on this floor opened and Steve Price stepped out onto the staircase.

'Morning, Mrs Smith,' he said.

'Could you help me, love?' Vera said. 'This is stuck. I can't get it open.'

He put his shoulder to the door and it opened enough for him to put his head round and see what was causing the obstruction. 'Oh, God,' he said and pushed himself through the gap and behind the door. Vera followed him and immediately wished she hadn't.

Adrian was sprawled on the floor behind the door. His face was blue and his eyes were open, bulging obscenely from the sockets, the whites suffused with blood. His hands were curled up like claws; the nail of one finger had been torn off and lay next to his body. Vomit encrusted his mouth and the front of his shirt.

Vera swayed and grabbed hold of Steve.

'Shall I . . . ?' He made as if to move towards the body.

'No, don't, there's nothing you can do.'

'What shall . . . ?'

'Have you got a phone?'

Steve dug in his bag.

'Phone the lodge. Bill will know what to do.'

She left him making the phone call and walked out of the room. Suddenly she felt very tired and very old, as if all the forty years of work in this place had caught up with her at once. Poor boy, she thought, why was it always the ones you liked who ended up this way? This university could be a cruel place. She got to her feet and started slowly down the stairs. She knew the police would want to speak to her but she couldn't bear to wait here a moment longer, she just couldn't bear to.

A couple of hours had passed since Mark had opened the champagne and Sam was feeling nicely light-headed. She looked across to where Mark and Brendan were laughing on the sofa.

'How did you meet?' she asked.

'Well,' Brendan said, 'we could pretty it up but basically I picked him up in a pub.'

Mark caught Sam's eye and smiled.

'Which one?'

'You did warn me about her being a private investigator,' Brendan said. 'It's like being interviewed by the mother of the bride.'

All Sam's goodwill left her in an instant. 'Just to ask where you met is hardly—'

Mark leaned over and put his hand on her knee. She glanced at him and then back at Brendan. Keep this all nice and easy, she thought. Try and be charming, even if you think he's an arse-hole. Mark ran the ball of his thumb over the large red lump on the first joint of Sam's thumb, then turned to Brendan holding out her hand.

'This should interest you,' he said. 'We were both born with extra fingers. Sam's was the whole thing, with joints and a nail. They cut it off when she was a baby.'

Brendan nodded. 'And yours?'

Mark showed him the side of his little finger where there was a small fleshy lump the size of a lentil. 'Not nearly as interesting, I'm afraid. There was a skin tag there, which was tied off with a suture and it just fell off. It didn't have bones or anything. What's the medical term for it?'

Brendan shook his head. 'I can't remember.'

'He's a doctor,' Mark said to Sam. 'Did I tell you?'

'No,' Sam said. 'But the term is polydactyly or, in our case, hexadactyly.'

'How do you know that?'

Sam shrugged. 'I was bored one afternoon and Googled.'

They were interrupted by a knock on the door and Mark got up and opened it.

'Oh, hi, how are you? This is a surprise...' Sam heard him say and turned round as a very familiar voice replied, 'I'm sorry, Mark, but this isn't a social call, it's police business.'

DS Phil Howard, Sam's ex-boyfriend, hobbled into the room followed by a younger, fair-haired man, who he introduced as DC Woods.

'What's happened to you?' Sam asked.

'London Marathon.'

'Did you get round?'

'Yes, of course I did.'

Phil was wearing brown chinos, Doc Martens and a brown leather jacket. He'd lost a lot of weight since giving up drink and taking up running a few months ago and his clothes hung loose on him. Sam noted with disapproval that he'd reverted to the shaved head look, which gave him an aggressive demeanour completely at odds with his temperament.

'Mark, I need to talk to you in private,' Phil said.

Mark frowned. 'Why, what's happened?'

Phil glanced at the champagne bottle sitting on top of the mound of books on the coffee table. 'Been celebrating something?'

Sam felt anxious. 'What's happened, Phil?'

Phil turned towards Mark. 'Do you know an Adrian Hunter?'

'Yes, of course I do, he's one of my students. What's happened? Is he in some sort of trouble?'

'I'm sorry, Mark, but there's no easy way to put this. He's been found dead in his rooms.'

Mark's face was frozen in shock. Squeezing the back of his neck, he looked down at the floor. He glanced at Brendan and Sam and then back to Phil. 'Oh God. How awful. When did this happen?'

'His scout found him this morning when she tried to get in to clean his room.'

'What happened?'

'That's not clear yet. We were hoping you might be able to help us. I need you to come down to the station.'

Mark nodded and walked like an automaton towards the door. He picked his grey overcoat off the hook. 'Right,' he said.

'I'll come with you,' Sam said.

Mark looked at Sam and Brendan. 'I'm sorry about this.' His gesture at the champagne glasses and bottle indicating that he meant the sudden termination of their celebrations.

Sam was the last to leave the room. The sun had finally deigned to come out and was shining through the window onto the champagne bottle and glasses. She suddenly felt ashamed. It seemed obscene that they had been celebrating love and new life while a young man was lying dead in his rooms. She crossed the room, snatched the empty bottle off the table and dropped it into the bin next to Mark's desk, before following the others down the staircase and out into a front quad now flooded with spring sunlight.

CHAPTER TWO

Mark stood up and stepped over the bench he'd been sitting on, pulling his trousers away from the backs of his thighs. He reached over his shoulder and pulled the dark green lambswool sweater he was wearing over his head and dropped it down onto the bench on top of his overcoat. He was in a muck sweat and he was entirely innocent. He'd never had so much as a parking ticket. How on earth did people who were guilty or had something to hide feel when waiting to be interviewed by the police?

The room Phil had put him in was small and claustrophobic and everything that could be – benches, table, tape recorder – was bolted down. Mark wished he could do the same to his heart, which was hammering so hard in his chest he felt it was about to jump out and skid across the floor. He tried to calm his breathing. *There's nothing to worry about. You've done nothing wrong. It's all right. You've done absolutely nothing wrong.* He repeated this again and again, but the message wasn't getting through to his respiratory system. He was panting like a cat that had travelled too far in a hot car.

He licked his lips and leaned back against the wall, the upper parts of which were covered with a material that looked like hessian and made him think instantly of padded cells and screaming lunatics. He'd only been in here twenty minutes, but already it felt like an eternity.

He hoped he'd be able to talk to Phil. Mark had known Phil since he first went out with Sam ten years ago and he'd always liked him. He was an easy-going bloke with a laid-back temperament and had been very good for Sam – solid and dependable, a pressure valve for his combustible sister. The fact that they'd lasted as long as they had was in large part due to Phil's placid good temper. At least Phil had given her life some kind of balance during those years when she'd been in full-time judo training. He'd always thought it was a shame they'd split up.

The door opened and Phil came in together with DC Woods. Woods was holding two cups in his hands and had a brown file tucked under his arm. He put the cups on the table and sat down.

Phil did the same and said to Mark, 'Tea all right?'

'Tea would be fantastic.'

Mark also sat down and reached gratefully for the tea that Woods had placed in front of him but it was in one of those wobbly, white plastic cups and it was too hot to pick up. He leaned forwards and blew on the surface of the hot fluid, willing it to cool down quickly. He was desperately thirsty.

Phil turned on the tape and after a preamble that stated the date and time, who the interview was with, what the case was and that Mark had been told he could have a solicitor present but had not wanted one, the interview got under way.

'Right,' Phil said. 'Could you tell me when you last saw Adrian Hunter?'

'Yesterday afternoon. We had a tutorial between four and five.'

'By himself or with someone else.'

'I teach in pairs. Juliet Bartlett was with him.'

'How did he seem to you?'

Mark shrugged. 'I don't know – same as usual really.'

'And what was that like?'

Mark scratched his eyebrow. 'I don't know – intense, funny, very bright.'

'How long had you been teaching him for?'

'Since the autumn, so this was going to be his third term with me.'

'Did he have exams coming up?'

'No, he was in his second year.'

Mark gingerly picked up the beaker by its white moulded lip and sipped. It was still too hot.

'Nothing appeared out of the ordinary?'

Mark stared at the table. 'He was a scholar. We expect our scholars to get firsts, but his essay yesterday could best be described as mediocre. I had spoken to him at the end of his first year and told him that I thought he was putting in the minimum amount of effort. One exceptional piece of work a term wasn't enough. He needed to work more consistently or he would be in trouble come finals. He did better for a while but this term he had fallen back into old habits. He was late with his essays and missed one tutorial altogether. I held him back at the end of the tutorial and confronted him. I said I didn't want to see such originality and intelligence going to waste but if he didn't get his act together we would have to take away his scholarship.'

'How did he react?'

'He apologised and then blamed the summer. He said it was hard to stay inside and study when you could be out on the river.'

'And what did you say?'

'Well, privately I had a degree of sympathy with him. I can't remember doing that much work myself in the summer of my second year, but I told him that wasn't an excuse and it certainly wouldn't satisfy my colleagues.'

'Did he appear depressed or distracted in any way?'

Mark sighed. 'It's difficult to answer that. Students often turn up to tutorials in a somewhat abnormal state.'

'What do you mean?'

'The well-organised ones will have spent at least a week producing their essays. The less well-organised will have waited until a couple of days before the tutorial, panicked, rushed around trying to get hold of the books on the reading list, maybe managing to get about half of them. They will then have locked themselves away for twenty-four hours to get the work done. Consequently, they sometimes turn up at tutorials looking in need of a good wash and either barely able to keep their eyes open or hard-wired on caffeine.'

'And was Hunter in that kind of state?'

'Adrian seemed pretty wired.'

'On drugs?'

Mark shook his head. 'I don't know. His was quite a hyper individual, a nervous character. It could just have been that or it could have been something else. Sometimes lack of sleep can produce that kind of nervy energy.'

'Did he seem upset by your conversation?'

'No, I would say he was fairly blasé about it. Frankly, it seemed to me to be water off a duck's back.'

'Were you aware of him having any other particular problems or pressures?'

'Students live pressurised existences. I'm not aware of him being under any other than the usual ones.'

'Do you know if there was any reason why he might have wanted to take his own life?'

'Is that what happened?'

'It's one of the possibilities we're investigating.'

Mark shook his head. 'No, I haven't.'

'Did you meet him in any other capacity other than as his tutor?'

'I'm sorry?'

'Did you have any other contact with him outside of tutorials?'

Mark frowned. 'I have an annual drinks party for all my students each summer. I also belong to a college dining club, which has members from the senior, middle and junior common rooms. Adrian was a member of that and I met him socially on those occasions. Is that what you mean?'

'Did you know he was gay?'

'What?'

'Did you know he was gay? It's a fairly straightforward question, Mark.'

'I don't see what that has to do with anything.'

'Answer the question.'

'I suspected he might be. I didn't know for certain but—'

'What made you think he was?'

Mark's voice was tight with anger. 'Oh, come on, Phil! How on earth am I supposed to answer that?'

'By telling me the truth.'

Mark glared at Phil and remained silent.

Phil leaned forwards and placed his clasped hands on the table. 'Did he tell you he was gay?'

'No.'

'You had no discussions about his sexuality?'

'Of course we didn't. The sexuality of my students is absolutely none of my business.'

'How do you feel about tutors who have affairs with their students?'

Mark felt the blood rush to his face. He stood up abruptly, knocking his cup of tea over in the process. Phil and Wood moved back quickly as hot liquid ran across the table towards them.

'Fail the course on homophobia, did you, Phil?'

'Sit down,' Phil said.

'How does your logic work? I'm gay so I must be sleeping with my students? Funnily enough, Phil, not all gay men want to jump on any man that moves – that is a stereotype.'

'Sit down,' Phil repeated. Then to Woods: 'Get something to clear this up.' He nodded at the tea-covered table and floor. Woods nodded and left the room.

Mark was still standing, breathing heavily.

'Sit down, Mark, and calm down.'

'And why the hell should I, when you're being so bloody offensive?'

Woods came back into the room with a bunch of paper towels in his hands. He mopped the tea off the table and floor and threw them and the now empty cup in a bin by the door. Then all three of them sat back down again.

'I'll ask you the same question,' Phil said. 'How do you feel about tutors having affairs with their students?'

Mark folded his arms. 'That it's an abuse of power; that any relationship of that sort is bound to be unequal and fraught with difficulties: that it is something that I would never, ever contemplate. Teacher – pupil, therapist – patient, boss – employee, Clinton – Lewinsky. What's the difference? It's quite simply an abuse of power and is going to end in trouble.'

'But you must have had students come on to you?'

'No, I haven't, as it happens.'

'Never?'

'Look, Phil, I have a responsibility towards them. I'm there to teach them not seduce them. I make sure I'm clear with my boundaries.'

'And when you socialise with your students those boundaries stay in place?'

'Yes.'

'Even when you've had a few drinks?'

'Yes.'

'Were you sleeping with Adrian Hunter?'

'Come on, Phil, you know me. I can't believe you're asking me that.'

But Phil wasn't saying anything about what he did or didn't believe and shortly afterwards he brought the interview to a close.

They were back in Mark's rooms and Sam was sitting on the sofa, watching her brother pace up and down. She had rarely seen him so distraught. She was the one with the temper. She was the one with the tendency to see red and fly off the handle.

'I mean, Phil was treating me like some fucking paedophile. It's the oldest prejudice in the book, isn't it? You're gay so you must fancy little boys.'

'Adrian Hunter was hardly a little boy, Mark.'

'You know what I mean. He made me feel like a dirty old man pawing away at my students.'

'He was only doing his job.'

'Well, it felt personal, Sam.' He kicked the bin next to his desk savagely and the champagne bottle clattered back and forth inside it. 'I would never, ever go out with one of my students. It would put both of us in a difficult position.'

'But people do, don't they? We know that. Do you remember Redman in St Cuthbert's?'

At St Cuthbert's, their dining room had looked out onto the fellows' car park, so they had been able to observe the dons' comings and goings. One don in particular seemed to have a new young blonde every night, as well as a wife who was bringing up his young family in North Oxford. Sam's mother, Jean, had disapproved and muttered darkly about never trusting men who wore suede shoes, had bouffant hair and drove soft-top sports cars. As a child Sam had rather enjoyed his flamboyance; by the time she was twenty and he was hitting on her she was more of her mother's opinion.

'I'm not saying people don't. I'm just saying I never would. Of course people do. It's human nature. It's like Clinton said – he did it because he could. But you've got young impressionable people in your care. What I don't understand is why they're even asking me the question.'

'Maybe Adrian had put a rumour about. Maybe he told someone that was going on.'

'But why would he?'

Sam shrugged. 'Maybe he was pissed off with you confronting him on the standard of his work and wanted to spread rumours to undermine you. Maybe it was personal kudos – look at me I'm sleeping with my tutor. Maybe because he wished he could.'

'They said they might want to have me in for more questioning.'

'That's just standard procedure. Did Adrian leave a note?'

'They didn't tell me.'

'Do you know how he died?'

He shook his head.

'Do you want me to do a bit of digging around, Mark? I can give Phil a call and see what I can find out.'

Mark was staring off into the middle distance.

'Mark?'

'What did you say?'

'Do you want me to see what I can find out?'

'I'm not sure, Sam. Isn't that just going to look as if I've got something to hide?'

'Not if I do it carefully enough.'

He shook his head. 'No. I don't want you getting involved.'

Mark sat down on the sofa and a pile of books, which had been leaning against the arm, slid across the floor. He leaned forwards and scooped them into some kind of order.

'So, what's the story with Brendan?' Sam asked.

Mark shrugged. 'I don't know really. I'm sorry about the May Day thing. I know we usually do it just the two of us but he asked . . . I tried to put him off but he was quite insistent.'

'It doesn't matter. Neither of us ever said we couldn't bring other people.'

'I know, but we haven't before.'

'Is he—'

Mark cut across her. 'I don't really know what he is. It's too early to say.'

'He's certainly very good-looking.'

Mark smiled slightly. 'He is, isn't he? It puzzled me a bit.'

'What's the puzzle? Surely you just enjoy it?'

'I'm just not sure what he sees in me.'

'Don't be stupid,' Sam said.

'This isn't false modesty or anything. I'm just not used to men who look as if they've walked off the fashion pages of *GQ* showing any interest in me.'

'Well, that makes two of us. You said he's a doctor?'

'Yes.'

'Where does he work?'

'Like I said, Sam, it's the early stages. I'll fill you in more if it looks like going anywhere.'

'Fine. Interrogation over.'

The phone on Mark's desk went and he got up to answer it.

'Yes, yes, of course . . . bring them straight over.' He put down the phone but remained standing, staring down at his desk, his back to Sam.

Sam stood up. 'Do you want me to go?'

He turned round. 'No. Would you mind staying? That was Bill at the lodge. Adrian's parents have asked to see me. He's bringing them over now.'

A couple of minutes later there was a knock on the door and Mark opened it.

'Please come in,' he said. 'I'm so very sorry for your loss.'

Mr and Mrs Hunter came in to the room, shook hands with Mark and sat down next to each other on the sofa. Mr Hunter was a broad, squat man with wavy orange hair, a prominent forehead and small bright blue eyes; he had the heavily freckled face of the true redhead. He was wearing a pinstriped suit, which flashed a scarlet lining as he sat down. His wife was wearing a cream linen trouser suit with a turquoise silk scarf tied round her neck.

Mark explained who Sam was and asked if they minded her being there.

'No, it's fine,' Mrs Hunter said. Mr Hunter stared at Sam and said nothing.

Mrs Hunter continued. 'We just don't understand how this could have happened. We've come from the police station and they say that it's not clear how he died. There's going to have to be an inquest.

23

They asked us if he was suicidal. We just can't...' She stopped and looked at her husband, who was sitting next to her in silence, and then back at Mark. 'Were you aware of there being any particular problems? The police said he had a tutorial with you the day before he died.'

Mark shook his head. 'I am so, so sorry. I am absolutely shocked by what has happened. It has taken me completely by surprise. But there was nothing to suggest in the tutorial that anything was wrong.'

'Did he seem upset?'

'No. He did not appear distressed. I had a brief conversation with him about the standard of his work but he didn't seem particularly perturbed by that.'

Mr Hunter's gaze snapped onto Mark. 'Was there anything the matter with his work?'

'This year it had been inconsistent in standard. I had spoken about it to him before. I was disappointed in his essay. He had produced some truly exceptional work for me and he certainly had the ability to get a first if he applied himself.'

'So you were putting pressure on him?'

Mark rubbed his forehead hard with the fingertips of his right hand. 'Yes, if you like, I was. I didn't want him to throw his scholarship or his degree away. It would have been such a waste.'

'Worried about losing St Barnabas's position on top of the Norrington Table?'

'I was more worried that your son would not fulfil his truly exceptional potential.'

Mrs Hunter rested her hand on her husband's arm. 'Adrian had told us nothing of this.'

'Perhaps that's not particularly surprising. Were there any problems over the Easter vacation?'

Mrs Hunter glanced at her husband and then looked back at Mark. 'No, we only saw him for a few days. The rest of the time he said he was staying in a friend's house in Oxford and was going to study.'

'Had you heard from him this term?'

'A couple of times. Each time I phoned he told me how busy he was. He was on the May Ball committee and seemed to be enjoying that.'

Mr Hunter sat back in the sofa. 'You were his moral tutor, weren't you? Isn't that what it's called?'

'Yes, I was.'

'If he'd had any problems he should have been able to come to you, shouldn't he? Isn't that the point? He should have been able to talk to you about what was worrying him?'

'I am so sorry, Mr Hunter, but for whatever reason Adrian wasn't able to do that with any of us. I wish that he had. He was an exceptional student and I felt privileged to have known him and taught him.'

Outside in the quad a sudden burst of laughter punctured the heavy silence in the room.

Mr Hunter stood up and his wife followed suit. He ran his hand down the red silk tie that matched the lining of his jacket. 'I do not believe for one moment that my son killed himself but if he did and I discover that you or the college have in any way behaved negligently in your behaviour towards him . . .'

The sentence was left menacingly unfinished.

He strode across the room, opened the door and stepped out onto the staircase. His wife followed more slowly. At the door she stopped and shook Mark's hand.

'Forgive my husband, Professor Falconer, we're both shocked and upset. When he's had time to consider . . .'

Mark nodded. 'I understand completely and I really am so terribly sorry about what has happened. If you want to talk to me at a later point then please don't hesitate to get in touch.'

'Adrian always spoke of you with a great deal of admiration and affection.'

She turned and followed her husband down the stairs.

Mark walked over to the window and looked down onto the High. Sam joined him.

'He's just upset, Mark, and wanting to blame someone for what has happened. You mustn't take any notice of what he said. He'll probably phone and apologise.'

Mark sighed. 'He's a QC, Sam, I don't think phoning and apologising is in his repertoire of personal skills. And actually, I think he's got a point. I was Adrian's moral tutor. Twelve hours before he died he was sitting on that sofa. Why couldn't I see that something was wrong?'

'Maybe nothing was wrong. We don't know how he died. We don't know if it was suicide. Maybe it was an accident.'

Mark shook his head. 'I should have noticed. I should have seen something.'

'But that's what I'm saying, Mark. Maybe there was nothing to see.'

'I knew he had mood swings. Sometimes when he came to tutorials he seemed elated, at others I could barely get a word out of him. I should have asked more questions.'

'Come on, you're a teacher not a psychiatrist.'

'I know that,' Mark snapped. 'But we both know people can flounder. Some people go under here and never really come back up. Maybe Adrian Hunter was drowning not waving and I was his tutor. This isn't some self-indulgent exercise in self-flagellation. This is a cold-eyed assessment of what I did and didn't do. I'm asking myself – could I have done more? And the answer is – yes, of course I could. Instead, I told him he needed to work harder. It was probably the worst thing I could do. Maybe his father was right I was just concerned about a first going begging.'

'That's ridiculous. You've never simply viewed them as exam takers. You've always been interested in their whole education. You've never been results driven.'

'Don't be so naïve, Sam. Everyone these days is results driven and I should have asked more questions.'

'Well, why didn't you?'

'I was too eager to be the good guy. I didn't want to interfere. It was the summer. They're allowed to enjoy themselves. They're not machines.'

'All that sounds fair enough.'

'Just excuses to make me feel better.'

Sam grabbed hold of his arm and he turned away from the window and looked down at her. 'Let me do some digging about. If you think Mr Hunter is going to start throwing his weight around, let me see what I can find out.'

'No, I don't want you to. The police will be crawling all over everyone as it is. It'll only make matters worse.'

'It'll all blow over, Mark.'

Mark ran his hand from the back of his neck to the front of his head, making his hair stick out in all directions.

'Why did you say that thing to Brendan earlier about my students falling in love with me?'

'I was exaggerating to make a point. You know how highly they think of you. I was just trying to bring you out in a good light.'

'Well, I wish you hadn't. Suppose they question Brendan. Suppose he says—'

'Now you're just being paranoid. They've got no reason to question Brendan. He's got nothing to do with this.'

'You'd be feeling paranoid if you were in my situation.'

'It's going to be OK, Mark. Try not to worry.'

'You know, I had this weird feeling today. Oxford can have a febrile atmosphere in May. It's a combination of spring and exam anxiety, and then there are the May Day celebrations, the paganism of it. This morning I felt really happy and I was looking forward to seeing you, but at the same time some bit of me was saying: Don't rely on this. It can't possibly last.'

Sam picked up her bag. 'I'm sorry I have to go back to London but Alan's back from holiday tomorrow. I'll phone you this evening. It's going to be all right, Mark.'

From the expression on her brother's face it was obvious he didn't believe her.

Sam stood at the X90 bus stop outside Queen's, thinking that the death of Adrian Hunter could not have occurred at a worse time. Mark was vulnerable at the moment. The truth was the whole family were ever since her father, Geoffrey Falconer, ex-member of the SAS, had walked back into their lives. His return would have been traumatic enough, given that Sam had been told he'd been killed in Oman when she was four years old, but even worse were the revelations of what sort of man her father was – a violent man who had raped her mother and beaten Mark and admitted to the murder of forty men in Northern Ireland. He'd turned up in Oxford asking Mark for his forgiveness and Mark had been moody and withdrawn ever since.

The bus appeared round the top bend of the High and Sam dug in her pocket for her ticket. Although her first impression of Brendan had not been particularly favourable she hoped he was going to stick around. Then at least there'd be someone else keeping an eye on Mark while she was in London. She climbed the steps into the bus, showed the driver her ticket and took her seat. The only good thing to say about her father at the moment was that he seemed to have disappeared again. Long may it continue, she thought.

CHAPTER THREE

Sam got back into London that afternoon and went straight to her office on the fifth floor of the Riverview building. It was a horrible concrete block on the north side of Putney Bridge but it overlooked the Thames and was only ten minutes' walk from where she lived on the New King's Road. Alan was due back from holiday the following morning; he was an ex-policeman who worked for her part time and his working methods were somewhat more methodical than her own. She needed to get the place organised before his return.

She opened the post, did some billing and filing and was just about to sit down with a pad of paper and pencil and jot down the details of any answer-phone messages when the phone rang. Usually she would have let the answer-phone take it, but seeking some distraction from the boredom of office work she picked it up.

'Gentle Way Investigations, Sam Falconer speaking, how can I help you?'

'Oh hi, Sam, it's Reg here.'

Sam put her hand over the receiver and mouthed a silent and prolonged scream into the office. Reg Ellison was her therapist, or rather he had been until Sam stopped seeing him without an explanation six weeks ago. He'd been trying to get in touch with her ever since. He'd managed a lot of friendly conversations with Alan and Sam's home answer phone but none with Sam herself.

'Hello?' Reg said.

'Actually, I'm just flying out of the office . . .'

'Look, I don't want to hold you up, Sam, but I promise I'll be quick.'

She sighed. 'OK – shoot.'

'First off, I want to apologise.'

Sam grunted in amusement. 'I didn't think therapists did that sort of thing.'

'Well, I don't know about the others but this one does, especially when he makes a complete idiot of himself. I had no right to tell you how fast you should be going in your work with me. All that stuff about surrender . . .'

'And horses plunging into woods and not jumping fences,' Sam said.

He laughed. 'Well, yes – that as well. Look, what I wanted to say was that I don't know, OK. I don't know how fast you should go. We're in this together. You set the pace and I'll be there alongside, whatever that pace is.'

'I thought you were disappointed in me.'

'I'm sorry if it seemed that way. No, I wasn't disappointed. Actually, I was more frightened than disappointed.'

'Why frightened?'

'Another client of mine . . .' He paused as if unsure how to go on. 'He committed suicide.'

'I'm sorry.'

'So I was worried. I felt I ought to have spotted the signs, that I should have been able to help him. I'm afraid it made me rather over-anxious in my dealings with some of my other clients. So what I want to say is that I'm sorry that I talked to you in that way. If I were you I would have thought I was an arrogant idiot and I would have quit.'

'That's all right,' Sam said, because she couldn't think of anything else to say.

'I can understand if you don't want to resume therapy with me but if you did I'd be delighted to work with you again. Alternatively I could recommend someone else.'

'Right.'

'How have you been?'

'OK – my father's not been around and that's made it a lot easier to keep on an even keel. Stuff's been going on with my brother but . . . spring's here – that helps. I don't know why but . . .' She petered out.

'Anyway, you were saying you were in a hurry, so I don't want to hold you up. But will you give some thought as to whether you'd like to resume working with me?'

'Sure,' Sam said. 'Of course I will.'

'Perhaps I could contact you in a week or so and you could tell me what you've decided.'

'That'd be fine.'

She said goodbye, put down the phone and swung round in her chair to look out of the floor-to-ceiling windows. The bisecting vapour trails of a couple of planes were the only marks in a cloudless blue sky. Down below in Bishop's Park people were strolling in the early-evening sunshine. Sam decided she wanted to be amongst them. She scooped all the papers spread over her desk into a folder and put them in the bottom drawer, then locked up the office and took the lift down to the ground floor. Greg, the receptionist, was on the phone and she waved goodbye to him and stepped out onto the pavement. Rush-hour traffic was inching along the road in front of her. She dodged between the cars and ran down the stone steps on the other side of the road into Bishop's Park.

She went straight to the Embankment and began walking towards Craven Cottage. In a boat on the river a man with a megaphone was shouting instructions to a rowing eight.

She'd been expecting Reg to give her a hard time, to criticise her for not being committed enough, to tell her how bad and wrong she was, but he hadn't done any of that. Instead, he'd been honest with her and owned up to what was going on for him. Now the ball was firmly back in her court. What would she do?

She thought back to what she'd said to him: spring helps. Helps what exactly? To keep the demons at bay? To lift depression? But was she depressed? How could you tell? At what point did a sort of low-level dissatisfaction, misery and anxiety morph into full-blown depression? And how did one not feel depressed? How was that possible?

She hadn't really felt right since being forced to give up judo three and a half years ago. She had been an elite athlete, winning four world championships in an illustrious career. It wasn't as if she'd ever chosen to retire; the choice had been taken away from her by a chronic shoulder injury, and she was still struggling to come to terms with the loss of the sport she loved.

But that wasn't the only thing she'd been struggling with. In the last conversation they'd had before she'd quit therapy, Reg had accused her of not confronting something, of constantly evading it. And he'd been absolutely right. The return of her father had triggered nightmares and flashbacks she'd never had before.

What did he do to you? What do you remember of him?

Those were the questions Reg had asked her. Those were the questions she was evading.

One thing she had revealed to him was that she had started self-harming. She thought back to what he had said on the phone and then she realised what he hadn't said. His client had killed himself. She had told him she was self-harming. Of course, she thought, he was worried I was going to kill myself, worried enough to spend six weeks trying to get hold of me. She ran her finger over the scar on her neck from when she had tried to do that exact thing as a small child shortly after her father disappeared.

Should she go back into therapy? It was hardly a panacea. Somehow it had clouded everything, like stirring a stick in the muddy bottom of a clear running river. She didn't know what to do; the six-week absence of her father had helped. She hoped it would continue. She hoped she'd never see him again. She hadn't been self-harming during that time, and felt she could just about hold things together as long as he was out of the picture. It wasn't just for Mark's sake that she hoped he stayed away.

She reached the football ground and stood leaning over rusty green railings looking at the graffiti of a woman's face that had been sprayed onto the outside wall of the stadium. The trouble was that the nightmares and flashbacks that had brought her to therapy in the first place were still there, as strong and disturbing as ever.

She turned and began walking back the way she had come, but this time she turned left off the riverside path and walked across the grass under the avenue of huge plane trees. She stopped and looked at the red granite memorial to those who had fought in the Spanish Civil War in the International Brigade in 1936. *We went because our open eyes could see no other way*, was carved onto the monument. Sam considered the words 'open eyes'. Not easy, she thought, to look with truly open eyes at the world around you, let alone your own life. Maybe with Reg alongside it would be easier.

She glanced up at the groups of people scattered across the park, some sitting on the grass, some walking their dogs. Not many of them would be willing to go off and fight for another country in the cause of freedom – they were more interested in how much their properties had risen in value and getting their children into the right schools. I'm hardly rushing to do it myself, she thought. Suddenly Sam wondered about her own father. He had been a soldier, a member of the SAS. What had motivated him? Why had he joined up? She'd never known.

She tugged a piece of rosemary from one of the bushes that surrounded the memorial. Rosemary was for remembrance. But what was the point of having therapy if you didn't want to remember? She held it to her nose then stuffed it in her pocket and headed for home, still undecided about what she would say to Reg.

The following morning she was back at the office, clutching two take-away coffees from Caffè Nero on Putney High Street. She was using the wrist of the hand holding one cup to wedge the other cup against her stomach, in order to free up a hand to open the door, when it sprung open and Alan stood there smiling at her.

He was tall, with short, black hair and several earrings in one ear. A tight, white T-shirt was stretched over his muscular, tanned frame.

'Missed me, I bet.'

'Too bloody right I have.'

Sam put the cups down on her desk and turned to hug him. Six weeks ago, protecting an antique dealer in Portobello Road, he'd been stabbed, and in the weeks following his return to work things had not been easy. He'd been tetchy, exhausted and forgetful, and in the end Sam had told him to go off somewhere hot and have loads of sex. By the looks of him – tanned and relaxed – he'd done exactly that.

'So,' he said, letting go of her. 'How are things?'

Sam took off her coat and threw it over the coat stand by the door. 'No, you first.'

He spread his arms out wide and grinned at her. 'As you see.'

She smiled. 'So what's that – pretty damn made up with yourself?'

'I always believe in following my boss's orders to the letter and now you see before you an altered man.'

Sam sat on the edge of her desk and laughed. 'Look at you, you sexy beast. You look great.'

Alan walked over to his own desk. A jungle of plants filled the area behind it. The equivalent space behind Sam's desk was devoid of a single green living thing. Alan moved from plant to plant, prodding his finger into the earth of various pots and grunting approvingly. 'Well done,' he said. 'I thought they'd all be dead.'

'You left me a two-page memo covered in yellow highlights and warning messages in bold, underlined, capitals. A four-year-old could have kept them alive.'

He lifted an African violet. 'You watered these from underneath, right?'

'No, I tipped water all over their – to quote from your memo – "fleshy, hairy leaves", and waited for them to rot.'

He laughed. 'You'll have green fingers by the time I finish with you.'

Sam stared down at the palms of her hands and thought that extremely unlikely.

Alan sat down and put his feet up on his desk. 'So, what's been going on here while I've been away?'

'Reg managed to catch up with me yesterday.'

'Ah. What did he have to say for himself?'

'He wanted to apologise.'

Alan frowned. 'I thought the whole point of therapists was that they were godlike, could see straight through you and made sure it was always your fault. In fact, I thought that's what they were paid to do.'

'Reg isn't like that at all, but he wants me to think about going back into therapy.'

'And?'

Sam shrugged. 'I haven't made up my mind yet.'

'Anything else happen?'

'Actually, I'm afraid I may have to dump a lot of stuff onto you.'

'Just what a man wants to hear on his first day back.'

Sam rubbed the skin under her right eye. 'I know. I'm sorry, but I've got a feeling I'm going to have to spend some time in Oxford with Mark.'

'What's he been up to?'

'One of his students, an undergraduate called Adrian Hunter, has been found dead in his rooms and the police have as good as accused Mark of having an affair with him.'

Alan dropped his feet back down to the ground with a thump. 'Why?'

'Mark doesn't know.'

'I presume he wasn't?'

'Of course he wasn't.'

'The police wouldn't ask him that question out of the blue. They must have had . . .'

'I know. Mark's really upset. He had a tutorial with Adrian the day before he died and thinks he should have noticed something was wrong. To add to the difficulties, Hunter's father's a QC, who is looking for someone to blame. He was pretty unpleasant to Mark.'

'What's he accusing Mark of doing?'

'Being negligent in his care of his son.'

'How did he die?'

'We don't know that. I asked Mark if he wanted me to find out what was going on but he's adamant he doesn't want me involved.'

'Do the parents know their son was gay?'

'I've no idea.'

'Often people come out at University. It's the first time they're away from home. They're not going to walk down the street with their partner and bump into their parents. They're more anonymous. But telling your parents . . . that can take more time.'

'His father didn't look like he'd be the easiest person to tell.'

'Mothers usually know. Fathers . . .' Alan blew out his cheeks. 'That's another story.'

'If Hunter's father finds out that the police suspect Mark of having an affair with his son all hell's going to break loose. What I want to do is find out the source of that story.'

'If it was Hunter you're on a hiding to nothing. He's dead – he can't change his story.'

Sam nodded. 'I know, but I could still do a bit of asking about. Anyway, on a lighter note, Mark's got a new man on the horizon.'

'Have you met him?'

'Yes. He looks as if he's just stepped out of an aftershave ad.'

'Hunky then?'

'He's got the whole chiselled-jaw, seal-eyed thing going on.'

'Yes, but is he a nice person?' Alan said in fake earnest tones.

Sam laughed. 'It's too early to tell. Mark seems a bit iffy about him. Says he's not used to very good-looking men being interested in him.'

'He sounds too good to be true.'

'At least he bites his fingernails.'

Alan laughed. 'What is it with women and hands? I just don't get it.'

'Well, what turns you on?'

'Freddie Ljungberg in Calvin Kleins is more my kind of thing.'

There was a knock on the office door and it swung open. A man wearing a long black raincoat with a small blue rucksack slung over one shoulder stood in the doorway. He ran his hand over dark brown hair neatly cut to disguise the beginnings of a receding hairline. Sam reckoned he was in his early forties.

'Can I help you?' she asked.

'Are you Sam Falconer?'

He had the trace of an accent that Sam struggled to place.

'Yes.'

'Ah, well then, reckon I'm where I want to be.'

'Usually clients come in via reception,' Sam said.

'Yes, sorry about that, but he was a bit tied up with a courier and so I just checked out which floor you were on, jumped in the lift and came straight up.'

'So what can we do for you?'

The man glanced at Alan and then back at Sam. 'Would you mind if we talked privately?'

Alan looked at Sam and she nodded. He got to his feet. 'No problem – phone me when you're done.'

After Alan had left the room, Sam indicated the chair opposite her desk. 'Would you like to sit down?'

The man dropped his rucksack next to the chair and took off his raincoat. Underneath it he was wearing an expensive-looking black suit and a pale blue open-necked shirt. He hung the raincoat on the back of the chair and sat down.

Sam moved a pad of paper in front of her and picked up a pen.

He linked his hands together in his lap and began to rotate his thumbs around each other. Sam smiled encouragingly.

'How can I help you?'

His thumbs stopped spinning and his eyes darted from his hands to her face. He had brown eyes; two deep lines bracketed his mouth. 'It's not easy to begin . . .'

Marital problems, Sam thought wearily.

'Perhaps if you could start with the nature of the case then we could go from there.'

'What do you mean?'

'Well, is it a domestic matter, for example?'

The man barked a short sharp laugh. 'No, no, nothing like that.' He took a deep breath and then lapsed into silence again.

Sam doodled on her pad and listened to a bluebottle droning against the windowpane and the distant roar of traffic on Putney Bridge.

'I'm here under false pretences really.'

Sam was getting a bit fed up with waiting for him to spit it out. 'Would you like some water?'

He shook his head. 'This might explain it.' He unzipped his rucksack and took out a paper. It had been rolled into a tight cylinder. He flattened it, found the piece he wanted, turned it round and handed it to Sam.

Sam saw the headline: *SAS soldier admits to murder of forty republicans*. Underneath was a picture of her father. Then she placed the man's accent – Northern Ireland.

She felt her stomach lurch as if the floor had suddenly dropped away. She stood up, her hands gripping the edge of her desk. 'What do you want?'

He was also standing now, staring steadily at her. 'I don't know how else to say this, so I think it's best if I just spit it out. I think your father, Geoffrey Falconer, killed my father in Belfast in 1974 and I'm looking for someone who might be able to tell me where his body is buried.'

The conversation she'd had with her father just after this article was published six weeks before flooded into Sam's head.

'You're going to have to watch yourself, Sam. They've named you in the article. It may not just be the press who come after you.'

'What do you mean?'

'Payback time. Old republican tactics. If you can't get the man go for his family. Get him where it hurts.'

'You really think there's a risk?'

'They've printed the list. Now forty republican families know I killed their relative ... I'm warning you, Sam – this is serious. If anything odd happens, anything at all, get the hell out.'

Sam stared at the man standing in front of her and at the door behind him. She'd have to go through one to get to the other. He was leaning down, reaching into his rucksack again. Sam sprinted round her desk, grabbed the back of his jacket, pulled him away from the bag and applied a half nelson.

'Jesus, woman, what the hell do you think you're doing?'

She pushed him against the wall and kicked his legs apart, then ran her hands over him, dropping the contents of his pockets onto the floor – keys, change, a mobile phone, a wallet, a Tube pass. 'Stay exactly where you are,' she hissed in his ear.

She grabbed his bag and turned it upside down – an iPod, newspaper and paperback, an apple, a small bottle of water and a chocolate brownie in Pret a Manger wrapping fell out. When she looked up, he'd turned round and was sitting on the floor with his legs stretched out in front of him and his hands clasped in his lap, watching her. He picked up the apple, which had rolled across the room towards him, and tossed it in the air.

'You know, if you wanted to bruise my apples you only had to ask. I like to be accommodating that way.' He raised his knees and rested his forearms on them. 'So, am I to take the answer as no, then?'

Sam dropped his empty bag to the ground and stood there, not knowing what to do.

'If I get to my feet are you going to clobber me again?'

She didn't answer.

'In that case, maybe I just won't risk it.' He bit loudly into the apple and chomped. 'Maybe I'll just sit here and eat my apple and wait for you to make up your mind that I'm not going to do you any harm.' He leaned his head back against the wall and closed his eyes. 'You know, when I was coming along here I was trying to envisage what sort of person you'd be – a female private investigator – and all I could come up with was all those femme fatales from the old films, the ones that teeter in with furs wrapped round their necks and tell Bogie all those lies and he ends up slapping or bedding or something. And then there were those sour-faced secretaries, weren't there? typing away and being disapproving of the boss. So, I couldn't think what you'd look like, but now I've met you I can see you're more Bogart than Dietrich, aren't you? Even though you've got the curls all right. But you punch above your weight, don't you, and I suppose now I feel a little like the woman who's been slapped, if you see what I mean – a bit of a role reversal there, but then I never was any sort of a hard man, that's for sure.' He opened his eyes. 'Would you have decided now about whether you were going to hit me again or not?'

Sam had been hypnotised by the man's stream of consciousness but when he stopped talking she snapped out of it. 'Get out,' she said.

'Why not hear what I've got to say? Then, if the answer's still "no" I won't trouble you again.'

One part of her was thinking, Get rid of him; the other part was curious as hell. After a brief struggle the curious part won. 'OK, you've got five minutes.'

He stood up and began to pick up all the things scattered around him on the floor. Sam did the same with the things she'd emptied from his rucksack.

'Have you got a bin?' he said, showing her the apple core in his hand.

She kicked the bin round the side of the desk towards him and he threw in the core and sat down.

'Where to begin?' He rubbed the top of his right ear and looked into the middle distance, then his gaze shifted directly onto Sam. 'It's like this, I'm not interested in the rights and wrongs, in blame or in vengeance, in any of that stuff. I don't want to hurt you or your father. My father's name's not even listed in the article but he went missing at the same time. He was a friend of some of the people who *are* listed. I want to find out if your father remembers him, if he remembers him being one of the ones who was killed. And if he was, all I want are the bones of my father to bury – that's it for me. But until I've got that I feel like bloody Hamlet, you know, haunted. It would mean a lot to my mother and my brother and my sister, my aunts and uncles, to the whole family, if we could have that, if we could just have his body.'

'I'm not in contact with my father at the moment,' Sam said.

'Did he tell you anything about this?'

She shook her head. 'I don't have a close relationship with him.'

He raised his eyebrows. 'Is there anything that you could tell me that might help?'

'I'm sorry,' Sam said. 'I don't think there is.'

'Could I hire you?'

'It's not a case I'd be willing to take on.'

'Is there no way I could get you to reconsider?'

'No.'

'Well, then . . .' He stood up and picked up his bag. 'That's that, isn't it?'

Sam didn't really believe he'd given up that easily, but she didn't care. At that moment all she wanted was to get him out of her office.

He put his bag on the chair and searched inside. 'You were sort of my last hope, actually. Maybe this will bring it all to some kind of end.'

Even though Sam knew there wasn't anything in the bag that could hurt her, she felt a surge of anxiety, but when he turned round he was holding a small piece of paper in his hand, which he dropped on her desk.

'Why don't you come along? You might be interested for yourself.'

She picked it up. It was a ticket for a theatre company called Torn Roots; they were performing at the King's Head pub on Upper Street in Islington.

'I'm part of a theatre group working with people from all over the world who have been affected by war and terrorism. We use theatre as a way for people to express their feelings and try to move beyond the trauma of whatever they've suffered.'

Sam stayed silent.

'I know it sounds a bit like therapy but it's also powerful drama. Come.'

She shook her head. 'I'm not sure I'll be able to.'

He shrugged. 'Whatever – tonight's our last night. Last chance saloon.' He swung his bag over his shoulder and held out his hand. 'My name's Rick McGann, by the way.'

Sam stared at his hand and then took it. As their hands separated he clenched and unclenched his fingers. 'I'll never play the piano again.'

For the first time since she'd met him, Sam laughed.

'Definitely more Bogart than Dietrich.'

After he'd gone, Sam picked up the ticket and tapped it against the nails of her left hand. She wasn't thinking of her father or the bodies of the men he had killed in Northern Ireland and she wasn't thinking about Bogart and Dietrich. In fact, she wasn't really thinking at all. She was recalling how she'd felt as her hands ran over Rick McGann's body, across the front of his chest, around his waist, up under his jacket and across his back, down the front of his legs and up along the back of his legs. She was seeing him sitting on the floor with his legs stretched out in front of him and the contents of his pockets scattered around him, laughing at her. His image seemed somehow to have burnt itself into her retina.

When she finally got round to a thought it was simply this: Dear God, here comes trouble.

CHAPTER FOUR

Alan returned to the office half an hour after Rick McGann had left.

'How long has he been gone? You could have phoned. I've gone hyper on the number of cups of coffee I've just had.'

Sam was sitting with her back to him, looking out of the window, and didn't reply.

'Ground control to Major Sam . . .'

Sam looked round. 'Sorry – what did you say, Alan?'

'Your circuit's dead, there's . . .'

She smiled. 'Shut up. Anyway I bet you've been chatting up that pretty Italian boy in Caffè Nero.'

'Maybe I was, maybe I wasn't.' He walked over to his desk and sat down. 'Matrimonial was my best guess.'

She shook her head. 'I wish it had been. He saw the article that was published in the *Daily Tribune* about my father. He thinks Dad was responsible for killing his father and wanted to know if I had any information that would help him find the body.'

Alan froze. 'What did you tell him?'

'Well, first I threw him against the wall and frisked him.'

Alan grunted in amusement. 'That's my mighty mouse.'

'Then I told him there wasn't anything I could do for him.'

'Which isn't true, is it?'

'No, it's not.'

'Have you still got those maps your father left with you?'

Sam nodded.

'Then what happened?'

'He asked if he could hire me. I said no and then he gave me this.'
She handed the ticket to Alan.

'Torn Roots? What's that – a bad day at the hairdresser's?'

'It's a play he's in.'

'It's tonight.'

'Yes.'

'Are you going?'

'I don't know.'

'Sam?'

She shrugged.

'Why?'

Sam grimaced. 'Well, Alan...'

'Yes.'

'When I threw him against the wall...'

Alan folded his arms. 'Yes.'

'And then, when I ran my hands over him...'

'Come off it, Sam. You frisked him once and now you're saying you're attracted to him? That would be quick even for me.'

Sam scratched the back of her head. 'You're right. I'm probably being ridiculous. I'm probably confusing the arousal you get from adrenaline with something else. I was frightened when he pulled out that newspaper article, so...'

But Alan wasn't buying it. 'If you felt attracted to him, you felt that in a different place to where you feel fear.'

Sam was staring into the middle distance. 'It's probably nothing.'

Alan sat down at his desk and blew out his cheeks.

'What did you think?' Sam asked. 'Did you think he was attractive?'

'What's that got to do with it? It doesn't matter what *I* think.'

'But would you say he was in a general sort of way?'

'Sam...'

'You know what I mean.'

Alan didn't say anything, he just raised his eyebrows at her.

She shook her head and looked down at her desk. 'Shit, it's the whole May Day thing – spring, new life, maybe seeing Mark with someone new. Mark was talking about the atmosphere in Oxford being febrile.'

'And what does that mean in plain English.'

'Feverish. Maybe I'm suffering from spring fever. The other day I was thinking that I wasn't sure I'd ever really fallen in love.'

'What about Phil?'

'Well, I used to joke about falling head over heels because we met on a judo mat and I practised with him, but it wasn't really like that. It was gentler. You know, Phil didn't make too many demands on me and he understood about the judo. It was easy to sort of fall into a relationship with him but I was never really smitten. I mean, I've had lust-ups of course . . .'

'Lust-ups?'

'You know. Short-term relationships based on sex.'

He laughed. 'Oh, those. Usually disastrous and, in your case, with superficial charismatics.'

Sam considered this for a second. 'Phil isn't like that.'

'No, but all your shorter term ones have been.'

'God, you're right. Why's that?'

'I don't know. Ask Reg.'

She picked up the ticket. 'Anyway, I think I will go to the theatre tonight.'

'No kidding. But one thing, Sam.'

Sam was rubbing her eyebrow with the end of a biro. 'Yup.'

'There are two things going on here: first, you're attracted to him. Second, he wants your help in finding the body of his father, or he says that's what he wants. Don't let the one influence your decision about the other. He's got a strong incentive to act cute with you. The whole situation is murky right from the off.'

'Like a muddy river,' Sam muttered.

'What?'

'Nothing,' Sam said. 'Murky – yes, I'll bear that in mind.'

That evening Sam sat on top of a number nineteen bus as it turned left at the top of Sloane Street and began the U-turn that would end up with it travelling towards Hyde Park Corner, Green Park and Piccadilly.

It had taken her a ridiculously long time to get ready to go out. For years and years, Sam had lived in tracksuits and trainers and the big baggy martial arts uniform, the *judogi* – soft, comfortable, loose clothes. Now, three and a half years after she'd retired from competition, she'd added jeans and fleeces to the mix but not much else. She tended to buy clothes from the local charity shops and, very occasionally, new stuff from Gap Kids. Being five foot one posed certain problems in adult clothes shops, and she was fed up with having to give herself four-inch turn-ups. Generally speaking, she wore her clothes until they fell to pieces. Recently she had forced herself to go into Top Shop on Oxford Street but had come out feeling sick and slightly disorientated and with the feeling reinforced that she had no idea how to look fashionable and feel comfortable at the same time.

All this became a problem when she met someone she was attracted to because she knew you were supposed to look as if you'd made an effort. In the end she had opted once again for the all-black look – jeans, shoes, jumper and leather jacket. The moths flying round her flat had eaten an enormous hole in the back of the jumper, but as long as she kept the jacket on she should be fine. The application of bright red lipstick had been the finishing touch.

The bus lurched to a halt and Sam was hurled forwards against the back of the seat in front of her. The number nineteen drivers were amongst the most psychotic in London. She righted herself and thought back to what Alan had said. He was absolutely right, of course.

Murky just about summed it up.

If she'd never been 'in love', it didn't mean she hadn't gone out with people, slept with them, gone through the motions of relationships. No, it didn't mean that, and the sex she'd generally enjoyed. It was all the other stuff she had a problem with; the things you were supposed to want to do in a relationship. The trouble was she didn't want to do any of them and as for living with someone, that had always been out of the question because she knew one thing above everything else: she had to have somewhere to go where she could be alone and unobserved. She had to have time to herself, for it was in solitude that she found tranquillity and a strong sense of herself.

Too much intimacy left her frayed and exhausted.

Phil had understood all this. He'd understood but he'd never found it easy because he had wanted to spend time with her, lots of it, and Sam had often found herself in the position of telling him why she had to be going now and not to take it personally. It was a miracle they'd lasted as long as they had.

But recently Sam had been thinking that maybe you reached a certain time in your life when such an attitude became simply pathetic. A couple of months ago someone described as a cat-loving loner had decapitated a man in Belsize Park. Cat-loving loner was a pretty accurate description of her. How many more years would it take for her to turn into a machete-wielding psycho? In essence, the question was this: would she turn into a right sad fucker and not even notice? In fact, had that happened already? And if it had was she prepared to do anything about it?

As the bus turned right at the top of Charing Cross Road into New Oxford Street, Sam thought of the first boy she'd ever slept with. Black-haired, loose-limbed and flat-stomached, she'd watched him standing on the waltzers in St Giles fair in Oxford, spinning the cars and making the girls scream. The music had been thumping out – Diana Ross singing 'Upside Down' and Sam had thought, Yes, you'll do – because she'd just wanted to be rid of it.

Virginity – who the hell wanted that?

She'd taken him to the University Parks and they'd squeezed through a gap in the railings and done it under the trees. Afterwards, lying on the grass with her hands behind her head, looking up at him as he tucked in his shirt, she'd laughed out loud.

He'd been instantly suspicious. 'What you laughing about?'

'The bloody relief to be rid of it,' she said.

Then his smile had mirrored hers. 'I'm moving on tomorrow.'

'I know.'

That's why she'd chosen this day, because tomorrow they'd be gone. No strings attached. Off he'd go and she'd be free of him.

He pulled the black leather belt tight and checked the buttons of his flies. In the background was the noise of the fair and fools falling in love. I'm no fool, Sam thought, looking at him. You haven't turned me upside down and I haven't fallen in love with you. You just helped me get rid of something I didn't want to have any more.

'Are you coming?'

Sam shook her head.

'See you next year,' he said.

She raised herself up on her elbows. 'Maybe . . .'

Then she'd watched him lope towards the railings and disappear and she'd known she'd never see him again.

With a jolt of alarm she realised who Rick McGann reminded her of. It was that boy, the boy she had so prided herself in waving goodbye to without a qualm. Well, there was a sort of poetic justice to that. She thought she'd been so clever about it, so very neat and tidy and now, here he was fifteen years later come back to haunt her.

Sam had been so lost in thought that she hadn't been paying attention to where she was. She looked out of the window and realised with a shock that the bus had gone past the King's Head and was about to round Highbury Corner. She swore, jumped to her feet, pushed the bell and headed for the steps.

All the Routemaster number nineteen buses had been taken out of service; Sam had loved the open platforms, which meant you could get on and off whenever you wanted. She stared at the doors in front of her and fumed. She hated these new ones; their suspensions made her feel sick. She had to wait for the bus to get to the stop in St Paul's Road before getting off and jogging her way back down Upper Street.

By the time Sam reached the pub she was late. She pushed her way through the crowds of drinkers to the theatre and showed her ticket to the usher. He pointed to the middle of the front row. Sam looked desperately to the back of the theatre, hoping that it wasn't full and that she could sneak into an empty seat, anywhere other than at the front, but the lights began to dim and she just had time to take her place before the performance began.

The piece was harrowing and involved personal testimonies from almost every strife-ridden part of the world – there were Israelis and Palestinians, Serbs and Croats, Sunni and Shiah, Protestants and Catholics and there were Chileans and Argentinians, there were white South Africans and black South Africans and there were people who had lost relatives on September 11th.

It was unremitting in its portrayal of the tragedy of conflict and the terrible consequences of communities torn apart by hatred and sectarian violence.

And there was no interval.

If there had been Sam would probably have left but positioned in the front, she was far too self-conscious to think of walking out right in the middle. Also, given the personal nature of the material, she felt it would have been disrespectful.

Rick's was the last testimony. He came on-stage lit up by a single spotlight and spoke:

My father disappeared in 1974 when I was ten years old. My mother was expecting him home for his tea as usual and he just didn't turn up. Over thirty years later she's still waiting. She still gets the tea ready but now it's for my brother. He was sixteen when Dad disappeared and doing well at school, but after Dad went missing he had to leave and go to work at my uncle's garage to help my mum. He's never left home. Still comes in every evening to my mother and the tea she was making for my father. At the age of sixteen he had to become the man of the family, but part of him never got older than sixteen. He says he can't leave her.

It's tortured my mother over the years. Suppose he just upped and left. People do that, after all. Suppose her Jimmy just abandoned her with three children to look after. She's old and tired now, but she's still wondering. She wants to know what happened. She wants to know where he is. She wants his body to bury.

I used to think I could save her, that if only I could find out what happened and find his body then she'd be able to die knowing and at peace, but it doesn't look like that's going to happen now.

I can't save my mother. Some days I feel as if I can barely save myself.

There was a time when I was filled with hatred, but I didn't even know who to hate.

I want an explanation but I know we may never get one.

In the end, all you can do is live with not knowing. The truth is one day in 1974 when I was ten years old my dad didn't come back for his tea and we don't know what happened to him. You cannot search for ever. Can you? At some point you have to put your hands up and say: it's over.

His gaze fell on Sam, or at any rate she thought it did, just as the lights cut out. Next, all those who had taken part came on-stage holding placards bearing large photos of their dead and missing. The placards jostled against each other, the lights gradually coming off the people holding them and shining just on the photos so they seemed suspended in the air. The lighting turned from white to blood red.

It remained like that for thirty seconds before the theatre was plunged into darkness.

After the applause died down Sam stayed in her seat while the rest of the audience got up and began to leave. The piece had left her extremely uncomfortable because it directly confronted the effects of violence and abuse on those left behind. It was the very thing she was frightened of doing with Reg. She felt upset. Suppose her father *had* been responsible for the death of Rick's. Forty people. That was the number Geoffrey Falconer had admitted killing. Forty families left wondering what had happened to their loved ones. So much extended suffering. Even though she wasn't responsible, she felt guilt by association. She sat there, not wanting to go out and face him, wondering if he'd told the others who she was and that she'd refused to help him, wondering how they'd feel about her. As the child of a perpetrator, where was her place in all this? Surely there wasn't one.

She got slowly to her feet and joined the last people leaving the theatre. Although she'd been affected by what she'd seen and felt sympathetic to what Rick had said, all her instincts were telling her to get the hell out and never see him again. This was complicated and potentially very, very dangerous. The trouble was she did have information that might help him; she just wasn't sure what the consequences of handing that information over would be.

She had decided to leave straight away but as she reached the doors of the pub, she felt a hand on her shoulder and turned to see Rick smiling at her.

'You came,' he said.

'Seems so,' Sam replied.

He gestured to where a large group of those who had taken part in the show were sitting. 'Come and have a drink with us.'

Sam shook her head. 'I'm sorry . . .'

'Oh come on,' he said, putting an arm round her shoulder. 'We won't bite, I promise.'

She allowed herself to be led back into the crowded pub to a table where seven pints of Guinness stood on a metal tray.

'Here,' he said, handing her one and picking one up himself. 'Cheers.' He tapped her glass with his.

Sam sipped in silence. Rick wiped the cream of the Guinness from his top lip. 'Ah, that's better – that kind of stuff doesn't half give you a thirst.'

Sam nodded.

'So, what did you think of it?'

'You don't pull any punches.'

'There'd be no point. To be honest, with this sort of theatre either it's truthful or it's nothing.'

'I suppose . . .'

A tall, thin woman with very short blonde hair, wearing glasses with narrow rectangular lenses surrounded by black frames came up and kissed him on the cheek. 'I loved it,' she said. 'Are you taking it to Edinburgh?'

He shook his head. 'The venues are so pricey. We wouldn't make any money there.'

'You'd get publicity.'

'I'm not so sure in amongst all that competition.'

'Well, let me know if you do. It'd be great to see you up there.'

Sam, who didn't have anything to contribute to the conversation and was feeling nervous and un-arty, was drinking her Guinness as if she'd just spent forty days in the desert. She was also heating up and wishing she hadn't chosen to wear a jumper with an enormous hole in the back. The woman left and Rick turned back to her. He looked at her empty glass with surprise.

'Another?'

She put her glass down on the table. 'I have to be going.'

'Well . . .'

She put her hands in her pockets and took a step backwards. Rick put down his pint, took a step towards her and kissed her on the cheek. Sam half smiled and turned towards the door. She had to go now. If she stayed she'd just get drunk.

'Sam . . . ?'

Oh sod it, she thought. How often does a man I'm attracted to cross my line of vision? She turned round. 'Let me get you one. Same again?'

His face split into a broad grin and he nodded. Sam picked up their empty glasses and pushed her way towards the bar. A couple of minutes later she was back, handing Rick a pint.

'So, how did you get involved in all this?' she asked.

'Well, there's this cliché in Northern Ireland, you know, that the men go out and fight and it's the women who are left to pick up the pieces and talk about peace. I didn't want to be one of those men – that was the beginning of it. It's too easy a path to go down. You start as a kid, picking up plastic bullets and selling them to American journalists and before you know where you are, you're throwing petrol bombs at Saracens and then driving taxis for the IRA. A lot of my friends went down that route.'

'How come you didn't?'

'It was really my mum and my brother. I was good at school and they insisted I get myself an education. I was the first one of my family to go to college and get a degree. After that, I became involved in a community theatre group called Crossing Borders and then with a theatre company called Tinderbox. We started putting together workshop programmes for schools, youth groups and adult community groups – we did plays on marching, policing and reconciliation between prisoners and victims. We also do anti-bullying workshops. I've been involved with Torn Roots for a couple of years now. It seemed a natural thing to extend the remit of the work to conflict worldwide.'

Sam sipped her pint.

He touched her arm. 'God, it makes me sound like some terrible do-gooder, doesn't it?'

She smiled.

'The truth is I do it because it makes me feel better and gives me hope. And those are pretty selfish reasons, aren't they?'

'Well, thank God for that,' Sam said. 'I was just about to put on some dark glasses.'

He raised his eyebrows.

'To stop myself being blinded by your halo.'

He laughed. 'I'm no saint, Sam, I tell you. You'll find that out soon enough.'

Give me a chance, Sam thought. Just give me half a chance and I'll take it.

A couple of hours later and Sam had lost count of the number of pints she'd had. All she knew was that saying anything, even the cat sat on the mat, would have been a challenge. She was sitting down, squashed between Bruno, a huge Croat with a crew cut, high cheekbones and a goatee beard, and a cousin of Rick's called Kieran McGann.

Kieran had a square solid physique and sandy hair. He looked older than Rick and was wearing a blue sweatshirt, jeans and a pair of heavily scuffed Timberlands. Rick was sitting on the other side of the table.

She closed her eyes and then, realising that she had reached the stage of drunkenness where that was not such a good idea, opened them again. Kieran was smiling at her.

'For someone who's pint sized herself you can't half pack it away.'

Sam grinned inanely back at him, tried to pat his knee but ended up patting her own. 'Have you come as a spectator or are you involved in some way?'

'A bit of both. Rick gets me work here and there when he can. I help out on the set. Anything technical that needs doing – general dogsbody, you know. It keeps me ticking over between jobs.'

'What do you do?'

'A bit of building work. Anything I can pick up.'

'What do you think of the show?'

He whispered in her ear. 'Between you and me I think it's a load of old bollocks.' He winked at her. 'An eye for an eye is my way of thinking about things.'

Sam laughed, thinking he was joking, but when she looked at him his face looked as if it was carved in stone; the only part of it moving was the muscle in his jaw. With a jolt of alarm she realised he was deadly serious.

'Well,' she said, keeping her tone light. 'It's a point of view.'

'Don't do an anti-bullying workshop just teach them how to box. Break someone's nose and they won't come after you again. Pick up a baseball bat and it always makes them think twice.'

'I teach self-defence classes,' Sam said. 'I agree it's important that people can look after themselves.'

'How did Rick get on with you today?'

'Sorry?'

'He came to see you, didn't he?'

'He told you about that?'

'Of course he did. I'm his cousin – it's my uncle we're talking about.'

'I'm afraid I'm not in a position to help him.'

'What are you doing here then?'

Sam shrugged. 'Free ticket – I was curious.'

'You're father's Geoffrey Falconer, isn't he? I read the article about him. He's still alive, isn't he?'

'Yes, but I'm not in contact with him. I can't help Rick.'

'Seems to me that's the least you could do. He's a good lad – Ricky. He does a lot for other people. It'd be good if someone could help him for a change. You know, tonight he did all right with his bit, but sometimes I've seen him do it and he barely gets through it. It can be heartbreaking to watch him. I've seen him struggle with it long enough. I reckon you should do something about it.'

'Look, I've genuinely no idea where my father is at the moment.'

'Oxford – isn't that where you were raised?'

'Yes, but my father's got nothing to do with Oxford.'

'Couldn't you find out where he is if you wanted to? You're a private investigator, aren't you?'

Sam didn't say anything.

He picked up his pint. 'That Blenheim's a beautiful place now, isn't it? I went round the grounds the other day.'

'What took you there?'

'Friends in the area.'

Sam nodded. 'As children we were always taken to Woodstock in the week before Christmas for lunch at the Bear.'

'We?'

'My brother and me.'

He raised his right shoulder, winced and then rotated it round and round.

Sam tapped her right shoulder. 'Dislocated three times. Brought my career to an end.'

'And what career was that?'

'Judo. What's the matter with yours?'

'General wear and tear. Neck, back, shoulder, knee ... take your pick. Work in the building industry long enough and something will start to give out.'

A tall woman with wavy dark brown shoulder-length hair walked up to the table. Rick stood up and greeted her.

He waved at Sam. 'Scoot out,' he said. 'I want you to meet someone.'

Sam was way beyond 'scooting'. She blundered past Bruno, stamping on his feet and falling backwards into his lap. He patted her amiably on the backside and continued the conversation he was having with the woman sitting opposite him. As Sam staggered out from behind the table, she realised that the woman had taken part in the performance. She was Chilean and her father had been part of the opposition to Pinochet's regime and had been murdered. She was wearing a bold red and white forties-style dress with a plunging neckline. Sam couldn't help but notice that it appeared to have been sprayed onto a classic hourglass figure.

Rick put his arm round the woman's waist and said, 'I'd like you to meet Isabel, my wife.'

Sam felt as if someone had instantly botoxed every muscle in her face and injected concrete into her jaw. She knew she was way too drunk to receive this piece of information with any degree of graciousness. She forced herself to smile and put out her hand. 'Very glad to meet you,' she said. 'I'm sorry, but I have to go now.'

She turned on her heels and headed straight for the doors. Rick caught up with her outside on the pavement. 'Hold on, Sam.'

She looked at him and wondered if he was as drunk as she was; shit, he didn't look it. He was scribbling on a piece of paper.

'If you change your mind. If there's anything you could tell me that might help me find him.'

He held out the piece of paper but Sam didn't take it. Her head was swimming and she was seeing about three bits of paper. When she still didn't take it, he leaned forward and stuffed it in her jacket pocket.

'Are you OK to get home?'

'No, I need a knight and a fucking white charger,' Sam snapped.

He blinked as if she'd slapped him. 'Sorry, I didn't mean— It's just . . .'

She turned away, saw her bus coming into view and lurched across the road to catch it. Inside she slumped onto a downstairs seat and banged her head gently against the window.

'What the hell do you think you're doing to yourself?' she muttered and then, lapsing into drunken self-pity, 'He was much too good-looking for you anyway.'

Now she had something else burnt into her retina: his beautiful bloody wife.

She groaned out loud, closed her eyes and fell into a drunken doze. She missed her stop on the King's Road and woke, as the bus was about to go over Battersea Bridge. She couldn't be bothered to go back up Beaufort Street to get the number twenty-two and instead decided to walk. She dug in her pocket and pulled out the piece of paper with Rick's number on it, scrunched it into a hard pellet and then flicked it into the river. She knew herself too well. If she kept it she'd phone. Now she couldn't. Half an hour later she got home, threw some food down for her hairy orang-utan of a cat, Frank Cooper, and crashed into a drink-soaked sleep.

CHAPTER FIVE

She surfaced first at six, staggered to the bathroom and then crawled back into bed, finally getting up around eight when Frank's gentle raking of her eyelids could no longer be ignored.

In the kitchen, she stood over the boiling kettle, trying to persuade herself that this wasn't the worst hangover she'd ever had and that the lining of her brain wasn't stuck to the inside of her skull. Her previous all-time worst ever hangover had been from four pints of Guinness and a bottle of red wine but this was four pints of Guinness and about ten bottles of self-loathing – and it was much, much worse.

Something was filling her with dread and it wasn't Rick McGann's wife or Adrian Hunter's father or indecision about therapy with Reg; there on the calendar in large red capital letters was the word VET. Today Frank had an appointment for his annual injections. She looked at him spread out on the kitchen table in a patch of sun and sighed. Several mugs of very strong coffee would need to slide down her throat before she could even begin to contemplate any action.

An hour later, feeling slightly more alert and having taken Frank's basket out of the cupboard as quietly as possible, Sam tentatively eased her hands under his armpits. Frank let out a low unearthly growl and twisted himself out of her hands with the agility of a contortionist. He bolted down the hall and scratched his way to the top of a bookcase, where he sat down, folded up his paws and examined Sam as if she were an unusual and disgusting insect that he was interested in looking at but wanted to keep as much distance from as possible.

Round one – Frank.

A couple of minutes later Sam was teetering on top of a ladder with an oven-glove-clad hand clasped round Frank's tail. As she began to drag him towards her he whipped round, clipped her across the nose with one paw and sank his teeth into the oven glove. Then he clawed his way over Sam's shoulder, sprang onto the sofa and disappeared into the bedroom.

In the bathroom she dabbed antiseptic on the cut on her nose and the claw marks on her shoulder. She went to look for him and found him under the wardrobe in the bedroom, his green eyes winking at her malevolently from among the dust balls.

Round two – Frank.

Time to call in the heavy squad.

She picked up the phone and explained the situation to her next-door neighbour, Edie.

Edie and Sam sat on the end of her bed with a plate of prawns at their feet. Edie was wearing a voluminous red T-shirt with *Costa del Sol – Benalmadena* printed on it in white letters, black tracksuit bottoms, yellow socks and furry light blue slippers with appliquéd kittens on them. Her hair was scraped back in a bun and contained not one thread of white amongst the brown, not bad for someone approaching eighty.

'Vets!' Edie snorted. 'Snowy lived to twenty-one and he never had a jab in his life. What happened to your nose?'

'What do you think happened, Edie?'

'Poor baby,' Edie said, waving a prawn in Frank's direction. 'You got her good and proper, didn't you?'

Edie, Sam thought, was the kind of person who could sow dissension among the saints.

Five minutes later Frank was creeping towards the dish; mind you, he always looked as if he was creeping because his stomach was so low to the ground. His lips had just curled around a prawn when Edie's hand clamped onto the back of his neck.

'Basket!' she shouted.

Sam opened the basket, Edie stuffed Frank inside, whipped her hand away and Sam slammed the lid shut and did up the straps that held it down.

Round three – Edie.

The surgery was only a fifteen-minute drive away but unfortunately it involved going over about a hundred traffic-calming bumps and Frank had the capacity to be sick on a straight, flat road with the car travelling at two miles an hour. So when Sam placed the basket on the examining table and opened it, both she and the vet, a young Australian called Nicky, took an involuntary step backwards.

Frank emerged and began sniffing the edge of the table while the vet grabbed some paper towels and began cleaning him and the basket. When she had finished she held his head in both hands and looked into his eyes. Frank blinked. Then she looked in his ears. Frank shook his head. Then she opened his mouth and looked at his teeth. Frank drooled.

'He has a build-up of tartar on his teeth,' she said.

Oh, give him the injection and shut up, Sam thought.

'What do you feed him?'

'Oh, you know, the usual.'

'Any dry food?'

Sam had a picture of Frank standing staring dumbstruck at some biscuits she had once put down for him.

'Occasionally.'

'You should try him with more hard food, it would be better for his gums.'

'Right,' Sam said, thinking she would do no such thing.

Nicky injected Frank in the back of the neck. 'Is he neutered?'

'Of course he is,' Sam blurted. 'I'm not completely irresponsible.'

This was even worse than being asked by the doctor how many units of alcohol you drank in a week.

'It's just he's very large.'

'He was big-boned even as a kitten.'

The vet picked Frank up and put him on some scales, then returned him to the table. 'Actually, he's obese.'

'He's not *that* fat.'

'Clinically obese.'

Frank sat down as if absorbing this new piece of information.

The vet sighed and stroked Frank's head. 'He's a lovely animal but he's the fattest cat I've come across in London.'

Both Sam and Frank looked equally stunned by this news.

Nicky made Frank stand up. 'When you look down on a cat from above you should be able to see a waist. Here.' She pointed.

Sam gawped. 'Cats have waists?'

'Yes. Healthy cats have waists, but Frank hasn't got one.'

'If I put him on a diet he'll scream the place down.'

'Well, if you don't he's at risk of developing high blood pressure, kidney disease . . .'

Sam scratched the top of Frank's head. 'All right. I'll try.'

The vet smiled. 'Good.'

'In the meantime, have you got anything for a cat who suffers from severe travel sickness?'

'We could give him some valium. How long is your journey?'

'About ten minutes.'

'I wouldn't recommend it for such a short distance.'

'And for me?'

As Sam was carrying Frank back into the flat her mobile rang. She put the basket down on the pavement and got out her phone. It was Mark.

'Where were you last night? I was trying to get hold of you.'

'I was at the theatre and turned my phone off, then I've had a hell of a time taking Frank to the vet. Anyway, what's happened?'

'You know you offered to do some digging around?'

'Yes.'

'Well, I've spoken to the Provost, Edward Payne, and he's pretty keen that you do.'

'Is there any more news about how Adrian died?'

'No, but Hunter's father is kicking up a huge fuss, and there's something else going on but I think it would be best if the Provost tells you about that himself. I've got tutorials all day but he said he could see you early afternoon.'

'Fine,' Sam said. 'I'll catch up with you after I've spoken to him.'

Sam stood admiring the maroon paintwork and gleaming brass fittings of the door in front of her. The small wooden plaque attached to it was covered in gold italic writing and informed her that she was exactly where she wanted to be – outside the lodgings of the Provost of St Barnabas's College. She rang the bell and then turned round to look behind her. Directly in front of the door there was a cobbled area surrounded by bollards, which were linked with chains. Two cars occupied the space. Private parking in central Oxford – it was as much of a rarity as the bits of the dodo that were left in the natural history museum.

The door opened and a woman with fine grey hair swept back in a bun, wearing a dress with a white background and loud splashes of colour across it, smiled at her.

'Hello,' Sam said. 'My name's Samantha Falconer. I've got an appointment with the Provost.'

'Oh yes, come in, come in. I'm Katherine, Edward's wife.' She stood to one side to let Sam enter. 'I'll just go and get him. Please take a seat. He won't be a minute.'

Sam sat down in an upright chair with a blue velvet seat and looked around her. The hall cut from one side of the house to another. There was a door at the other end leading into a yard where more cars were parked.

For no good reason she could think of, Sam felt as if she were a naughty child waiting for the headmaster to turn up and tell her off. Heads of Oxford colleges could have that effect on you. To ease her anxiety she got up and looked at a still life that was hanging on the wall to the left of the front door – lilies, pomegranate and a dead gold finch all surrounded by an extraordinarily garish, gold-leaf frame. At first she had thought it was painted but as she got closer she saw that it was a mosaic, the whole thing being made of different coloured marble. The seeds of the pomegranate were ruby red glass.

She heard a door being opened and turned to see a man came out of a door further down the hall. The Provost of St Barnabas's was a neat, dapper man dressed in a dark suit with the white triangle of a handkerchief showing in his top pocket. He had the tanned, leathery skin of a man who had spent many years in a hot climate. He walked briskly up to Sam and shook her hand with the sort of bone-crunching brutality that Sam was usually accused of.

'We've met once before, haven't we, when you came to dine with Mark in hall? How very nice to see you again. Thank you so much for coming.'

He gestured at the marble picture. 'It's odd, isn't it?'

'I thought it was painted.'

'Everyone does. Persephone ate the pomegranate and because of that had to spend a third of the year in hell.'

Only a third? Sam thought. Well, Persephone must be doing all right for herself.

'I inherited it. It's ghastly, of course, but I'm fond of it, so what can one do?'

Reframe it, sell it, put it in a cupboard were a few of the options that occurred to Sam as she followed the Provost into his study.

Two windows looked out onto a large square garden in which a magnolia was in full bloom. Beyond the magnolia, golden Oxford stone gleamed in the spring sunshine. The Provost's desk was placed at a right angle to the furthest window and faced out into the room. He sat down behind it and gestured for Sam to sit in the chair opposite. It was covered in a large stack of papers. Sam picked them up and asked him where she should put them.

'Oh anywhere, anywhere,' he said.

Sam looked around her but the only clear space was a narrow path that ran from the door to the desk. The rickety table behind her was covered with books and papers, as was every inch of floor space. She stood, spinning round, holding the papers.

'I'm sorry. Here, let me.' The Provost reached over the desk, took them from her, sighed and dropped them heavily onto the floor next to a large wicker waste-paper basket. He waved at the room. 'I'm afraid it's getting beyond a joke.'

The rainforest probably felt the same way.

'I'll have to tidy up soon or Katherine will let our daily woman Mrs Prior loose in here and all hell will break loose. Last time that happened I lost things . . . well, things I still haven't found – an index, a tax form . . .'

The phone went on his desk. 'Excuse me,' he said and picked it up.

Sam looked around the room. There were floor-to-ceiling book-shelves behind her and also behind the Provost. On the wall facing the windows was the portrait of an effete man with pink cheeks and lips wearing a powdered wig. His expression was one of the utmost pomposity and humourlessness. On the floor underneath the portrait was an ugly three-bar electric heater, which Sam presumed was never used because it would have set fire to the piles of books that rested against it. The Provost had obviously never heard of the phrase fire-hazard.

The Provost put down the phone just as the door opened and his wife came in carrying a tray covered with coffee things.

'Splendid, splendid,' the Provost said, rubbing his hand together. 'Coffee all right?'

'Fine,' Sam said.

Once the coffee had been poured and his wife had left the room, the Provost sat forwards in his chair and said, 'Thank you so much for coming over so quickly. I really am most grateful to you.'

'I only spoke briefly with Mark on the phone, but am I right in thinking you would like me to see what I can find out about Adrian Hunter?'

'Yes, that's certainly part of it. I had a rather difficult meeting with Mr Hunter and his wife yesterday.'

Sam nodded. 'I was with Mark when he met them.'

'Yes? What was your impression of Mr Hunter?'

'That he was very angry and looking for someone to blame for what had happened to his son.'

'Yes. He was certainly highly agitated when I spoke to him. I told him that we would conduct our own internal investigation into what had happened and let him have the result as soon as possible.'

Sam nodded. 'What have you heard from the police?'

'Very little as yet.'

'Have they confirmed how he died?'

'I believe they are awaiting the result of toxicology reports, forensics and such like.'

'Mark said that there was something else you wanted some assistance with.'

'Yes, it is something that would require the utmost discretion.'

Sam resisted the temptation to say 'utmost discretion is my second name'. Instead she said, 'I keep all my clients' affairs confidential as a matter of course.'

'Would you be willing to sign a confidentiality agreement?'

Sam prodded the pile of books sitting on the floor to her right to make sure it was stable and, finding that it was, balanced her cup and saucer on top of it. 'Not really.'

'Could I ask why not?'

'Well, what would you say if I asked you to take an IQ test?'

'And your point is?'

'My point is you're head of an Oxford college; implicit in your position is an assumption of your intelligence. To ask you to do an IQ test would be insulting. I'm a private investigator – private. Asking me to sign a confidentiality clause is insulting. It seems to me either you trust me or you don't. You know my background and my stepfather, Peter Goodman; Mark has been at the college for fifteen years. I think what counts here more than any piece of paper I might sign is mutual trust. Signing a confidentiality agreement won't create trust and if you don't trust me you shouldn't think of using me.'

He had been looking at her intently while she was speaking, a finger running lightly back and forth over his top lip. He picked up a piece of paper off his desk, glanced at it, then placed it flat again.

'The law tutor won't be happy.'

'Lawyers never are. They're a pessimistic bunch, always warning their clients of the worst that can happen.'

He smiled and drained his cup.

Sam wondered if she'd pushed her luck. Why didn't she just sign the bloody thing?

'Look, I was brought up in an Oxford college. I couldn't be better placed to investigate anything you want me to and with, as you said, the utmost discretion.'

The Provost slammed his open hand hard against the window and Sam jumped. Outside in the garden, she saw a squirrel leap off a bag of nuts hanging from the magnolia and race across the grass and up the trunk of a large copper beech.

'Perhaps you might take a look at this.'

He handed Sam a piece of paper. It was handwritten on plain paper.

> *Come 23 December it'll be your head on a plate, your mouth stuffed with an orange. Come January 1 it'll be your eyes stuck with needles.*

'What's the relevance of the dates?'

'They're feasts – the Boar's Head and the Needle and Thread – but not this college's.'

Sam frowned. 'Which one, then?'

'Queen's.'

'Why Queen's?'

'My old college.'

'So this was sent to you, then?'

'Yes.'

'When did you get it?'

'Yesterday afternoon.'

'Have you shown this to the police?'

'No.'

'But it's a death threat.'

'Oh, that's putting it rather too strongly, don't you think? It's too amateur for that. Just someone letting off a little steam.'

'Why didn't you go to the police?'

'Well, like I said, it didn't seem serious enough and of course there was no guarantee that it wouldn't be made public and I didn't want policemen tramping round the college upsetting everyone.'

'But that's exactly what you've got happening.'

'I know, but it's not something *I* set in motion.'

'Don't you think you should tell them now?'

'I was rather hoping not to. I was rather hoping it might be settled without their involvement.'

'Do you think this has anything to do with what's happened to Adrian Hunter?'

'If I thought that for one minute I would, of course, inform the police, but I really don't think it has. I don't want to tell the police now because I fear that they may think the same thing and then a horrible misunderstanding may occur.'

Sam's brain was beginning to ache. Talking to this man was like playing chess with someone who you knew was always going to beat you. She looked out of the window and looked at a great tit, which was pecking at the bag of nuts hanging from the magnolia.

'Who do you think sent it?'

'I don't know for sure.'

'But you have your suspicions?'

'Yes.'

'And they are?'

He folded his hands together but didn't reply.

Smoke and fucking mirrors, Sam thought.

'Who else knows about this?'

'My secretary – she's the one who opened the letter – and of course my wife.'

'Do you know if anyone else has received one?'

'I presume not.'

'Why?'

'Because I would have got to hear about it.'

'But they haven't got to hear about this, have they?'

'No, but I am top of the pile, if you see what I mean.'

Sam laughed. 'From what Peter has told me sometimes a chilly and rather isolated place to be, which, surely, at times makes you the last person to know.'

He smiled. 'At times undoubtedly, but in this matter I don't think so.'

A wave of impatience swept over Sam. 'So, are you going to tell me who you think it is and what you'd like me to do?'

'I should stress that I don't know for certain.' He took off his glasses and rubbed his eyes. 'It was actually my wife's idea to talk to you about it.'

'Perhaps I could talk to her then? Maybe that would speed things up a bit.'

His face lit up. 'Yes, what a good idea.' He put his glasses back on, sprung to his feet and headed for the door.

Sam followed him out of his study and into the living room where his wife was sitting on a sofa, holding a newspaper folded at the crossword. She took off her glasses and looked at them with surprise.

'Darling, have a word with Samantha here,' the Provost said and bolted from the room.

Sam sat down next to Katherine.

'I'm sorry about my husband, dear, he does so hate things to get messy.'

'Peter's the same.'

'Oh, is he? Well, at least you're used to it.'

'Could you tell me why you thought your husband should talk to me?'

'He got that wretched letter and I really didn't think we should just ignore it, especially with what's happened now in the college. He's very capable of putting his head in the sand, but someone's died and I think it's about time he stood upright and shook the sand out of his ears.'

'Who do you think sent it?'

'I'm pretty certain it was Kenneth Adams or someone involved with him. Did Mark tell you about him?'

'Retired from teaching a year ago but still lives in the college and refuses to give up his college rooms.'

'Yes, that's right.'

'And has a drink problem.'

'Yes.'

'And has been the cause of some unpleasantness as a result.'

'You see what I mean about it being an untidy situation?'

'So what happened?'

'Well, there was an incident, shall we say, that made it quite obvious to everyone that something had to be done about him. He was told he had to leave and was given a deadline. When the deadline expired he was removed.'

Sam raised her eyebrows in surprise. Oxford colleges were notoriously conservative institutions. Her stepfather Peter's favourite quote about Oxford was Lord David Cecil's: 'It is impossible to reform the university. One might as well try and reform a cheese.' Her mind boggled at the thought of what it was that the man might have done to force the college to act so quickly.

Curiosity overwhelmed her. 'What exactly did he do?'

'Well, shall we say it involved a degree of personal exposure in rather a public place. It was such a shame really, the whole thing, but drink ... well, he is not a happy drunk, that's for sure.'

'So you think he wrote the note to your husband?'

'I don't know. He is one of those dons who save all their malice for their colleagues and the best of themselves for their students. As a consequence, he has a coterie of devoted ex-pupils. It is strange how often the most vicious and vindictive of individuals can be the most charming and devoted of tutors.'

'Where is he living now?'

'Somewhere off the Iffley Road with his nephew, I believe.'

'Lucky nephew.'

'The whole episode was most unpleasant but the situation could not be allowed to continue. People felt they could not bring their friends to dine because he was behaving so boorishly. The college behaved very well with him, too well you might say. They allowed him to stay a year after he had retired when he really should not have been here. But then there was the incident and it was decided he had to go. Some people do not cope well with retirement and if they have a propensity for the bottle staying in an Oxford college is not good for them. There is simply too much good wine readily available. It's a recipe for disaster.'

Sam nodded.

'Obviously his nephew did not want him but then in the end he was not the college's responsibility, was he?'

'Who was involved in the decision to evict him?'

'Ultimately it's the decision of the Governing Body.'

'Do you know who actually told him? I presume there were face-to-face discussions.'

'I don't know the answer to that, I'm afraid. You'd have to ask my husband.'

'Has anything else been going on that might explain the letter? Has anyone else got a grudge against your husband? Is there anyone else he might have upset?'

'Not really, no . . .' She paused. 'Well . . . there was . . . but I don't think that's really relevant.'

'Anything you can think of would be useful.'

'Some people we know very slightly came round with their son, seeking advice.' As she said the last word she ghosted a pair of inverted commas in the air. 'It's amazing how often old friendships are renewed when people's children reach university age.'

Sam laughed.

'I'm sure you know the kind of thing – what colleges they should apply to, which ones to avoid. Of course the underlying request, which is never stated, is can you help get my child in.'

Sam nodded. 'Peter always used to say that he had absolutely nothing to do with admissions.'

'Yes, exactly, that's what Edward says, but of course they never believe it. They think the heads of Oxford colleges are like Tudor monarchs, tyrants who can do what they like. As you know, the reality is very far removed from that.'

Sam smiled. 'There were always a few members of the Governing Body Peter would have fancied stretching on the rack.'

Katherine laughed.

'So what happened?'

'They came to tea. We chatted about colleges. A week later several rather good cases of claret turned up from them.'

Sam grunted in amusement.

'Exactly. Edward phoned and reiterated that he had no influence over admissions. The father said he understood but wanted him to keep it anyway. His son applied here and failed to get in.'

'What happened to the claret?'

'Oh, we drank it, it was excellent.'

'And then?'

'He phoned Edward up in a fury and threatened him. Said he'd broken a promise, but of course he'd done no such thing. You know what these people are like. They don't take kindly to being turned down and they think anyone can be bought. When they don't get their own way . . .'

'Did your husband take the threats seriously?'

'No, not really. He put it down to a sort of temper tantrum. It was the son I felt sorry for. He seemed a nice boy, but it wasn't an easy situation for him to be in.'

Sam stood up. 'Perhaps I should have another word with your husband.'

'Of course.'

Back in the study, Sam found the Provost writing at his desk. He put down his pen.

'Your wife's been most helpful. Could you tell me who was involved in actually telling Kenneth Adams he had to leave? I presume he wasn't just sent a letter.'

'Letters had proved completely ineffective on previous occasions. In the end it was the bursar and Mark.'

'Why Mark?'

'I think he offered, actually. He didn't feel it should fall solely on the bursar's shoulders. People weren't exactly lining up to do it, but it was also felt that Mark would do it as tactfully as possible. He was one of the few members of the Governing Body who had any time for him.'

'But Mark hasn't received a note?'

'No. Mark was very good to him. He got some of his students and college servants to help him pack up his rooms and apparently they were in a terrible state. If you think this is bad . . .' He made a gesture that encompassed his own study. 'This is nothing, I believe, in comparison.'

'When did Adams move out?'

'Last week.'

Sam stood up. 'I presume you have his address?'

'I can certainly get it for you.'

'Could you do that and I'll go straight over.'

The Provost looked startled.

'I don't want to mess about. It seems to me the best way to sort this out is to go and ask him.'

'Yes, I see.'

The Provost picked up his phone, spoke to someone, then wrote something down on a piece of paper, which he handed to Sam.

'Right. Could I take a copy of the note?'

'You can have this one.'

Sam put the note in her bag and the Provost came round from behind his desk and followed her out of the study and into the hall. He held out his hand. 'Thank you for coming.'

This time Sam was prepared for the bone-crunching handshake. He opened the front door and Sam stepped through it.

'Oh, one thing.'

'Yes?'

'I'm presuming you didn't recognise the writing?'

'Correct.'

'What was the postmark?'

'There wasn't one. It was just placed in my open pigeonhole in college in an unmarked envelope.'

'So pretty much anyone who has access to the college or the pigeon-post could have put it there?'

'I'm afraid so, yes.'

Outside in the Turl, Sam stood for a moment in the spring sunshine. She turned round and looked up at the façade of St Barnabas's. To outsiders Oxford colleges looked like oases of tranquillity. The reality, of course, could be very different. Colleges, after all, contained people and people in Sam's experience were rarely tranquil. But even so, an alarming number of things seemed to be coinciding in St Barnabas's – Adrian Hunter's death, Kenneth Adams's eviction and now this note. The Provost had sought to play it all down but Sam knew that if she'd been sent it, she'd have been considerably more concerned than he appeared to be. She ducked round a group of tracksuit-clad cyclists heading for the river and set off for the High.

CHAPTER SIX

Sam stood outside Queen's waiting for a bus to take her to the Iffley Road. She'd driven to Oxford that afternoon and considered taking her car now but what with the one-way system and the horrors of Oxford's perpetually changing traffic system, she thought the bus would be easier. She took out her mobile and phoned Phil.

'It's me. The Provost of St Barnabas's has asked me to look into the circumstances surrounding the death of Adrian Hunter and I was wondering if there was anything you could tell me.'

'No. The investigation is on-going.'

'What did the autopsy come up with?'

'We're waiting on forensics.'

'What do you think happened?'

'I'm not going to speculate, Sam.'

'Oh come on, Phil, you must have some idea. What was the cause of death?'

'I'm sitting my Inspector exams this autumn and we've got a new boss. I'm not going to stick my neck out for you, Sam. There's nothing I can tell you.'

Sam sighed. 'Did you have to be so heavy-handed when you interviewed Mark? You really upset him.'

'Adrian Hunter is dead and I'm investigating that death. I'm a police officer not a fucking primary school teacher. I don't care if he was upset. It's not my job to be polite to my ex-girlfriend's brother for old times' sake.'

'But what made you ask him if he was sleeping with him?'

'I'm not going there, Sam.'

The phone went dead.

Twenty minutes later she got off the bus, turned left off Iffley Road and after a five-minute walk stopped in front of the address the Provost had given her. She rang the bell and stood back, admiring the purple blossom of the wisteria that had snaked its way up the front of the house and was hanging down from the guttering.

A tall thin man, wearing a green tweed jacket and worn brown cords opened the door. He was leaning heavily on a stick with his left hand and clinging onto the doorframe with his right. He had the florid complexion of the heavy drinker.

'I don't know where the bloody meters are and if you're a Jehovah's Witness I've read Revelation and it's a loathsome pile of twaddle.'

'I'm Mark Falconer's sister. I wonder if I could have a word with you.'

'Mark, you say?'

He didn't say anything else, just turned round, leaving the door open, and walked back into the house. Sam followed him along a hall lined with boxes into a front room filled with even more of them. Adams dropped heavily into an armchair, the only chair in the room and Sam sat down on one of the boxes.

'They've dumped me here because they don't know what to do with me.'

'You haven't had time to unpack.'

'I don't know how long I'm going to be here. It's hardly worth it. So, what did you say you were called?'

'Sam.'

'Is that what your parents christened you?'

'That was Samantha.'

'Well, that's what I'll call you. I don't believe in diminutives.'

Sam puffed out her cheeks.

'So, what does Mark's sister want with me?'

'I don't want to waste your time so I'll get straight to the point.' Sam took out the note and handed it to him. 'This was sent to the Provost last week.'

Adams peered at it through greasy glasses speckled with dandruff and then roared with laughter. 'Thank you so much for coming, you've cheered me up no end. Fancy a drink?'

Sam didn't think he meant anything as mild as tea or coffee. 'No, I'm fine.'

'You're not one of those ghastly teetotallers, are you? It's never a good sign. Look for the people with livers the consistency of pâté and you'll find they're the best in the world.'

Sam wasn't that far from holding the same opinion.

'I drink, just not at this time of the day.'

'More and more my feeling is, why wait? It probably has something to do with retirement. I think old Dean Aldrich of Christ Church put it rather well three hundred years ago:

> *'If all be true that I do think*
> *There are five reasons we should drink:*
> *Good wine – a friend – or being dry,*
> *Or lest we should be, by and by,*
> *Or any other reason why.'*

A bottle of whisky stood on the mantelpiece next to a glass. He waved at it. 'Would you mind?'

Sam got up and handed him the bottle and glass. He poured himself an ample measure and then placed the bottle with great care on the floor next to his chair.

'So, that miserable bastard thinks I sent it, does he?'

Sam couldn't quite help from smiling. 'Not necessarily. He doesn't know who sent it but he's asked me to try and find out. He said you had a good reason for feeling upset.'

'Upset! Is that what he said? Live in a place for forty years of your life—'

Sam cut him off. 'Look, I want to be up front with you.'

'Up front?' he said with a heavy sneer.

'Straight with you,' Sam tried.

'Straight as opposed to what exactly – deviant or wiggly?'

Sam was beginning to feel like a Roget's Thesaurus. 'I want to tell you the truth.'

He grunted and gulped some more whisky.

'I don't really care who sent this.' She tapped the note. 'A student's died in the college. The Provost asked me to look into this privately. He hasn't told the police about the note but wants to be clear that it isn't involved with the other matters. I've told him I'll do my best to find out.'

Adams sniffed. 'He's too embarrassed to let on. Doesn't want this out in the open, does he?'

'Did you send this?'

He took a vast handkerchief of uncertain history out of his pocket and wiped his nose. 'Don't be ridiculous.'

'Can you think of anyone who might have?'

He shrugged. 'There are always good reasons to hate.'

'Do you recognise the handwriting?'

'No.'

'Could it be one of your ex-students holding a grievance on your behalf?'

'I hope they have better things to do with their time than waste it on other people's grievances. Personally, I find that there are always so many of one's own to hold; taking on other people's would be unnecessarily onerous. Anyway, do you know how many students I've had in my career? Do you think I remember the miserable scrawl of every wretched one of them?'

Sam heard the front door open and close and turned round to see a man standing in the door holding two heavy bags of shopping.

'Ah, Nephew,' Adams said.

'Uncle.'

Sam felt as if she'd been deposited in the middle of *A Christmas Carol* with Scrooge and Fred. Unfortunately the obvious part remaining for her was Tiny Tim or rather Tiny Sam.

'This is Mark's sister, Samantha. The Provost has sent her to spy on me.'

Adams's nephew put down the shopping bags. He had round, pale blue slightly protruding eyes and a blond pudding-basin haircut that sat on his head like a wig. He was boyish-looking, but the lines round his eyes placed him in his late forties or early fifties. His eyes darted from Sam to the glass in his uncle's hand.

'Excellent, excellent – Mark was a great help to us, wasn't he, Uncle? Very kind.'

This uncle/nephew business was beginning to get on Sam's nerves.

'I was asking your uncle if he knew who might have sent the Provost this?' She handed him the note.

He read it, then looked up, frowning. 'Head on a plate? Eyes stuck with needles?'

'Queen's, Nephew, Queen's.'

'Ah yes, of course – *Graecum est.*'

'Yes, exactly.'

Sam looked from one to the other. '*Graecum* . . . ?'

'The origins of the Boar's Head feast. A student of Queen's was studying his Greek grammar on Boar's Hill, when he was surprised by a charging boar. He killed it by stuffing his grammar down its throat, saying *Graecum est* or, in other words, "It is Greek."'

'And the Needle and Thread?' Sam asked.

'You know that one, Nephew.'

'I forget, I forget.'

'Forget! You went to it, didn't you, at the beginning of the year? How can you forget? Needle and Thread is a pun on the name of the founder Robert de Eglesfield – in the French it is *"Aiguilles et fils"*. Guests are given needles threaded with different coloured silks depending on their subject.'

'Well, well.' The nephew handed the note back to Sam. 'I'm afraid I can't help you with this.' He took off his beige raincoat and draped it over some boxes. 'Would you like some tea?' he asked Sam.

'Not a drop of milk in the place,' his uncle said with grim satisfaction.

'I came prepared.' He lifted the plastic bags at his feet. 'Shall I make you some coffee, Uncle?'

'Coffee! What would I want with coffee, you bloody fool?'

The nephew raised his eyebrows good-naturedly at Sam and left the room. Sam followed him into the kitchen. She perched on a stool and watched him fill the kettle.

'You'll have to forgive my uncle. He's not himself at the moment. Well, in some ways, of course, he is, very much so. He's always been irascible, but at the moment he's especially so. The move has disorientated him and rendered him, shall we say, more despondent than usual.'

'Of course, it must be very difficult to move from somewhere you've lived for forty years.'

'Rather like throwing a naked baby out into the snow.'

The kettle had boiled and Sam watched him pour some water into a yellow pot and carefully swill it round before tipping it down the sink.

'Do you know who might have written this?'

'I'm afraid not.'

'Do you think it could be because of what's happened to your uncle?'

'I really don't know.'

'Are you his closest relative?'

'For my sins. He's managed to fall out with just about everyone else. He has a knack for it. Unfortunately, I have a knack for doing exactly the opposite. Uncle delights in telling me it is because I have the personality of a blancmange.'

Sam smiled. 'But the Provost said that many of his ex-students are devoted to him.'

'That's true. He was an inspiring teacher. The best of himself he kept for his pupils. He never published much but he's got a remarkable list of people he taught.'

He reeled off a list that included several MPs, an ex-Chancellor of the Exchequer, a couple of TV and newspaper journalists and a well-known television historian.

'Good grief,' Sam said.

'Some dons really aren't interested in teaching, you know. What they want to do is research and writing but in order to do that they have to teach, and some of them, frankly, just aren't any good at it. Being very clever does not per se make you a good teacher but Uncle was a very good teacher, whether you had a first-class brain or a second-class one. You would think he would have only been interested in the very bright ones but that wasn't the case. And he was always very generous in supporting them after they left the university. He has a fondness even for his thirds.'

He had finished making the tea and now handed Sam a mug.

'Was anyone particularly upset about him being removed from the college?'

'Not that I know of.'

'Could he have sent the note himself?'

'It's not his handwriting. I suppose he could have got someone to write it out for him but it's not really his way. He has no qualms about being exceptionally rude to people straight to their faces. Why bother with this? If he'd written something like it, he'd be much more likely to sign his name to it. He'd want the Provost to know he sent it.'

'How do you feel about what has happened?'

He sighed. 'Sad, mainly, and also rather put upon I have to admit. I think it's a shame it had to happen this way. They kept Auden in Christ Church, didn't they?'

'Yes, but rather a long time ago and not without some difficulty.'

'It's the drink that's a problem. He gets depressed and then he drinks and the drink makes him more depressed and then he has to drink more. It's a vicious circle. He doesn't help himself, I admit that.'

'Is this his new home?'

'We got it on a six-month lease. I don't know what we're going to do after that. Shall we rejoin him?'

Sam nodded and followed him back into the sitting room. They both sat down on different boxes.

'Been whispering away about me in there, have you – drinking your *tea*?' Adams sneered.

'Pretty much,' Sam said. 'Your nephew was saying a lot of nice things about you.'

'More fool him.'

'I tend to agree.'

He smiled slightly. 'So how's Mark? I like your brother, he's sensible unlike some of them on the Governing Body – bunch of second-raters lead by a Captain Mainwaring.'

'He's OK.'

'And you said a student had died?'

'Yes.'

'Well, I should imagine that's keeping the Provost busy. He was kind to me, Mark, very kind. Helped us pack up. Brought along some students and college servants to help.'

Sam put down her mug. 'I should be going.'

'Pass on a message to the Provost, will you?' Adams said. 'Tell him the note mirrors my feelings exactly. Tell him—'

'Uncle, come now—'

'Don't Uncle me . . .'

Sam left them to their bickering.

As she was sitting in the bus heading back into Oxford her mobile rang. It was Alan.

'How's it going?' he asked.

'Slowly.'

'Rick called.'

'What did he want?'

'To speak to you.'

Sam sighed. 'I hope you told him to fuck off and go and talk to his bloody beautiful wife.'

'No, I didn't. I told him I'd pass the message on. He wanted to make sure you'd got back all right after the theatre.'

'No, he didn't. He wanted to schmooze me into giving him the information he wants about his father.'

'And now he's got a wife you're not going to help him?'

'Even I am not that petty, Alan, but I'm not going to put myself out for him, no.'

'You all right, Sam?'

'I'm fine, Alan.'

'Incidentally, Rick left me his number.'

'I'm not going to get involved with him, Alan. He gave it to me when we parted outside the King's Head and I've already thrown it away once.'

'Well, I suppose he wants to make sure you've got it again.'

'I'm not phoning him, Alan.'

'I didn't say you would.'

Sam went straight back to St Barnabas's and told the Provost the outcome of her conversation. The only other obvious candidate for Sam to talk to was the man who had sent the claret, but when she asked the Provost about this he seemed horrified that his wife had mentioned the episode and was adamant that he didn't want him approached. Sam asked if she could speak to the college secretary, Mrs Prendergast.

'Why?' he asked.

'Because in my experience the college secretaries know everything that goes on in a college.'

The Provost smiled and picked up the phone. When he had

finished the call, he stood up and said he could take Sam over to see her.

They walked in silence across a small courtyard and then turned left along a paved path flanked on either side by blackened, crumbling stone walls. At the end of the path was a carpet of pink blossom, which had fallen from the cherry tree in the Provost's garden.

The college secretary's office was in front quad on the first floor.

'She doesn't know about the letter,' the Provost said as they climbed the stairs.

'Would you like a bet?' Sam said.

He knocked on a door, pushed it open and then, somewhat to Sam's surprise, turned and ran down the stairs.

'Come,' Sam heard from inside. The pitch of the voice suggested at least a forty-a-day habit but when Sam entered the office there was no smell of smoke, only air freshener.

Mrs Prendergast had a rigid helmet of ash-blonde hair that would have defied a typhoon. She was wearing a green twin set, a brown pleated skirt and flat brown shoes. She stood up behind her desk as Sam came into the room and looked her up and down from a height of at least six foot.

She gestured at the chair opposite. 'Sit,' she said.

Sam decided she was probably the sort of woman who treated everyone in the same way – like dogs. She took out the note and handed it to her.

'The Provost received this in his pigeon hole and I was wanting to gauge your opinion of it.'

Mrs Prendergast read it and then placed it to one side.

Sam continued, 'The Provost has told me about what happened with Kenneth Adams and I've just visited him to see if he might have anything to say on the matter.'

Her face softened momentarily. 'How is he?'

'A little disorientated.'

'No wonder.'

'But he says he has nothing to do with it. I wondered if you might know of anyone who might have sent this on his behalf?'

'People were upset about what happened,' she said slowly.

'People?'

'Members of staff. Kenneth had been with us a very long time.'

'Was he popular?'

'With the staff – very. He was always charming and was very generous at Christmas.'

Sam frowned. 'From what the Provost said he was not so charming with the fellows.'

'I couldn't possibly comment on that.'

'Would you say anyone in particular was upset?'

'Leave this with me.'

'I'm sorry?'

'I will look into it.'

'The Provost wanted this looked into with the utmost discretion.'

'And you think I'm incapable of that?'

'Oh, good God, no,' Sam stuttered. 'The reason that he did not go to the police was because he did not want it mixed up with the death of Adrian Hunter. He was worried that if—'

'You do not have to spell out to me the Provost's concerns.'

'Right.'

'I don't know why he didn't come to me with this straight away.'

Pure terror was Sam's best guess.

Mrs Prendergast continued, 'These things are not best dealt with by outsiders.'

'I agree with you completely,' Sam said.

The college secretary placed her hands flat on her desk and stood up. Sam, anticipating imminent dismissal, followed suit.

'One thing,' Sam said. 'Could you tell me what that is?'

She pointed to a metal board covered in a large number of brightly coloured magnetic beetles. Mrs Prendergast folded her arms and smiled.

'Each one represents a member of the Governing Body.'

'And their position on the board?'

'My approval rating.'

Sam couldn't help laughing. 'Where's the Provost?'

Mrs Prendergast looked at the board and frowned then she lifted her foot and bent down. 'Crushed under foot,' she said, a beatific expression spreading across her face.

Confronted with Mark's strained, pale face later that afternoon when she'd caught up with him in his rooms, Sam suggested they go out for a walk. After a brisk turn round Christ Church meadow they ended up sitting at a trestle table outside the Head of the River pub, watching the swans swimming back and forth and the college eights turning round at Folly Bridge and rowing back towards the boathouses in the early-evening sunshine.

'Have you heard any more from the police?' she asked.

He shook his head. 'But I know they've been all over the college asking questions.'

'I couldn't get a word out of Phil.'

'How did you get on with the Provost?'

'Well, things became a lot clearer once I'd spoken to his wife.'

'The power behind the throne. Some of the dons have nicknamed her Richelieu. You know what the Provost's previous career was?'

'No.'

'He was a diplomat. He was stationed in some of the most notorious trouble spots in the world. Stick a pin in a map marking coups and riots of the last twenty years and he will probably have been posted to three-quarters of them and she went everywhere with him.'

'I liked her. She seemed very sensible and pragmatic. Did the Provost show you the letter?'

'Yes.'

'What do you think?'

'A malicious prank.'

'Nothing more?'

'I wouldn't have thought so.'

'Do you think it links in with Adams being removed from the college?'

'It could do, I suppose. Some people were very upset about the way it was handled.'

'You spoke to him yourself.'

'Yes, together with the bursar. I felt very strongly that one of the fellows should be involved. It couldn't just be dumped on the bursar. It was unfair.'

'I bet there weren't many volunteers for that job.'

'Well, I said I'd do it, so no one needed to.'

'What did Adams do when you talked to him?'

'He became very upset. That malicious carapace just crumbled. It was harrowing. He started saying he didn't know where he could go or what would become of him. I spoke to Colin, his nephew, and then liaised with him to find him somewhere to go.'

'So you were the most involved of all the fellows in the move?'

'Yes. I got some people together to help pack up his rooms. Adrian was one of them.'

'Adrian?'

'Yes.'

'Do you think his death could be linked to Adams's expulsion?'

Mark shook his head. 'He was helping him. So was I. That doesn't make any sense.'

'Couldn't you just have got a removal company?'

'It was forty years of a man's life in there, Sam. I wanted it done with some degree of decorum and tact. We took a great deal of trouble to make lists of the contents of each box and keep everything as orderly as possible.'

'Was Adams there while you did it?'

'For the first half of the day, then I got Colin to take him away. He sat there drinking whisky and railing at everyone. It was exhausting.'

'Do you think Adams could have sent the note?'

'I think that's very unlikely. It's not his style. Maybe Colin could have.'

'He seemed altogether too mild-mannered to me. He said his uncle described him as having the personality of a blancmange.'

'He wasn't like a blancmange in his dealing with me, I can tell you. He struck me as more than capable of looking after his own interests.'

'Do you know what he does?'

'I'm not sure – a librarian, a teacher. Something like that.'

'If the note had nothing to do with what has happened to Adams, is there any other reason why someone might have sent such a note to the Provost?'

Mark ran a finger down the condensation on his glass. 'He's only been here since the beginning of the academic year. It's not really long enough to have fallen out with anyone.'

'Was there any controversy over his appointment?'

Mark laughed. 'There was what you could call a thorough discussion about it.'

'Was he a unanimous choice?'

'Not altogether. There were two bodies of opinion. First, that we should make another internal appointment. As you know, the two previous Provosts have also been dons of St Barnabas's. Second, that it was time for an external appointment. There was a strong feeling amongst some of us that it was time for someone with no connection to the college.'

'Why?'

'A breath of fresh air? New ideas? A change? A high-profile candidate can increase the profile of the college.'

'Oh, that reminds me,' Sam said, 'how many Oxford dons does it take to change a light bulb?'

Mark shrugged.

She continued. 'Change . . . ?'

He laughed. 'That's a good one.'

'If it had been an internal appointment who would have been next in line?'

'Petheridge, the classics tutor. He's the senior fellow.'

'Was he upset to be passed over?'

'It's difficult to say. He is rather a scatty individual. I'm not sure he would have been an ideal candidate. My impression is that he was somewhat relieved. He would not have enjoyed the social side of the job – drinks parties for undergraduates, that kind of thing. He's a shy man and his wife is . . . well, a polite description would be highly strung.'

'And an impolite one?'

'Oh, bonkers – serious loony tunes.'

'So what was he like when Edward Payne arrived on the scene?'

'I would say from day one he has gone out of his way to be very welcoming.'

'And how is the Provost generally viewed after two and a half terms in the job?'

'Favourably – once we'd all got over the redecoration costs of the Lodgings. The benefit of an internal appointment is that they rarely want to live in the Lodgings – they already have houses in North Oxford and rooms in college. New provosts and their wives always want the place done up.'

'Not an altogether unreasonable request,' Sam said. 'Presumably it's good for the college to have them living there.'

'That's true, but it was a particularly large bill because no one had been living in there for the last ten years.'

'For heaven's sake, Mark. Oxford colleges are filthy rich.'

'I know, put they can be surprisingly mean when it comes to carpets and wallpaper.'

'But not when it comes to their wine cellars.'

'Good God, no.'

'Could you arrange for me to meet Petheridge?'

'I'll phone him tonight if you like and see if he can talk to you tomorrow but as soon as you clap eyes on him I think you'll see he couldn't have sent that letter.'

Sam looked at her brother's empty glass. 'Another?'

He nodded.

A couple of minutes later she was back with their drinks.

'I know you've got a lot on your plate at the moment, Mark, but there was something that happened in London that I need to talk to you about.'

Mark picked up his pint and drank.

'A man came to see me who wanted me to help him find his father's body.'

'That's unusual – you're usually looking for living people, aren't you?'

'He thinks Dad was responsible for his father's death. He wants me to find out if he killed him and if he did where he's buried.'

'Is this because of the *Daily Tribune* article?'

Sam nodded. 'I thought I should warn you in case they approach you too.'

'You know, it's bad enough he ever came back, but this—'

'You haven't seen him again, have you?'

Mark shook his head. 'I don't ever want to set eyes on him again, Sam, and I don't really want to talk about this now. I've got enough on my plate.'

Sam hadn't told her brother about the photocopies of the documents her father had left with her, or how she felt about Rick McGann. Now was definitely not the time. She'd warned him and that would have to be enough for the moment. She looked at her watch.

'Shall we try the college bar now? Maybe I'll be able to talk to some of Adrian Hunter's contemporaries.'

Mark drained his pint and stood up. 'Let's go.'

CHAPTER SEVEN

Sam followed Mark down the steps into the smoke-filled bar of the Junior Common Room. Conversation stopped for a moment, as everyone turned to look at them. Only a handful of people were down here. Two men were playing pool, and a man and a woman were sitting on stools, talking to the woman behind the bar.

'It's quiet,' Mark said. 'Everyone must still be nursing May Day hangovers. Do you want anything to drink?'

'Orange juice,' Sam said, having already downed enough for one evening at the Head of the River.

They had agreed on the walk over that Mark would introduce her to the people there and then make his excuses. It would be easier for people to talk to Sam without him around and also without them knowing she was his sister.

The woman behind the bar greeted Mark and he introduced her to Sam as Robin McConnell, the president of the JCR. She was small, with short dark hair, and wore a denim shirt and jeans. She poured out the orange juice and Mark paid for it. The couple who had been talking to Robin drifted away to watch the pool game.

'Sam's been asked by the Provost to look into the circumstances surrounding Adrian Hunter's death,' Mark said. 'Would you mind talking to her?'

Robin groaned.

'What?' he said.

'The police ... journalists ... I've been doing nothing but answering questions for the last couple of days.'

'Well, she's a good listener,' he said. He turned to Sam. 'I'm off to London early in the morning, so I'll catch up with you tomorrow evening.'

Sam picked up her orange juice and watched her brother leave the bar.

'Can I buy you a drink?' Sam asked.

'Sure.' Robin poured herself a pint and Sam paid for it.

'Did you know Adrian well?'

'He was down here most evenings.'

'Was he well liked?'

'I wouldn't go that far. He knew how to get up too many people's noses to be described as well liked.'

'How did he do that?'

'He was mouthy, opinionated, in your face. He could be very arrogant, but he could also be a good laugh. It depended what mood he was in.'

'Did he have any particularly good friends?'

'Most of his social life seemed to revolve around people in other colleges. I saw him in here quite a few times with people I didn't recognise. I think he went to one of those public schools that are an Oxbridge factory. He probably came up with twenty or thirty contemporaries who he'd been at school with for years. They tend to stick together when they get here. They can be very cliquey.'

'Was that how it was for you?'

She laughed. 'You're joking. I didn't come here to hang out with people I went to school with. What the hell would be the point of that?'

'People are frightened to step outside of what they know,' Sam said.

Robin shrugged.

'Did Adrian strike you as the kind of person who would kill himself?'

'How can you tell? He could be excessive in the things he said. You know – go way too far with something. It's like sometimes he didn't know how to put the brake on. It could be pretty uncomfortable viewing.'

'Was there anyone in particular he upset?'

'The people he upset are too numerous to mention. Most of us had out heads chewed off by him at one time or another.'

'Did you know he was having trouble with his work?'

'Trouble – what do you mean?'

'He wasn't working hard enough. He was at risk of having his scholarship taken away.'

'You're joking? That would have killed him. He loved that

scholarship, I can tell you. I've heard him throw that in a few people's faces before now.'

'In what sort of way.'

'Oh, accusing people of having pedestrian minds, that kind of thing.'

'Charming.'

'The thing is, he could be when he put his mind to it. He could be a real sweetie. He was doing a good job on the May Ball committee. He had lots of good ideas and was also effective at following them up, not just saying 'how about this' without considering the practicalities.'

A cry came up from the pool table and one of the men held his cue over his head and whooped.

'Is there anything else you could tell me about him? Were there any rumours, for example?'

'What kind of rumours?'

'I don't know – any kind.'

She looked over Sam's shoulder as a woman came into the bar. 'You could talk to Juliet, she had tutorials with him.'

Juliet Bartlett had a long pale face and brown straight hair that reached almost to her waist, and she was wearing a white cotton shirt and a floral skirt that fell to her ankles. She walked up to the bar and Robin introduced her to Sam.

'Do you know if there were any rumours about Adrian?' Robin asked.

'Other than the fact he was sleeping with Professor Falconer,' she replied.

'That's ridiculous,' Robin said.

'Where did that rumour originate?' Sam asked.

'With Adrian. He told me he was.'

'And did you tell the police?' Sam asked.

'Yes, I did. I felt I had to. I also told them that I didn't believe it for one second.'

'In what circumstances did Adrian say that to you?'

'After the last tutorial I had with him. Professor Falconer asked him to stay behind. I bumped into Adrian a couple of hours later in the quad and I asked him what that was about and he said it to me then.'

'But you didn't believe him?'

'No. I thought it was his way of covering over the fact he was being given a talking to about the standard of his work. The essay he read out was rubbish. Professor Falconer was obviously not that impressed. It wasn't even in his handwriting. He'd borrowed it from someone else and it was on a slightly different subject to the essay title Professor Falconer had given us. He couldn't even read the handwriting.'

'Why did you tell the police if you didn't believe it yourself?'

'Because it was the last thing he said to me and the next day he turned up dead. I thought I had to . . . in case it had any relevance to what had happened.'

'Is there anything else you could tell me about him?'

'He was an idiot. He was ten times cleverer than me and he was just pissing it all away here. I'm not surprised that Professor Falconer was getting exasperated with him. I'd asked if I could have tutorials with someone else for the rest of the term because I was worried that my work would suffer.'

Sam drained her orange juice and stood up. 'Thanks a lot for your time,' she said.

Sam let herself back into Mark's rooms. A single futon had been laid out on the floor along with a pillow, sheets and a duvet. In Sam's opinion, Juliet Bartlett was something of a drip and she wished she'd kept her mouth shut but at least now she had an explanation for the way in which the police had dealt with Mark. His bedroom door was closed. It was late and he was getting up early the following day. She decided to tell him what she had discovered in the morning.

On top of the duvet was a note:

> Spoke to Petheridge. He said he could see you at three
> o'clock in Worcester gardens tomorrow. He'll tell the porters
> to expect you.
> He said he's training frogs. Consider yourself warned and
> Good Luck!

*

Katherine Payne opened her front door at eight o'clock the following morning looking for a bottle of milk. The bottle of milk was on the doorstep as usual, along with a white plastic bag. She bent down and pulled apart the handles so she could look inside. She frowned, put her hand into the bag and then withdrew it quickly, as if she'd been stung. Picking up the milk bottle but leaving the bag where it was, she closed the door and walked back into the dining room where her husband was having his breakfast.

'Edward,' she said, 'I think there's something you should come and look at.'

Her husband looked at her over the top of his glasses and lowered his paper. 'What is it?'

'I think it's best you see for yourself.'

The ringing phone on Mark's desk woke Sam. She looked at her watch and saw it was half past eight. She swore. She had wanted to speak to Mark before he went to London but now it would have to wait until this evening. She dragged herself off the floor, walked over to his desk and picked up the receiver.

'Mark Falconer's phone.'

'Is that Samantha?'

'Yes. I'm afraid Mark's in London all day.'

'It's the Provost here. It was you I was hoping to speak to. I wonder if you could come over.'

'Now?'

'Yes, as soon as you can.'

'I'll be over in twenty minutes.'

Sam showered and got dressed and, with her stomach grumbling for a breakfast she hadn't eaten, walked over to the Lodgings.

'I am so glad we managed to catch you,' the Provost said, leading her into the dining room. 'Something happened this morning.'

The pig's head sat on a blue willow-pattern dish; needles had been inserted into its eye sockets.

Sam stared at it and frowned. It seemed rather small. She tried to imagine a body attached to it and couldn't. She remembered a production of *Macbeth* when a gale of laughter had swept over the actors, as a head that looked as if it belonged with the shrunken ones in the Pitt Rivers museum was paraded onto the stage at the end of the performance.

'It was on the doorstep this morning,' Katherine said.

All three of them stared at it.

'It must have given you quite a shock.' Sam said.

'Yes, it was somewhat unexpected.'

'The boar's head of the note, I suppose,' Sam said.

'Indeed.'

'And the needles of the Needle and Thread.'

'Yes.'

'Was there another note?'

Katherine Payne shook her head.

Sam pulled the dish towards her and pulled open the pig's mouth. It was empty. 'I think you should definitely tell the police now,' she said.

'We have great confidence in you being able to sort this matter out,' the Provost said calmly. 'I do not want this made public. The college is experiencing enough adverse publicity from what has happened with poor Adrian. This would just fan the flames of media interest. I do not want the college's reputation to be affected by what so far are a series of rather childish pranks.'

Sam looked at the pig's head. 'So far,' she said. She turned to Katherine Payne. 'What do you think?'

'I agree with my husband. If there are other occurrences then we will have to reconsider, but for the moment I think you should carry on your enquiries as discreetly as possible.'

Sam sighed. 'I understand your concerns about publicity, but I would strongly advise bringing in the police.'

'The police have better things to do with their time than run around after this,' the Provost said. 'I will, of course, keep the matter under review, but for the moment I am going to rely on your services.'

Sam sighed. 'Right,' she said. 'I'm going to go round all the butchers in the covered market and see what I can find out. If the head was bought there it's a sufficiently unusual item for someone to remember who they sold it to.'

Morning sunlight was slanting across the Turl as Sam stepped out of St Barnabas's College and began walking towards Market Street. Students were on their way to lectures by bike and on foot, and Oxford looked idyllic, done up in its best spring finery. She stopped off for some breakfast at a greasy spoon, picked up some ground coffee from Cardews and then headed straight for Hedges, the butcher's in the middle of the market. She didn't have to wait long before she was noticed.

Barry was in his fifties and wearing a straw boater. He put down his knife and wiped his hands on his impressively bloodstained apron, then swept his boater off his head and delivered a flamboyant Three Musketeers bow.

Sam laughed and blushed. 'Cut it out, Barry,' she said.

'How come we don't see you any more?'

'I've not lived here for the last three years,' Sam said. 'That might have something to do with it.'

'Where was it you moved to?'

'London.'

He pulled a face. 'Why'd you go there? You'll come back eventually. They all do, you know. You're Oxford born and bred.'

'Not born.'

'As good as. How long have I known you now? Since you were a little blonde five-year-old pipsqueak carrying your mother's shopping.'

Sam smiled. 'So not much change there.'

'What can I get you?' He turned and gestured at the meat spread out in the counters behind him.

'Actually, I was wondering if you'd do me a favour. I'm looking for someone who might have bought a pig's head over the last couple of days.'

Barry frowned. 'Pig's head? We get asked for things like suckling pig when the May Balls are on, but they're later in the month. Then there's the Boar's Head at Queen's, but that's at Christmas.'

'Would you ask around for me? Anything you could find out would be helpful.'

'Hold on.'

Sam watched as he talked to each of his colleagues in turn and then turned back to her with a shrug. 'I don't think it was bought here. I'll ask around the other butchers for you if you like.'

'Thanks,' Sam said and handed him a card.

'Pig's head. That's an unusual thing to ask for. If it was bought in the market someone should remember it. Why are you interested in that?'

'This morning it turned up somewhere it shouldn't have.'

At three o'clock that afternoon Sam presented herself at Worcester College's lodge.

'I've come to see Professor Petheridge,' she said to the porter and then followed his directions.

As she emerged from the college buildings into the gardens, she saw an elderly man squatting down with his back to her, in what could best be described as a wicket-keeping position. Around him stood a circle of undergraduates all looking down at something on the grass. Beyond them was a lake covered with ducks and geese.

Suddenly a collective 'Oooo . . .' went up and several of the undergraduates stepped abruptly backwards.

Sam walked up to the group and saw that they were watching a large green frog. It jumped and the circle moved back again.

'You see,' Professor Petheridge was saying, 'the mechanics of the way he jumps. This is what we are looking for in your movement. The way his feet are positioned and then the way his whole body is taken up with the leap, like flight.' He stood up. 'This is the kind of movement I will be looking for as you leap between the pontoons.'

He was very tall and thin, with a mass of curly grey hair and grey eyes. Everything about him seemed to be slipping and sliding: the horn-rimmed glasses on his nose, his shirt, which had come out of his trousers, and his blue cotton jacket, which seemed to swamp him and sat crookedly on his shoulders. His feet, Sam noticed, were enormous.

He turned and caught sight of Sam. 'And you are?'

'Mark Falconer's sister. I think he spoke to you yesterday evening.'

'Of course.' He turned back to the group. 'Please go off now and practise jumping like this frog.'

'If I try jumping like that frog, Professor Petheridge, I am going to end up dislocating my knees,' said a podgy young man with lank hair and a sour expression on his face.

'Knees! And why should you be worrying about your knees at your time of life?' Petheridge snapped. 'At my age perhaps, but at yours – it's ridiculous. Look, I will show you.'

He squatted down and then sprang across the lawn. His glasses flew off the end of his nose and his jacket flapped over the top of his head. Several pens fell from his top pocket. He stood up, wrestling his head free of his jacket. Sam picked up his glasses and handed them back to him. She noticed that several of the undergraduates had covered their mouths with their hands.

'If I can do it so can you – and look, my knees are perfectly all right. Now go off and practise in pairs.'

He was breathing heavily.

'Shall we sit down?' Sam suggested, pointing to a bench over by the lake.

'If you feel you must,' he said, taking a large handkerchief out of his pocket and wiping his face.

'What are you doing here exactly?' Sam asked.

'Frogs, frogs,' he said.

Sam frowned.

'*The Frogs* by Aristophanes.'

'Ah.'

'In the original Greek.'

'Will anyone come?'

'Of course they will. It is part of the A-level syllabus. We'll get school children from all over the country. We are on for four days and we have already almost sold out.'

'Well done.'

'*Batrachoi*,' he said.

Sam didn't say anything because she thought he might be trying to clear some phlegm.

'Brekeke-kex, koax, koax.'

Sam sighed. Having grown up surrounded by very clever people talking way over her head, she didn't generally expect to understand what came out of the mouths of academics. Her response had always been to fix a suitably bland, slightly enquiring expression on her face and wait until they talked themselves into a more comprehensible vein. The key, she had discovered, after much trial and error, was waiting and not exposing one's complete level of ignorance. She did that now.

'*Batrachoi* – the Greek word for frogs. Koax, koax is onomatopoeic. The sound of the word is supposed to mimic the croak that a frog makes. We are going to have pontoons on the lake in the shape of enormous lily pads. And our frogs will leap from one to another. It will be glorious. We are very lucky of course to be able to use the lake. Worcester have been most generous. We are going to boom the Crazy Frog theme from loud speakers to create a modern ambience.'

Sam found herself strangely tempted by the prospect of seeing the play, if only to find out if any of the actors survived the first night.

'Now, what was it you wanted to talk to me about?'

'The Provost has received a threatening letter and there has been another incident this morning and I wanted to talk to you as one of the senior members of St Barnabas's to see if you had any idea who might be responsible.'

'The Provost threatened? How very theatrical.'

Sam handed him the letter and he read it.

'You know the connection?'

She nodded. 'Queen's.'

'Yes, the Provost's old college.'

'And what was this incident you spoke of?'

'A pig's head left on his doorstep this morning.'

'How very disagreeable for him. What line of enquiry have you been pursuing?'

'I wondered if it might in any way be linked to the removal of Kenneth Adams from the college.'

'Ah, yes. Poor Ken. The whole affair was most unfortunate, very regrettable.'

'But I've spoken to him and he denied knowing anything about it. It seems unlikely that he would have done this himself. Maybe someone was upset about his treatment and acting on his behalf but without his knowledge.'

'Could be, could be.'

'Is there any light you could throw on the matter?'

'Light?' An orange-beaked goose had climbed out of the lake and was pecking at the grass round there feet. 'Goosy goosy gander,' the professor said absentmindedly.

'Yes, anyone you can think of who was particularly upset by what happened to Adams or anyone who might hold a grudge against the Provost.'

'Of the Governing Body I am probably the most likely one to be holding a grudge against the Provost,' he said, looking at Sam with clear grey eyes. 'And I presume that is why you are here. Some of my colleagues, I think, feel that I might have felt hard done by – because an outsider was appointed to the post of Provost – but I can assure you I felt nothing but relief. As you can see, I make an unlikely figurehead for the college. I am not saying, of course, that it wouldn't have appealed to my pride and vanity, but all in all I think I would not have made a very good job of it. It would have been a strain on my wife and I was frankly rather relieved when the job was offered elsewhere. I like the new man and have gone out of my way to welcome him. He seems eminently sensible and has a much higher public profile than myself, which is good for the status of the college. You would not see him leaping around the garden imitating the actions of a frog and he is rather good on the *Today* programme. I fear I would not fare as well faced with the redoubtable Mr Humphrys.'

Sam smiled. 'Is there anyone else you can think of who it might be?'

'Have you met the college secretary?'

'Mrs Prendergast? Yes, I've spoken to her on the basis that college secretaries know everything that is going on ...'

'Quite so, quite so ... Well, you will have observed that she is a rather ... well, put it this way, you would not imagine that she would be much affected by affairs of the heart.'

'No, you wouldn't.'

'Love, etc.'

'She came across as a very armoured individual.'

'Yes, with the protective covering of an armadillo, indeed. To look at her you would not think that she had once been head over heels in love with a member of the Governing Body.'

'Who?'

'Kenneth Adams – they had an affair over many years.'

'Was this widely known in college?'

'No, I wouldn't say so.'

'May I ask how you know?'

'She had summoned me one time. I can't remember the reason, I probably hadn't paid my battels. The horses occasionally entice me. I have the vague recollection that my summons coincided with the end of a rather disappointing Cheltenham. It was something of that sort at any rate, and when I entered her office I was very surprised to find her in tears. I asked her what was the matter and she told me. I believe I was the first and only person she told and I vowed that I would keep it secret.'

'And you told no one?'

'I am rather good at keeping secrets,' he said lightly. 'A lifetime's practice. And I felt sorry for her. To find such a formidable woman in such a state of disarray was unnerving, and afterwards I found her surprisingly benign in her attitude towards me. I can't pretend that wasn't convenient at times. My beetle always hovers near the top of the board.'

'How long ago was this?'

He blew out his cheeks. 'A good twenty years ago at least. Mrs Prendergast was a very handsome woman in her youth – an altogether softer presence. It is perhaps difficult to imagine that now.'

'Do you know how long the affair continued?'

'No, but even if it had ceased I would say that from what I have observed she retained quite a soft spot for Ken. She would have felt sad to see him go.'

'How did you feel about it?'

'That it had all the inevitability of Greek tragedy. The man is a drunk. It was only a matter of time before he did something that would force the college's hand.'

'Well, thank you very much for your time,' Sam said. 'And good luck with the play.'

They both stood up and walked over to where the students were practising their jumps. Petheridge stared at an empty box lying open on the grass.

'Where's the frog?' he shouted. Everyone stopped jumping. 'The frog's not mine.' There was a note of panic in his voice. 'It's a neighbour's and it has to be found. Spread out everyone.'

Sam left them all walking slowly over the lawn. As she reached the college buildings she heard a cry. Turning round, she saw Professor Petheridge standing on the edge of the lake, staring out at the water and tearing at his hair.

Crazy Frog had escaped.

CHAPTER EIGHT

As Sam was walking back into town she passed the Playhouse. A poster caught her eye – Torn Roots. She hadn't realised that they were coming to Oxford. Her thoughts turned to Rick McGann and his wife. Give it up, girl, she thought. That is a road you really don't want to go down. Maybe it was old-fashioned but she had no intention of becoming involved with a married man.

Her phone went as she was crossing the Broad in front of Waterstone's. It was Adrian Hunter's mother.

'I hope you don't mind me phoning. I got your number from the Provost. He told me he'd asked you to look into the circumstances surrounding Adrian's death.'

'That's right.'

'I was wondering if you could meet me. I'm staying at the Old Parsonage Hotel.'

'Is your husband with you?'

'No, he has a case that is keeping him in London. It may seem callous to you but I encouraged him to go back to work. I thought it would be good for him. He's so very upset and having nothing to do was allowing him to dwell on things.'

'I understand. When would you like to meet?'

'Could you come now? We could have a drink here in the hotel bar.'

Sam looked at her watch. 'I'll be there in five minutes.'

Mrs Hunter was waiting for her in reception. They took their drinks and found themselves a sofa.

'Thank you for coming so quickly,' Mrs Hunter said. 'I very much wanted to speak to you without my husband here.'

Sam nodded and sipped her glass of white wine.

'I apologise for his behaviour in your brother's rooms.'

'It was completely understandable,' Sam said. 'Both of you must be in a state of shock and disbelief.'

'Yes.' She placed her hands flat on her thighs and looked down at them. 'I knew Adrian was gay. He told me during the Easter vacation. I had naturally suspected for some time and was relieved that he had told me, but neither of us had decided on the best manner to broach the subject with my husband.'

'You hadn't told him?'

'No. They did not have the easiest of relationships and somehow the time never seemed to be right.'

'How do you think your husband would have reacted?'

A noisy group of people entered the bar and Mrs Hunter glanced towards them. Then she looked back at Sam. 'I think he would have been mortified. I wish I could say otherwise but knowing him as I do that is all I could imagine. He would have viewed it as a bad reflection on himself.'

'Tricky,' Sam said.

'Exactly. The reason why I'm telling you this is two-fold. First, I don't know if it has any relevance to your investigation. I wanted to make sure you knew and I did not want it overlooked if it had any significance. Second, if at all possible, I would like it kept from my husband.'

'Have you spoken to the police about this?'

'Yes.'

'It may be hard to keep it quiet. Inquests are public and if it's mentioned there . . .'

'I'm aware of that, but no one is saying at the moment that his sexuality was a significant factor in his death, are they?'

'At the moment I don't think it's clear to anyone what caused his death. Have you had any further information from the police?'

'No. Have you found anything significant?'

'His work appears to have been a problem, but Mark said Adrian seemed unconcerned when he spoke to him about it. Did anything else happen during the Easter vacation?'

'He was distant and rather depressed while he was home. I put it down to problems he was having with his father. It's a difficult time. He hadn't completely left home but he didn't want to be there. It bored him. He was almost independent and being at home at that age has its frustrations.'

'There was nothing else?'

Mrs Hunter shook her head.

'Did he mention that he was seeing anyone special?'

'A boyfriend, you mean?'

'Yes.'

'I think it was enough for him to tell me he was gay. To have presented me with a boyfriend as well would have been a little too much too soon.'

'Did he have any particularly close friends I could talk to?'

'He saw a lot of his old school friends.' She reeled off a list of names and colleges, which Sam wrote down.

'You mentioned that he stayed in a friend's house during the vacation. Do you have the address?'

'No, I'm afraid not. We could get hold of Adrian on his mobile and we sent any post to the college. He was only there a week or so.'

A few minutes later a phone call to Mrs Hunter's mobile brought their conversation to an end.

Mark didn't come back to his rooms that night. He had told Sam that he was meeting some friends straight from the train station and wasn't sure when he'd be back. Sam had wondered if Brendan might be among the friends but had resisted teasing him. Mark was too irritable and tense to tease at the moment. So when she woke up the following morning and found he wasn't there she assumed that he had spent the night elsewhere, perhaps at Brendan's, and then gone straight to deliver a lecture. Sam made herself some coffee with the grounds she'd bought from Cardews and then sat down on the sofa with a piece of paper and a pen. At the top of the paper she wrote 'To Do' and then made the following list:

1. Try Phil again – forensics/toxicology report. How did Hunter die? Suicide, murder, accident . . .
2. Talk to Mrs Prendergast re Kenneth Adams
3. Check out about pig's head with Barry

4. Contact friends of Adrian Hunter – where was he staying Easter vacation?
5. Kenneth Adams's nephew?

She was just deciding which to embark on first when her mobile rang. It was Phil.

'Do you know where Mark is?'

'I think he's lecturing this morning.'

Phil sighed. 'I spoke to him yesterday evening and told him we needed to talk to him again. He said he'd come to the station this morning and he hasn't turned up.'

'Maybe he got held up in London. He was at a conference there all day yesterday.'

'Well, if you see him will you tell him to call me?'

'Sure.' Sam looked at her list and decided to chance her arm. 'Is there anything you could tell me about how Adrian Hunter died yet?'

'No. If you see Mark get him to call me at once.'

'Phil—'

'I'm not going there, Sam. I don't know why the Provost's involved you. He should just let us get on with the job.'

'Still playing it by the book and thinking it'll get you a promotion?'

'Oh, grow up.'

The phone went dead. So, schmoozing her ex-boyfriend had gone well. She looked at her list. Next up was Mrs Prendergast.

Mrs Prendergast was looking resplendent in a green tweed suit. She was also bashing seven bells out of her keyboard and didn't look as if she wanted to be interrupted.

'Sorry to disturb you,' Sam said, poking her head round the door.

Mrs Prendergast sniffed. 'The people who say that rarely are.'

'I'm sure you're right,' Sam said in her most oleaginous manner, 'but I was wondering if you'd had any more thoughts about the letter.'

'I have had plenty of thoughts about the letter.'

Sam came into the room, closed the door behind her and leaned against it.

Mrs Prendergast had folded her arms and was staring at her. She said nothing.

'Would you be willing to share your thoughts with me?' Sam stammered.

'I am pursuing certain lines of investigation that will shortly come to fruition. Until that time I think it best I remain silent.'

'You couldn't perhaps give me some indication . . . ?'

'No.'

'Are you aware that a pig's head was left on the Lodgings doorstep yesterday morning?'

'No, I was not . . . I . . .'

'I am concerned that matters are escalating and that we need to get to the bottom of things sooner rather than later. Do you see what I mean?'

She nodded. 'A pig's head.'

'With needles in the eyes.'

'That is really most unnecessary.'

Interesting way of describing it, Sam thought. She continued. 'Yesterday I had a chat with Professor Petheridge.'

Mrs Prendergast didn't say anything.

'I was concerned that he might be holding a grudge against the Provost because he was passed over for that position himself.'

'I can assure you that Professor Petheridge is amongst the least harmful of the Governing Body. That is frankly a ridiculous suggestion.'

'Well, having met him I agree with you wholeheartedly, but in the course of our conversation he brought another matter to my attention. He told me there was someone else who had, shall we say, a strong attachment to Kenneth Adams and therefore might feel that he had been particularly hard done by.'

Mrs Prendergast looked at Sam in the way a rattlesnake might look at a mouse.

'I have absolutely no idea what you are talking about, but I will say this: it was quite clear to me that Kenneth had crossed a line in his behaviour. He is a deeply unhappy man who was always going to struggle with retirement. His family has always been the college and his students. It is not altogether surprising that he found it difficult to leave. That is all I have to say on the matter. I think his removal was sad but I could also see the necessity of the action taken. I will let you know if my other lines of enquiry come to fruition.'

And with that dismissal she turned her back on Sam and returned to her keyboard.

Sam stood for a moment in the quadrangle looking at Alex, the college gardener, planting red geraniums into the borders of the lawns. She recognised in herself a tendency to swing between prickly malice and slushy nostalgia in her feelings towards Oxford. Over the last few years prickly malice had generally gained the upper hand but now, looking at the red of the geraniums and the vivid green of the lawns, she felt that ebb away. She sat down on the stone steps that sloped down to the lawns and for a few moments enjoyed the warmth of the sun on the back of her neck and the smell of newly cut grass and recently turned-over earth. Then she got up and headed once again for the market.

This time, Barry wasn't there. It was his day off. After checking that he hadn't left a message for her she walked back to Mark's rooms and sat down with the list of Adrian's friends Mrs Hunter had given her. She wrote notes to all the people on there, explaining who she was and why she wanted to speak to them. She included her mobile number and asked them to phone her as soon as they got the note. Then she walked down to the lodge and put the notes in the internal postal system, which moved post free between all the colleges. They would get them that evening, so hopefully they'd contact her that evening or tomorrow morning. Then she went back to Mark's rooms to wait for his return. She'd tried his mobile a couple of times but still hadn't managed to talk to him about her conversation the previous night with Juliet Bartlett.

But Mark didn't return.

As the afternoon wore on, and there was still no sign of her brother and no call from him, she was unable to quell her growing anxiety. Perhaps he's in an afternoon seminar, she thought. Perhaps he didn't get my calls before going in. He'll phone when he comes out. He'll be back by six. He wasn't.

Finally she cracked and phoned her parents. She hadn't wanted to because she wasn't exactly sure what Mark had said to them. She knew he'd spoken to them after Adrian Hunter died, he'd had to because there'd been something about it in the *Oxford Mail*, but she didn't know what he had told them about being questioned by the police. Not much was her best guess. Her mother picked up the phone.

'Hi, Mum. Mark's not there, is he?'

'No. I haven't spoken to him since he phoned a couple of days ago to tell us about what happened to that poor boy. Is he all right?'

'Yes, yes, I'm sure he's fine. It's just I was expecting him back in his rooms and he's not here. I thought he might be with you.'

'You'd tell me if something was the matter?'

'Yes, of course.'

'When I spoke to him he sounded very upset about what had happened to Adrian.'

'Yes, he was.'

'And now you don't know where he is?'

'I'm sure he'll turn up.' Even to her own ears Sam's voice sounded falsely light-hearted.

'If I hear from him I'll let you know. Will we be seeing anything of you while you're down?'

'Yes, definitely. Everything's a bit up in the air at the moment but once I know what I'm doing...'

'You'll let us know if you get hold of him.'

'Yes, of course.'

Sam put down the phone and sighed. Well, her attempts to downplay how worried she was hadn't fooled her mother one bit and speaking to her had just made her more anxious.

Phil phoned again.

'I don't know where he is,' Sam said. 'He's not been back here all day.'

'We need to speak to him, Sam. He's doing himself no favours with this kind of behaviour.'

'What kind of behaviour?'

'He's probably gone on a bender. He did that before, didn't he? We had to drag him out of the Red Lion. Have you checked there?'

'No.'

'What about your parents?'

'I've just spoken to them. They've not seen or heard from him in the last couple of days.'

'Check the pub, Sam. He's probably there.'

Sam decided to take his advice. As she was pushing her way into the Red Lion her mobile rang.

'Mark?' she said.

'No,' a stranger's voice replied. 'You sent a note to college giving this number to phone. My name's Charlie Stroud.'

'Thanks a lot for getting back to me,' Sam said. 'Can I buy you a drink? I'm in the Red Lion.'

They arranged to meet in twenty minutes. Meantime, Sam looked around the pub and then had a word with George, the landlord, who told her Mark hadn't been in all day.

Charlie Stroud turned out to be the podgy undergraduate with the lank hair who had told Petheridge that his knees would dislocate if he jumped like a frog.

'You?' he said, coming up to Sam at the bar.

'How are the knees?' she asked.

'Petheridge is going to kill us all if he has his way. He is intending that we jump between the pontoons while wearing frog masks that almost completely obscure our sight. We are arguing with him about the distance between the pontoons. He says that to maximise the drama they should be as far apart as possible. The audience should think that we are going to miss.'

'God,' Sam said.

'Exactly.' He pulled up his trousers to reveal a lengthy abrasion down his shin and then showed her the backs of his hands, which were covered in scrapes and bruises. 'It hurts like hell when you do.'

Sam brought them some drinks and they sat down. 'I'm very sorry about Adrian,' she said. 'It must have been a terrible shock. Was he a close friend?'

'He wasn't a particularly easy man to get close to but we'd been all the way through school together.'

'Is there anything you could tell me that might explain what's happened?'

'He was a bit of a mess.'

'What do you mean?'

'His behaviour had become more and more erratic this year. I thought he'd calm down once he came out. It was hardly a surprise to those of us who'd known him a long time, but it didn't appear to be the answer to his problems. He still continued to drink heavily and he was mixing the drink with drugs.'

'Are you sure?'

'Absolutely – he could supply you with anything you wanted, from grass upwards, and all kinds of pills, and he was taking a fair few of them himself.'

'You think he overdosed, then?'

'It wouldn't surprise me at all. This term things really fell apart for him. He became severely depressed. He'd told his mother about his sexuality in the Easter holiday but not his father. I told him he should come off all the drugs he was taking but he told me to piss off.'

'Do you know where he got the drugs from?'

'I saw him with someone once and wondered. He wasn't one of us, older and very good-looking. I thought he might have been his lover . . . Adrian kept all that part of his life separate from us.'

'Would you recognise the man again?'

'Perhaps. He wasn't someone you'd forget in a hurry.'

'Have you told any of this to the police?'

He shook his head. 'They haven't asked to speak to me, and talking to the police about drugs is tricky.'

Sam nodded. 'Thanks a lot for talking to me.'

'He was a prickly fellow, Adrian, and he was in over his head, but if he was taking something dodgy it could have been any of us.'

Sam nodded.

Charlie drained his drink and stood up to leave. 'You know Petheridge wants us to dress in tight bright green tunics cut very short so as to reveal an artificial phallus.'

'God!' Sam said.

'He says that this would be in full conformity with the ritual aspects of a Dionysian festival. What do you think?'

'Resist him at all costs,' Sam said.

'It's difficult enough just learning the Greek.'

'He told me you were sold out.'

'Yes,' Charlie said gloomily. 'He told us that as well. News is spreading round the university like wild fire. Anyone who knows any of us is going to turn up just to see if we manage to survive to the end of the evening.'

'I'm tempted myself,' Sam said.

She stayed in the Red Lion until closing time, then made her way slowly back to St Barnabas's.

Mark's rooms were empty. She checked her phone – no message. He'd been missing now for twenty-four hours.

She sat down on the sofa, shifting her shoulders in an attempt to ease the tension that had locked in there and was beginning to crawl remorselessly up her neck over the top of her skull and into her eyes. It did no good. Anxiety had been building in her all day as if she had a key in the centre of her chest and an invisible hand was turning it and turning it. She had an image of herself as an old tin toy that was being wound up until it broke. She tried to take a deep breath but felt that she could only half fill her lungs, that the anxiety was sitting in the other half like concrete.

Sam had lost count of the number of missing persons cases she had taken on since working for and then taking over the Gentle Way Investigations agency three years ago. She had lost count of the number of times she had counselled people whose loved ones had gone missing to take one day at a time. She knew and had repeated all the statistics endlessly.

Of the 210,000 people that would be reported missing each year the vast majority returned within seventy-two hours. Abduction, which is what people feared the most, was by far the least likely reason for someone to disappear and only one per cent of adults went missing as a result of being a victim of crime or force by others.

She had referred clients to the National Missing Persons Help Line, she had phoned hospitals and morgues, she had liaised with the police and social services, she had checked credit card statements and phone bills and she had interviewed countless families, friends and colleagues.

She had tried, as their anxiety grew with each passing day, to reassure them that everything possible was being done to find their loved ones. But this was the first time that someone she knew had gone missing.

She ran through the checklist of reasons why adults went missing and applied them to Mark.

1. Family conflict/relationship problem – not really. He had a much better relationship than Sam with their mother and stepfather and Brendan was too newly arrived and Mark too indifferent to him to be the source of any problem. However, he had been very upset by their father's return.
2. Debt – not a problem as far as Sam knew.
3. Illness/accident – not illness, at any rate. Perhaps an accident but he'd gone to London on the train. It wasn't as if he could have been involved in a road traffic accident.
4. General anxiety or stress – well, some, certainly, because of what had happened with Adrian Hunter, but surely not enough to make him disappear. It just made him appear guilty.
5. Depression/amnesia – no.
6. Alcohol/drugs – he'd certainly been drinking heavily a while back and that had been directly linked to her father's return. He might have gone on an almighty bender, but when he'd done that a few months back he'd gone to the Red Lion and he'd never got so drunk that he'd disappeared for twenty-four hours before.

And then the final and scariest one – abduction. Most feared, least likely – that phrase went round and round in her head. Well, there was no way that had happened.

'Mark,' she said out loud, 'where the hell are you?'

Sam couldn't imagine her life without Mark. He was a crucial part of her security and identity, but there was no getting away from the fact that the recent return of their father had ushered in an unusually rocky patch in their relationship and this had a lot to do with the very different assessments the two siblings had of him.

Sam, only four years old when their father disappeared, had idolised him as a dead hero her whole life and that had fuelled a large part of her own success in her judo career. He had been a fighter, she was a fighter and a World Champion in her chosen sport. Mark, eight years older than Sam, had no illusions about what sort of man Geoffrey Falconer had been; he had the scars on his forehead to prove it.

When, nine months ago, Geoffrey Falconer had walked out of the past very much alive, Sam had been forced to come to terms with the reality of who her father was and a very different story had emerged.

A story of his faked death and involvement in an assassination squad in Northern Ireland. A story coloured by his violent and abusive behaviour towards his family.

The dead hero had come back into Sam's life as a living monster, and all kinds of painful memories had started to stir. He claimed he was looking for reconciliation and forgiveness. Well, perhaps he was. But that hadn't made things any easier as far as Sam and her family were concerned. He may have disappeared for the last couple of months and Sam may have got some sort of balance back, but she also knew that balance was precarious and dependent on his continuing absence.

Narrative wreckage is what Reg had called it. 'Everyone has a story of their lives, of their families, of their relationships, of the past. True or false, everyone has a story. It's part of who we are. Yours was of a dead hero father. Your story has just been torn up.'

One part of her narrative that Sam believed could never be torn up was the part that involved the strength of her relationship with her brother. It was a rock-solid and reliable part of her life. It was an intrinsic part of who she was.

But where the hell was he?

CHAPTER NINE

After a night's sleep from which she awoke more exhausted than when she went to bed, Sam spent the morning on the phone trying to track down Mark's movements. What she found out was the following. He had attended the seminar in London. He'd gone for a drink with some of the other participants between six and seven in the evening and then said he had to catch his train. From phoning round friends of his in Oxford she'd found out that he'd been expected at a birthday celebration at Le Petit Blanc but hadn't attended or phoned to make his excuses. The following morning he had failed to turn up to give a lecture on Shakespeare's sonnets and he hadn't phoned in to cancel that either. Basically, from the point that he left the pub in London no one had seen or heard from him. Another phone call to her parents again drew a blank.

That afternoon she packed her stuff into an overnight bag; she'd arranged to spend the night at her parents. She left a note for Mark to phone her at once if he came back and set out for St Aldate's police station. There she asked to speak to Phil. The desk sergeant told her to take a seat and she sat down under a pinboard fluttering with notices, opposite a man whose right leg was jiggling up and down like a pneumatic drill. He was wearing a white tracksuit, loose trainers and no socks. Sam stared at the blue veins on the instep of his foot and then tried to position herself so that she couldn't see the movement of his leg but everything she tried failed, the knee continued to jump up and down and then the man began to chew his nails. In the end, all she could think of to block him out was to close her eyes. The trouble was how he looked was exactly how she felt – edgy as hell.

'Sam.'

Her eyes sprang open and she saw Phil standing in front of her.

'Well?' he said. 'Where is he?'

'I've no idea, Phil.'

'Christ, Sam! All hell's broken loose here.'

'Why?'

He sighed and rubbed the palm of his hand over his face. 'Come on,' he said and led the way through a door, along a linoleum-covered corridor to a large open-plan office. The blond-haired DC Woods was the only other presence in the far corner of the room. Phil sat down and pulled over a chair from the desk behind him so that Sam could sit next to him.

'Mr Hunter pulled some strings and insisted on seeing everything we had on his son's death.'

'Right.'

'That included the notes of our interview with Mark.'

'Oh, shit, his wife said he didn't even know his son was gay. Neither of them had got round to telling him.'

'He's furious. It's why we were going to talk to Mark again. Hunter insisted and wanted to be there when it took place.'

'How come he gets to tell you what to do?'

'Friends in high places.'

'Surely that's not by the book, is it?'

'Book's well and truly torn up on this one, Sam. He can't accept his son's death. At the moment it's looking like Adrian OD'd, but it's not clear if that was intentional or accidental. Hunter's father has latched on to the fact that there's evidence Adrian was in a fight before he died. We're doing tests on his clothing to find out if the bloodstains are just his or if someone else's are on there. If Adrian was in a fight and that contributed towards his death then he'll find that easier to deal with than the other scenarios. He's looking for another reason and he's decided Mark's it.'

'But I spoke to Juliet Bartlett. Even she didn't believe it. She said she thought Adrian was just covering up for the fact he was struggling with his work and Mark was calling him on it.'

'I know, but you can see that once she told us what Adrian had said we had to follow up on it. We had to ask Mark.'

'And now Hunter's got the wrong end of the stick.'

'He's jumped the gun. Instead of waiting for the forensics, he's obsessed with Mark. When Mark failed to turn up he went ballistic. He's insisting we treat Mark as a murder suspect.'

'That's ridiculous.'

'The man's son's just died, he's not behaving rationally.'

'So, is that what's going to happen?'

'I don't know, but a hell of a lot of pressure is coming down the line for us to find Mark.'

'Maybe that's not such a bad thing. At least you'll be forced to look for him.'

'I'm sorry about what's happened with Mark, Sam, but for us to be out there looking for him in these circumstances is a complete waste of time.'

'If I give you his mobile number will you check his records?'

Phil nodded. 'Give it to me.'

Sam scribbled it down on a piece of paper. 'The only other thing I can think to do is to check on Brendan.'

'Who?'

'He was there when you came to Mark's rooms on May morning.'

'The Marlboro man?'

'That's the one. I met him for the first time then. Mark's just got involved with him. I don't know much about him.'

'You think Mark could be with him?'

'It's a possibility.'

'What's his surname?'

'I don't know.'

'Telephone number or address?'

She shook her head. 'All I know is his first name and that he's a doctor. Mark was being a bit coy about his level of interest.'

'Presumably he lives in Oxford?'

'I don't even know that.'

Phil groaned. 'Do you know how many hospitals there are in Oxford?'

'Nuffield, Radcliffe, Churchill, Warneford . . .'

Phil pushed back his chair and ran his hands over the stubble on his head.

'Did you tell Mark about Adrian's father when you asked him to come to the station for more questioning?' Sam asked.

'No, I just said we had a few more details to check up on.'

'What's worrying me is that Mark must have known that if he didn't turn up it would look suspicious. It's like sticking a notice on his forehead saying, "I have something to hide." He's not stupid. He'd know it was the worst thing he could do.'

Phil nodded. 'Maybe he'll turn up today with some perfectly good excuse for what has happened.'

'It's what I say to my clients,' Sam said, 'and I don't think they usually believe me either.'

On leaving the station, Sam walked up St Aldate's across Carfax and into Cornmarket. The council were digging it up and it was a mess of no-go areas, barriers and piles of concrete slabs. It was hopeless, Sam thought, nothing that anyone did to this street could in any way redeem it. All the character and charm had been beaten out of it years ago. A group of teenagers were hanging around outside McDonald's in the evening sunshine.

As she crossed St Giles and headed for the Banbury Road, Sam's pace slowed then slowed again. Outside the Old Parsonage Hotel she stopped and rested against a wall. She had to get straight in her head what she was going to say to her mother and stepfather. Maybe the best thing would be to treat them like clients. Calm them down, reassure them and stress that everything possible was being done to find Mark. Yes, that would be the correct approach.

Park Town was an eighteenth-century crescent just off the bottom of the Banbury Road. A couple of minutes later Sam was standing on their doorstep ringing the bell. Her mother, Jean, opened the door; she was tall and dark like Mark, with a bob of black hair that reached exactly to the level of her chin. The only unruly aspect of her mother's appearance was her nose, which although long and elegant had a slight kink in the middle.

'Hi, Mum,' Sam said, then felt her throat close up.

Her mother took one look at her, pulled her into the hall, closed the front door and hugged her. 'Look,' she said, holding Sam at arm's length. 'I'm sure there's a perfectly reasonable explanation for what has happened. We just have to stay calm and take each day as it comes.'

Sam hung back, allowing her mother to lead the way into the kitchen, and blinked away tears. Her mother was a brusque, rather remote woman, seeing her face suffused with worry and empathy had caught Sam completely off guard.

Well, that had gone as planned.

'Have you eaten?'

Sam shook her head.

'I'll get you something. Peter will be back later.'

The kitchen ran the width of the house. The windows by the sink looked out onto the garden at the back and a large round table was positioned at the other end of the room. Sam took off her coat and slung it on the back of a chair and sat down.

'Omelette all right?'

Sam nodded. She didn't really feel hungry; she just wanted the reassurance of being cooked for by her mother. She watched as her mother put on a blue and white striped apron to protect her black wool trousers and burnt orange linen shirt, broke two eggs into a white china bowl and began to beat the living daylights out of them.

'Mushrooms and potatoes all right?'

'Great.'

For a while neither of them spoke. The only noise was the sizzling of the frying food. Sam looked round the kitchen. Her mother and stepfather had contrasting tastes when it came to art. Her mother was traditional, her stepfather, Peter, modern. They had divided the rooms in the house between them and Peter had got the kitchen and his study and her mother had got the living room and the hall. It was an orderly compromise. Sam looked at some new paintings hanging on the walls and thought not for the first time that more interesting things must go on in Peter's head than he was ever willing to let on.

Her mother slid the omelette onto a plate, took off her apron and put the plate down in front of Sam. She took two glasses out of an overhead cupboard, picked up a bottle of red wine, which had been standing next to the gas hob, and came and sat down at the table. She took the stopper out of the bottle and poured them both some wine.

Sam tucked in, finding her appetite had returned with a vengeance. Despite the difficulties in their relationship, one thing Sam had always appreciated about her mother was her cooking.

'I don't know what's worse,' her mother said, looking into her wine glass. 'That poor boy's death or the fact that Mark's disappeared. The two aren't connected, are they?'

Sam shook her head. 'I've just come from talking to Phil at the police station. He doesn't think so.'

Sam's mother sighed. 'He hadn't been to see us for a while. Maybe if I'd asked him round he . . .'

'Don't torture yourself with that, Mum. You see lots of him. He'd got himself a new boyfriend – he was busy, that's all.'

'We hadn't met him.'

'Well, he probably wanted to make sure it was serious before bothering you.'

'Yes,' she said slowly. 'That was probably it.' She folded her hands in her lap and stared at her wine glass.

Sam stabbed a potato with her fork. 'This is delicious.'

'You know it's never been a problem for us?'

'What?'

'His sexuality.'

'Yes, of course.'

'But *he* knows that, doesn't he, Sam?'

Sam reached for her wine glass. 'Yes, I'm sure he does.'

'You don't think anything happened with this boy, do you?'

'No – he taught him. That was it. Absolutely nothing happened.'

'But the police—'

'The police are being bounced on by Adrian's father, Mum. That's all.'

Her mother watched her eat for a few minutes. When Sam looked up she saw a smile cross her mother's face.

'What?' she said.

'Do you remember when I tried to get you both to eat more slowly?'

Sam laughed. Much to her mother's embarrassment Mark and her had always been ferociously fast eaters. Her mother's approach to meals was that they were social events, not just times when you shovelled in as much food as possible and then made a run for it. Being the wife of the head of an Oxford college meant that during term time they often had people to stay and those people came to dinner.

One time her mother had told them that they were not to finish their food until the slowest person had finished. On that occasion they had a particularly garrulous slow-eating Bishop. Mark and Sam raced through the meal as usual but then left a sprout each on their plate. They watched and waited and as the Bishop placed his final forkful in his mouth, they stabbed their sprouts clattered their knives and forks onto their plates and looked at their mother in triumph. It was the last time she had made that particular suggestion.

'Michael Winner says that all Scorpios attack their food,' Sam said.

Her mother put her head in her hands. 'Please don't say that to Peter – not in the present circumstances.'

Sam laughed. Her stepfather, Peter, was a mathematician; to talk to him about astrology was to cause him extreme mental anguish. It had always been a fantastically easy way to wind him up. She pushed her plate away from her and reached for the wine glass.

'What are you going to do?' her mother asked.

Sam sipped her wine and put down the glass. 'Try and find him.'

'In tandem with the police?'

'In tandem with Phil, at any rate.'

Sam's mother frowned and swilled her wine round and round.

'Mum, I can't just sit around doing nothing.'

The front door opened and closed and shortly afterwards Peter walked into the kitchen. He was tall like Sam's mother and had dark Italian good looks. He was wearing a pale green linen suit and white open-necked shirt.

'Sam,' he said, 'you're here.'

Sam stood up and he hugged her warmly. Something he never usually did.

He kissed her mother and then nodded at the wine. 'I might have some of that.' He went and got himself a glass and then joined them at the table.

'Any news?' he asked.

'I'm afraid not,' Sam said. 'I've just come from the police station. There was nothing new.'

'Have you any idea where he might be?'

She shook her head.

'I've just come from talking to Edward Payne. He was telling me how very helpful you are being over the problems in St Barnabas's.'

Sam sighed. Today she had made absolutely no progress with those problems whatsoever.

'It's nice to see you, Sam.'

'You too.'

Peter smiled a tight smile and looked from Sam to her mother and then to his wine glass.

A few minutes later Sam made her excuses and went to bed, unable to stand the silent anxiety emanating from her parents. She paused on the landing, seeing the light on in Mark's old bedroom. She pushed open the door and went inside. Books from his childhood lined the wall. Her mother was constantly trying to get him to either give them away or take them but because of the shortage of space in his rooms in college and his emotional attachment to his books, he wouldn't do either.

She looked at the familiar titles, running her finger over the spines: *Stig of the Dump*, *The Silver Sword*, *Custer's Gold*, *Where Eagles Dare*, *White Eagles Over Serbia*, *Moonfleet*, *Treasure Island*, *Maddon's Rock*, *the Cruel Sea*, *Day of the Jackal*, then the black spines of Hardy and the orange ones of Greene and Waugh and then the yellow spines of a line of Zane Grey westerns.

She'd read most of them herself, trying to play catch-up with her voracious reader of an older brother. At the bottom was a pile of Tintin and Asterix books.

An argument they had had one long tedious car journey when they were children came back to her. They had both made lists of their top-five Tintin books, then swapped lists.

She heard Mark's voice clearly in her head: '*Tintin in Tibet* at number one! You're joking. Why?'

'Because I love the turquoise anorak he wears and for the scenes in the ice caves,' Sam replied.

'There is no question that the all time best Tintin book is *Prisoner of the Sun*.'

'What's your reason?'

'Where else does Captain Haddock get spat in the face by a llama. Where else does Tintin swing through a waterfall with Snowy strapped to his back?'

Sam smiled at the memory. They'd never managed to agree on that one. She picked up the pile of Tintin books. At the door she stopped and turned round and looked at the bookshelves again. She had an image of someone being the sum of all the books they had read in their lives. Mark's attachment to his books had always been a visceral thing.

She crossed the room and placed her hand against the spines of the books as if in touching them she was touching Mark himself, imagining that behind these spines were his heart and lungs, his blood and sinews, as if she had her hand on his chest and could feel his heart thumping. Literature was his lifeblood and the great thing about Mark had always been that he was in no way snobbish about it; he could get as enthusiastic about a Tintin book as a Yeats poem.

After a couple of pages of *Tintin in Tibet* she fell asleep.

She was in a field of long grass. It was summer and she was a child; she could smell the hot grass and feel the sun beating down on her. She stumbled against something and looking down saw that it was a hand. 'Hello,' she said and took hold of it and pulled. The hand was warm but surprisingly light. As she pulled there was no resistance and soon she saw that the arm had been severed from the body – veins tendons, muscles and the white glare of a bone were all visible at the top of the arm where it should have been joined to the torso. Blood was pumping onto the ground at her feet. She let go and moved on and found another arm, then two legs, then the torso. Everywhere she looked the earth was red with blood. But where was the head? Then she heard Mark's voice. 'Quick, quick – you have to find me. Hurry – soon it'll be too late. Too late. Sam, you're too late.'

Sam woke bathed in sweat. A police car's siren wailed in the distance. She lay there for a while and then got up and tiptoed downstairs to the kitchen. The light was on and Peter was standing over the kettle.

'Bad dreams,' Sam said and sat down at the table.

'Would you like something?' Peter asked.

'What are you making?'

'I hadn't quite decided.'

'Tea would be good.'

'Yes,' he said. 'Of course.'

He made a pot of tea and put it on the table, then brought over two cups and the bottle of milk. He sat down and rubbed his face. Sam poured the milk into the cups and then poured out the tea.

It was Peter who spoke first. 'I was thinking earlier how reassuring it is to have an expert in these kinds of things in the family.' He picked up his cup and blew on the surface of the tea.

Sam stared blankly at him and then realised he was paying her a compliment. She was astonished. She wasn't used to Peter saying anything positive about what she did for a living. Among the ferociously highly achieving and competitive families of North Oxford, saying your daughter was a private eye wasn't much to boast about. You were in the territory of double firsts, top marks in the Civil Service exams and speech writing for senior politicians. To cap it all they were probably married to men who looked like George Clooney and had triplets.

'Good,' she said. 'I'm glad.'

'There's nothing the police are keeping from us, is there?'

'I don't think so, no.'

He nodded. They sat there, drinking their tea, listening to the first birds welcoming in a rainy and blustery spring day.

Later that morning Sam stood in Valerie Jenkins's rooms in front of a picture of a nude woman. Valerie Jenkins was the French and Philosophy tutor and Mark's closest ally in St Barnabas's. If anyone in the college had any idea of where he was it would be her. The picture was the work of a notoriously reclusive but famous British painter. The woman had been painted from behind and Sam wondered if the rumours were true, that this was Valerie and that she'd been paid for services rendered with this painting. Not, the rumours added, that she needed to be paid for anything. She was so rich it was said that she had taken her divorce settlement in wine from her French aristocratic wine-growing ex-husband.

At the moment Valerie was on the phone, looking out of the window down into the quad. She turned round and pulled a face at Sam, indicating that the person on the other end was going on and on and she couldn't get him to stop.

Sam mouthed. 'It's OK,' and sat down on a sofa covered with a luxuriant fake wolfskin throw.

These rooms were stylish and comfortable in a way that Mark's patently weren't. Chaos was not the defining characteristic here; books were kept mainly in their place. The chairs and sofas were covered with throws, and a vase of parrot tulips stood on the coffee table between the sofa and the chairs. The parts of the walls not covered by books were hung with paintings, the white buildings and blue skies of Greece in one, the bright pink of bougainvillea growing over a courtyard in another.

Macavity, the St Barnabas's College cat, a thuggish tabby with raggedy ears, close-set eyes and huge hairy feet, was snoring in what could best be described as a sheepskin hammock attached to the side of a radiator. The cat was no fool, he'd spotted a fellow sensualist within about half an hour of Valerie's moving into college five years ago and now there was a dish and water bowl and a neat stack of Sheba packets piled up on a piece of newspaper near the door. Valerie, Sam thought, was not the kind of woman to allow a cat to get obese.

She put the phone down. 'I'm sorry about that, Sam – committees, committees, committees – the bane of academic life.'

Valerie was in her fifties, tall as a beanpole with grey hair cut stylishly short. She was wearing a pale blue cut-velvet scarf, which matched her eyes. She stood out from her colleagues in one very important way: she was the only one who ever wore black leather trousers. On her feet she had pointed high-heeled boots, which made Sam think of pig-sticking. She was the kind of woman who wouldn't have been seen dead wearing sensible shoes or riding a bicycle sedately along the Banbury Road with a tweed skirt inching its way over her knees. Her preferred mode of transport was a bright-red Yamaha motorbike.

She sat down next to Sam and placed both arms along the back of the sofa.

'When did you last speak to Mark?' Sam asked.

'Four days ago. We sat next to each other at high table. He was very upset about what had happened to Adrian. He came back here after we'd eaten and sat where you're sitting and his foot was going up and down.' She jigged her own foot up and down. 'And I told him to stop it. It was getting on my nerves and he said he wasn't even aware he was doing it. He was depressed about the interview at the police station. He said that the way they had talked to him made him feel dirty. Of course, he was upset about the boy's death. He was very fond of him. He was worried that the pressure he had put on him about his work might have contributed to his death.'

'Was there anything else that was upsetting him?'

'You know a couple of months ago there was all that stuff about your father; Mark was knocked sideways by that. Do you think anything could have happened there? We had talked at length about the ethics of forgiveness, how to forgive, the consequences of withholding forgiveness. How does one know if one has?'

Sam shook her head. 'My father's been completely out of the picture for the last couple of months. Mark would have told me if anything was going on there.'

'But for Mark, you know, it was a terrible experience to meet your father again. I was worried about him then. I thought he could allow his feelings to overwhelm him completely. He has not been the same since that time – more depressed, more brooding over things. Maybe this thing with Adrian was the last straw for him. On top of everything else.'

Sam felt a knot of anxiety tighten in her stomach. 'Did he ever talk to you about Brendan?'

'Who is Brendan?'

'A man he had just met. He was with him when I came up for May Day morning.'

Valerie shook her head. 'Perhaps he was keeping him to himself. You know how it is in the first stages – one wants to keep the bubble intact. Also, it can take a while before one is fit for company.'

'The only thing I know about him is that he's a doctor. I don't even know his surname. Did Mark tell you anything about him?'

'I'm afraid not. I'm sorry, Sam. I've been racking my brains to think if there was any indication in my conversation with him that would be of any help now but there's nothing that stands out. I'm sure he'll turn up soon. Maybe he just needed to get away for a few days to clear his head.'

'Have you heard about the letter the Provost received?'

'And the pig's head,' Valerie said. 'Everyone in the college knows about it.'

'How did you find out?'

'You know how it is in Oxford colleges. It is impossible to keep such things secret for any length of time.'

'What do you think?'

Valerie snorted. 'These men,' she said dismissively. 'They go to public school and then to college, then they spend their lives living in college ...'

'Kenneth Adams, you mean?'

'They never grow up. Everything is laid on for them and in their emotions they are no better than adolescents. A note, a pig's head – it is the ridiculous melodrama of teenagers, a schoolboy prank ... childish and hysterical. It will all blow over.'

Sam stood up and Macavity stopped snoring and opened an eye to see if she was going anywhere near the packets of Sheba. When she didn't, he sighed and closed his eyes again. Her phone rang.

'Sorry, Valerie,' she said and answered it. It was Phil.

'I thought I should warn you: they're getting a search warrant for Mark's rooms. They'll be going in tomorrow morning.'

'That's ridiculous, Phil.'

'Have you got stuff there?'

'No, I stayed at my parents' last night. But it makes no sense, Phil.'

'I know. I'm not arguing that it does but some of the forensics have come back. There is someone else's blood on Adrian's clothes and we're going to check it against Mark's DNA.'

'Thanks for the warning anyway.'

She closed up the phone and told Valerie. Valerie pulled open a drawer in her desk and turned round holding a key. 'This may be useful. It gives access to the main entrance of the college and the gate at the back where there is no lodge and no porters to see you. You have the keys to his rooms?'

Sam nodded. 'Thanks, Valerie.'

'Such a nice man,' Valerie said. 'Not a stuffy bone in his body.' She put her hand on Sam's arm. 'And so very proud of you.'

Sam bit down on her lower lip and busied herself with stroking Macavity.

CHAPTER TEN

That night Sam couldn't sleep. She tossed and turned until two o'clock and then, seeing the key Valerie had given her on her bedside table, came to a decision. She'd go to his rooms. OK, it wasn't rational but tomorrow the police would be tramping through them. Perhaps she might find something that would explain everything. Also, somewhere lurking at the back of her mind was another reason for going. If she found anything incriminating she could remove it. She got dressed and let herself quietly out of her parents' house into the silent streets of North Oxford.

Twenty minutes later Sam slid the key into the lock of the wooden gates at the back of St Barnabas's and stepped into the fellows' car park. Following the same route she had taken that morning with the Provost she swiftly crossed the yard and continued along the passage towards the main part of the college. The sweet smell of cherry blossom hung in the still night air. She reached up and gently shook a branch, feeling the petals fall onto the top of her head and her outstretched hand like a gentle benediction. Keeping to the shadows Sam turned right and made her way towards Mark's staircase.

Oxford colleges changed at night. During the day, filled with the hustle and bustle of undergraduate life, you could persuade yourself that they were modern institutions, but in the stillness and quiet of the night, the past claimed them, the war memorials took on a different quality, the buildings seemed heavier, more solemn, more ancient. In the starkness of moonlight St Barnabas's was a chilly, eerie place; its stone no longer golden but bone white.

She stopped at the bottom of Mark's staircase and shivered. No undergraduate had managed to make much impact on Oxford life since Byron decided to keep a bear in his rooms. The place defied any attempt to shock or influence; it was like a padded cell that had experienced every kind of lunatic but had simply absorbed everything thrown at it and endured, leaving its occupants exhausted and defeated. Even Hitler hadn't had the temerity to bomb it.

In the middle of front quad Macavity was digging up the geraniums that Sam had seen the college gardener planting out so carefully only days before. For a second he froze and stared at Sam and then continued tearing at the newly dug-over earth. As she began to climb the stairs she heard the chapel bell strike three.

Inside Mark's rooms Sam stood stock-still, leaning against the door, waiting for her eyes to adjust to the darkness. The curtains had been drawn and the room was pitch black. All she could hear was the rapid beating of her heart. What on earth was she doing here?

When she'd opened the door, she'd half expected Mark to come out of his bedroom, scratching his head and blinking in surprise. She had observed the phenomenon in her clients when someone went missing. It was a bit like losing your purse. You kept looking in the last place you'd seen it – your pocket or your bag – you looked and you looked until, exhausted and bewildered, you had to face the reality that some bastard had pinched it. That was the real reason she'd had to come back because she simply couldn't believe he wasn't here.

Gradually shapes began to form out of the darkness: the sofa and chairs, the books, Mark's desk over by the window and his computer. Sam slumped down in an armchair, feeling hopeless. Where should she begin?

A noise from Mark's bedroom made her freeze. She waited, listening for any follow-up sound but when none came she ignored it. It was probably just the floorboards creaking or another pile of books falling over. She reached into the pocket on the knee of her trousers and took out a small torch, stood up and turned it on.

She sat down at Mark's desk and opened all the drawers in turn. Her mother had bought the walnut bureau from the twin brothers who had run an antique shop in Ship Street. When Mark moved into his rooms in St Barnabas's she had given the desk to him, and Sam had helped him get it up here. She remembered him standing with his hands on his hips, once they'd got it up the staircase, saying, 'Isn't it fantastic?'

It wasn't really because there wasn't enough room for his legs under it and he had to twist his body into terrible positions to use it, but he had always loved it because of the secret and hidden drawers it had. Sam checked all these as well as the more obvious ones but found nothing of interest.

In the bathroom she stood holding his toothbrush. She could take it but what would be the point. They could get DNA from a single hair on his pillow or his hairbrush. There was no way she could go all over these rooms removing every trace of him. She sighed and dropped it back into the glass and turned towards the bedroom.

The curtains were drawn in here too. The bed was a tangle of twisted blankets and sheets and books were scattered on the floor. A slim leather volume lay on his bedside table. Sam knew what it was immediately; Mark always kept it there – Shakespeare's sonnets. She sat down on the bed and held it in her hands, rubbing her thumb over the gold tooling, the soft, wood-like swirls on the surface of the leather. She pocketed the book and then picked up his pillow and buried her face in it.

A crash jerked her head out of the pillow. Then someone swore.

She jumped to her feet. A shape emerged from the shadows and charged straight at her. Sam didn't have time to think or even to step out of the way. She was pushed savagely to one side and fell, smashing her head on the edge of the bedside table. She scrambled to her feet and ran out of the room. She could hear someone running down the staircase and set off in pursuit. Taking the steps three at a time, she crash-landed at the bottom of the staircase and sprawled forwards onto her hands and knees out in the quad. She was struggling to get to her feet when a crushing blow landed on the back of her head and she passed out.

'Sam?' The voice seemed very far away but somehow familiar. 'Sam, can you hear me?'

She felt a hand on her cheek and swam gradually back up into consciousness. Phil was bending over her. She groaned and felt the back of her head. Her hand came away sticky with blood. She winced and closed her eyes again. When she reopened them she saw she was lying on a hospital bed.

'What the hell happened?'

'Pretty much my question to you,' Phil said.

'Where am I?'

'Casualty.'

'How did I get here?'

'The night porter was doing his rounds and found you unconscious at the bottom of Mark's staircase. He called an ambulance and then the police and here we all are. It appears that someone had been inside Mark's rooms, because the door had been left open.'

Sam put her head in her hands and groaned.

'Do you want to tell me what happened?'

'Someone hit me.'

'No kidding, I thought you just ran backwards into a wall.'

'If you're going to be sarcastic I'm not going to cooperate.'

'Were you in Mark's rooms?'

'Oh, what the fuck do you think, Phil?' She winced as searing pains shot into her head.

Phil ran his hand up the back of his neck and over the top of his head. 'Sam . . .'

'Of course I was in Mark's rooms.'

'How did you get in?'

'That doesn't matter. I was in there and then someone came at me, pushed me out of the way and ran out of the room. I followed and then at the bottom of the staircase I poked my head out and whack.'

'Someone was already in there?'

She nodded.

'Man? Woman?'

'Man.'

'Did you see his face?'

'No, it all happened too quickly. It was dark in there and he came at me with such speed I didn't have time to clock him. It felt like standing in the path of Jonah Lomu.'

'Did you find anything in Mark's rooms?'

'No.'

'Come on, Sam.'

'Look, I didn't. I'm telling you the truth. To be honest I got there and then I wondered what on earth I was doing. I think the only reason I went was because I just can't believe he's disappeared. I went to see if he was there.'

'What about this?' Phil held out the book of sonnets.

'You get your kicks now from frisking unconscious women? Very nice, Phil.'

'It fell out of your pocket. I suppose I could have just left it there. Maybe you'd have preferred it.'

Sam sighed. 'Look, I took it from his bedside table. It's just pure sentimentality on my part. There's nothing significant or helpful about it.'

A white-coated doctor joined them. He shone a light into Sam's eyes, made her follow his finger, without moving her head, and whacked her knees a couple of times with a rubber hammer. He told her he wanted her to have a scan but Sam, despite his and Phil's protestations, jumped off the bed and told him it wouldn't be necessary.

Half an hour later Sam let herself quietly back into her parents' house and collapsed into bed. Her head still hurt like hell and her pride had definitely been dented.

She was woken by her mother's hand on her shoulder.

'Is it Mark?' Sam said. 'Have they found him?'

Her mother shook her head.

Sam sat up and glanced at her alarm clock. She'd only been asleep an hour and she had a crashing headache and the kind of sickness in her stomach that presaged a migraine.

'What is it, Mum?'

'This just came in the post.'

Her mother handed her a card. On the outside was a picture of Christ carrying a lamb on his shoulders. For a minute Sam thought it was a Christmas card. She opened it and read it.

The Holy Sacrifice of the Mass
will be offered
for the repose of the soul of
Mark Falconer
with sincere sympathy
from

———————————

The space underneath had been left empty.

A wave of nausea swept through Sam. She looked at her mother. 'I don't understand. What is this?'

'It's a Catholic sympathy card. They send them out when someone dies to let you know that they are going to say a mass for the dead person.'

'Who's sent it? Why are they . . . ?' Her head felt woolly, the light from the window was hurting her eyes. She closed them then opened them again. 'Are they telling us he's dead?'

Her mother's face was ashen, her lipstick a vivid red slash against a grey background as if all the blood had run into her lips.

'Are they telling us he's dead?' Sam repeated, this time more loudly.

Her mother looked down at the floor, blinking rapidly.

Sam reached for her phone. 'I better get hold of Phil.'

Twenty minutes later, Phil, Peter, her mother and Sam were all sitting round the kitchen table. Sam was still in her pyjamas. Her headache was affecting her ability to see and think clearly. She rested her head in her hands and tried to keep the nausea under some kind of control. She was waiting for the painkillers to take effect – ten minutes to go.

'Are you all right, Sam?' Phil asked.

'I'll be fine, just waiting for the painkillers to kick in, then I'll be with you.'

'What do you think is going on?' Peter asked Phil.

'Someone is trying to scare you.'

'Do you think Mark's still alive?'

'If they've killed him why send this to you? There'd be no point. I think this is probably a preamble to soften you up. The threat is, if you don't do as we ask, then we'll kill him.'

Most feared, least likely . . . one per cent . . . abduction . . .

The words were spinning around in Sam's head. 'But why have they done it?'

Phil clasped his hands together and placed them on the table. 'What exactly *is* the situation with your father at the moment?'

Sam raised her head from her hands. 'I haven't seen him since the day after the article came out in the *Daily Tribune*. He hasn't been around for the last few months.'

'Do you know where he is?'

She shook her head.

'What about you both?' Phil said, turning to Sam's mother and stepfather.

'The same,' Sam's mother said. 'We haven't seen him. What's this got to do with him? Do you think he's taken Mark?'

'But that doesn't make any sense,' Sam said. 'Last time he saw Mark he was asking for his forgiveness; he's hardly going to kidnap him.'

'Maybe it's about revenge?' Peter said.

'Against Mark? But he hasn't got those kinds of enemies.'

'I was thinking more about your father. He has.'

Sam got up and went to the sink to pour herself a glass of water. What was it her father had said? If you can't get the man go for his family. Sam turned round. 'If that's the case surely we're all at risk.'

Silence fell over everyone in the room.

Phil cleared his throat. 'Do you have any way of getting hold of him?'

Sam didn't say anything. She sat back down at the table, closed her eyes and held her forehead with her right hand. It was the last thing on earth she wanted to do. It was bad enough that Mark had disappeared and now she was going to have to go looking for her father. She thought of what she'd said to Reg about being on an even keel. Not any more she wasn't. When she looked up they were all staring at her.

She sighed. 'I suppose I can try.'

Phil leaned across and touched her arm. 'It might be a good idea. Meanwhile, we wait.'

'What for?'

'Well, if this was meant as a softening-up exercise the next thing will be a demand of some sort.'

'For what?' Sam said.

'I don't know.'

The painkillers had still not taken effect.

'Have you got any other information on Mark?' Sam asked.

Phil shook his head. 'His credit card hasn't been used since he went missing. We got his phone records. After the call he took from me there's only one incoming call but it's from a pay-as-you-go registered to a fictitious name and address. Since that call the phone hasn't been used.'

'What about Brendan?'

'We're waiting for the hospitals to come back to us – nothing so far. Without a surname it's taking much longer. You look done in, Sam. You should try and get some sleep.'

She nodded. He was right. She couldn't think straight with the pain banging away in her head. She'd have to try and sleep it off. Maybe when she'd slept she'd have a clearer picture of things, because there was something she was sure she was missing, like something moving on the edge of her peripheral vision that she couldn't quite see yet.

She stood up unsteadily. 'You're right. If I don't nip this in the bud I could be stuck with it for days.'

Upstairs she lowered herself into bed and was immediately asleep.

When she woke there was a split second of calm before she remembered everything that had happened. It was like the first morning after someone has died when you wake and for a moment feel all right before you feel the loss and it all comes crashing down on you.

Then she remembered the card. *Mass will be offered for the repose of the soul of Mark Falconer,* and she felt as if a hand had closed over her throat and someone had stabbed her in the stomach.

Tentatively she raised her head from the pillow and much to her relief felt no pain. She sat up and squeezed the back of her neck and waggled her head a bit. Thank God, it was gone. Now she'd be able to think straight. What was it that she couldn't put together before? She swung her legs onto the ground, rubbed the back of her head and yawned. She looked at the clock on her mobile phone. Two o'clock in the afternoon.

One thing she hadn't mentioned to Phil was the possibility that this card might be linked to the Provost's note and the pig's head. If those two incidents were tied in with the removal of Kenneth Adams from the college then Mark could also be a target because he had been actively involved in moving him. So could Adrian, if it came to that – he'd been there packing up his books. Admittedly, the note and the pig's head had been directed at the Provost but suppose the perpetrator was now casting his or her net to include anyone that had been involved – that could easily include Mark and Adrian as well. Adams himself had not appeared vindictive about Mark, but someone else, looking at what had happened from the outside, might have thought Mark was as much to blame as anyone. Mark had been missing for four days. His absence was known about in the college. Someone could have seen it as an opportunity to make more mischief.

She considered why she hadn't mentioned any of this to Phil or her parents. It was partly because she hadn't quite been able to put all the connections together. But she had also been motivated by loyalty to the Provost. She needed to have a conversation with him before she got the police involved. She phoned St Barnabas's and asked to speak to him. His wife said he was in committees all day and was expected back at five. That gave her three hours.

She dressed quickly, touched base with her mother, made a copy of the sympathy card and an hour later was standing outside Kenneth Adams's house ringing the bell. The wisteria was now looking decidedly the worse for wear, as was Adams when he eventually opened the door.

The front room was in better order this time. A desk and chair had been set up in the window that looked into the front garden and a couple of armchairs had been placed round the fireplace. In one of these sat his nephew, Colin. There were still a lot of boxes but they had mainly been lined up against the walls.

Adams sat down. 'So, what have you come to accuse us of this time?'

'I wanted to fill you in with what has happened.'

'I doubt it. You're sniffing around for more information, I suppose.'

'A pig's head was left on the Provost's doorstep.'

'Ha,' Adams laughed. 'I'm delighted to hear it.'

'And this morning my parents received this.' She handed a copy of the sympathy card to Adams.

Adams read it and frowned, then handed it to his nephew. Adams rubbed his eyebrow and a fine mist of scurf drifted through the air.

'What does Mark think of this?'

'He's disappeared.'

'What do you mean?'

'He's been missing for four days. The point is this,' Sam continued, 'so far the mischief that's gone on in the college has not been reported to the police. The Provost has not wanted them involved, but I'm going to go and talk to him this afternoon. If this sympathy card is part of the other things that are going on in the college I want the police involved and I'm going to tell him that. The other incidents can be written off as malicious pranks but this card ... Now, is there anything that you can tell me?'

Adams swilled his whisky round his glass. 'I've told you, I don't know anything about these incidents and I like your brother. This has nothing to do with me.'

'What about others acting on your behalf?' She glanced at Colin.

'I can't be held responsible for their actions.'

'If you know who they are and you do nothing, I think you can, actually.'

'Well, I don't know who they are so I can't ask them to stop, can I?'

Sam stood up to leave. Colin, who had said nothing in the course of the conversation, followed her to the door.

'I'm sorry about Mark,' he said. 'You must be very worried.'

Sam turned round on the doorstep. She looked at him and Valerie's words came back to her – *no better than adolescents, a schoolboy prank*. He was one of those men who would still be looking boyish in his coffin.

'Because of the sympathy note a lot of heat is going to come down the line. It's going to be out of my hands now.'

His pale rather bulbous blue eyes smiled at Sam. 'Well, the sooner it stops the better for all of us. Although, of course, Uncle and I will miss these little visits.'

'I'm so very sorry about what has happened with Mark,' the Provost said, ushering Sam into his study. 'You must be worried sick.'

Sam was surprised. Emotional intelligence wasn't what she expected from academics. It came as a refreshing change.

'I am,' she said. 'We all are. Peter and my mother.'

'Any more news?'

'Of a sort,' Sam said, handing him the copy of the sympathy card.

'Oh,' he said, 'good grief.'

'It was sent to my parents' house. I'm worried that it may be part of the other things going on in the college. I would like to tell the police about the note and the pig's head.'

The Provost frowned. 'Of course, of course, if you feel you must, but I would think that this was a different kettle of fish altogether.'

'Why?'

'Well, the note and the pig's head were targeted directly at me, weren't they? This is completely different. I assume what you are thinking is that this targets Mark but actually it doesn't. Mark isn't here to receive it, is he? This targets you and your parents.'

'But suppose the person who sent it doesn't know that Mark has disappeared? He sends it to frighten him.'

'But then why send it to your parents? Why not send it directly to Mark? Also, if we are assuming that the perpetrator of the previous malicious incidents is involved with the college in some way, and the note to me certainly shows an insider's knowledge of Oxford life, surely that person would know that Mark wasn't here to be affected by the card.'

He was right, Sam thought. In that case, Mark couldn't be the target.

'I confronted Adams and his nephew. If they are responsible it may warn them off.'

He nodded. 'Any luck in tracing the buyer of the pig's head?'

'I'm waiting for a butcher in the market to get back to me.'

'I can quite see why you would want to involve the police, but my personal feeling is that there may be three separate things going on here at the moment. First, Adrian Hunter's death and the circumstances surrounding that. Second, the note and the pig's head sent to me with perhaps the connection to Kenneth Adams. Third, Mark's disappearance and this card sent to your parents. Have you considered that the three may be in no way related? I can see that it is tempting to look for connections but trying to force them can, in my experience, blinker one from discovering the truth.'

Sam rubbed her forehead. 'But surely all these things happening so close together, and in the same place, is just too much of a coincidence?'

'But they say bad news comes in threes.'

'Did the police search Mark's rooms this morning?'

He nodded. 'They didn't tell me what they were looking for.'

'From conversations I've had with the police I think they believe that it's a clear-cut case of Adrian taking too many drugs with too much alcohol. Mr Hunter, however, is not satisfied with that. Adrian had been in a fight before he died and there was someone else's blood on his clothes. He's insisting they check it against Mark's DNA. I spoke to a friend of Adrian's who said that he was known for being able to supply every sort of drug you can think of—'

The Provost groaned. 'Drugs?'

'I'm afraid so. He said he'd seen Adrian with a man he didn't recognise and who he thought might be his dealer. He did say that this term Adrian had barely been holding it together. His friend advised him to come off everything but obviously he didn't. A week later he was dead.'

'I don't understand why the police would think that Adrian had been in a fight with Mark.'

'Adrian Hunter told his tutorial partner, Juliet Bartlett, that he was having a relationship with Mark, and she told the police this. The police asked Mark about it in their first interview with him and he denied it. He wasn't. There's absolutely no way he was. Even Juliet said she didn't believe Adrian. It's just something she felt she had to tell the police when Adrian died. Mr Hunter read the notes of that interview and is now bringing pressure to bear on the police about Mark being involved in some way in his son's death. Mark's disappearance hasn't helped matters. I think the police succumbed to pressure from Mr Hunter and got a search warrant. They won't have found anything there.'

'And if you're so sure of that, what were you doing there in the middle of the night?'

Sam blushed. She had obviously been wrong about the Provost being the last to know about what was going on in the college.

'I'm not sure why I went. I suppose I just can't believe he's not there.'

'And you ended up being hit on the head.'

Sam didn't say anything.

'Were his rooms closed when you arrived?'

'Yes.'

'So the most likely explanation is that someone had his keys.'

She nodded.

'Who do you think it was?'

She shook her head. 'I have absolutely no idea.' She stood up, wanting the grilling to end. 'I'm sure you'll understand that I'm going to have to concentrate on finding out what has happened to Mark.'

'Naturally, but in due course you'll keep me informed of how things are progressing in the other matters?'

'I will.'

Sam went to Brown's to have some supper. She wished to avoid an anxious meal with her parents and needed some time to collect her thoughts.

She ordered herself the steak and Guinness pie with chips and considered what to do next. The more she thought about it, the more she thought the Provost was right. Mark wasn't the target and the card wasn't part of some malicious prank going on in the college.

The waiter came with her order and she peeled the top off the pie and watched the steam rise up off the meat and gravy.

Her mind had been so focused on Adrian Hunter and the other dramas taking place in St Barnabas's that she had only been looking at Mark going missing against that background. But something else had taken place in the last week. Rick McGann had turned up at her office asking for her help in finding his father's body. She remembered what Phil had said: *What exactly is the situation with your father at the moment?*

By the time she had come to the end of the meal she was certain of her next course of action. She couldn't just hang around in Oxford waiting. She had to do something.

As she entered her parents' house the murmur of voices drew her to the living room.

Her mother and stepfather were sitting on the sofa. Two candelabra had been lit on the mantelpiece and the flames of the candles were reflected in the gold-framed mirror behind them. There was no other light on in the room. Sam felt an overwhelming desire to slam on every light in the house, to smash the palm of her hand down on every flame. Candles were for remembering the dead. But she didn't say anything. The truth was her mother often lit candles. There was nothing unusual about it. So instead she sat down, trying to keep her feelings under control.

'Are you feeling better?' her mother asked.

'Much. Thank you.'

'Do you want something to eat?'

Sam shook her head. 'No, I've eaten.'

'Have you thought what you're going to do?' Peter asked.

Before she could answer her mother said, 'We've been thinking that in these circumstances, knowing where your father is might be helpful.'

Sam blinked in surprise. She knew Phil had suggested it before but she hadn't expected her mother to agree. 'I've been thinking the same. I wasn't lying before to the police, you know. I've no idea where he is.'

'How about Max? Wasn't your father working for him before?'

Sam nodded. 'I could ask him.' Max was Sam's godfather; he had joined the SAS at the same time as Sam's father and now ran a security business.

Sam looked at Peter. 'What do you think?'

'Reluctantly, I agree with your mother.'

'The last person in the world I want to go looking for is my father,' Sam said.

'I know,' he said. 'But if he can help?'

Sam nodded. She thought back to the last time she'd spoken to her father:

'How will I know where you are?' she'd said.

'I'll be in touch.'

'Where will you go?'

'Best I don't tell you. Then you'll have nothing to hide.'

And he hadn't been in touch since. He had taken the dog tags she had always worn round her neck. They were his, but she had worn them since he disappeared when she was four years old. She remembered his parting words to her.

I might need you. If I send them you'll know it's me.

That was all very well but what about this situation now, when she needed him?

She said goodbye to her parents and half an hour later Sam was turning off the Headington roundabout onto the A40 and was on her way back to London.

She got back to her flat at midnight and phoned Max. There was a message on his voicemail saying that anyone wanting him should phone the office. It was too late to do that; it would have to wait until morning.

As she'd come back into the block Sam had noticed that Edie's lights were on and now she let herself out onto the landing, pushed open Edie's letterbox and delivered a low flat whistle into Edie's hall. After a few minutes of silence, followed by the rattling of chains and keys and locks, Edie peered out at her.

Given the fact it was half past midnight she appeared extremely awake.

'I saw your light was on,' Sam said. 'Otherwise I wouldn't have—'

Edie grabbed hold of her arm and pulled her inside. The flat smelled faintly of mothballs. Next to the front door were two large orange plastic bags provided by the council for recycling.

'Do you want me to put these out for you?' Sam asked.

'What, babes?'

'The recycling – don't they come in the morning?'

Edie laughed. 'Don't touch that, it's my baccie.'

Sam smiled. Over the last couple of years Edie had taken up tobacco smuggling, going on progressively more and more trips to France, Belgium and Spain.

'I've got someone turning up for that soon. Would you take it down to the door for me when they come? My knees aren't up to it any more.'

'I . . .'

'They'll be here any minute, love. You take down the bags and then they'll give you an envelope. Just put it through my letterbox. I don't want to talk to them myself. If I do I have to ask them in for a drink and I can't be doing with all that.'

'OK.'

Sam sighed. She didn't really want to get involved in Edie's dodgy dealings but she relied on Edie to look after Frank when she was away and needed to keep her sweet. At that moment Frank strolled out of Edie's kitchen, sat down next to her and began to rub his face absentmindedly on her blue furry slippers.

Looked at from above Frank was almost completely spherical. No waist was to be seen.

'Oh my God,' Sam said. 'You remember what I told you about Frank being on a diet.'

Edie snorted and folded her arms. 'I always give him the best.'

'Oh, I know, Edie, I'm not saying you don't. It's just the vet said Frank was the fattest cat she'd seen in London and—'

'Vets don't know nothing. They're just after your money. My Snowy was twice the size of Frankie and he lived to twenty-one. If Frank's the fattest cat she's seen in London she hasn't seen many cats. Did they try to get you to buy that horrible hard food for him?'

'Well, yes, they did.'

'That's not fit for pigs. I won't give it to him.'

Sam gave up the fight. Edie was a fat cat woman and that was the end of it. 'I need the file I asked you to look after a couple of months ago.'

Edie frowned.

'I think you put it in here.' Sam tapped the top of the three-drawer green filing cabinet she was leaning against.

Edie nodded, bent down and lifted a bit of carpet by the entrance to her kitchen. When she stood up she had a key in her hand. She opened the filing cabinet, pulled open the bottom drawer and took out a file, which she handed to Sam.

'Thanks.'

While Sam opened it and checked its contents, Edie leaned on the top of the cabinet, writing something on a piece of paper. 'Tack this to the front door,' she said, 'and they'll know to ring your bell not mine.'

Sam nodded. 'Come on, Frank,' she said. She went to pick him up but he made a run for it, scampering off into the kitchen. Well, he didn't scamper exactly. Sam wasn't in the mood for hide-and-seek at this time of night, so she left him and began dragging the two bags out of Edie's onto the landing. She ran down the stairs and stuck the note on the main door and then returned to her own flat.

She made herself a cup of tea, sat down in her front room and took out the four pieces of paper that the file contained. The first sheet was her father's statement, the second had the names of people he had been involved in killing, the last two were maps marking the burial sites that had been used to dispose of the bodies.

Briefly she scanned what her father had written, reminding herself of its contents, certain phrases catching her eye:

I know they will try and silence me. They've killed all the others . . . unlawful killing of Catholics on the streets of Belfast . . . I do not know the names of all those I killed . . . memories and nightmares have almost destroyed me . . . there have already been attempts on my life . . . I want to set the record straight . . . I want the bodies properly buried . . .

She looked down the list of names and thought about Rick McGann. Surely it was just too great a coincidence that Rick had walked into her office in Putney and two days later Mark had disappeared. She wondered which of these men Rick's father had known. She wondered if Rick was really a man of peace and reconciliation as he claimed. These maps were her bargaining counter. They hadn't been published in the newspaper. No one knew about them, but they were exactly what Rick wanted.

Quarter of an hour later the doorbell rang and Sam dragged the sacks down to a ferrety-looking woman who slung them in the back of a dirty white van. She slammed the doors and handed Sam a thick white envelope, which Sam shoved through Edie's letterbox. She listened but didn't hear the envelope hit the ground.

CHAPTER ELEVEN

First thing the following morning Sam contacted Max's office. Paula picked up the phone – she was Max's girlfriend and also worked as his receptionist.

'Oh hi, Sam, how are you?'

'Fine, thanks. Can I speak to Max?'

'He's not in the office today.'

'Where can I get hold of him? When I phoned his mobile yesterday the message told me to phone the office.'

'We're not expecting him in until the beginning of next week.'

'Why? Is he on holiday or something?'

'Not exactly.'

Silence.

'Look, Paula, it's really urgent that I talk with him.'

'Is it anything that I could help you with?'

Sam felt managed and held at arm's length and it was beginning to piss her off.

'Is my father working with him at the moment?'

'I . . . look, Sam, I think it would be best if Max—'

'Is he going to be phoning into the office?'

'Not necessarily. It depends on certain factors.'

'Why can't you just tell me where he is?'

She heard a sigh on the phone. 'I'm sorry, Sam, but I can't talk to you about this. We're expecting him back at the beginning of next week. Phone then. I'm sure he'll be pleased to hear from you.'

The phone went dead.

Pleased to hear from me, Sam thought. Well, that'd be a first.

*

Sam went straight to her office in Putney. Alan was on the phone when she entered the room and she slumped down in her chair, swung it round and looked out of the window down onto Putney Bridge and the bottom of Putney High Street. The sky was overcast and grey and the tide was up. The river looked smooth and unruffled, like a large slug slithering under the bridge. Four Canada geese were flying across the river in the direction of the Wetland Centre at Barnes.

Alan put down the phone and she swung back round to face him.

'Well, look what the cat dragged in,' he said. 'Long time no see, no hear, no bloody anything. How long do you think you can leave me here running the show while you go poncing round the bloody ivory towers? You have got a business to run, you know? It may have escaped your attention but I'm grinding out our daily bread and butter while—'

'Hold on, Alan,' Sam said. 'I'm sorry I haven't been in touch.'

'You've been gone a week and you haven't even phoned in to see how I've been doing . . .'

'Look, I'm sorry, OK, but all hell's broken loose down there.'

'Been dropping their tea cups, have they? Getting ink stains on their gowns?'

'Alan—'

'I've been dealing with the jealous husband from hell. I've followed his wife everywhere and not a sniff of anything going on. I write up the report. I speak to him on the phone. You'd think he'd be happy but, oh no, instead he accuses me of not doing my job properly. He knows something is going on and he tells me if I don't find something he won't pay the bill—'

Sam held up her hand. 'Shut up a minute, Alan. I'm sorry I didn't phone in, but let me explain what's been going on.'

A couple of minutes later Alan was updated and considerably calmer.

'So how long's Mark been missing?'

'This is the fifth day.'

'Do you think he could have had some kind of nervous breakdown?'

Sam shook her head. 'I don't know.'

'Do you think he was involved in some way in Hunter's death?'

'No way, Alan, absolutely not.'

'But suppose—'

'No, Alan, I'm not even willing to speculate on that one.'

'But if he's been taken by someone – why? And why haven't they been in contact with you or your parents?'

Sam shook her head. 'The sympathy card was contact of a sort.'

'How are you doing with it?'

'Five days,' Sam said. 'It's been five days.'

He nodded.

'What does his new man have to say about things?'

'I've no idea. All I know is his first name and that he's a doctor. Mark hadn't told me anything more than that. I gave those details to Phil, but so far he hasn't had any luck tracing him.'

'What are you going to do next?'

'Have you still got Rick McGann's number?'

He nodded. 'Is that advisable, Sam?'

'Look, Rick McGann turned up here a week ago – two days before Mark went missing. I'm not saying he's done anything, but I need to sound him out.'

'Yes, you do, but with a great deal of caution.'

Sam put her head in her hands. 'Oh Jesus, Alan. Rick McGann and his bloody beautiful wife.'

'Just out of curiosity, on a scale from one to ten, ten being the highest, how attractive do you find him?'

'None of that matters any more.'

'Humour me.'

Sam leaned forwards and banged her head gently against her desk. Then she sat back in her chair. 'About one hundred and sodding fifty.'

'Even though you know he's got a wife?'

'Well, that piece of information brought it down from two hundred.'

'And you've got four planets in Scorpio,' Alan muttered.

'Don't go on about the four planets business, Alan, you know it just pisses me off.'

Alan waved a piece of paper at her. 'Well, lucky for you I kept the number.'

*

They met in a café at the bottom of Upper Street. Rick was already sitting at a table when she arrived. Sam had been hoping that her feelings for him would have diminished, but unfortunately when she clapped eyes on him her response was exactly the same as the two previous times they'd met – uncomfortably high levels of attraction.

The café was seething. Nearby, a woman sat with her mobile clamped to her ear. Her little boy was sitting in a high chair and kicking his feet against the underside of the table, his face was smeared in chocolate and he was delicately picking up the remnants of a piece of chocolate cake and dropping them onto the floor.

Rick was wearing the same outfit he'd had on when he'd come to her office: black coat jacket and trousers, blue open-necked shirt.

He stood up. 'What can I get you?'

'No, it's all right. I'll get it. What do you want?' She pointed to his cup. 'Another?'

'Thanks – cappuccino.'

'Cake?'

'One of the abiding principles by which I lead my life is never to say no to offers of cake.'

Sam smiled. 'Any sort in particular?'

He shook his head. 'Any cake will do.'

A couple of minutes later, Sam was placing two cups and two pieces of chocolate cake on the table.

'Good choice.' He gestured at the little boy. 'I was about to get down on my hands and knees there and have a go at his.'

'Thanks for seeing me so quickly,' Sam said.

'Jesus, you sound like you've got toothache and I'm the emergency dentist.'

She laughed. 'The truth is I need to ask a favour.'

He looked up from stirring his coffee.

Sam took out the photocopy of the sympathy card and handed it to Rick. 'This was sent to my parents' house in Oxford.'

He read it in silence and then handed it back.

'This Mark Falconer?'

'He's my brother.'

He bit his lip, but didn't say anything immediately. Next to them the chocolate-smeared boy was starting to scream. 'Where is he, Sam?'

'I don't know. He's been missing for five days.'

'Missing?'

'Yes.'

'You know what this is, right?'

'A sick joke?'

He shook his head. 'The IRA used to send them to people they were warning out of Northern Ireland. The only difference is that here,' he pointed at the empty lines that came after the words *with sincere sympathy from*, 'they put words like *your friends in Connelly House, Crumlin Road and Long Kesh*.'

'I don't understand,' Sam said. 'What does that mean?'

'Connelly House is the headquarters of the Sinn Fein in Belfast. Crumlin Road was where suspected terrorists were held. Long Kesh is more commonly known as the H-Block. It's a way of saying the IRA are after you. Kieran got sent one. It's what made him come to England. He hasn't been back since and it was over twenty years ago he received it.'

'So does this mean they've got Mark?'

He shrugged. 'It's their style, Sam.'

'But what do they want with him? He teaches English at an Oxford college.'

'Have you had any other communication?'

'No, not yet. The thing is, I've not had any contact with my father for the last couple of months. In fact, since that newspaper article came out. I've been making enquiries but at the moment I can't get hold of him.'

'Why not?'

Something about the way he asked made Sam pause. 'I just can't, that's all.'

She looked down at the table. He's in on it, she thought. It's too much of a coincidence. His words from the Torn Roots performance echoed in her head. *There was a time when I was filled with hatred* . . . He turned up asking where his father might be buried and then Mark went missing and now there was this card.

'Where the hell is he, Rick?'

'What?'

At the next table a full-scale tantrum was now taking place. The little boy was arching his back, kicking with all his might and had turned puce.

'Look, you came to me wanting information about your father, wanting to know where his body might be. Two days later my brother goes missing. You grew up in Belfast in the seventies. You told me about throwing petrol bombs at Saracans and picking up plastic bullets for journalists. Now where the fuck is my brother?'

Rick thumped his cup down in its saucer, making the spoon jump onto the table. 'Jesus, you don't get it, do you? You're just one of those idiots who think that if you're Catholic and you grew up in Northern Ireland then you must be connected to the IRA. Did you have your eyes shut and your ears blocked through the whole play the other night? Everything I've done with my life has been about peace and reconciliation. I came to you for information about my father's body not to threaten you or your family. I've made that quite clear. I didn't send this card. It's got nothing to do with me.'

The child had stopped screaming and was staring at both of them, obviously feeling out-tantrumed.

Sam stood up. 'OK, I'm sorry, but what the hell would you be thinking if you were in my shoes?'

He didn't say anything at first, tapping his spoon against his plate, then he looked up at her and nodded.

Sam sat back down. 'Are there any people you could talk to?'

He sighed. 'Perhaps.'

'Help me and I'll see what I can find out about your father.'

He nodded. 'I'll make some calls.'

'Thanks. I saw Torn Roots was going to Oxford. Maybe we could meet up there if you have something for me.'

He nodded. 'I'll call and see if you're in town when we get there.' He paused. 'By the way, Sam, you know the other night after the play?'

'Yes.'

'You went tearing out of there in a hell of a hurry.'

'I'd had too much to drink. If I'd stayed any longer I'd never have got home.'

'Oh, right. Nothing else was upsetting you?'

'Why do you think I was upset?'

'Weren't you?'

'Tired and emotional, that's all.'

'Kieran didn't upset you, did he?'

'Kieran? No. Why?'

'I just wondered. He doesn't have the same approach as the rest of us. I'd told him about you and was hoping he wasn't giving you a hard time. Sometimes he's a bit overprotective. He's under a lot of pressure at the moment and I'm worried about him. When my dad went missing he was like another big brother to me.'

'Sounds like you're the one who's protective of him.'

'Well, I owe him.'

'Anyway, he was fine. He wanted me to help you, that's all. To be honest I was so drunk I can't really remember what we were talking about.'

'There was something I meant to explain when I introduced Isabel. The thing is, I do it as a joke really.'

'A joke? How charming of you. This is my wife – ha, ha, ha . . .'

'No, listen. I mean she is my wife and everything, but it's an immigration thing. She didn't want to go back to Chile and her visa was due to run out. I was unattached and said why not. We had a good party and then she went home with Boris, who's her boyfriend.'

'That was very understanding of you.'

'I like to think so. I'd had a thing with her, you know, before.'

'A thing?'

'Yes, but a while back now. She's too much of a firebrand for me. God, you wouldn't believe the rows, it was bloody exhausting. But she and Boris, that's a good match, they sort of burn each other out.'

'But you still introduce her as your wife.'

'Well, she's gorgeous, isn't she?'

'She is.'

'I mean, it's a male vanity thing. You know this gorgeous woman is my wife. It's pathetic, I know. I only tend to do it when I've had a few.'

'So why did you do that to me?'

'I was drunk. I was showing off. You tore out of there so fast you missed the punchline.'

'So why did you want to tell me that now?'

'No reason, really.'

They looked at each other.

'Just so that we're straight,' Rick said.

'We are,' Sam said, seeking refuge from the prolonged eye contact by pretending to look for something in her bag.

Sam rolled over and looked at her alarm. Six in the morning. The mobile on her bedside table was ringing. Who on earth was this? It was the kind of time you phoned to tell people someone had died. She grabbed the phone, sending a yellow plastic container of evening primrose oil spinning to the ground.

'What is it?'

'Samantha Falconer?' The voice sounded weird, as though it was being filtered through something that was distorting it.

'Yes. Who's this?'

'If you want to see your brother alive you'll shut up and listen.'

Sam sat bolt upright, her phone clamped to her ear. 'Who is this?'

'Shut up and listen.'

Sam shut up.

'Get your father on the end of the phone in twelve hours or you'll never have regretted anything so much in your whole fucking life.'

'But—'

'Tell the police and we'll kill him.'

'But how do I know you've got him? How do I know—'

'Sam, is that you?' The voice was a dry croak.

'Mark . . . ?'

But all she heard was a fit of coughing.

The phone went quiet and there was a delay until the voice returned. 'Get your father. You've got twelve hours.'

'But I don't know where he is. I haven't seen him for two months. I can't get him.'

'You know how to trace missing people, don't you? Why do you think we took your brother and not you?'

'Hold on—'

'Six this evening. Make sure he's there.'

'But I won't be able to. It's too short a time.'

'If you get in touch with the police we'll know about it and we'll kill him.'

The phone went dead.

She put her head in her hands and tried to control her breathing.

She felt as if someone had plunged a needle full of adrenaline into her heart.

Twelve hours.

Twelve hours to trace her father.

It wasn't enough time.

She dialled Alan's number and a sleepy voice answered.

'Alan something's happened.' Her voice was trembling. 'Could you get over here?'

'What's the time?'

'It's five past six. I just got a phone call about Mark. I've got twelve hours to get my father on the end of the phone or he said he'd kill him.'

She heard a sharp intake of breath. 'I'll be there as soon as I can.'

Half an hour later Alan was sitting in her kitchen rubbing the dust off the leaves of her money plant.

'What am I going to do, Alan?'

'Well, obviously you have to tell the police.'

'I can't do that. They said they'd kill him.'

'Of course they're going to say that, but what other option have you got? You can't possibly think you can handle this yourself, Sam. It's gone way beyond that.'

'He said they'd know. He said they'd find out. I can't risk it. Suppose he has contacts in the police? I can't do it.'

'Well, what are you proposing to do?'

'Find my father.'

'How?'

'I'm going to try Paula again. If she knows what the situation is, she may be more forthcoming.'

'And if you can't find out that way?'

'There's only one other thing I can think of.' She handed Alan a sheaf of A4 paper. He looked through it. It contained photocopies of credit cards, a driver's licence in the name of a James Parker and a copy of a photo of a woman with two small children on a beach.

He finished looking through it and looked up. 'I don't understand. What is all this?'

'It's the identity my father was given when he left Northern Ireland. In January when he turned up here and he'd been shot, he left his wallet by accident. I copied the contents. That's what you're looking at.'

Alan shuffled the pages. 'So, James Parker is your father?'

She nodded. 'And the Norfolk address on the driving licence, I presume, is where his second family live.'

'Have you ever had any contact with them before?'

Sam shook her head.

'Do they know about you?'

'I've no idea what they know.'

Alan sighed. 'You sure you want to prise open that particular can of worms, Sam?'

'No, I'm not. But suppose my father's with them. Or suppose they know where he is? I don't want to do it, but it's a path I have to pursue. After talking to Paula again, it's the only thing I can think of to do.'

'I still think you should tell the police. At least tell Phil.'

'No.' Sam shook her head. 'He's going for promotion at the moment, so it's all by the book. I wouldn't trust him with it.'

'I really think you're over your head here, Sam. The police have people trained in hostage negotiation. They send them all over the world. They're experts, and you don't know what the fuck you're doing. You have to tell them he's been kidnapped. They don't even know that yet, do they? All they know is that Mark's disappeared and a card has been sent.'

'I'm going to go my own way with this, Alan. Are you going to help me or not?'

He walked over to her and put his arm round her. 'Of course I am, darling. Don't be ridiculous.'

'Will you track down a telephone number for me?' Sam said. 'I'm going to concentrate on Paula.'

The gag tore at the corner of his mouth, creating a trickle of blood onto his tongue. He couldn't feel his hands or feet; he flexed them, trying to get some sensation into fingers and toes numb from the binding ropes, but the little feeling he managed to generate was agonising. The blindfold tied tightly around his face made his eyes itch and throb. Mark sucked in air through his nose, smelled dust and damp and something else sickly and cloying, an insistent disturbing smell. However deeply he breathed, he didn't feel as if he was getting enough air into his lungs. He tried again but this time the dust caught in his throat and he began to choke.

He had no idea how long he'd been held, he'd tried to work it out from the change in temperature and the far-off noise of a television – he thought it was three or four days, but wasn't sure. What had happened to him? Bits and pieces floated in his mind like so much flotsam and jetsam on the surface of the sea, but when he tried to pull them all together into a whole picture the bits floated away from each other, refusing to be joined into a coherent whole.

He remembered getting off the train and walking across the station car park and past the Royal Oxford Hotel. He was in Hythe Bridge Street when he heard steps behind him, running. He hadn't bothered to look round but had stopped and stepped to one side, imagining that it was a group of runners and then . . . This is where the pieces of the puzzle floated apart because then there was nothing, absolutely nothing, until he'd come round here.

When he'd regained conciousness his first thought had been that maybe his father had done this to him, but as the days passed and he had more time to think about it he realised that didn't make any sense. When he'd met up with him his father had seemed genuine in his search for forgiveness. Why would someone who was asking for forgiveness one day kidnap him the next? Unless he was insane, unless . . . but he hadn't seemed insane – exhausted, burnt out maybe, but insane . . . ? But if it wasn't Geoffrey, then who? He was an Oxford don, not a banker or the relative of a millionaire. Who had done this to him and what on earth did they want?

The only thing that had changed in his life recently, excluding events with his father, was Brendan and he had been highly inquisitive about his background. Mark had put it down to the natural interest to get to know everything about a new lover, but maybe there was something more sinister about the questioning. One thing he did remember was that Brendan had phoned him on the train. Just to say hi, he said. But it meant that he knew when his train was due in; Brendan knew exactly when he would be walking down Hythe Bridge Street, when he could be taken.

The longer this went on the more certain he was that he was going to die. The first time his kidnapper removed his gag to give him a drink Mark had tried talking to him. *What's the matter? What have I done to you? What do you want?* But all he'd received in reply was a blow to the head and the swift removal of the water he desperately needed. There had been questions flung at him at the very beginning, in a voice he didn't recognise, questions he had no answers to, but now there was silence. And the silence was worse. If the kidnapper talked to him, replied to him, he would have to acknowledge he was a human being. In silence he could turn him into a thing. A thing didn't need food and water. A thing was a means to an end. Mark had stopped trying to engage him now, not so fearful of the violence as of the withdrawal of water.

Soon he would be too weak even to try to escape.

He struggled into a sitting position and began shunting himself forwards. If he could find a wall or something to brace himself against maybe he could stand up. He inched forwards, feet first. He heard a door open and close, not sure if someone had come into this place where he was being held, or if the noise was further away. He imagined someone standing in a doorway looking at him. He stopped and listened but after a few minutes' waiting he continued, cautiously shuffling forwards until he hit something.

He prodded it with his feet. Something was protruding low to the ground and then there was something rising up above the protrusion. He prodded it harder.

Pain exploded in his shins. Someone seized his hair and yanked his head backwards and he fell back onto the floor. Then he heard a voice hissing close to his ear.

'Don't move a fucking muscle. You move one inch from where I leave you and I'll kill you with as much thought as if you were a rat. Can you smell that? Can you? Hope your sister's good at her job or you'll be just the same, just a pile of stinking dead meat.'

Then he heard footsteps walking away and a door closing. He lay quite still, his shin throbbing and throbbing in time to the pounding in his head.

Sam. He'd heard her on the phone. He knew she was out there. He knew she would be looking for him.

She will be coming for me, he thought, she'll be doing absolutely everything to find me, but now he was beginning to wonder if he would still be alive for her to find.

He lay rigid with terror, surrounded by the sweet sickly smell of decay, trying to find something to reassure himself with, but in the end all he could come up with was Sam. She was it, his only hope.

It took Alan half an hour to track down the number. Sam phoned at seven, hoping they were early risers, not much caring if they weren't.

The voice that answered was male, youngish.

All Sam could think of was to tell the truth.

'My name's Samantha Falconer. My father's name's Geoffrey Falconer. I think you'll know him as James Parker.'

No answer.

'Is he there? Can I speak to him?'

'I don't know what you're talking about.'

'Please,' she said. 'I don't have time to explain. It's extremely urgent that I get hold of him.'

'You must have the wrong number.'

'Hold on,' Sam said. 'Could you tell me who you are?'

'Jack.'

'Jack Parker? Are you his son?'

Silence.

'Look, Jack, please. I have to speak to him.'

'What's the urgency?'

'My brother's been kidnapped. They want my father on the line by six this evening. I have to try—'

'Your brother's been kidnapped?' The sarcasm in his voice was obvious. 'Is this some sort of joke?'

'Look, I know this is awkward and I'm not surprised you're suspicious and I'm sorry. Usually I'd have come to see you in person but I don't have time.'

'How do I know that you are who you say you are?'

'You can go on the internet. There are pictures of me on judo websites. I was a world champion. You can see what I look like. I'm the spitting image of him. There was the article about him in the *Daily Tribune*. I understand this is difficult on the phone but please . . .'

He sighed. 'He comes and goes. Last time we saw him was a couple of weeks ago.'

Sam felt hope drain from her. 'Do you know where he went?'

'He said he was going back to London.'

'Have you got a contact address for him?'

'When he's in London he sometimes stays in Finsbury Park at 19, Mimosa Crescent.' He gave her the number. 'The mate he stays with is Billy.'

'Thanks,' Sam said. 'I'm sorry about this. I realise it's not the best of circumstances to introduce myself. Perhaps when this is over . . .'

'Yeah,' he said, the sarcasm back in his voice. 'Perhaps . . .' And he hung up.

She phoned the number Jack had given her and got an answerphone message: 'If you want to leave a message for Alf, Jenny, Al, Rob or Billy please do so after the beep.'

'My name's Samantha Falconer. I urgently need to talk to James Parker. If anyone knows where he is please could you contact me or let him know that I'm trying to get hold of him.' She left her number and hung up.

She didn't have time to wait in the hope that someone would phone her back. She looked at Alan. 'Will you come with me?'

'How could I miss a trip to Finsbury Park?' Alan said. 'But first you have to give me a bin bag and five minutes.'

'What for?'

'To clean out your car.'

'How do you know it needs it?'

Alan raised his eyebrows.

'All right, all right,' Sam said, opening the cupboard under the sink. 'I'll give you a hand.'

They parked and looked at the house. It was a Victorian four-storey, semi-detached in desperate need of repair. Black refuse bags spilled out of a pair of old metal bins, but there was at least as much rubbish floating around loose in the front garden as there was in the bins.

Sam phoned Paula again, leaving a message for her at Max's flat and the office, then they got out of the car and crossed the road, stepping round the remains of a spaghetti bolognese, which had been spilled on the stone path leading up to the house. Obviously it wasn't a household that bothered to tip the bin men at Christmas. As they walked up the steps to the front door, a fierce little tortoiseshell cat hissed at them from the sill of a bay window.

Sam tried the bell, but when that made no noise she used the knocker. There was no reply.

'Let's try the back,' Alan said.

They walked along the side of the house, which led into a wild and overgrown garden. Halfway along, a makeshift washing line had been strung up between two gnarled thorn trees and a faded pair of jeans with holes in the knees sagged on the line. They'd gone slightly green, probably from being left hanging out there since the previous summer.

At the far end of the garden in a cleared area was an old rusty swing. The wind was pushing it back and forth and the chains, which held the seat to the frame, were screeching in protest.

Sam put her hands to her ears and closed her eyes. With the sound, images flooded her head. She looked down and saw blood on her hands and the face of a man streaked also with blood. A tear rolled slowly down his cheek, leaving a white track. She had to hold onto someone. She reached out and grabbed hold of Alan.

'Sam?'

She opened her eyes to see Alan staring anxiously at her. She looked down at the palms of her hands then back at Alan's face.

'Are you all right?'

She was still gripping onto him. Her overwhelming feeling was that someone had been torn from her. Mark, she thought. Has someone just killed him?

She let go of Alan and put a hand over her eyes, struggling to regain control.

He put his arm across her shoulders and pulled her to him. The images were receding now; the only thing that remained was the screech of the chains on the swing blowing back and forth in the wind.

'Sorry,' she said a few moments later.

Alan gave her a reassuring squeeze but didn't push her for any explanation.

Loud music was booming from the basement.

'Someone's in,' he said.

He cupped his hands round his eyes to block out the light and peered through a dirty window, then he slapped his hand hard against the glass and made a gesture to indicate to the person inside that he should go and open the front door.

'Looks a bit rat-like,' he said as they once again climbed the stone steps to the front door.

'The cat?'

'No, him downstairs.'

The door was opened by a skinny man of medium height who Sam reckoned was probably in his fifties but wearing the clothes of a twenty-year-old. He had big baggy trousers hanging halfway off his arse and a large silver chain dangling between his belt and his pocket.

'What is it?' he said. 'I'm working.'

He did not, Sam thought, look like a man who knew the meaning of the word.

'I left a message on your answer-phone about James Parker,' Sam said.

'Well, I didn't hear it. I've been working in the basement all morning.' He pointed to the headphones hanging round his neck.

'Do you know where he is?'

'Who are you?'

'I'm his daughter.'

'I haven't seen him for at least a week. He doesn't live here all the time. I've no idea where he is.' He began to close the door on them. Alan stepped swiftly past him into the hall.

'Now hold on, you—'

'We're in a hurry,' Alan said. 'We wouldn't be here if it wasn't urgent. Is there anyone else we could ask?'

'I don't know and I don't have the time to—'

Alan took a couple of steps towards him, which backed the man against the handlebars of a bike that was leaning against the wall.

'Go and find out,' he said, 'and we'll wait here for you. It won't take you that long and then we can leave you alone and you can get on with your work.'

The man swore but was obviously intimidated enough by Alan's bulk to do what he said. He thumped up the stairs like a recalcitrant teenager.

'I love it when you get all butch and manly,' Sam said.

'I have my moments.'

The cat had come rushing into the house behind Alan and was clawing at a door. He pushed it open and the cat rushed inside. Alan and Sam followed into a large room that doubled as kitchen and living room. Sam found a packet of cat biscuits and thinking of Frank and the tartar on his teeth rattled some out on a dish and the cat fell on them as if it hadn't seen food in a week. Sam looked down and saw what the vet had meant about cats having waists.

Three enormous windows looking out onto the garden meant that the room was light but also incredibly cold and damp. The window frames had been painted a horrible pastel blue, which made the place seem even colder.

'God, it's warmer outside than in,' said Alan.

Sam eyed the lid of the swing bin that looked as if it had experienced death by a thousand teabags and then bent down to look at something growing a grey hairy coat on the floor next to it. She had just managed to ascertain that it wasn't a mouse, when she heard steps coming back down the stairs and turned as another man came into the room.

He was small with jet-black hair and brown eyes, wearing a blue sweatshirt and loose white cotton trousers that reminded Sam of martial arts trousers. On his feet he wore black Chinese slippers.

'Hi,' he said. 'I'm Billy. You're looking for James?'

'Yes,' Sam said. 'It's urgent I speak to him.'

'I heard your message but I've no idea where he is, otherwise I would have phoned. He's been gone a week.'

'Any idea where he went?'

'Look, James does his own thing. Sometimes he needs a place to stay and I let him stay here. I've got two rooms upstairs and he can doss down in one of them. He contributes to the house, is good at unblocking the filter on the washing machine and keeps out of people's way. He phoned a fortnight ago and asked if he could come up. I said yes. He stayed a week and that's the last time I saw him.'

'How do you know him?'

'I used to work out on the rigs with him.'

'Rigs?'

'Oil rigs off the Norfolk coast. We were both on the health and safety side.'

'Could I have a look at the room he used?'

'Sure, he never leaves anything but you're welcome to.'

They climbed the three flights of stairs to the top floor. He pushed open a door and they followed him in. The room was empty except for a grubby futon on the floor and a battered wicker waste-paper basket. Sam picked it up and peered inside. There were some tissues, a squashed packet of cigarettes and a couple of crumpled receipts.

Billy leaned against the wall. 'One thing. I came in here when he was packing up to leave and he asked me if I had any sun block. I presumed he was going on holiday, or at any rate somewhere hot. He was talking about how when he was young he'd taken all kinds of risks, which he never would now, you know, because he's so blond. I offered him some but he said it wasn't strong enough. He said he didn't take any chances now.'

'Do you know Max?'

'He's spoken about him as a mate but I've not met him. He's never brought anyone here.'

'Do you know if he was seeing Max in the week before he left?'

'I don't know.'

'OK,' Sam said. 'Thanks for your help.'

'If he phones, I'll let him know you need to talk to him.'

Alan and Sam let themselves out and got back in the car. Sam stared at her watch. Eleven o'clock. Panic rose up in her. She smashed her hands down on the dashboard.

'Seven hours to go and what have we found out, Alan? That he may be somewhere hot. What the hell am I going to do now? What can I do if he's out of the country?'

'What about telling the police now? At least they'll have time to set something up and give you some advice on how to handle the call. What have you got to lose?'

'I'm frightened to, Alan. He said he'd kill him.'

'Yes, but he said he'd kill him if you couldn't get your dad there and it doesn't look as if you can.'

Sam's phone rang and she grabbed it.

'Sam, it's Paula. I've been out of the office and only just picked up your messages. What is it?'

'Thank God you phoned.'

Sam told her about the phone call she'd received. 'So you can see I have to get hold of my father. Do you think Max knows where he is?'

'Can you get yourself to the office?' Paula asked.

'I haven't got time. If I haven't got Dad on the line by six this evening—'

'I can't talk about this over the phone. Get yourself over here and I promise you, Sam, I'll explain.'

'Come on, Paula, tell me now.'

'It won't make any difference, Sam, I promise.'

Sam swore. 'OK, we'll come straight away.'

Max's business was based in a building on the north side of the Thames near Embankment tube, and an hour later Sam and Alan were following Paula into his office. Paula was six foot in heels and towered over Sam. She was also blonde and blue-eyed; it was not unlike meeting Dolly Parton on stilts.

The first time Sam had met Paula she'd been intimidated by the war paint, the long red nails and the Max Factor, but she'd always been OK to deal with and Sam admired the caustic sense of humour that she unleashed periodically in Max's direction. She reckoned that Paula and Max were probably well matched in their mutual unfaithfulness to each other.

Paula sat down in a black leather and chrome chair, kicked off her shoes and began to massage her feet.

'I'm sorry to be so vague on the phone, but Max left very strict instructions when he went.'

Sam walked over to the window and looked out at the view. Max's offices were situated in a glass-fronted building on the bank of the Thames. From here she looked along the length of the river to where the London Eye was circling so slowly that it appeared to be standing still.

'So where's Max?' Sam asked.

'Iraq, I'm afraid.'

Sam swung round from the window. 'Oh, no!'

'It's been an incredibly lucrative source of business for us. It's the combination of a deadly insurgency and the availability of billions of dollars of aid money. We can charge $500 to $1,500 a day for our more skilled operatives and with those sorts of sums on offer there's no shortage of SAS and SBS men quitting the army to cash in.'

'I've read about it in the papers.'

'Well, there's a small fortune to be made, but there are certain operational difficulties.'

'I can imagine.'

'The main one is that we are supposed to be able to make do with defensive weapons only but our teams are coming under fire from insurgents who have heavy machine guns and rocket-propelled grenades. And our boys are not supposed to be carrying anything heavier than an AK47 and a pistol.'

'So what's Max doing out there?'

'Two of our boys were killed in Fallujah.'

'I'm sorry.'

Paula shrugged. 'It's the nature of the business. If we've got people out there in the sorts of numbers we have, we're going to take some hits. But Max wants the bodies back. He says that's the least we can do for the relatives.'

'So he's out there trying to get them?'

'Yes, but we haven't heard from him for the last forty-eight hours.'

'Were you expecting that?'

She held her hand out palm downwards and then rocked it from side to side. 'Twenty-four maybe. But not forty-eight. We've got other guys out there who are trying to make contact.'

'Do you know where he was?'

'A town four miles east of Fallujah. He'd arranged to meet someone who he'd been told could help them.'

'When was he due back in England?'

'He didn't know. You know what Max is like. He said he'd stay as long as it took.'

'But presumably he's got satellite phones and all that kind of stuff?'

'He's got everything you could imagine.'

'Do you know if Max had been in contact with my father?'

'Well, that's the thing, Sam, I'm really sorry, but I'm afraid your father's out there with him.'

'Oh shit.'

'Max was glad to have him along. He's an old mate and they've watched each other's backs over the years. Max told him what he was going to do and your father offered.'

Sam put her hands to her head. She was on her own and way out of her depth. She felt the blood drain from her face. What could she do to save Mark now?

CHAPTER TWELVE

The four men sat in the back of the café, glasses of tea resting on the table in front of them; the air was thick with the sweet smell of tobacco. Three of the men were crouched together but one with sandy hair sat back, observing them and their surroundings.

Geoffrey Falconer looked at the fly washing its legs on the back of his hand. Sweat ran out of his eyebrows into the corners of his eyes, it stung and he blinked a couple of times. When he looked again the fly was still there – cheeky sod. He pressed his hand flat against his side, absorbing the trickle of sweat that was sliding down from his armpit into his shirt. The rickety old fan clanking round and round above his head was sending down a fine mist of dust from the ceiling, which had covered their tea with a fine scum. To have a fan fall on your head, now that would be a bloody ridiculous way to die in a place like this. Four miles east of Fallujah must count as one of the most dangerous places on earth.

Mind you, there were always ridiculous ways to die in a war zone and that's what Iraq still was. One night in Baghdad listening to the muffled thump of bombs going off – he'd counted five – had confirmed that in his mind.

Max had had unspecified business on their first night. A woman was Geoffrey's best bet, probably a journalist, so he'd gone down into the foyer of the hotel alone. It had been heaving with truculent, ill-disciplined mercenaries swaggering around with their rifles and pistols showing, talking 'security'. They were all here: South Africans, Croats, Russians, Aussies, ex-French Foreign Legion and, of course, the British and Americans.

Geoffrey had avoided the gun-slingers in their ridiculous dark glasses, who were drinking too much, and sat down next to an undistinguished-looking bloke having a Coke at the bar. There was something about his quiet manner and low profile that made him wonder and he'd guessed right: the man was ex-SAS, in charge of a team guarding BP and Motorola executives.

They'd got chatting. He'd quit the SAS a couple of months ago. Everyone was wanting out, he said. The money's so good. Going private he could earn four or five times his previous salary. It was too good an opportunity to miss. Sure, you were playing Russian roulette with your retirement but at least you were earning decent money. He'd been dismissive of the increasingly rowdy group behind them. They're scraping the barrel there, mate. Those guys think it's a game, a cross between the Alaskan gold rush and the bloody OK Corral. Half of them haven't got a clue.

Now Geoffrey looked at Max and the two Iraqis and tried to gauge from their expressions how negotiations were going. Max was in his mid-fifties, and still had the moustache he had first grown after joining the SAS all those years ago. The ginger was flecked with grey now and there were a hell of a lot more freckles on his face but he hadn't allowed office life to expand his waistline too much.

Max patted the two pockets of his denim shirt and then the pockets on the thighs of his trousers and brought out a packet of cigarettes. He held them out to Geoffrey, who shook his head, and then to the two men in front of him. The interpreter took one with a wide smile of thanks, exposing his missing lower teeth, and Max lit the man's cigarette before doing the same to his own. The other man, wearing a long white robe, refused; he was the only one of the four of them who appeared unaffected by the oppressive heat.

Coming out here had brought home to Geoffrey that this was a young man's game. What the fuck did he think he was doing? He'd needed to get away and what better place? Max had said. Iraq's a good place to disappear. To die, Max, he'd replied. It's a good place to die. No one's going to die, Max said. But he'd been wrong, hadn't he? Those two boys had died, been dragged through the street, their headless bodies hung from the bridge. Come with me – for old times' sake, Max had said. Help me bring the bodies back.

But, God, this place was dangerous, and at the back of his mind he'd wondered if he'd ever get back alive.

He certainly knew something about dangerous places. Oman, Northern Ireland, and after what he'd been involved with there, every day of his life that followed. Thirty years of checking under his car for bombs, waiting for the front door to come splintering off its hinges in the middle of the night, expecting the balaclava-covered face, torture and then death.

It still happened, Good Friday Agreement notwithstanding. A couple of days before he'd flown out to Iraq, a man he'd served with in Northern Ireland, a sniper, who'd given evidence to the Bloody Sunday Inquiry, had been found dead in his car from stomach wounds, a 9mm on the seat next to him. There'd been some rubbish about it being a suicide – no soldier on earth would ever willingly shoot himself in the stomach. You only had to see that once, and you'd never choose that way to go. No, he'd got careless and they'd caught up with him. It was as simple as that.

He was tired of watching his back. Sometimes he thought it would be a relief to die, to have it over with. There'd been a few times in the last couple of years, especially when he'd been drinking, when the thought had crossed his mind to help them out and just do it himself. He knew it was only a matter of time. The newspaper article had seen to that. They'd catch up with him as well. And he was getting older. Maybe one day he'd just let them. It would be easy enough to do, to stop checking the car, to stop looking behind him, to stop covering his tracks. He didn't deserve an easy death. Maybe that's why he'd agreed to come.

But the minute he'd stepped off the plane he'd wanted to turn round and get right back on it again. The palms of his hands had felt as if he'd just grabbed hold of a nettle. That prickle in his hands was what he'd always felt in dangerous situations. Iraq had the heat of Oman and the danger of Northern Ireland. It was a godforsaken combination.

The white-robed Iraqi sat back suddenly in his chair. He held out his hands and shrugged his shoulders in a take-it-or-leave-it gesture. Geoffrey looked at Max. He spoke to his interpreter in a tight low voice that Geoffrey didn't catch. Then something caught his eye. He looked out of the café and saw a car draw up on the opposite side of the street. The air above the dusty road rippled in the heat. Two men got out and came across to the café and began talking to the man behind the bar.

'Jesus,' Max said.

'What is it?'

'They say they can give us the bodies but not the heads. Without the heads they could be anyone.'

'Tell them they have tattoos you'll be able to identify them by.'

'They haven't.'

'Tell them they have. They'll think that you'll know if it's them or not.'

The two men had left the bar now and also the barman. Geoffrey looked at the empty bar and then back out into the street at the parked car.

Max was back in conversation with his interpreter.

Geoffrey touched his arm. 'Max . . .'

He held out his hand. 'Just a minute, Geoff.'

Maybe it was nothing.

Geoffrey Falconer pushed his finger against his ear. Ever since that mortar had exploded in his observation post in Oman he'd had tinnitus in his right ear. He'd been lucky. The man with him had been splattered all over the place. There wasn't a piece of him left you could recognise and it was only his first week out there. Walking away from that with a bit of ringing in the ears, he counted himself definitely among the lucky ones.

He heard a rumble outside in the street. A noise he recognised. There was an American base up the road a couple of miles; they'd passed a few tanks on the way here. He saw the convoy passing in front of the parked car.

He reached out his hand and touched Max's shoulder. 'Max . . .' But it was as if his words had been sucked right out of the air.

And now a weird thing happened: the pressure in his ears had changed. For a second it was as if there was a complete absence of noise and everything had gone into slow motion. Geoffrey saw the mirrors behind the bar jump off the walls. Then all the glass at the front of the café was flying towards them, mixed up with tables and chairs. He threw himself at Max and their interpreter at the same time as his ears registered the explosion.

CHAPTER THIRTEEN

A hand on her shoulder shook her awake. Sam opened her eyes and saw Phil standing by the bed, a cup of tea in his hand. He carefully pushed it onto her cluttered bedside table.

'An hour, Sam.'

'Thanks.' Her mouth was dry. She reached for the tea.

From the bottom of the bed came a muffled growl and the menacing glitter of Frank Cooper's green eyes.

'He still hates me,' Phil said.

Not surprisingly, Phil had never recovered from the time Frank had decided his lap was a trampoline and jumped up and down on it with full claw extension.

'He doesn't, Phil, he's always like this. He's got terrible bed manners, he growls if he's disturbed.'

'We're all set out here.'

'I'll be out in a second.'

He turned and left her room.

She propped herself up on her elbow. The tea hitting her stomach unsettled the fear, which began to move like a circling shark.

It was five o'clock – an hour to go before the call.

An hour to go before she would have to tell the man holding Mark that she didn't have her father there and that she had no idea when or if she would ever be able to get him.

The shark began to speed up.

She sat up and hugged her knees. She'd gone to the police in the end as Alan had suggested. She didn't see what else she could do. When she thought about taking the call, she knew she had to. Paula telling her that her father was in Iraq was the end of the road she could travel alone. Now she needed all the help she could get.

Phil had been furious with her at first.

'What the hell do you think you're playing at, Sam? Why on earth didn't you come to us straight away?'

'Because he said if I did he'd kill Mark. I wanted to see if I could find my father. Now I know I'm not going to be able to. I've come to you because I've got nowhere else to go.'

Phil had shouted at her a bit more but then had swung into action. When she'd told him, there'd been six hours to go before the call but in those six hours a hell of a lot had happened and now Sam's flat creaked with the presence of the people Phil had called in. Both Sam's lines had been tapped on the basis that he might try her landline this time and then there'd been DCI Fiona Thompson, an expert from the Serious Crimes Squad, who had given Sam a crash course in hostage negotiation. It had only ended a couple of hours ago when she'd suggested that Sam try and get some rest. At first she'd protested that there was no way she'd be able to sleep but in fact as soon as her head hit the pillow she'd crashed into welcome oblivion.

Sam swung her legs onto the floor and stretched her spine. She listened to the mutter of voices elsewhere in her flat. Someone walked along the hall in the direction of the kitchen. She got up and stood in the doorway to her front room.

Phil was sitting on a red two-seater sofa. Over to the left was a large table, which took up about a quarter of the room. Fiona Thompson was sitting there next to a man who was tapping away at a laptop. On the table next to Sam's mobile were a pair of headphones and several pieces of paper. They all stopped what they were doing and turned to stare at Sam as she came into the room.

Fiona Thompson stood up. She had fine straight brown hair that fell to the level of her shoulders and green eyes set in a pale face. She was wearing a black jacket and trousers, a blue and white striped shirt and flat black lace-up shoes. She was taller than Sam but not by much and Sam guessed probably in her mid-forties.

'Did you manage to get some rest?'

Sam nodded. 'A bit.'

'If it's OK with you, I thought we could go through some of the material we were talking about before. I've made a list of simple bullet points for you to have in front of you as you're taking the call.'

Sam sat down at the table and Fiona handed her a sheet of paper. The first section was a list titled 'Do'. Underneath that was another titled 'Don't'.

Sam sighed and read down the list.

Do:
1. *Show concern*
2. *Empathise and explore common ground*
3. *Seek alternative solutions – it is our problem to sort out. How can we do that?*
4. *Probe the cause of the problem*

Then came the Don't list:

1. *Don't be too probing*
2. *Don't get angry – keep your voice level*
3. *Don't get judgemental*

Sam closed her eyes and put her hands to her head.

'I know it seems impossible,' Fiona said. 'But you must keep in mind what your goal is. Your goal is to get him to let go of Mark, to ensure his safety. Getting angry won't help that. Attacking him won't help that. You have to look for common ground, empathise. You're trying to find out what has led him to do this. You're looking to present him with alternatives, other ways round the problem. Why does he want your father? What does your father have that he wants? Can you help him? Do you see what I'm saying?'

Sam sighed. 'Sure, I see what you're saying but what do I do about the fact that what I really want to do is rip out the man's liver and wipe him from the surface of the earth?'

'Excessive emotion won't help, Sam. You need to put that away for the moment. It won't help you get what you want, which is your brother back safely. What you need to focus on is the result you want, not what you're feeling towards the hostage taker. I know it's hard but this list has been compiled from thousands of hostage situations. We've learned what works best. You have to trust me on this. Getting emotional, getting angry, mouthing off at him – none of that will get you what you want. It will just make the situation more dangerous, more prone to deterioration. You are looking to establish some kind of rapport with this man. That's what matters. The more you can drain the emotion out of the situation the better.'

'How many hostage situations have you been involved with?'

'This is my twentieth.'

'How many resolved themselves safely?'

'All my hostages have got out alive. I've had a couple of deaths by cops of the hostage takers. They walk out waving a gun, knowing a full SO19 team is waiting for them. Usually they haven't even had bullets in the gun.'

'So a hundred per cent success rate, then.'

'Not in my eyes. My aim is to get both out alive. If we lose a hostage taker that's not a success.'

'But at least the innocents escape unhurt.'

'I try not to look at it like that – innocent/guilty. It's not a distinction that I find helpful. Often hostage takers are desperate. They don't know what else to do.'

'But you're a policewoman, surely that's what it's all about – the distinction between the innocent and the guilty?'

'Maybe it is for some people. It's never been what motivates me.'

The man tapping at the laptop interrupted. 'DCI Thompson is what we call a bleeding-heart liberal.'

Fiona smiled.

'She is also, incidentally, one of the best we've got at this kind of situation. You'd do well to listen to her. All the top brass do.'

Sam sat back in her chair and folded her arms. 'So if you don't look at the situation as someone being guilty and someone being innocent, what do you do?'

'Well, in this situation – he wants to get your father on the phone. Why? What does he want from him? What has your father done to him? You told me your father was in the SAS in Northern Ireland. What happened? You need to try and look at it from his point of view. He's risking a lot – his life, his freedom. He's desperate. What's making him do that? How can the situation be resolved from his point of view? What's triggered this?'

'But I don't give a shit about him. All I want is for him to let go of my brother.'

Fiona put her hand on Sam's arm. 'Listen to me, Sam. If you start to give a shit about him that's much more likely to happen.'

I can't, Sam thought, he's the enemy and pretending any different is just a whole load of bullshit.

'How did you get involved in this kind of work anyway?'

'I was raising two teenage sons. I thought a course on hostage negotiation might help.'

Sam laughed. 'Who's the hostage in that situation?'

'They're held hostage by their hormones and I'm a hostage of them and their hormones.'

'Did it help?'

'Not really. The only answer as far as I can see is that they grow up and leave home. The other option is sending them to live with their father, but he's not that keen on the idea.'

Sam looked at her watch.

Fifteen minutes to go.

The call came in on Sam's mobile on the dot of six. She grabbed it but Fiona put a restraining hand on her arm.

'Let it ring a couple of times,' she said. 'Take a deep breath.'

Sam did as she was told, although every ring of the phone felt as if it was vibrating along her nerve endings.

Fiona let it ring five times. 'OK,' she said. 'Let's do it.'

Sam picked up the phone and Fiona put on the headphones.

'Sam Falconer speaking.'

'Put your father on the line.'

'Look, I'm sorry, I haven't got him here, but I do know where he is and when he's likely to be able to talk to you.'

'Did you not understand what I said to you?'

'What I know is that it's very important for you to talk to my father. I've done everything I can in the last twelve hours to find where he is and meet your request. I know how important this is to you.'

'Do you think I'm someone who makes idle promises? Is that what you think? That you can mess around with me and that it'll be all right?'

'I don't think that, no, but my father is in Iraq and out of phone contact. He has been for the last forty-eight hours. I only just found that out this afternoon. We're hoping that he'll be back in the country by the beginning of next week and then we'll be able to arrange for you to talk to him.'

'You're lying.'

'I swear to you I'm not. I want to do everything in my power to help us resolve this situation. I swear to you that I'm telling the truth. I've asked the people he's working with to do everything they can to try and contact him and tell him how urgent it is that he comes back into the country.'

There was silence on the line. Sam glanced at Fiona who gave her the thumbs-up and indicated by pointing to her lips and making circular movements with her finger that Sam should keep talking.

'Why is it that you want to talk to my father?'

'None of your fucking business.'

'Is there anything that I can help you with?'

'Shut up.' The tone was savage and abrupt.

'I want to help you. Tell me what I can do to help?'

'Shut up and listen to me.'

Fiona placed a finger across her lips.

'I'm listening.'

'You think you're being so clever, don't you? That you've got me over a barrel with your reasonableness, with your, "I've done everything in my power." With your, "Tell me what I can do to help." But you're forgetting I'm the one with the power. I'm the one who's got your brother. I'm the one who can hurt him and maybe I'll give you a reminder of that right now.'

Sam looked at Fiona who was scribbling on a pad of paper. She pushed it in front of Sam. *Tell him you know he has the power.* But when Sam began to speak into the phone there was no reply.

She heard noises on the end of the line. He was on the move.

Then she heard the man's voice, but not close up to the phone, say, 'Speak to your sister.'

'Sam?' It was Mark's voice.

'Mark, are you all right? Has he—'

And then she heard Mark again. 'What are you doing? No, please don't. I—'

'Mark?' Sam shouted.

And then she heard him scream.

She was on her feet now, staring blankly at the reminder in front of her. *Don't get angry. Don't get too judgemental. Seek common ground.* The words floated off the page, mocking her. Her free hand smashed down on the paper and scrunched it up in her fist. She was aware of Fiona trying to get her attention but she ignored her, her whole being concentrating on the moment when he would come back on the line.

She heard his breathing first. Fast. Ragged.

'Who has the power?'

Sam felt sick. Her legs were shaking. *Seek common ground.*

She opened her mouth to speak but the words stuck in her throat. She heard him laugh.

Perhaps there was common ground but...

'What did my father do to you?' she said. 'Did he hurt you? He hurt me and Mark when we were children. Look at Mark's forehead. You see those scars? My father did that to him. It's my father you want, not Mark.'

'And what did he do to you?'

It was what Reg had asked her. Sam didn't reply. She looked up, suddenly aware of the other people in the room.

'Four days,' he said. 'Make sure he's there.'

'Wait – put Mark on the line.'

'You don't get to order me around.'

'I have to know he's alive. I just need to know he's alive.'

There was a couple of seconds' pause. 'Sam...?' Mark sounded as if he was talking through gritted teeth.

He was alive.

Then the kidnapper was back on the line. 'Four days – same time.'

The line went dead.

No one spoke. Outside there was the rumble of rush-hour traffic building up in the New King's Road. The front door of the block opened and slammed shut. Sam dropped her mobile on the table.

'You did really well,' Fiona said.

Sam narrowed her eyes. 'He tortured my brother and made me listen while he did it. How does that constitute doing really well?'

'But you got something from him.'

'What exactly?'

'Time,' Fiona said. 'You got more time and you know your brother is still alive.'

'I don't even know if having any more time's going to do any good. They haven't been able to contact my father out there.'

She brushed past Phil and opened the front door. Phil grabbed her arm.

'Where are you going?'

'I have to run this one off, Phil. I can't stay here.'

'But where are you going?' he repeated. 'Shall I come with you?'

She shook her head. 'I need to be by myself.'

'But we need to talk about what to do next.'

'Later,' Sam said.

She ran down the stairs to the main door to the block and pushed her way out onto the pavement. Mark's screams were ringing in her ears. Clear her head. She had to clear her head. She began running swiftly towards Putney Bridge. Try not to think about it. Try to block it out. Don't dwell on it. Don't . . . Faster and faster she ran. Don't think about what he did to him. Don't think about him being in pain. Try not to think. She felt as if the rage and upset she was feeling would overwhelm her. Keep moving. Keep running. Try and keep ahead of it.

It was a beautiful spring evening but to Sam it might just as well have been the middle of the night. Across Putney Bridge, then right and along the front of the boathouses, along the tow path and then left towards the Wetland Centre and on and on Sam ran. She had to keep moving.

This is what it meant to love another person – agony, worry and terror. Love threw open the door and crashed the most well built of defences. Sam, who had always been so careful to keep something back, knew now why she had done it. The risk of loss, the risk of pain, was too great. Who but an idiot would put herself there? Who has the power? He was holding hostage someone she loved more than anyone in the world and he had tortured him and made her listen. But the only reason he had that power was because she loved Mark. If she was indifferent to him then he could do what he liked and she could walk away with a shrug of the shoulders.

Faster and faster she ran. She wasn't thinking where she was going, she wasn't thinking at all, she was trying and failing to keep it all at bay, to keep the screams from her head. Be indifferent. Cut yourself off. Remove yourself from it. Try not to love him so much ... but that was impossible.

She had to save him. She had to. But to do that she needed her father. She needed him. She could not think the words without feeling sick. Need implied vulnerability and of all the people in the world she didn't want to feel vulnerable with, her father was top of the list. But then Mark's screams echoed in her head. She heard his screams and knew she would do anything, including asking her father for help, in order to save her brother.

Four days. There was no guarantee that her father would be back in the country by then. There was no guarantee that he'd come back alive. And if he didn't, what would happen to Mark? She would have to go back to Oxford, she would have to begin from the beginning. She would have to track down where Mark was being held. There had to be a trail of some sort that she could follow. She would go back and begin again.

As Sam placed her key in her front door she felt the blister on the back of her heel burst. Phil and Fiona were still there, sitting in the front room waiting for her. She sat down in a chair opposite them and bent down to undo the laces of her shoes.

'Did it help?' Fiona asked.

Sam sat back in the chair. 'Now I'm upset, traumatised and I have blisters.' She peeled off her socks and poked at the damage. 'Did they get a trace on the phone?'

'No luck there, I'm afraid. It was blocked.'

'So we're no closer to finding out where they are?'

'No, but like I said before, you've bought us a bit of time.'

'But it's not enough. Four days. That's nothing. There's no way I can be sure that we'll get my father back into the country and on the end of the line in time. Even if we did get him here, there's no guarantee he'd be willing to do it.'

'Come on, Sam,' Phil said. 'Mark is his son.'

'And my father's my father, Phil. I think we have to go on the basis that we won't have him here come the next call. I think we have to put everything into tracing the exact chain of events leading up to

Mark going missing and hope that we'll be able to find where he's being held.'

Phil nodded. 'I agree. We pursue that course and at the same time we try and make contact with your father. We also have to consider what the kidnapper wants with him. There was that article in the paper, wasn't there, saying that he had been responsible for the murder of all those republicans. The men he killed were named.'

Rick McGann floated back into Sam's head. She hadn't mentioned him to Phil or DCI Thompson. She knew they'd want to interview him but first Sam wanted to wait and see what he came up with.

'I'm not sure what we can do with that,' Sam said.

'We can ask the police in Northern Ireland if they can come up with anything.'

'I can't see that working, Phil. Why should any of the families help if they think it's doing a favour for the man who may have killed their relative?'

'I know, but we can try at least.'

'Have you got any further with tracing Brendan?' Sam asked.

Phil shook his head. 'Not yet.'

'You searched Mark's rooms?'

'Yes.'

'Was there a photo of Brendan among Mark's things?'

'I don't think so. I'd have to check.'

'So you haven't been able to show his photo around?'

'No.'

'Do you think your boss would let me put together a photofit?'

'I can try him. You really think Brendan's involved?'

'I don't know, but he was someone new in Mark's life just before all this happened. When I asked him how they met he said he picked Mark up in a pub. If we've got a photo to show then we can go round the gay pubs and clubs in Oxford and see if anyone knows anything about him. We could also show it to people in the hospital.'

'I'll see what I can do,' Phil said.

Sam looked at her watch. 'I'll phone Paula and see if they've had any luck tracking down Dad.'

Sam spoke to Paula and updated her with what had happened.

'Any luck in making contact with them?'

'Nothing yet, I'm afraid, but . . .'

'But what?'

'There's nothing certain yet but there's been a report.'

'What sort of report?'

'We don't know if it's anything, Sam.'

'Just tell me, Paula.'

'OK, there's been a report of an explosion in a town four miles to the east of Fallujah. It was where we last had contact with them. I mean, we don't know if they were still there and of course there are bombs going off all over the place but we're sending a team out there . . .'

'If you hear anything, Paula, anything definite, please let me know as soon as possible. And if you make contact with him tell him it's incredibly urgent I speak to him.'

'I will, Sam. What are you going to do?'

'Go back to Oxford and start all over again.'

CHAPTER FOURTEEN

Sam drove back to Oxford with Alan the following morning hoping that his presence in the gay pubs and clubs that evening would help in tracing Brendan. She left Alan at her parents' house and went straight to the police station, but after a couple of hours in a stuffy room she was still no closer to producing an accurate picture of Brendan.

She peered at the computer screen. 'I'm sorry, but it still doesn't look like him.'

'Any bit in particular?'

Sam scowled. 'The eyes are all wrong.'

'Shape? Colour? Position?'

'I don't know. The whole way they sit in the face. I think there should be more of a gap between the top of the eye and the underneath of the eyebrow. I think.'

Liz, the woman sitting in front of the screen, made some adjustments and the face changed.

'No, now it's wrong, but wrong in a completely different way.'

Liz took a deep breath. 'Maybe it would be best if we take a break.'

Sam nodded, stood up and stretched. Liz also stood up. She was wearing a scoop-necked white T-shirt and a large engagement ring, which had announced itself each time her hands sped over the keys. She had been exhibiting the patience of a saint for the last couple of hours.

'I'm going to get myself some coffee. Can I get you anything?'

'What's the coffee like here?'

'Terrible.'

'Tea, thanks.'

Sam walked round the computer terminal, stretching her neck and wiggling her shoulders. She'd thought she'd be good at this. After all, she had spent several hours in Brendan's presence; she'd had long enough to observe him. But she'd been amazed how difficult it was to build a face from scratch, from its different features. How big was his nose? How broad was his face? How high was his forehead? She'd got the hair OK but as for the rest of it . . .

Liz came back into the room carrying two cups and handed one to Sam. She sat back down in front of the terminal and started to shake a paper tube containing sugar.

Sam put her tea on the floor and squatted down with her back to the wall. 'I'm finding this a complete nightmare. How on earth do people manage this if they've just been attacked?'

'It's really hard. Ideally we want to get hold of people within two hours of them seeing the perpetrator. After that, accurate recognition decreases significantly.'

'Do you ever catch people with these?'

Liz tore the top off the tube and poured the sugar into her coffee. 'We do. A couple of years ago they caught a rapist from one. An off-duty policeman recognised a man from the photofit and followed him home. He was arrested and convicted of four rapes.' She sipped her coffee. 'The trouble with the present system is that people tend to recognise faces as whole entities not as a collection of separate features. They're going to start trials with a new system called EvoFIT next year.'

'How will that work?'

'Well, instead of choosing different features you'll be presented with sixty different faces with a random selection of features. You chose six that most closely represent the person you're trying to describe and then from those six the computer generates another sixty and so on and so on. In only a few cycles it can produce very good results.'

'Anything must be better than this,' Sam said. 'It's like pulling teeth.'

Liz smiled sympathetically.

Phil came into the room. 'How's it going?' He walked round behind Liz to look at the computer screen.

'See for yourself,' Sam said.

Phil leaned over Liz's shoulder and looked at the screen. There was a slight pause before he said: 'Ridiculously badly.'

'Don't exaggerate, it's not kind.'

'Look, let me have a go.'

He sat down next to Liz, and Sam got up and came over to watch.

'OK, to start with his nose is smaller and his eyes are set further apart. Also he's not so long from the top of his cheekbones to the bottom of his chin and his chin isn't so pointed. His whole face has to be squarer, more chiselled.'

Fifteen minutes later Brendan's face had appeared on the screen.

'How did you do that?' Sam asked.

'I'm a policeman, Sam. I'm trained to be observant.'

'But I'm a private investigator.'

'You've always been laughably bad at faces,' Phil said. 'Comically bad.'

Rick McGann's face zoomed into Sam's mind, clear in every detail. She'd have been able to put together a pretty good composite of him – no problem. She wondered if he had any information for her yet. It had been two days.

'Well, it was easy for you,' Sam said. 'I'd done all the hard work. Roll on EvoFIT is what I say.'

'I'm not so sure about that,' Phil said. 'They don't know how that's going to work with real-life witnesses and also there's the worry that if they present the witness with lots of faces then those images will contaminate their memories. It's different from making someone create a face from scratch. Anyway, with Brendan maybe you just didn't want to see him.'

'What do you mean?'

'Well, you know how you and Mark are.'

'How's that?'

'Come on, Sam. Exceptionally close. You've never taken to his partners in the past.'

'That's not true.'

'Tell me one you liked.'

Sam frowned.

'See – none of them.'

'Well, he has bad taste in partners.'

'Whereas you, of course, have excellent taste.'

'Naturally,' Sam said. 'Excellent, excellent taste.'

'I feel there's something in this exchange I'm not quite getting,' Liz said as the printer started to hum and the first photo emerged.

As Sam came out of the police station into St Aldate's she bumped into Mr Hunter. Now the rims of his eyes were as red as his hair.

'Where the hell's your brother disappeared to?'

'Hold on . . . ' Sam began.

His finger was jabbing the air in front of her nose. 'Where is he? Does he think he can just run away from all this? You can tell him from me that I'll come after him. He won't be able to escape me. If he laid a finger on my—'

'He didn't and his disappearance has nothing to do with Adrian's death.'

'I don't believe you.'

Sam shrugged. 'Well, don't then. You can check it out with DS Howard.'

She tried to walk past him but he blocked her. 'I'm still talking to you.'

Sam stopped. 'Look, Mr Hunter, if you're looking for someone to blame it should be whoever was supplying your son with drugs.'

He grabbed hold of her upper arms. 'Why was there bruising on his arms and why were his knuckles grazed? Why was there a bruise on his temple? He'd been in a fight before he died. Have you got an explanation for any of that? Have you?'

'Take your hands off me,' Sam said calmly.

Mr Hunter let go of her.

'What have the police said about the bruises?'

'The police don't know what they're talking about.'

'I'm terribly sorry about what happened to Adrian, but my brother had nothing to do with it. If you insist on the police fixating on him they're going to miss other avenues of investigation. Why don't you back off and let them get on with their job?'

He gave her a look of utter disgust and walked past her into the police station. Sam continued up St Aldate's. Bruises, grazed knuckles, a knock on the head . . . who had Adrian been fighting with?

Her phone rang as she reached Carfax. It was Barry.

'You know the pig's head?' he said. 'I think I might have something for you.'

A couple of minutes later and Sam was outside Hedges. Barry introduced her to Jim, a young lad who'd been away on holiday for the last few days. He wasn't much older than seventeen, Sam thought, and had the acne to prove it. He said he'd sold a pig's head to a schoolboy the day before he went on holiday.

'What did he look like?' Sam asked.

He shrugged. After her ordeal with the photofit Sam felt sympathetic.

'Blond, brown, black hair?'

'Brown.'

'Taller or shorter than you?'

'Taller.'

'What was he wearing?'

'School uniform.'

'Do you know the school?'

He shook his head. 'But it was a posh one.'

'Did you talk to him at all about why he'd bought it?'

'Yeah – he said his teacher must be going off his head. He'd told him to buy it for their art class. He seemed pretty pissed off about it as well.'

'Did he say anything else that could help me trace him?'

He shook his head.

'If you remember anything else could you get in contact with me? Barry's got my number.'

'What's in it for me?'

'Oi,' Barry said. 'The amount of meat her mum's bought here over the years she gets that information for free.'

Sam smiled. 'Twenty quid,' she whispered, and the boy grinned.

When Sam finally trudged back to Park Town it was to find Alan with her mother in the garden. She had given her and Peter an edited version of what had happened in the last twenty-four hours, agreeing with Phil to omit Mark's screams.

Her mother's charm offensive was obviously well under way. Walking across the lawn towards them, Sam felt a rush of affection for her mother. However traumatised or upset, she had the knack of never forgetting her manners. Sam supposed it had something to do with the stiff upper lip. It wasn't a characteristic that she had inherited but she admired it in other people.

'Your mother was just telling me about when you got drunk and climbed out onto the roof and heckled the actors who were taking part in a play in your garden.'

Sam smiled. 'It was a terrible play and a particularly boring scene where a woman drones on and on and as far as I remember she was wearing some sort of sheet.'

'*The Dog Beneath the Skin*,' Sam's mother said. 'I've never forgotten it.'

'God, that's right, by Auden. A truly terrible play. It was Mark's fault actually. Some friends of his had finished their finals. They were celebrating and anyway they deserved to be heckled.'

'The following morning the director came and complained,' Sam's mother said.

'And what did you say?' Alan asked.

'I said I was sorry but I hadn't heard anything. A complete lie, of course. And that maybe the noise had been drunken undergraduates in the street on their way back to Teddy Hall. And then I said I was sure it wouldn't happen again and could they make sure that when they took down the seating they picked up all the cigarette butts off my lawn.'

Sam reached up and cupped one of the pinky-white flowers of the magnolia and petals fell off onto the ground. 'Where was Peter?'

Her mother smiled. 'Hiding in the study. You know as a general rule of thumb it was never good news when the actors were wearing sheets. It usually meant the previous year had blown the wardrobe budget.'

They had all turned and were walking back towards the house.

'My favourite play was *The Devils* because I persuaded Mum that I could stay up late on the basis that it's hell to sleep when you've got nuns being exorcised in the garden. There was this final scene when they screamed the place down and lit up the library with bright red floodlights. At least that one was dramatic.'

That evening Sam and Alan set off on foot for the centre of town.

'I notice you steered clear of mentioning the gay pubs and clubs when you were explaining to your parents what we were going to be doing this evening,' Alan said.

Sam sighed. 'You know how it is, Alan. They know he's gay. He knows they know and no one ever talks about it directly. They'd probably be fine about it or maybe they'd think gay pubs were dens of iniquity.'

Alan laughed. 'Dens of iniquity – mmm, that would be nice ... '

They walked on in silence for a couple of minutes. It had been a bright clear day but now a cold wind was blowing. They crossed St Giles and headed past the Martyrs' Memorial towards Cornmarket.

'Your mother,' Alan said thoughtfully, 'is unexpectedly camp.'

'Not now, Alan.'

Thirty seconds passed.

Sam glanced sideways at him. 'What on earth makes you say that anyway?'

'She's camp in that way that people are in a completely unknowing and innocent way.'

'In my opinion there is absolutely nothing camp about my mother whatsoever.'

'I bet she has coteries of gay men who absolutely adore her.'

'For what?'

'Oh, her elegant good taste – she's very just so, isn't she? She's beautifully dressed, lives in this very elegant house ... '

'Just so is one thing, camp is quite another.'

'She's got a sort of girlish innocence to her.'

'No, she hasn't.'

'But your stepfather lacks normal response times.'

'Yes.'

'Talking to him, every question dies. There's absolutely no conversational bounce-back at all.'

'He's a mathematician, Alan, not Stephen Fry.'

'He's a bit unsettling, not unpleasant, just unsettling. There is no aspect of camp in your stepfather whatsoever, rather like yourself.'

Sam felt unexpectedly disappointed.

'But at least I've got you.'

'True.'

'So I'm camp by association.'

'That's right.'

'Well, thank God for that,' Sam said, pushing her hand through the crook of his elbow. 'When everything else is falling apart at least I can hold on to the fact that I'm camp by association.'

The Castle Tavern was a big pub with a mock-Tudor exterior. A rainbow flag flying from the roof announced its character and the pub sign, which also had a rainbow background, was painted with a black silhouette of a castle. Or at any rate that's what Sam thought it was.

'Very post-modern,' Alan said, ducking his head under a hanging basket of red geraniums swinging wildly in the wind.

Inside Sam and Alan leaned on the wooden bar next to a large vase of lilies and waited for a man in a pink and white striped shirt to reach them. The pub was seething, its white wooden sash windows hurled open as wide as possible to let some cool air in to the stuffy interior. Sam looked at the drink choices – Guinness, Carlsberg, 1664, Stella Artois – and after a momentary flirtation with 1664 asked for what she always drank, Guinness. Alan ordered a pint of Stella.

A young man with a tanned face and wearing a white vest that showed off an equally tanned body and bulging biceps leaned backwards on his bar stool and gave Alan the once-over.

As the barman brought back her change, Sam took the photofit of Brendan out of her bag and asked if he recognised him.

'Have you got some identification?'

'We're not from the police. We're private investigators looking into the disappearance of Mark Falconer. He's my brother. He was going out with this man just before he disappeared but all he told me about him was that his first name was Brendan and that he was a doctor.'

'Hold on a minute.' He took the photo and walked over to the till and showed it to two of his colleagues. One of them pointed to someone in the main part of the pub and the man in the pink striped shirt came out from behind the bar and disappeared from sight.

A couple of minutes later he returned with another man at his side. He handed the photofit back to Sam. 'Have a word with Chris, here, he might be able to help.'

A group of people got up from some seats behind them and the three of them sat down.

The man the barman had brought over looked more like the straight guy than the queer eye. He was bearded and had the kind of body hair that would have made him a good cast member of *Carry on Screaming*. Sam, who knew enough about the modern aesthetics of gay beauty to know that an absence of body hair figured pretty high, wondered how he managed his love life. She introduced herself and Alan and asked him if he knew Brendan.

'Yes, I'm pretty certain it's him.'

'Do you know what his surname is?'

'McNally, but we know him as Doctor Zhivago.'

'Why?'

'Because all that doctor stuff was rubbish – fiction. He certainly wasn't a doctor. Oxford is a small place and the gay scene in Oxford is even smaller. People get found out pretty quickly if they're telling lies.'

'When was the last time you saw him?'

Chris scratched his beard. 'About a week ago, I think.'

Sam frowned. Mark had gone missing a week ago. 'Could you tell me exactly? It's important.'

He dug in the rucksack at his feet and took out a slim, dark blue pocket diary with a gold crest on it. He flicked through the pages and then looked up at Sam. 'Last Wednesday.'

'Was he here?'

'No, it was at the Oxford Gay and Lesbian centre in Northgate Hall.'

'Who was he with?'

'I'm not sure but I could make a few phone calls and see if anyone knows.'

'How long has he been on the scene?'

'A year or so, I think. I've seen him in all the usual places.'

'How do you know he's not a doctor?'

'A friend was in a car accident and ended up at the Churchill. Brendan wheeled him up to the X-ray department. He tried to pretend otherwise but it was obvious he was a porter.'

'The Churchill?'

'Yes.'

'Why do you think he'd lie about something like that?'

'If he says he's a doctor people are impressed; it's easier for him to pick up.'

'But he's so easily found out.'

'Maybe he's someone who moves on quickly when that happens, gets a job somewhere else and does the same thing. Maybe he never gets involved enough for it to matter. It's easy enough to do if you lie, keep the relationships short, and as soon as you're found out, move on. Who knows, maybe he's got a wife and kids somewhere and he's just dipping in and out.'

'Do you know anyone who'd know where he lives?'

Chris turned away from the table and looked towards the crowd at the bar. 'There might be someone. Hold on a minute, I'll have a look downstairs.'

'I knew when I met Brendan something was wrong.'

'Yes,' Alan replied. 'He was too good-looking for Mark.'

'It wasn't just that.'

'No, you were jealous.'

'No, Alan, that's what I thought at first. But what I was picking up on was that Brendan was lying.'

'Have you never lied? Have you never felt defensive?'

'Of course I have but—'

'He probably felt as if a Jack Russell had latched on to his ankle.'

'What the hell do you mean?'

'It's obvious, isn't it? You're incredibly possessive of Mark.'

Sam folded her arms and didn't say anything. She felt furious but wasn't exactly clear about how she and Alan had got to this stand-off so quickly.

Alan's face was a set mask of hostility.

Count to ten, Sam thought. Start now.

One, two, three . . . 'Well?' Alan snapped. *Four, five, six* . . .

'What's happening here?' Sam said.

'You're being a smug judgemental bastard.'

Seven, eight, nine, ten.

'I don't think I am, Alan.'

'Yes, you are. He's a liar. You were right. Oh, what a relief.'

'Alan!'

'You don't know anything about that man's life.'

'No, I don't, that's true, but I'm allowed to feel protective of my brother.'

'It's a miracle that any gay man survives into adulthood at all. Do you know what the statistics are on suicides of young gay men, or the homelessness statistics, or, if it comes to that, how many leave education as early as possible because they can't stand the bullying?'

'Alan . . .'

'So what if he's got a wife and children? Maybe he didn't know he was gay until recently, maybe he doesn't know what he is. Maybe he loves his wife and wants to have sex with men. Frankly, it's miraculous that any of us grow up to be fully functional, happy, well-adjusted adults.' Alan was on his feet, shouting at her. 'Just because Section 28's been repealed and they've allowed Julian Clary back on the television doesn't mean there's not a fucking war on and now they're telling us we can't be bishops.'

'But I've never seen you inside a church in your life.'

'That's not the point and you know it.'

He grabbed his jacket from the back of his chair and held out his hand. 'Give me the keys otherwise I'll have to wake up your parents.'

Sam handed them over and watched him head for the door and push his way out of the pub. She sat there considering what she had said and wondering if he was justified in getting angry with her. Alan rarely lost his temper but when he did he took a long time to regain his equilibrium. Although her instinct was to run after him, she knew there was no point in talking to him until he'd cooled off.

She had just finished her pint when Chris came back to her table with a man he introduced as Gary. Gary was wearing a green T-shirt, which announced in white lettering: *Happiness is a good joint.* Underneath the words was the picture of a plumber's joint and under the picture the words: *Mack's plumbing hardware sales.*

'Has your friend gone?' Chris seemed disappointed.

'I'm afraid so.'

The two men sat down. Gary had short blond hair fluffed up at the front and a couple of silver bangles on his wrist. His enlarged pupils and bloodshot eyes indicated that earlier in the evening he'd taken something substantially stronger than the pint of lager he was currently holding. He grinned at Sam as Chris handed the photo back to her.

'What can you tell me about him?' Sam said, tapping the photofit with her finger.

'Good in bed,' Gary giggled.

God give me strength, Sam thought.

'When did you go out with him?'

'A couple of months ago.'

'Did he tell you much about himself?'

'My mouth was occupied in more interesting things than small talk, darling.'

Sam wished Alan were still here. He would charm him or at least engage with the banter, when all Sam wanted to do was slap him. She looked at Chris, who rolled his eyes.

'Did you go back to his place?'

'Well, that was a dump! I tell you. I couldn't have gone out with him for long, not with him living in a place like that. I do have certain standards. Such a good-looking man living in that tip.'

Sam saw the light at the end of the tunnel.

'Could you tell me his address?'

'It'll cost you.'

'What do you want?'

'Well, Chris here's a bit smitten with your friend, isn't he?'

Sam looked at Chris in surprise and wondered fleetingly what Alan would feel about a man with the body hair density of a small bear.

'I'll swap the address for your friend's telephone number.'

'Done.' Sam got out her mobile, scrolled through the phonebook and wrote out Alan's number on the back of a flyer. She tore the flyer in half and handed the unused half and her pen to Gary, who began writing.

'Best to wait a bit before phoning,' she said, handing the piece of paper to Chris. 'He's not in the best of tempers.'

Chris nodded and pocketed the number. Gary pushed his piece of paper across the table to Sam and stood up. 'Nice doing business with you,' he said. Then to Chris: 'You can buy me a pint.'

Sam handed Chris her card. 'Thanks a lot for your help. If anything else comes to mind, I'd really appreciate you letting me know. Or, of course, you can call Alan.'

Chris nodded and walked over to join a group of men at the bar.

Sam looked around her. People were starting to pair off. Conversations were intensifying as drink oiled the wheels of social intercourse. She thought about what Alan had said about her being possessive of Mark. He was right, of course. Her bond with her brother had been forged in the crucible of a traumatic childhood. Those bonds held them together in a very specific and powerful way. In the past people had misinterpreted the nature of the connection and it had amused them both. The bonds that tied them together were not sexual, they were the product of a violent childhood survived by the skin of their teeth. If you were cast adrift in a raging storm you clung to the person next to you; you held on for dear life. That is what they had done with each other.

She thought of Rick and felt depressed about relationships and about all the old clichés, such as can one ever truly know another person. She wondered, as she often had, whether she and Mark would ever settle down, find someone to love, someone to love them.

Then she thought of Rick McGann again and of her hands running over his chest and down the front of his thighs and along the inside . . . she shook her head. When real life became overcomplicated, the desire to jump into a fantasy increased a thousand fold. What she didn't know was how he felt about her. But if he was indifferent, why had he bothered telling her about Isabel not really being his wife? Why bother with that unless . . . ? She remembered what Alan had said to her about it being murky from the off. He was right, of course he was, but she wondered if Rick had come up with anything. Torn Roots was due at the Playhouse some time this week. Perhaps he was already in town.

Outside the pub she paused to zip up her leather jacket. The bitter cold wind gusting in her face was moving the May blossom along the pavements in pink and white rivulets. In the distance the wail of a police siren could be heard. Sam looked at the address Gary had handed her and considered her options. Wait until morning. Hand it over to Phil. Or go and investigate herself now. Sam thought of the hours ticking away until the next call. She hadn't heard from Paula about her father.

Then she heard Mark's screams ringing in her ears.

Suppose he was at this address? Suppose he was hurt or dying? She had to go now but she'd also let Phil know what she was doing.

Maybe he could meet her there. She started walking briskly towards the High, putting a call into Phil as she went. He didn't pick up and she got his voicemail.

'Phil, it's Sam, I've got an address for Brendan. His surname's McNally and he's not a doctor, he's a porter at the Churchill. I'm going to go and pick up the car from my parents' and then drive over there and have a look. Could you meet me?' She looked at her watch. 'It's twelve forty-five now. I'll probably be there in about twenty minutes.'

Then she gave the address and hung up.

CHAPTER FIFTEEN

Bullingdon Road ran between Cowley and Iffley Road and it took Sam about fifteen minutes to drive there. She parked and peered across at number twenty-three. At first she thought Gary must have given her the wrong address because the house was boarded up and from the outside looked completely uninhabited. But then she thought of what he had said about the state of the place Brendan lived in. Maybe this had been a squat.

The house reminded her of one on Lettice Street close to where she lived in London. It was on the route between her flat and Oddbins on Fulham Road, so she passed it with extreme regularity. An enormous privet hedge had been allowed to expand about a foot over the pavement and to grow as high as the first-floor window ledges and white paint edged each red brick. The blue of the woodwork had last been fashionable in the late seventies.

A month back she had spent a week sitting outside it in order to write a report for a couple intending to buy an adjoining property. The report Sam gave them stated that the occupants were as quiet as church mice all week round, including Fridays and Saturdays, but that her clients should watch out for the stress-filled couple with three small boys who lived on the other side of the house they were intending to buy, especially when they'd had too much to drink and had screaming arguments about why her mother wouldn't contribute to the school fees. Appearances could be deceptive. Their house might have wooden floors, white woodwork and cheerful window boxes but Sam wouldn't have wanted to live anywhere near them.

Leaning against the car looking at this house now, Sam considered her options. Wait until morning. Wait for Phil. Go in and investigate.

What would she say to the defence class that she taught? Don't go anywhere near it was her first thought. Don't be so bloody stupid. Never put yourself needlessly at risk.

But then this wasn't a theoretical situation. Mark might be in there. He might be hurt and in need of help.

He might be dying.

Fuck it. Fuck common sense. Get in there and have a look. If she called the police they'd have to get a warrant and that would take time. She opened her phone and tried Phil; again she got his voicemail. She left a message telling him what she was going to do, snapped her phone shut and reached under the passenger seat for her torch.

The wooden door that led into the back garden had lost one of its hinges and creaked mournfully as Sam pushed through it into the darkness beyond. She had her torch focused on where she was putting her feet and recoiled, heart hammering, as something brushed against her face. She redirected the beam of the torch above her head and saw a hanging basket, very different from the one hanging outside the Castle Tavern. Attached by rusty brackets to the side of the house, its dead brown roots trailed through the wire mesh. A first-floor light came on in the house next door, spilling some light into this garden and showing it to be little better than a rubbish tip. She heard the noise of flushing water, but from number twenty-three came no sound whatsoever.

The sickly rotten smell of rubbish filled the air.

Sam walked along the path that led to the back of the house and peered into the back room. She tried the windows and then the door. The locks on the windows looked as if they'd rusted shut but the door bulged when Sam leaned her weight against it and the lock gave way easily in a shower of woodworm dust.

Inside there was the acrid smell of cat's piss mixed with another smell, insistent and sickly, overriding everything else. But that smell didn't appear to be coming from here, it seemed to be coming from further inside the house.

This room had been used for storage and was filled with the detritus of people's lives: boxes, broken chairs, old stereos and old suitcases, oozing notebooks, clothes and broken records. She picked her way through the mess until she stood in the doorway leading to the rest of the house. To her right were two rooms. One contained a rusty washing machine and an old bath, the other was filled with the same sort of stuff she had just seen. A staircase led up to the rest of the house.

Sam started up the stairs, treading carefully and holding onto the banister for fear that she might put her foot through rotten floorboards. At the top of this flight was the main hall and off it a large kitchen and an empty bedroom; neither of them contained the source of the smell. Sam continued up the next flight of stairs, the stench growing stronger and stronger as she ascended.

Perhaps an animal had got trapped up here and died; perhaps a lavatory was blocked. Her brain scrambled to seek alternative sources for the smell. Anything that would mean it wasn't a dead body, that it wasn't Mark. Anything but that.

Sam began to bargain: she'd give more to charity, she'd fill in her tax return early, she'd go to the dentist. She'd be a nicer, better person, she wouldn't judge people so quickly, she'd eat better, she'd defrost the fridge. She'd be nicer to Frank, she'd feed him organic bacon by hand, she'd try and read Proust, she'd buy a hoover that wasn't possessed by Satan, she'd jog.

Bargaining with every cell in her body, Sam reached the landing and pushed open the first door she came to. The beam of her torch picked out wooden floors, an original white marble fireplace, a stained pillow over in the corner and empty shelves looking sad and forlorn. The door to the next room only opened a couple of inches when she first tried it. She pushed harder and just managed to squeeze through. She gagged and brought her hand up to cover her nose and mouth. The source of the smell was in here. Not Mark. Make it anybody else, anything, but for God's sake not Mark. She kept the torch at her feet, too scared to raise it and see what was there. The moon, however, was not sensitive to Sam's need to wait. Slowly and silently it flooded the room with light and Sam could do nothing but look.

This room was smaller than the one she'd just left and had two windows that looked out into the back garden. An old leather sofa with a collapsed base rested against the wall to Sam's left, its springs poking through the cushions. A torn poster of Che Guevara hung by one drawing pin from grubby white woodchip wallpaper. On the facing wall was a poster of *Apocalypse Now*, Marlon Brandon's head, suspended against a night sky, melting in orange flames. The sound of the rusty swing flooded Sam's head, the feeling that someone was going to be torn from her returned. Had it been a premonition before, a warning that this was the place she was going to find Mark?

She took a step forwards and felt something crunch under her feet, she shone the torch at the floor and saw what at first glance looked like scrabble letters, then in the corner she saw a computer of enormous antiquity, the keyboard of which had shed its plastic letters and it was these that skittered under Sam's feet. So far so good, but then where was the smell coming from?

As slowly and silently as it had arrived, the moonlight vanished and Sam was left only with the light of her torch. She directed it into the far corner of the room, revealing a broken black wooden desk, a stained mattress and then something huddled under a chipboard shelf covered in blankets. Sam's feet wouldn't move; she felt as if someone had nailed them to the floor. She sent a message from her brain to her feet. Move. But the message was not transmitting. She forced herself to walk towards the huddle. It could have been a bundle of bedclothes dragged off the bed and flung in the corner.

If it wasn't for the smell.

Was she really going to touch the blankets? Turn them over? Look for a face?

With her hand over her mouth she turned away and walked over to one of the windows. It opened easily; at least that would ease the stench. For a moment she hung out of the window, taking deep breaths, then she looked back into the room, paralysed by indecision. She couldn't bring herself to look.

A noise snagged her attention.

Someone was moving around downstairs.

Her way out was back down the stairs into the basement, past whoever or whatever was producing that noise. In a moment of blind panic she considered crawling out of the window, but even for Sam that was too reckless to contemplate. Well, I'm not going to hang around waiting to be found, she thought, and I'm not going to try and tiptoe out of here. No, I'm going to run for my fucking life. She walked across to the door, opened it, took a deep breath and sprinted for the stairs. Down the first flight of stairs, down the second, with the carpet sliding from under her feet, past the front door and down the stairs into the basement she tore, running as fast as she could through the clutter of the house, and finally out into the back garden. She gulped the fresh air with relief and, hearing a voice behind her, sprinted round the corner of the house and ran head first into a large immovable object. She bounced off it and turned to run back into the garden but as she turned someone grabbed her. Then she heard a voice.

'Sam, what the fuck do you think you're doing?'

She looked up at her assailant and saw it was Phil.

'Shit, it's you. I think there's a body in there,' she gasped. 'I couldn't bring myself to look. In that room.' She pointed above their heads. 'The smell . . .'

Phil looked up at the open window and nodded at DC Woods, who, as it turned out, had been the immovable object.

'Go and wait in your car,' Phil said, and he and DC Woods disappeared into the bottom of the house.

Sam crossed the road and got into her car. She sat waiting for Phil, waiting for him to tell her that it wasn't her brother in there, to tell her that her life wasn't just about to end.

Five minutes later and Phil was squatting down next to the open window of her car. 'It's not him.'

Sam felt the air escape from her lungs, as if someone had just performed the Heimlich manoeuvre on her. She leaned her forehead against the wheel.

'SOCOs won't be too happy with you tramping all over a crime scene.'

Sam raised her head and cleared her throat. 'I'm not too happy with having discovered a body I thought was my brother's. Is it Brendan?'

'No, it's an older man but there is no ID on the body. How did you get this address?'

'This bloke I met at the Castle Tavern said he came back here one time with Brendan. They called him Doctor Zhivago because the whole doctor thing was a fiction.'

'How long ago did he come back here with him?'

'A couple of months.'

'Did he say the building was closed up then?'

'No, I think they must have been recently evicted.'

'You know better than to do this by yourself, Sam. What happened to Alan?'

'We had an argument. I'm still not sure what that was all about. Anyway, usually I wouldn't have come here by myself. I'm not a complete idiot. My first instinct is not to go blundering into a derelict house in the middle of the night like some dumb heroine in a horror film. But I couldn't get hold of you and I thought Mark might be being held here or he might be injured or dying or . . . so that's why I went in. It was a calculated risk and anyway you'd have been held up by search warrants and the like.'

He shook his head. 'All the same . . . it's not going to help things if you start behaving recklessly.'

He stood up and Sam watched him walk over to a police car that had just drawn up on the other side of the road.

She got out of the car and leaned against it. She felt as if she couldn't get enough fresh air into her lungs. A tubby man wearing a red hooded fleece, jeans and trainers and carrying a small rucksack on his back was coming out of a house opposite number twenty-three.

He nodded at her. 'What's all this then?'

'Body's been discovered. Have you noticed anything going on recently.'

He shook his head. 'House has been boarded up a month.'

'And before that?'

'Housing association place.'

'Did you know any of them?'

'People came and went there. Some I knew better than others. They were OK on the whole. Kept themselves to themselves. No trouble. The house was in bad condition but that wasn't their fault. The housing association hadn't done anything to it for years. Just took the rent and left them to it.'

'Did you know any of them by name?'

He shook his head. 'To say hello to – that was it.'

'Would you mind looking at a photofit?'

'If it's quick.'

Sam opened her car door and grabbed the picture of Brendan from her bag and showed it to him.

'Sure, he was one of them. Kept strange hours like me. We were always the first ones on the street to leave in the morning.'

'What do you do?'

'Run the newsagent at the top of the street.' He looked at his watch. 'I need to get going.'

'The police will probably want to talk to you.'

'I thought that's who you were.'

Sam shook her head. 'Afraid not.'

She watched him hurry up the street in the direction of Cowley Road. She walked over to where Phil was talking to a man wearing a white zip-up body suit. Their conversation ended as she reached them.

Phil stopped writing and closed his notebook.

'What are you going to do?' Sam asked.

'Once we get an accurate idea of how long he's been dead then we'll start going through the people reported missing around that time. We'll do a door to door.'

'A bloke in that house recognised the picture of Brendan. He runs a newsagent at the top of the road. Said the house was boarded up a month ago and before that it belonged to a housing association.'

'That might be useful. We can get a list of tenants from the association. If the council or housing association had a duty to re-house them they'll know where they are . . .'

Sam nodded. She felt exhausted, drained of everything other than despair. 'You're going to search the whole house?'

'Of course.'

'That'll be fun, like picking through a rubbish tip.'

'Go home, Sam. You look awful. Get some sleep. I'll update you if anything comes up. What did you and Alan argue about anyway? I thought he was here to help you out.'

'I don't really know,' Sam said. 'But I think it was my fault.'

Phil walked away from her back towards the house.

Sam watched as the body, zipped up in a white bag, was carried out and placed in the back of an ambulance. Dawn was lightening the sky and a blackbird was singing at the top of its voice. She shivered in the damp air and got back in her car.

The sun was coming up as Sam drove slowly over Magdalen Bridge, and mist was rising up off the river like steam off the back of a racehorse; the golden Oxford stone looked at its most beautiful in the early-morning light. She glanced up at the tower. How long was it since she'd been up there with Mark and Brendan, welcoming in the spring on that soggy miserable morning? The days that had followed felt like a lifetime. This morning the beauty and serenity only enhanced Sam's feelings of misery.

Back outside her parents' house Sam turned off the engine and looked at her watch. She'd given Alan the keys to let himself back in and didn't have another set. Five thirty was too early to wake everyone up. She lowered her seat and closed her eyes.

She's walking through the farmhouse, a shotgun pushed against her spine. 'In there,' he says. 'Through that door.' Sam looks at the strange padded door. 'No, please,' she says, 'not there.' The push becomes a shove. She opens the door and steps inside, hears the door being locked behind her. A huge head hovers in the air in front of her, the face melting in orange flames. And now it's no longer Marlon Brandon's face but Mark's. The rotting smell of death fills the room. She reaches out her hands to touch it. The cheek moves under her fingers, the skin comes away. At least he can't feel it, she thinks, looking at the closed eyes. But the eyes spring open, the mouth becomes a silent scream of agony. The whites of the eyes are blood red. She turns to run. 'You're killing me,' the head screams. 'Why are you killing me?' She hears the grate of metal upon metal, the child's swing slowly swinging in the wind. She throws herself at the door, tearing at it with her hands, struggling with all her strength, but knowing that there is no way out, that she will have to turn and face the head again but it will be closer this time and the smell will be worse and she will not survive it. She turns and sees—

Sam sat up so quickly she jammed her hand on the car horn. For a second she didn't know where she was. Gradually she registered the inside of the car, and Peter leaning down and peering at her through the car window. She rubbed her eyes, opened the car door and got out. He was holding his bike, ready for the short journey into work.

'I wasn't sure if I should wake you or not.'

'It's fine, I didn't want to wake everyone up too early.'

'No keys?'

'I gave them to Alan.'

'Any luck with your investigations?'

Sam didn't really want to tell him about the dead body, she felt it would require too much explanation and there was nothing definite yet, no ID, it would only worry him unnecessarily. 'Yes, we got some information to follow up on.'

'Will you be here when I come back?'

'I'm not sure – I think so, yes.'

'Good. By the way the Provost of St Barnabas's phoned. He said he needed to talk to you.'

'Has something else happened?'

'He didn't tell me. I'll catch up with you later.'

Peter got on his bike and pedalled sedately away. What a civilised way to go to work, Sam thought, as she turned towards the house.

She went straight upstairs to the bathroom, tore off her clothes and stepped into the shower. Usually she hated showers – she got water in her ears and dropped the soap and could never get the temperature and water pressure right – but after what had happened she could not have contemplated lying in a bath. She wanted the smell of death washed off her and down the plughole as quickly as possible. She moved so that the water was drumming on the back of her neck, and closed her eyes. She immediately felt dizzy and put out her hands to brace herself against the blue tiles, then she picked up the soap and scrubbed every inch of herself until her skin was raw and protesting. Even then she didn't feel altogether clean. She wished she could stay under the water longer, she wished she could stay there all day. She dried herself and put on a dark blue towelling dressing gown of Peter's, which was hanging on the bathroom door. Her clothes lay where she had dropped them. How many times would she have to wash them before she felt happy about wearing them again? She wasn't sure they could ever be washed enough.

The thought crossed her mind that if she just left them there her mother would pick them up. It was a child's thought, she knew, but at the moment she just couldn't bear to touch them. She left the bathroom and went downstairs.

In the kitchen Alan was sitting at a table covered in used breakfast items.

'We were worried about you,' Sam's mother said, coming into the kitchen behind her.

'I'm sorry. I fell asleep outside in the car. I didn't want to wake you up too early.'

Seeing a half-full cafetière sitting on the table, Sam got a mug, poured herself some coffee and sat down next to Alan. She was trying to fathom how he was feeling about her. He certainly wasn't seeking much eye contact, but it was difficult with her mother there. Perhaps he was embarrassed by his behaviour or perhaps he was waiting for her to apologise.

The phone rang and Sam's mother left the room.

Sam reached across and touched his arm. 'Alan, I'm so sorry if anything I said yesterday upset you. You know I adore you. You're one of the most important people in my life. I can't bear to argue with you. I'll apologise as much as you like but please can we never do that again, especially not at the moment.'

Alan placed his hand over the top of hers where it rested on his arm. 'Sorry, darling, I don't know what came over me. I was thinking about it all night.'

Things were going to be all right between them.

'I particularly liked the bit when you said that even though Section 28 had been repealed and Julian Clary was back on the television it didn't mean there wasn't a war on.'

He smiled. 'Yes, that bit was particularly good. A sort of Jean Claude van Damme meets Bette Davis moment. So how did you get on after I left?'

'I got an address for Brendan.'

'Do you want us to follow it up this morning?'

'I've already been there. The place is boarded up.'

He frowned. 'You went there last night?'

'Yes.'

'By yourself?'

'There was a body there—'

'A body?'

'It wasn't Mark.'

'You went into a derelict building in the middle of the night alone?'

Sam could see Alan wrestling with his temper.

'It's all right, Alan, you can shout. Phil did.'

'I don't see that I can flounce off in a temper and then complain when you do a Lone Ranger but, for God's sake, woman, you teach self-defence classes. If I'd done something like that you'd have been *furious* with me.'

'You're right, Alan. But suppose Mark had been in there, badly hurt; suppose I hadn't gone in and he'd died . . .' She picked up her coffee but her hand was shaking so much she put it down again. 'God, I can't get the smell of that body out of my nose.'

'OK, but suppose Mark had been there with whoever kidnapped him. What would you have done then? We're talking about an extremely dangerous individual here. You know that, right?'

Sam nodded. She placed her finger over some pepper, which had fallen out of the bottom of the pepper grinder, then licked off the grounds. The pepper burnt the end of her tongue. Yes, she knew that.

Alan took a deep breath. 'What do you want to do today?'

But before she could reply Sam's phone rang and she dug in her bag for it.

'Hi, Sam, it's Rick. Are you back in Oxford?'

Sam's stomach did some strange tap dance. 'Yes, I am.'

'Sorry not to have been in touch before but I had nothing to report.'

'And now?'

'Now I have. We came up last night. We're here till Thursday, then back down to Brighton and Sussex University. We're working all day. Should be done about six. Could you meet me then?'

'Yeah, that should be fine,' Sam said, trying to sound nonchalant, trying not to sound like someone with a tap-dancing stomach.

She told him where to meet her and ended the call. She leaned her elbows on the table, covered her face with her hands and groaned.

'Rick and Sam,' Alan said.

Sam dropped her hands away from her face and wagged a finger at him. 'Don't start.'

'I'm not starting anything. I was just thinking that in *Casablanca*, the true love affair is between Rick and Sam.'

'Don't be ridiculous, that's rubbish.'

'Well, he's the one there when Rick's sobbing into his whisky.'

'Sam goes off to the Blue Parrot with Ferrari and Rick goes off with Captain Renault.'

Alan laughed. 'God, I've trained you well.'

CHAPTER SIXTEEN

As Sam stepped through the main gates of St Barnabas's a couple of hours later it was immediately obvious why the Provost wanted to speak to her. The beautiful lawns she had so enjoyed looking at a few days ago had been desecrated. An area four feet long and the width of the lawn had been torn up and white paint had been poured all over it.

A group of people stood staring down at the damage. Bill, the head porter, was amongst them. Sam walked over to him.

'When did this happen?'

'Last night.'

'Did anyone see who . . .'

He shook his head. 'The night porter only saw it at the end of his shift.'

Sam sat down on the stone steps that ran down to the grass and rubbed her face. She'd only had a couple of hours' sleep and her thoughts felt muddy, but even muddy she could compute that this was different from the pig's head and the note. They had been aimed solely at the Provost, this was a very public attack on the college as a whole. However much Edward Payne had wanted to keep it all under wraps, he wouldn't be able to now. She got up and set off for the Lodgings.

A few minutes later, outside in the Provost's garden, Sam looked carefully at the rusty deckchair the Provost had indicated she should sit down in and then lowered herself cautiously into it. The pinky red canope of a copper beech spread above their heads.

'You'll tell the police now,' she said.

He nodded.

'I'm sorry I haven't been much help. The incidents seem to be getting worse.'

'Nonsense. You've been most helpful. I wondered if there'd been any progress on the pig's head?'

'Nothing concrete. I'm sorry, but with things being as they are with Mark I've not been able to focus my attention ... but if the police are involved ...'

He nodded. 'Out of interest, who do you think is responsible?'

'Kenneth Adams's nephew, I think. He's probably going to be the most badly affected by Adams's eviction from the college. He told me he's the only member of the family who hasn't fallen out with him, so he's inevitably going to be drawn into the carer's role, doing his shopping, that sort of thing, and dealing with the consequences of his drinking. Also he knew about the Boar's Head and the Needle and Thread. Do you know if Adams ever gave his college key back?'

'I doubt it. I can check, but it's not as if he can't come into the college. It's just that he's not living here any more.'

'So his nephew could have used it to get into the college last night?'

'Yes. Do you think Adams knows?'

Sam shifted her weight in the deckchair and it wobbled precariously. 'I don't think so, no. He wouldn't want the lawns torn up. After all those years at the college, he must have some affection for the place.'

'Might you try to make the nephew see reason? Perhaps if you confronted him ... ?'

Sam nodded. 'I'll try. It's just I haven't got anything to go on at the moment other than a hunch. It would help if I had some definite evidence to link him to what's happened. I could then threaten him with taking the evidence to the police if he didn't stop.'

The Provost stood up and Sam followed suit. 'No word yet on Mark?'

She shook her head. 'I bumped into Mr Hunter outside the police station a couple of days ago. He wasn't a happy man.'

The Provost sighed. 'Have the police matched Mark's DNA to the blood on Adrian's clothes?'

'I haven't heard anything from them but I can tell you it won't match.'

'It would help if we could find out who Adrian was fighting with.'

Sam nodded. 'You're right, but the police are well aware that my brother's disappearance has nothing to do with Adrian. The only reason they've done the test is to placate Mr Hunter.'

He nodded. 'Are there any developments in your brother's case?'

'I'm sorry,' Sam said. 'There's nothing I can tell you about that at the moment.'

Standing in the Turl a few minutes later, Sam couldn't make up her mind what to do next. It was too soon to get any information out of the police about the body she'd found at Bullingdon Road. And she knew that they would be making enquiries at the Churchill about Brendan. She was meeting Rick at six, so she had the afternoon to kill. At least the note, pig's head and paint were a distraction from the knot of fear in her stomach, which twisted every time she thought about Mark, every time she thought of the clock ticking down to the next call.

She phoned Kenneth Adams and got the name of his nephew's work place, which turned out to be a large boys school on the Woodstock Road. Then she phoned the school and left a message saying she had to speak with him urgently and would be at the school in forty minutes. Confronting him at work might shake some of the complacency out of him.

When she arrived at the school, a short bus ride later, she found him waiting for her on the pavement outside the school grounds looking flustered.

'What is it?' he said. 'Has something happened to Uncle?'

He indicated that they should cross the road and led the way into the cricket grounds where white-clad boys were practising in the nets.

'No, nothing like that. The lawns at St Barnabas's have been torn up and white paint poured over them.'

'And you haven't found who did it yet?'

'No.'

'The note, the pig's head, the lawn – oh dear, oh dear. Why do you need to see me?'

A cricket ball rolled towards them. He took his hands out of his pockets, picked it up and threw it back to the boy running towards them. Sam saw white paint on the edges of his thumbnails. He stuffed his hands back into the baggy green tweed jacket he was wearing.

'I think you're responsible for what's been happening,' she said. 'And this is a warning for you to stop. What happened to the lawns constitutes criminal damage and the matter is now in the hands of the police. If they find evidence linking you to what's happened that'll be the end of your teaching career.'

He smiled. 'What makes you so certain it's me?'

'You know about the Boar's Head and the Needle and Thread. You had access to the college with your uncle's key. You are the person who has been most personally affected by your uncle's eviction from the college. A pig's head was sold to a public school boy who said his teacher had told him to buy it for an art class. Do you teach art?'

'Yes, I do.'

'You also have white paint on your hands.'

He laughed. 'If you're an art teacher you always have paint on your hands. And I'd like to point out that recently there was a long correspondence in *The Times* about the Boar's Head. So you can add the circulation figures of that paper to the number of people who know about that.'

'What about the Needle and Thread?'

He shrugged. 'I admit that is somewhat more obscure. Actually, I'm rather flattered you think it's me. No one has ever thought I had the capacity for any criminal activity before. But I'm afraid you've got it wrong. I'm much too diffident to engage in acts of malice. You can talk to any of the boys I teach and you won't find any of them knowing anything about a pig's head.'

He looked at his hands and with the nail of one thumb removed the paint from the other. He placed the small scroll of white paint in the palm of his hand and then blew it into the air. 'If that was your evidence. I think you'd agree it's rather flimsy. You need to be looking elsewhere.'

Unexpectedly and inconveniently Sam found herself believing him. He was accurate, she thought, in his assessment of himself. He did seem too diffident to engage in acts of malice. They had circled the cricket pitch by now and were back on the pavement, looking across the road at the school. But if it wasn't him who was she left with? Professor Petheridge? Mrs Prendergast?

She sighed. 'Who do you think it is?'

'Maybe it has nothing to do with my uncle at all. Maybe there is someone out there who is angry with the Provost and the college for entirely different reasons.'

'Such as?'

'I'm not a private investigator. I am a mere art teacher. How the hell should I know?' He looked at his watch. 'I have to get back.'

Sam watched him disappear through the school gates. All the evidence incriminated Colin, but now she didn't believe it was him. Someone, however, was doing a pretty good job of setting him up.

They had agreed to meet in the Quod Bar on the High at six o'clock that evening. As Sam pushed through the door, she saw Rick leaning on the bar, chatting to the woman serving him. If Sam's stomach had tap-danced earlier at the sound of his voice, at the sight of him it now did something that was more *Last Tango in Paris* than *Top Hat*. She was just contemplating taking a quick walk round the block and giving herself a good talking-to, when Rick turned and saw her. He waved and she walked over to the bar.

He took hold of her elbow and kissed her on the cheek. The tangoing intensified.

'What can I get you?'

Sam looked at the glass of white wine in front of him and pointed to it. 'That'll do fine.'

'I'll get a bottle.'

Get three. Get five. Get thirty, Sam thought. She'd need about a bottle and a half to even approach a relaxed state. She sat down and Rick joined her a couple of minutes later with a bottle and two glasses.

'How did it go today?' she asked.

'All right, thanks. The kids were great, really into the kind of stuff we were doing. Children are great, aren't they? I want to have a whole handful.'

Sam didn't quite manage to keep her face in neutral.

He laughed. 'You don't want them, then?'

How on earth had they got on to this territory so quickly? It was ridiculous, they'd only just sat down.

'I wouldn't say I've completely ruled it out. You never can tell, can you, what's going to happen to you in life?'

'Who you might meet,' Rick said. 'I think that makes a whole load of difference. I've seen it with friends of mine. They get together with the right person and away they go . . .'

Rick raised his glass. 'To a resolution of the present situation.'

Sam clinked her glass against his. And what was that exactly?

Rick unbuttoned the cuffs of his white linen shirt and rolled up his sleeves. Sam looked at the black swirl of hairs on his arms and at the long flat fingers. She wondered what those fingers would feel like on her body; she wondered what they would feel like inside her, what he would feel like.

'God, woman, what are you thinking about? You look so sad.'

Sam laughed but didn't reply. This was revenge indeed. All those years ago she'd thought she'd been so clever with that boy from the waltzer, so clever to skip the embarrassment of puppy love and infatuation. It had all been so neat. They'd had sex and then he went away the next day. Phil had never had the same effect on her as Rick, with Phil it had been a steady, safe thing, nothing had really seemed at risk there because Sam had always been safe in the knowledge that he was more in love with her than she was with him. But now with Rick she felt ridiculously vulnerable and when she thought about sex she looked sad.

Yes, that boy was back from the fair, wielding Cupid's bow with a vengeance, her head was pressed back and she was spinning so fast she felt sick. Love sick.

Sam took a large gulp of wine, then felt his hand on her arm. 'Are you all right, Sam?'

Oh. So that's what it felt like to feel his hand on her.

'Yes, I'm fine. I'm sorry, this thing with my brother . . .' She reached for the bottle and refilled their glasses.

'You're very close to him.' A statement not a question.

Sam sighed. 'I had a client who lost his twin a couple of months ago and he said he felt lopsided without him. Now I know exactly what he meant.'

'What's the news on him?'

'I was about to ask you for yours.'

He took his hand off her arm and twisted the stem of his wine glass round and round. 'It's a tricky thing, isn't it, trust? It doesn't come that easily to me either. With my background that's no great surprise. Feeling safe, believing people won't betray me. God, all of that, I have to work on it every single day. I used to think I'd reach a point where it would come automatically but now I think it never will. Each time it's a choice, isn't it?'

'I suppose it is.'

Sam reached for the bottle again. She didn't know what to do. She didn't know if she could trust him and if she told him she was attracted to him, God, that was something he could use. Lust could be mighty inconvenient. She felt exhausted and upset. But then something in her rebelled. Fuck caution. She would tell him some of the truth. She would see how he did with that and then she'd see about the rest.

'Mark has been taken hostage. I spoke to the person who's taken him. He wants my father on the end of the phone in two days' time or he'll kill Mark. He tortured Mark while I was listening. I heard him screaming . . .'

Sam stopped. She remembered her gran once saying to her that the only way not to cry at funerals was not to sing the hymns. Well, she was singing now and she felt the tears rising up her throat. She swallowed. She felt she was at the wheel of a car that had just hit black ice. She couldn't stop and there was nothing she could do until it crashed.

'And I can't get him because he's in Iraq. They think he might have been hurt in an explosion near Fallujah. He could be dead, and if he is then what am I going to do? I've been down here trying to go back over everything, to trace what might have happened to Mark, but I'm no closer to knowing where he might be being held and I'm going to have to speak to the man again on the phone . . .'

He hadn't said anything or done anything while she babbled on but he had listened intently. Sam realised with relief that he wasn't frightened by strong emotions; he wasn't going to walk away, nor was he going to try and save her. He could hold his ground with it.

'Jesus, you must be frantic.'

'I feel like I'm locked into something that just has to be played out to its conclusion come what may. There's almost nothing that I can do to affect the outcome. And I'm so, so tired. I'm so tired even this . . .' she picked up her wine glass, 'isn't having any effect on me.'

He opened his mouth to say something but Sam cut across him. 'A couple of months ago my father left me a whole load of stuff to look after. There were two maps with places marked on them where they buried the bodies of the men they killed. I don't have them on me but I can let you have them. If my father comes back from Iraq in one piece I'll ask him if he knows anything about your dad.'

Rick was watching her intently.

'I don't know if it'll be any good to you but I think my father may well be willing to help. I think he came back seeking some sort of redemption, looking for forgiveness.'

'Why did you decide to tell me now?'

'It's like you said before. It's a choice each time, isn't it, to trust someone or not to.'

'As simple as that?'

'Yes,' Sam said, although of course it wasn't.

She was trusting him with the information about Mark and her father to see how he behaved. But one thing had now become clearer in her mind. She would not tell him how she felt about him or try to find out what his feelings for her might be until this was all over. Whatever happened, she mustn't sleep with him. Sam was a Scorpio; refraining from sex with a man she found attractive was not the first thought that entered her head. The first thing that entered her head was ripping his clothes from his back and unbuckling his belt. Restraint depressed her. She stared at the empty bottle and sighed.

'Anyway,' Sam said, 'you said you'd found out something that might help.'

He was staring into the middle distance.

'Rick?'

'Oh, sorry, yes, yes.' He looked at the empty bottle. 'Another?'

'My shout,' Sam said, getting up.

She brought the second bottle back and filled both their glasses. He still seemed in a daze.

'So, what was it?' Sam asked.

He looked at her as if he hadn't noticed that she'd just sat down.

'I did a bit of asking about. Came up with some names for you.' He took a piece of paper from the pocket of his jeans and pushed it across the table towards her.

'They'd be worth checking out.'

'Thanks,' Sam said. 'You know that I'll hand these to the police.'

He nodded.

'And you don't mind?'

'Look, Sam, I can't be doing with all that tribal bollocks. I've had enough of that to last me a lifetime. That's not who I am any more. If they've done nothing, they've got nothing to worry about, have they?'

Sam thought that was rather naive, but on the other hand she didn't really care. She had the list of names and maybe it would help them find the person holding Mark. That was all that mattered.

By the time the barman threw them out, the wine had definitely taken its toll on Sam. She stood awkwardly in the High not knowing quite how to part.

'Thanks for the names,' she said.

'I hope they help. When could you let me see the maps?'

'I don't know when I'm next going to be in London but I'll phone you when I know myself. As for asking my father, I just don't know what's going to happen there. I still don't know if Paula's managed to make contact with him . . .'

He nodded and then leaned forward to kiss her on the cheek. In her mind's eye Sam turned her head and found his lips, placed her hand against the side of his face and held him there a while.

In reality she stood there passively and then turned and began crossing the High in the direction of Radcliffe Square.

'See you then,' he shouted after her.

She waved her hand but didn't look back. A couple were walking towards her entwined in each other's arms. The night was mild and everywhere she looked people were strolling arm in arm.

She stopped and leaned against the walls of All Souls, looking at the Radcliffe Camera. It had seen it all, she thought. Young love one summer followed by the trauma of finals the next. It wasn't offering any opinion on the matter of her love life. Sam closed her eyes and imagined how good his mouth would feel against hers. She sighed heavily, pushed herself away from the wall and headed towards Jericho, crossing the area the Morris dancers had occupied on May Day. The thoughts circulating in her mind would have been ones thoroughly approved of by the beer-drinking fertility bush.

Twenty minutes later, she was outside Phil's house in Walton Street, banging on the door. He opened it in his pyjamas. 'What is it, Sam? Has something happened?'

Sam barged past him. 'Got some coffee?'

He turned and followed her into the kitchen. 'You're pissed.'

'Well spotted. Oh, I forgot, you're a policeman, you're trained to be observant.' She sat down heavily and smiled at him.

Phil didn't smile back. He filled the kettle and put a spoon of instant into a red mug. When the kettle had boiled he poured water into the cup, stirred it and put the cup and a bottle of milk on the table and sat down.

On the way here Sam had been thinking if she couldn't sleep with Rick at least she could sleep with Phil. They'd slept together twice in the last six months. Why not add to it? She was too drunk to consider if he'd mind. She didn't stop to ask him instead she leaned across the table and kissed him.

He looked startled then irritated.

'What?' Sam said.

'I think that should be my line. Or rather, what the hell do you think you're doing?'

Sam sighed and felt her feelings of lust receding. 'Nothing I haven't done before.'

'If you remember, it was you who split up with me. It was then me who suggested we get back together again. It was you who said let's not have that conversation. Now it's you kissing me.'

'Is that a no then?'

'I don't even know the question you're asking.'

'Oh God, Phil, are you playing hard to get?'

'What's the fucking question, Sam?'

Fancy a quick shag? was the first thought that came into Sam's mind. But even she knew that in the circumstances it would be best not to articulate that one. So instead she said, 'I'm sleeping so badly – sex helps.'

'Have you any idea how insulting that sounds?'

Sam sighed. This was all going to hell in a hand basket.

'I think you're confusing me with a fucking sleeping pill.'

'I promise I'll still respect you in the morning.'

'You don't know the meaning of the word. I don't think you ever had any respect for me, even back then. I don't know how we lasted as long as we did.'

Indolence, Sam thought, I was too lazy to break it up and having sex on tap and somewhere to go on a Saturday night was useful.

'I kept making excuses for you. I thought once the pressure of training had calmed down, once this event was over, things would change, but they never did. You seem to think it's OK to be in a relationship and give the absolute minimum of yourself and use it as some recreational pit stop for sex. I don't think you have the slightest interest in me. You're a selfish person, Sam, and I don't know why I stayed with you as long as I did – probably because I didn't think I deserved any better. You can't just sleep with me when the fancy takes you. It's insulting.'

Sam felt exhausted. She didn't want a row. She tried to think of some suitably witty riposte, failed and instead opted for, 'You're right,' followed by, 'I'm sorry.'

She drained her coffee, got to her feet and made for the door.

She stood on his doorstep, looking up and down the street. She blamed his recent sobriety. In the good old days they would have got drunk together and then Phil would have had no qualms about going to bed. Since he'd stopped drinking he'd become a right pain in the arse, interested in promotion, resistant to seduction and, most distressing of all, sort of moral.

In a city filled with thousands of undergraduates there must be someone who was desperate to get laid. There was a cocktail bar not far away; she'd try her luck there.

Sam lay squashed between the wall and a young man whose name she had found out approximately four hours ago was Greg Smith. He'd been easy enough to pick up. Sam had waved a bottle of wine in his face and asked him if he'd like to join her. That seemed to have done the trick. Having been brought up in an Oxford college and gone to God knows how many of her parents' parties, Sam knew all the questions. She could ask them without even hearing the words come out of her mouth. What year are you in? What subject are you studying? Are you enjoying it? What are you going to do when you leave? In Greg's case the answers were: second year, English, sort of and haven't a clue – I'd like to try acting but my parents say do law and you can always become a barrister.

The sex had been frantic, short-lived and rather brutish. The condom was barely on before becoming sadly redundant. It was exactly what she deserved, Sam thought. Greg Smith seemed happy enough though, asleep on his back, mouth open and snoring loudly. He had a broad tanned face and black curly hair, his nose was long and straight other than its tip, which pointed almost at his forehead. She'd liked his shirt – the blue background and white design and short sleeves seemed faintly tropical – and his body, square but lean.

Sam had kept herself well hidden behind the barrage of questions she threw in his direction. If you carried on asking them questions it kept them away from you, didn't it? He'd been happy to keep answering and answering and answering. And all Sam had thought was how much of this do we have to go through before we can get down to it.

She looked at him affectionately. She didn't blame him; she blamed herself. He'd been sweet enough but also desperate and very anxious – not a great combination. She envied him the oblivion of sleep, it's what she craved more than anything else, but what she was left with was a terrible headache and the dry mouth of the extremely hung-over. She needed water and painkillers urgently.

She slid out of the bottom of the bed and, despite the mattress being shot and moving a lot, Greg Smith didn't wake, he merely turned over on his side with a grunt. That was a relief. Sam didn't fancy a conversation with him. Not much to talk about really.

Shirt, trousers, shoes and socks she managed to find but where the hell were her pants? Rolled up in a ball in the bottom of the bed next to Greg Smith's malodorous feet. She dressed hurriedly. There was nothing like bad sex to sober you up quickly. She found a piece of paper and a pen on his desk and after several failed attempts settled for, *It's your life not your parents' – try the acting. Good luck.* She picked her jacket off the door hook, let herself quietly out of the room and ran down the steps into the quadrangle. Now there was the lodge to negotiate. Fortunately she was coming along one side of the quad at the same time as a group of young men in tracksuits were heading towards the main gates of the college, rowers off for an early-morning outing. Sam slid through the door behind them and out into the High.

CHAPTER SEVENTEEN

Screaming and shouting echoed in Sam's head as she clawed her way back to consciousness. She sat up and groaned as the hangover immediately claimed her. It slowly dawned on her that the screams hadn't stopped; they were not coming from the inside of her head or from her nightmares, but from downstairs.

He's dead was her first thought.

Her second, Oh God, it's my mother making that noise.

She was halfway across the room when Alan burst through the door.

'Sam . . .'

'What's going on? What's the matter with Mum?'

'You better come downstairs.'

'What's happened?'

'Just come, will you.'

Sam ran down the stairs into the kitchen.

Her mother and Peter were standing up. The room looked orderly other than a chair, which was lying on its side. Sam righted it and looked from one to the other. Had they been fighting? Her mother's arms were tightly folded and she was biting down so hard on her lower lip, she looked as if she were about to draw blood. Peter was looking down at the floor, his hand repeatedly smoothing his hair back from his forehead, as if trying to comfort himself.

'What's happened?' Sam asked.

No one said anything.

'Alan?'

On the table was a pile of post. On the top was a small padded envelope. Alan picked it up and peered inside. He swallowed and looked at her. 'Sam, I don't know . . .'

She held out her hand. 'Let me see.'

Alan handed it to her and she held the envelope upside down over the palm of her hand and shook. When nothing happened she reached inside and pulled out the contents.

Then slowly it registered what it was. She began to sway, her legs felt wobbly as though she'd suddenly lost all muscle power. Alan grabbed her and then a chair was pushed against the back of her legs. She heard Alan on the phone talking. She felt herself starting to shake, her legs first and then spreading up her torso and along her arms and into her teeth.

In the end the only bit of her not shaking was the hand that had closed over Mark's little finger.

'Sam . . .' Alan crouched by her side. 'I've called the police, they're coming straight over.'

Sam closed her eyes. The screaming was back, not her mother's this time but Mark's and with it the screech of metal on metal, the rusty swing blowing back and forth in the wind. She felt his finger in the palm of her hand. She felt Alan's hand on her arm. 'Let go of it, Sam.'

She didn't open her eyes. This was all she had of her brother. No way was she going to let go of it. In her mind she made her fist not a series of fingers and a thumb but a sealed metal unit impervious to forced entry. No one would take this away from her.

'Sam, let go.'

She couldn't speak. The screaming in her head was getting louder and louder. Alan was still talking to her but she couldn't hear what he was saying. Now he was trying to prise her fingers open. She looked at him impassively. That wouldn't get him very far. She stood up and gently pushed him away from her.

'Come near me again and I'll kill you,' she said, her voice matter-of-fact, devoid of feeling.

Her mother was saying something now, and Peter, but she couldn't hear them above the noise in her head. She walked out of the kitchen and back upstairs, still holding her brother's little finger.

In the bathroom she locked the door behind her. Looking at her reflection in the mirror over the sink she barely recognised herself. Red-rimmed eyes with deep black smudges underneath stared blankly back at her. Mark's screams mingled with the screech of rusty metal were growing louder and louder. She saw a glass tumbler next to the sink with a bubble in its base. I'm the bubble she thought. I'm trapped and can't breathe and there's glass all around me and the noise is getting louder and louder. If I can just break the glass I'll be free and the noise will stop. She picked up the glass and smashed it with all her might against the mirror, her reflection splintered and fragmented into thousands of pieces, shards of glass fell into the sink. But the base of the tumbler remained intact – the bubble had not burst. She picked up the jagged base and closed her hand around it, feeling the glass beginning to cut, squeezed it tighter.

The door of the bathroom flew open and Alan grabbed hold of her. He seized hold of her hands and turned them wrist up. Blood was trickling from the one holding the piece of glass. He squeezed her wrist until she opened her hand and the piece of glass fell into the sink, then he grabbed a towel and mopped away the blood.

The screaming in her head still hadn't stopped.

She looked down at her hand. The cuts weren't that deep. If they were deeper maybe it would stop. She watched them slowly fill with blood. She pushed past Alan and went into the bedroom and that's where Phil found her a few seconds later, curled up in the corner of the room, staring out of the window across the garden, one hand covering her ear, the other still gripping onto the finger. He'd taken hold of the hand covering her ear and held it in his, he'd held onto it until she was ready to open the other one. After that someone else came she didn't recognise. He took hold of her hand and bandaged it. 'I feel like a computer that's about to explode,' she remembered saying. Then she remembered taking a glass of water, swallowing a pill and then nothing else, the relief of oblivion and of the plug finally being pulled.

She was rising from the bottom of the sea but too quickly, doubled up in agony because she was coming up too fast. She couldn't slow herself and the quicker she came to the surface the more pain she was in. She tried to struggle back down, back into the pitch darkness of the ocean but however hard she tried she couldn't slow her ascent to the

surface. She was coming up too rapidly and she was going to
die.

She woke to screams, this time her own.

The room was in darkness but a shadow sitting in a chair next to her bed stirred and a sidelight came on. She turned away from the light, not wanting to be seen. She looked down at her hands, one bandaged, the other empty, and remembered. She curled up, away from the person who had turned on the light, wanting to be left alone in the dark, wanting time to try and pull herself back together. If she could find the bits to pull.

'Sam?'

The voice was unexpected but instantly recognisable – Reg.

Sam looked round. 'What . . . ?' But it was such a relief to see him she couldn't finish the sentence.

Reg stretched his back and smiled at her.

The top of his head was bald and shone in the light of the lamp but there was the glint of grey stubble above his ears. He was wearing blue cotton trousers and a loose white shirt. His face was tanned and he had brown almond-shaped eyes. His right foot was resting against his left thigh. Despite his Buddha-like stomach, he had the bendy easy-in-his-body quality of a man who could get himself into the most extreme of yoga positions without any difficulties at all.

She swallowed and eventually managed, 'What are you doing here?'

'Alan phoned me. He said you could use some help right now. He asked me to come down.'

'I didn't realise you made house calls.'

'I don't usually, but he said you could do with some support.'

She sighed. 'He told you I was cracking up, I expect.'

'He was really concerned for you, Sam. He said you were under an intolerable amount of pressure.'

It was weird seeing Reg in this room in her parents' house. She'd only ever seen him in his own consulting room. He seemed somehow smaller here, more contained.

'Have you met my parents?'

'Only briefly. Alan told them I was a good friend who'd exert a calming influence on you.'

'They don't know you're my therapist?'

'No, and I suppose strictly speaking I'm not. You'd stopped seeing me.'

'But you still came.'

'Yes.'

Sam pressed her fingers against her closed eyes. 'I don't think you can help me. There's just too much.'

'Shall we try anyway and see what happens?'

She nodded. 'But I wouldn't know where to start.'

'Alan and Phil have filled me in on the details of what has happened, so there's no need for you to tell me that.'

God – how embarrassing. Now they'd all met him.

'Sam?'

'I'm sorry, Reg, but would you mind if I got dressed. It's just . . .'

'No, of course not. I'll wait outside.'

He got up and left the room. Sam scrambled into her clothes, feeling the fear growing in her stomach. She felt like she'd been skinned. Maybe with her clothes on she wouldn't feel so cold, so exposed. A couple of minutes later she pushed open the door and he came back in.

She glanced at her watch and then at him. 'What's the time?'

He looked at his own watch. 'Two thirty.'

'At night?'

He smiled. 'Yes.'

'Are you sure you're OK to do this?'

'Yes, fine.'

'How long have you been here?'

'I got here about six.'

'And have you been in here most of the time?'

'We didn't know when you might wake up. No one thought it was a good idea for you to wake up alone.'

'No.'

Sam was standing awkwardly in the middle of the room with her hands in her pockets. Reg dragged the chair he'd been sitting in from the side of the bed over to another chair, positioned next to the window, and turned on a nearby standing lamp.

'OK?' he said.

Sam nodded and walked towards him, feeling like a prisoner

walking to her execution. Reg kicked off his shoes and sat down. Here we go, Sam thought, shit, here we go.

She shrugged. 'I don't know where to begin.'

'Wherever you want.'

'The last call I took with the man holding Mark. I heard Mark screaming. Since hearing that . . .'

'Yes?'

'I've been hearing screaming in my head ever since, but it's not Mark's. It's someone else but it's in my dreams and in my nightmares. Sometimes it's there when I'm awake. I can't clear my head of it. And I'm going to have to take another call and I don't think I can stand it but I have to.' She glanced at her watch. 'I have to take it in just over thirty-six hours.'

Reg's eyes went to her damaged hand. 'Did that make it stop?'

She shook her head. 'Not completely.'

'Did you think it would?'

She nodded.

'Have you been self-harming since you stopped seeing me?'

She shook her head. 'No, this is the first time.'

'How did you feel when you heard Mark screaming?'

'I felt as if someone had threaded barbed wire into my entrails and was slowly pulling it out. I felt a sharp pain in my upper chest and I felt as if my head had been put in a pressure cooker.' Sam looked down at her hands. They had begun to shake.

'And what were you saying to yourself?'

'I have to save him. It's up to me to save him but I can't. I mustn't cry out, it'll only make things worse. It's impossible. I'm powerless. I have to get away. There's nothing I can do but listen. I'm going to die.'

Sam closed her eyes as other images came.

'Sam? Tell me what you're seeing. Tell me where you are.'

'There are horrible noises. I've been woken up and I'm frightened. I want my mother. I'm about four years old. I push open the door and there are shapes writhing in the darkness but the noises are like an animal in pain. They're not noises I can recognise. I'm standing in the doorway too frightened to go in and then someone's knee catches the side of my head, someone's gone past me into the room. Then I hear Mark's voice and he's tearing at the shapes in the dark, pulling at them. Then I see that my father has him by the throat and he shoves him violently away from him and there's the crash of breaking glass . . .'

'Sam?'

'Now I'm looking down at Mark and he's lying on his back in a pool of blood and shattered glass, I touch his forehead and the skin moves under my hand like his forehead is a slice of salmon you could lift off. He's not moving and I'm tearing at him, telling him to get up. My hands are on his face but the skin keeps sliding as I touch it and I know it's all my fault. I'm making it worse and worse. I should never have woken up. I should never have pushed open the door. He's dead and then someone starts screaming.'

'Sam, it's all right.'

'The screaming is going on and on.'

'Who's screaming, Sam?'

'Then my father's standing over me and staring down at Mark and his face is blank and I'm holding onto his leg and holding my arms up to him. I have to get him away from Mark. I have to distract him.'

Sam's breathing was coming in huge gulps. She was the bubble again, trapped in the bottom of the glass.

'He picks me up and he smells sour and I put my hands on his face and round his neck and he holds me tightly and then we're outside and he's sitting on the swing and we're swinging backwards and forwards and he's holding me so tightly I can't breathe.'

Sam sat forwards, gasping for breath, hands on her knees, wheezing.

'He's holding me so tightly and the swing is squeaking backwards and forwards and then . . .'

Sam was coughing now, coughing and gasping for breath.

'Sam, open your eyes and look at me.' Her eyes sprang open. The pupils of Reg's eyes looked vast and black like caverns. 'Take a deep breath, Sam. Slowly. And another. Let it out slowly. Slow and steady.'

This continued for ten breaths.

'And then what happened?'

Sam closed her eyes. 'His body began to shake and the more he shook the tighter he was holding on to me. He was crying and crying and crying and I was holding onto him and saying it was all right that everything was going to be all right. The lights came on in the house and people began walking towards us. When I looked at his face it was covered in blood where I'd touched him but the tears had cut tracks through the blood and then they tried to take him away from me. I wouldn't let him go and I'm fighting and kicking at the people who are there, but in the end they tear me away from me and take him away and still there's just the screaming going on and on...'

'Who's screaming, Sam?'

She had her hands over her face.

'Sam?'

She opened her eyes and sighed. 'I am.'

Reg sat back in his chair. 'How are you feeling?'

Sam shrugged.

'The barbed wire?'

Still there.

'The pressure cooker?'

Hissing.

'The pain in your chest?'

Intolerable.

'I'm all right, thanks.'

Reg was frowning. Sam could tell he didn't believe her. She closed her eyes, felt the tears slide down her cheeks, brushed them away.

'They're all still there, aren't they?'

'I'll be all right.'

'But right now you're not...'

Sam ran her fingers across her forehead. No, right now she was nowhere approaching all right.

'Do you know when this was?'

'My father came back from Oman and went on a bender. He came home, attacked my mother and threw Mark into a glass cabinet. It was the last time I saw him before he turned up nine months ago.'

'Have you recalled it before?'

She shook her head.

'A long time to hold that inside you.'

'Why now? Why do I remember it now?'

'It takes a lot to bring something like that to the surface. Something you've spent your whole life trying hard to forget. Everything you've been going through recently is pretty traumatic by any standards. You were trying to protect Mark then. You're doing the same now.'

The silence grew between them. The birds were beginning to sing outside. Reg got up and walked over to the curtains and drew them back. The sky was lightening.

Sam rocked her head back as far as it would go and then forward. The pain was moving about in her head, at the moment it seemed to have jammed up in the nerve endings in her teeth.

'How about a walk?' Reg said.

'Now?'

'It looks like a beautiful morning. How often do you see the dawn come up?'

Recently, rather more often than she would have liked.

'All right,' she said reluctantly.

Reg sat back down and pushed his feet back into his shoes.

Outside the house Reg turned to her. 'I'm in your hands.'

'That way.' Sam pointed behind him towards the Banbury Road.

They walked in silence through the quiet streets of North Oxford, cutting across Banbury Road and then Woodstock Road until they reached Kingston Street. The cool dawn air was soothing and so was the walking. There were very few people about, only a milk float was moving on the streets. At this time in the morning only the birds were noisy. From Kingston Street they made their way to Aristotle Bridge, pausing to look down at the boats moored alongside the canal, sealed silent pods, like chrysalises just before they split their skins and turn into butterflies. They crossed the railway line and then there was Port Meadow, a large slab of pastureland, spread out before them with the sun rising through the early-morning mist.

'This used to flood and freeze when I was a child. We used to go ice-skating.'

They walked out into the meadow, towards where the cattle and ponies were grazing. Sam had always loved Port Meadow. How many places were there these days that had been left untouched for a thousand years? It felt ancient and eerie. But after a couple of minutes she asked Reg if he'd mind going back.

'I feel like a hare that's about to be swooped on by a hawk,' she said.

He nodded and they walked back to the gate that led to the footpath that ran along the side of the canal. They leaned against it looking out at the meadow. The teeth of the barbed wire seemed to have dulled a bit and the cool morning air had taken the edge off the pressure cooker but the pain in her chest was as acute.

'How are you doing?' Reg asked.

She shrugged. 'King Charles escaped at night across here with five thousand, five hundred men during the Civil War.'

He smiled slightly. 'I think you're answering a different question to the one I asked.'

'Do you think it makes any difference?'

'What?'

'Therapy. In the end, do you think it makes a blind bit of difference?'

'I can't answer that for you. I know it made a big difference to me. I believe it makes a difference to other people or I wouldn't do it. Otherwise I'd be taking money under false pretences.'

'There are lots of people who are willing to do that.'

'Perhaps, but I don't think I'm one of them.'

Sam did a rough calculation of how much money she must owe him. If he'd been there since six the previous evening and it was approaching six in the morning now, that made twelve hours. He charged fifty pounds for a session of fifty minutes. Christ!

'How much do I owe you?'

'You got this one for free.'

'Why?'

'By way of apology.'

Sam frowned. 'Don't be stupid, Reg, you apologised on the phone. That was the end of it. This has taken up a huge amount of your time. You must have had to cancel other sessions.'

'I don't want your money, Sam. What I do want is for you to consider coming back into therapy.'

'God, you're like a Jesuit.'

'I've been accused of many things but never that.'

'I just don't know, Reg.'

'At least consider it. What we did today – that's just fire fighting.'

Sam thrust her hands into the pocket of her coat and pulled out the rosemary she'd picked in Bishop's Park. She held it to her nose. 'What if I say no, do I have to pay then?'

He smiled. 'Buy me breakfast and we're quits.'

'Deal.'

She took Reg to a café in the covered market. It was mainly filled with the men who'd been off-loading goods for the fish, meat and vegetable stalls, men who wanted to be able to smoke over big fried greasy breakfasts and read the sports pages in silence. Reg ordered sausages, eggs, beans and toast and attacked it with gusto. Sam couldn't stomach any food and settled for a cup of tea.

'I suppose that's why I've never been able to stand men crying,' she said.

Reg wiped his mouth with a paper napkin and looked at her.

'Someone once said to me I was happier walking towards a man wielding a knife than one who was crying, and they were absolutely right.'

'What do you feel about a crying man?'

'Panic. Fear.'

'Because . . .'

'I have to save them but I know that I can't. So I have to get away or I'll be destroyed. I'll fail. They'll die.'

'And . . . ?'

'They'll be taken away from me. I'll be abandoned, deserted, left all alone.'

'So a crying man means abandonment?'

'Yes.'

Reg smiled. 'You know, I spend half my working life telling men it's OK to cry and that if they do, they won't be ridiculed or . . . ' He paused.

'Abandoned?'

'Well, yes.' He stabbed a piece of sausage and dipped it in the yolk of his egg. 'Not every man who cries is going to be taken away from you.'

'No. But it's such a powerful thing, you know, I'm halfway out of the room before I can even engage rational thought. My whole being goes into automatic – get out, get out.'

'You could try staying next time.'

'It's a blind panic thing, Reg.'

Reg put down his knife and fork. 'You have a choice.'

'It doesn't feel like I have.'

'You've obviously never been to a rugby international with a Welshman.'

'But I thought they'd started winning recently. There's that bloke who shaves his legs and wears silver boots.'

He laughed. 'My father was Welsh, worked down the mines all his life until that was all brought to an end. My mother died about the same time. He'd always loved rugby. We had a cousin who played for Swansea and he used to get us tickets for the international matches at Cardiff. Well, Dad just stopped going, completely refused, used to send us off but said he wanted to watch it at home and he was in good health and we couldn't work it out. But then one time my car broke down on the way to the game. We'd left a lot of time because we were going to go to the pub so we managed to get back to Dad's place for the start of the match. As I came through the front door I heard the national anthems being played, but when I walked into the sitting room he was sitting there sobbing. Not just crying but really sobbing.'

'What did you do?'

'Well, I didn't know what to do. I just froze, staring at him. Thank God for my uncles. They got us all out of there and saw to my dad. He was this very tough man and I hadn't seen him cry when he lost his job or when my mother died but he knew he couldn't stand in a crowd with thousands of Welshmen singing "Land of My Fathers" and not lose it completely, so he preferred to stay at home and watch it by himself.'

'Poor man.'

'Afterwards, I thought, Why didn't I just go over to him and put my arms round him? But at the time I couldn't. I was just completely frozen, horrified, really.'

'What *did* you do?'

'What I usually did, at that time. Went out and got blind drunk with my mates.'

'Did you ever talk to him about it?'

He shook his head. 'My life was very different then. I had no idea how to talk to him about things like that.'

For a couple of minutes they lapsed into silence. Sam was the one who broke it.

'I think I'm falling in love.'

'With all that's going on I'm surprised you've had the time.'

'He's sort of involved.'

'Oh.'

'The thing is he feels familiar. I feel like I've known him all my life.'

Reg pushed away his plate. 'Has he had a traumatic upbringing?'

Sam frowned. 'Why do you say that?'

'Traumatised people – survivors – they often recognise each other. They recognise the trauma.'

'Like attracts like, you mean.'

'Sort of.'

'So what are you saying?'

'Nothing, I'm just saying that can happen. I presume he hasn't cried yet.'

Sam smiled. 'No.'

'And what are you going to do if he does?'

Sam sighed. 'Run for my life?'

He laughed. 'Well, good luck.'

Sam reached into her pocket to pull out her wallet. A piece of paper fluttered onto the floor and she picked it up. It was the list of names Rick had given her. Shit, she'd not even given them to Phil yet. Everything crashed in on her at once: the body in Bullingdon Road, what had happened to her father, and the forthcoming phone call. She had to get on; she had to speak to Phil. She walked over to the counter to pay. One cooked breakfast and two cups of tea came to £5.27. Back at their table she told Reg.

He stood up, brushing some toast crumbs from the front of his shirt. 'It's the cheapest therapy I reckon you'll ever get,' he said, reaching for his coat.

CHAPTER EIGHTEEN

Mark swore as the vehicle he was being transported in stopped suddenly and he fell against something sharp. The pain that had started off localised in his hand now seared up his arm, tearing into everything in its path – flesh, tendons and bones.

He swallowed, trying to get some saliva into his parched mouth. In the earlier part of his captivity, he had been given some water and food but for a long time there'd been nothing, and now he could think of nothing but water. Awake or asleep it dominated his thoughts, he dreamed of oceans, of lakes and rivers and waterfalls. Now he knew why people would drink their own urine, would do anything to stop the ravening, overwhelming thirst. More than the fear of death, more than the pain in his arm, his thirst consumed him.

Time had ceased to function normally. Blindfolded, unable to see if it was day or night, he existed in a suspended state. He slept and woke, drifting in and out with no concept of how long he had been unconscious. His dreams and nightmares had the vividness of reality because they were all he could see. I could go mad, he thought, and no one would care, no one would even know. In the beginning he'd tried to keep some kind of track of time from the temperature, the muffled noise of the television and the sound of birds, but since he'd been moved he'd let all that go. He could have been held a week or a month. It didn't matter because either way it felt like an eternity, it felt like it would never end.

He'd been moved soon after his finger was cut off. It was the first time he registered there'd been two of them. He'd felt his feet being untied and hands under his arms hoisting him to his feet.

'Up,' the voice hissed. 'Get up.'

But he couldn't, his legs wouldn't support him. It was as if they had no bones in them and he'd not been able to feel his feet and collapsed. It had taken a few attempts before he could support his own weight and eventually he'd been able to stagger with a person supporting him on either side, guiding him downstairs and then out into fresh air. God, the relief to be away from that smell, from the sickly sweet odour of decomposition, the relief to know that the smell wasn't coming from him, that he wasn't rotting to his death.

At first he hadn't known where he was but then an engine had started up and he'd realised he was in some kind of vehicle. And still they had barely spoken to him. His time was coming to an end. He was being driven to his grave. The questions that had consumed him at the beginning – Who? and Why? – seemed somehow irrelevant. He needed to conserve all his resources for just staying alive.

A lake in the Swiss Alps appeared in his mind's eye. He was as large as the mountains with a vast open cavern of a mouth; he opened his mouth and the lake tilted and cascaded down his throat. He drank down the delicious sweet water, he drank and he drank until he was satisfied.

The vehicle lurched again and he hit his head. The weird thing was that the inside of this van smelled of books, a smell he loved. It evoked memories of being taken to the library as a child. The cover of *Sam Pig* by Alison Uttley swam suddenly into his head, vivid in every detail followed by *Swallows and Amazons* by Arthur Ransome. He wondered if he had conjured the smell of a library to comfort himself, he wondered if the last thing he would smell before he died would be books.

In the St Aldate's police station, Sam sat waiting for Phil to come and get her. A few minutes earlier she'd said goodbye to Reg in Market Street, standing with her hands in her pockets like some awkward adolescent, battling more bloody tears.

Reg had touched her lightly on the arm. 'Phone me, Sam. When it's over. During. Whenever you want. You've got my number.'

'Will you tell my parents and Alan that I'm going to the police station?'

He nodded.

'Thanks,' she said. 'Thanks for coming.'

She'd just about managed to hold it together, but now here was Phil coming towards her, solid, reliable Phil.

He looked down at her anxiously. 'Are you sure you should be here, Sam?'

'Yeah, I'm...' She was going to say fine but somehow the lie defeated her.

'Come on,' he said.

He led the way to an office and closed the door, turned towards Sam and hugged her. She allowed herself to be held for about thirty seconds and then gently pushed him away. It was all she could bear.

She rubbed at a sodden patch on his shirt. 'I'll ruin your shirt.'

'Well, that would be a right tragedy.'

'I'm sorry about the other night.'

'Forget it.'

'The finger was his, wasn't it?'

He nodded. 'There was enough of a print left on it to compare it to the ones we took before he went missing.'

'I knew it was his, as soon as I saw it – there was the lump where he'd had the extra little finger removed.'

'There was something else in the Jiffy bag it was sent in.'

Sam folded her arms.

'A note with the phrase *Skin and blister* – does that mean anything to you?'

Sam closed her eyes as the memory came crashing in.

'Sam?'

She looked up. 'It's what my gran used to say to Mark about me. Where's your skin and blister? Baby sister.'

'Right.'

'He's saying the finger's for me. I've heard nothing from Paula about my father and what's happening in Iraq and I'm going to have to talk to this man again this evening. What am I going to say?'

Phil didn't reply.

'What did you find out from the hospital about Brendan?'

'He's not been into work for a fortnight. The first week he was due to take off as holiday anyway but then he didn't come back and no one's heard from him.'

'What contact details do they have for him?'

'The Bullingdon Road address. They're not that sad to see the back of him though. Turns out they thought he was stealing drugs. They didn't have any evidence, but each time they moved him the thefts started up on his floor. They were on the verge of pulling him in when he disappeared.'

'What was he stealing?'

'Anything he could get his hands on – painkillers, diamorphine, coproxamol, valium, beta blockers, anti-depressants, seroxat, prozac. You name it . . .'

'So he disappeared at the same time as Mark?'

'Yes.'

'It's too much of a coincidence, isn't it, Phil? Brendan has to be involved, doesn't he?'

'I don't know. Suppose he just happened to be with Mark when he was snatched. He could have been caught up in it, killed and dumped somewhere. Or there could have been another reason for him making himself scarce. If he knew the hospital suspected him of stealing he may have thought it was time to move on. He had to move out of Bullingdon Road, didn't he? Maybe he's got a new job and moved to a different town.'

'Or he's the one who's taken Mark. Mark said he was puzzled by his interest in him, didn't he? Maybe he was trying to find out about my father and when Mark didn't come across he pursued more extreme ends to get what he wanted. He knew I was a PI and he knew Mark and I were very close, so he used that to try and get hold of my father. The kidnapper said that's why he'd taken Mark, not me, because he knew I'd be better at tracking down Dad.'

'But we still don't have the connection between Brendan and your father. We've sent his name off to the PSNI and we'll see what they come back with about him.'

Sam put her hand in her pocket and took out the list of names Rick had given her. 'These might be worth asking them about as well.'

Phil glanced at them. 'Who are they?'

'People who might have a reason to feel angry towards my father.'

'Who gave this to you?'

'Someone who thinks my father killed his.' As the words came out of her mouth she knew it was a mistake to have told him.

'What do you mean?'

'He's not involved with Mark. He came to me completely separately from all this.'

'Well, isn't that just a bit of an enormous coincidence? You don't think they could be approaching you from both sides. Mark gets Brendan, you get this bloke.'

'Look, I know he's not involved.'

'How did he come by these names then?'

'He was brought up on the Ballymurphy Estate in west Belfast. He's a Catholic. I asked him if he'd put his ear to the ground for me. That's all.'

'And these are the names he came up with?'

'Yes.'

'So he still has contacts there?'

'It's not him, Phil.'

'Give me his name then.'

Sam shook her head, thinking about what Rick had said about betrayal. 'I won't. He was doing me a favour. I'm not going to hand him over to the police when he hasn't done anything.'

'When did you first meet him?'

'I don't know, about nine days ago.'

'Nine days?'

'Yes, about that.'

'At exactly the same time that Mark goes missing this man just happens to turn up.'

'He'd seen the article in the paper about Dad, Phil – he was responding to that.'

'What did he want from you?'

'I told you. He's convinced Dad killed his father. His father went missing at that same time mentioned in the paper. He wants to know where his father's body is.'

'Jesus, Sam, what on earth made you think that this wasn't something you should tell us? He's got an obvious motive.'

'Whoever's holding Mark is out for revenge. It's about payback. This man is not like that. His whole life is about something the polar opposite to that. He works for reconciliation, creating trust, healing wounds. I mean, he does anti-bullying workshops in schools, for God's sake. He's not the kind of man who would cut off someone's finger.'

'You seem to know an awful lot about him.'

'I'm telling you he has nothing to do with this.'

'Give me his name then and we can check that out.'

'I'm not giving you his name.'

'He might not be the sort of person who cuts off someone's finger but suppose he's working with someone who is?'

The door opened and a gaunt man in a blue suit came in. He glanced back and forth at the two of them.

'Who's this, Howard?'

'Sam Falconer, boss.'

'DI Hopkins,' the man said, holding out his hand.

Sam took it.

He gestured outside to Phil. 'Can I have a word?'

The two men left and closed the door behind them.

Sam suddenly felt exhausted. She slumped down in a chair. Was Phil right? Was she being a fool about Rick? She thought about what Reg had said, that her sense of familiarity had come from recognising someone as traumatised as she was. She knew she couldn't see him clearly. She closed her eyes and tried to think it through dispassion-ately. She tried to look at the facts of the matter entirely separately from the fact that she wanted to rip Rick's shirt off. She failed miserably. All she could think of was him unbuttoning the cuffs of his shirt and rolling up his sleeves, of the swirls made by the hairs on his arms and those long flat fingers, twisting his wine glass round and round.

Her phone rang and she answered it.

'Sam, it's Paula. We've just heard they're OK. They were caught up in the explosion. They're being held by the Americans in a military camp outside Fallujah.'

'Have you spoken to them?'

'No, we've only just heard they're alive. We've got people there working to get them released.'

Sam felt an overwhelming sense of relief followed swiftly by panic. The next call was that evening.

'How long is that going to take?'

'I'm sorry but I've no idea. The Americans are extremely pissed off. The explosion killed four of their men. No one's managed to gain access to Max or your father yet. All we know is that they're alive and the Americans are checking that they are who they say they are.'

At six that evening she'd be on the end of the phone and she'd have to say, No, he's not here. No, I haven't got him. Please don't hurt my brother. And then the screaming would begin in earnest.

'Sam, are you still there?'

'It'll be too late, Paula. I need him here by six this evening.'

With her left finger and thumb, Sam felt around the base of the little finger of her right hand, feeling the bone, feeling the place the knife might cut through it.

'We'll do everything we can to get him back in the country as quickly as possible, but I have to be honest with you. You won't have him back by then. A couple of days maybe.'

'I need to talk to him as soon as possible.'

'I promise you, Sam, we'll do everything we can.'

'Thanks, Paula.'

Sam was closing up her phone as Phil and DI Hopkins came back into the room and she told them what Paula had said. Hopkins sat down and gestured for Sam to do the same. Phil remained standing.

'Phil's told me about this.' He placed the list of names on the table. 'We need to know who gave these names to you.'

'I've already gone through this with Phil. He gave the list to me as a favour, in good faith, not so that he could be hauled in by the police and interrogated. I won't tell you who he is and that's all there is to it.'

'You realise that you could be putting your brother's life at risk.'

'Don't you think that if I thought that for one minute I'd give you the name just like that? I'm telling you he has nothing to do with what's happened to Mark.'

'The very fact that he's given you these names connects him. It means we must talk to him.'

'Look, hauling him in is not going to get us any closer to finding Mark. Checking out those names might.'

Hopkins sighed. The silence in the room was interrupted by a car backfiring in St Aldate's.

Sam stood up and leaned against the wall next to Phil. 'Have you been able to identify the body in the house yet?'

'Dougie Malone. He was a local homeless man, used to hang out outside St Michael's.'

'Was he squatting?'

'We don't know – maybe he broke in there for the night.'

'How did he die?'

'Someone cut his throat. Apart from the blood produced by that we have also come across a lot of blood in another room in the house, which we are having tested. There wasn't just blood but also some other human material.'

Sam was trying to take on board what he was telling her. 'You mean Mark might have been held there? His finger might have been cut off there?'

He nodded. 'We're testing it to see if it's his.'

'What do you think happened?'

'Perhaps poor old Dougie blundered in there thinking the house was empty and saw something he shouldn't have.'

'Surely he wouldn't have been killed just because of that?'

Sam saw Phil and Hopkins exchange a look. 'The man who cut off Mark's finger isn't squeamish about violence or killing,' Phil said.

'But just to casually kill him . . .'

'Maybe he saw Mark, and whoever killed him didn't trust him not to blab to his mates. Given the kind of relationship Dougie had with Special Brew it wouldn't take much time in his company to realise that he couldn't be relied upon to keep his mouth shut. Maybe Dougie fancied a bit of blackmail and didn't realise the kind of person he was dealing with.'

Oh God, Sam thought, and this is the person who's got hold of Mark. A person who'd killed someone just for being in the wrong place at the wrong time.

'What about tracing the people who lived in the house?'

'We've just brought the first one in for questioning – Helen Sawyer.'

'Would you let me watch the interview?'

Phil glanced at Hopkins, who sighed but nodded.

Sam leaned her forehead against the glass that allowed her to look into the room where the questioning was going to take place but not be observed. The young woman sitting at the table had frizzy auburn hair that fell to her shoulders and a pale face. She was wearing a tie-dye T-shirt, black jeans and red ox-blood Doc Martens boots. Her long legs were thrown out in front of her and crossed at the ankle and a jean jacket hung on the back of the chair she was sitting on. A bag spilling papers and books rested on the floor next to her. She was examining her hair for split ends.

A uniformed policeman came into the room carrying a cup, which he placed in front of her.

She stood up. 'Do you know how long they're going to be? I've got exams in two weeks, I don't have time to waste . . .'

'They'll get to you as soon as they can.'

She peered into the cup but did not appear to like what she saw and began walking up and down the room. The policeman sat down and watched her.

A few minutes later Phil entered the room, sat down, turned on the tape recorder and got the interview under way.

'How long did you live at 23 Bullingdon Road?'

'I'd been there about two years. The house was short-term housing, it had been for about eleven years. The rent was very cheap because of that but the downside was that they could chuck us out on a month's notice and that's what happened.'

'What are the names of the other people who were living in the house when you had to move out?'

She folded her arms. 'Why do you want those? I don't understand. Is this something to do with them signing on?'

'No. Who else lived in the house while you were there?'

'I'm not going to give you a list of any names until I know what this is all about.'

Phil placed his clasped hands on the table. 'A body's been found there.'

The woman's mouth gaped. 'A body?'

'Yes, and so we need to trace all the people who were living there.'

'Right.'

A list of names swiftly followed. The uniformed officer left the room with it and returned a couple of minutes later.

'Those people were all in the house at the time you had to move?'

She nodded, stared into her cup and this time decided to take a sip.

Phil pushed the photofit of Brendan across the table towards her. 'Do you recognise him?'

'Yes, that's Brendan McNally.'

'Why didn't you mention him?'

'He wasn't strictly a tenant, he sort of muscled in under false pretences.'

'What do you mean?'

'The room belonged to Robbie but he worked on six-month contracts in Brussels and then came back to the UK. He wanted a cheap base for his stuff so he kept a room but when he went away he sub-let it. In the past he'd sub-let to someone we all knew, Jay, but this last time Brendan turned up and there was no explanation. He was just there and then we realised he was the new tenant. It's not supposed to work like that; we're all supposed to meet and OK whoever comes into the house but in Brendan's case we were presented with a fait accompli.'

'Did anyone try to contact Robbie?'

'What was he going to do about it?'

'And no one said anything?'

'Brendan wasn't the sort of man it was particularly easy to challenge.'

'What do you mean?'

She sighed. 'He was a bit of a charmer really. Also, in fairness to him, he kept himself pretty much to himself. There wasn't much of a community spirit in the house. People came and went fairly independently of each other. He wasn't any trouble.'

'So you didn't see much of him?'

'Bumped into him every now and again in the kitchen.'

'Which room was his?'

'The one by the front door.'

'What did he do?'

'I was never really sure but he came and went at strange hours – very early. I think he worked at a hospital, I wasn't sure . . .'

'So no one said anything to him?'

'Well, it took a while for us all to realise what had happened. By then it seemed too late to do anything about it. He'd been living in the house for a month and we'd sort of got used to him.'

'Was Brendan living in the house when you were all evicted?'

'Yes.'

'Do you know where he went?'

She shook her head. 'His name wasn't on the housing association's books, it was Robbie's, so they had no responsibility to rehouse him. Mind you, they didn't make much effort with the rest of us either.'

'You've no idea where he might have gone?'

'No. Maybe the others in the house will have some idea, but I don't know. He was the last one to leave though. I suppose because he didn't have anywhere else to go.'

Phil showed her a photo of Mark. 'Do you know this man?'

She frowned. 'I've seen his face in the paper, haven't I?'

'Yes, you could have done, but other than that was he someone you saw in Brendan's company?'

She frowned. 'He didn't bring many people back to the house. None of us did, for obvious reasons.'

'Is there anything else you could tell us about him?'

She began to shake her head, then stopped, and started inspecting her hair for split ends again. She sighed and looked back up at Phil. 'There is one thing. You know that student who died recently?'

'Adrian Hunter?'

She nodded. 'Well, Brendan knew him. He was one of the few people he ever brought back to the house. He stayed for a couple of weeks over Easter.'

'What was the connection?'

She shrugged, looking wary.

'Was it drugs? Was Brendan supplying him?'

'I don't know anything about that.'

'Was he supplying them to the rest of you?'

She didn't answer.

'Was he a friend of Brendan's or a lover?'

'I don't know. I suppose I presumed he was his lover. To be honest, I assumed Brendan was setting himself up with somewhere else to stay. The way he'd come into our house was pretty shifty. I thought he was looking for someone to move in with. But then when I realised Adrian was living in college I thought I must be mistaken.'

'Why didn't you come forward with this information before?'

'Look, I'm not a bloody snitch. I may not have particularly liked Brendan but I wasn't going to go out of my way to land him in trouble. I didn't think anything of it. Anyway, I've got finals in two weeks. I didn't have time to waste. I haven't got time to waste now.'

'Some of his pills helping you with a bit of late-night revision, were they? God forbid anything else should get in the way of your exams,' Phil snapped.

She blushed and then returned to her split ends and shortly afterwards Phil brought the interview to a close.

Sam was standing against the wall of the interview room, which had now been emptied of everyone other than Phil. She thought of what Charlie Stroud had said about the man he'd seen Adrian with. But if Brendan and Adrian had been lovers what was Brendan doing hanging round her brother? It was a risky thing for him to do if he was supplying drugs to students. Mark was hardly going to approve of that.

'When you first came to Mark's rooms,' Sam said, 'to tell him Adrian was dead, Brendan was there but he didn't turn a hair, did he? He gave absolutely no indication that he knew him at all.'

'He obviously didn't want us knowing he had any link to him. Especially if the link between them was drugs and especially if Adrian had died as a consequence of drugs he was supplying to him.'

'Do you have a definite cause of death now?'

Phil shook his head. 'He died from breathing in his own vomit. As I told you, the blood tests came back stuffed with all sorts – seroxat, valium and very high levels of alcohol. Then there was also the evidence of a fight having taken place just before he died. He'd hit his head but there's not enough evidence to suggest that he was suffering from concussion. It hadn't fractured his skull or created any bleeding or bruising of the brain. In other words, they can't say for definite that the fight caused him to be sick. It seems more likely that it may have contributed to him OD-ing on the coproxamol. Mixing that with all the other things in his system and the whisky. He may have known he was in trouble and been trying to get to the door for help when he passed out and threw up. The body was found lying against the door. We don't have enough evidence to point to suicide or murder at the moment.

'One thing we haven't been able to find out is who he had the fight with. If we get that bit we'll have a clearer picture of what happened the evening before he died. Is there anything else you can add?'

Sam shook her head. 'Not at the moment, I'm afraid. But the thing is, Phil, now we know that Brendan had a perfectly good reason for wanting to disappear. The hospital were on to him and if he was supplying Adrian he may have thought that sooner or later the police would come calling. He's got a good reason to disappear that is entirely separate from anything to do with Mark.'

'That's true, but Dougie Malone was found murdered in Bullingdon Road and Brendan's the connection to the house, unless, that is, another of the tenants was involved in some way.'

'How long will it take you to track them all down?'

He shrugged. 'We're doing it now.'

'Have you got any of those photofits of Brendan around the place?'

'Sure.'

'Can I have one? There's someone I want to show it to.'

Sam made a phone call and caught up with Charlie Stroud outside St Mary's in Radcliffe Square. She showed him the photofit.

'Is that the man you saw Adrian with?'

Charlie nodded. He was even greyer and pastier than before.

'Are you all right?' Sam asked.

'Tired,' he said. 'Tutorials are piling up and the play is taking a lot of my time.'

'How's it going?'

'Petheridge says it's going to be a triumph.' He paused. 'There's something . . .'

He seemed about to say something else but stopped and then started again.

'How did Adrian die?'

'There's going to be an inquest. At the moment the police are still trying to piece it all together.'

'Was this man involved?'

'Maybe.'

He turned away from her.

'Charlie . . .'

He turned round.

'If there's anything else you could tell me . . .'

He shook his head and kept walking.

Alan and Sam drove back to London in the early afternoon. Alan's flat was on the twenty-sixth floor of a high rise in Hammersmith. Sam leaned over the edge of his balcony, looking down at the traffic jamming the flyover. Twenty minutes ago they'd been down there sitting in it. Alan had asked her if she wanted to come in and she'd accepted gratefully. Anything to distract her from the fact that in a couple of hours she would be sitting in her flat waiting for a call from a man who had tortured her brother and without her father to offer him. She looked at her watch for the fifth time in the last twenty minutes and tried not to think about what would happen then. Alan had offered her beer, wine or tea, and she'd chosen tea. After her drunken episode the other night she'd decided she should try and steer away from alcohol for the foreseeable future. Drizzle drove her back inside.

Minimalism, order, cleanliness – all these things characterised Alan's flat. It was restful, Sam thought, but not something she could ever manage herself. Semi-circular silver light surrounds, attached flush to the wall, reflected light upwards against the white walls. A black-and-white framed photo of a man with prominent cheekbones smiling into the camera stood on the mantelpiece. In front of it was a row of tealights.

Is that what I'll be doing soon? Sam thought, as she slumped down on a black leather sofa. Will Mark be framed and remembered each night with a lit candle?

Alan walked out of the kitchen carrying two cups. He placed them on coasters on a glass-topped table in front of the sofa and sat down beside her.

Sam reached for the cup. 'Does it always rain this much in May?'

Alan shrugged. 'Flaming June's going to have to be a bloody inferno to make up for it.'

On the drive back to London, Sam had filled Alan in on what had happened in the police station and on the link between Adrian Hunter and Brendan. The trouble was that increasingly she feared that in pursuing Brendan they were going down a blind alley. OK, it was true that Brendan was linked to Adrian, Dougie and Mark – and two of them were dead, the other injured. But she was not convinced he had taken Mark. And if it wasn't him, then who was she left with? Rick? The people on the list he'd given her? It was now ten days since Mark had gone missing and four days since the last call. Four days since his finger had been cut off. Sam doubted he'd seen a doctor in that time. She couldn't begin to imagine what kind of state he'd be in, if, that is, he was still alive.

She replaced her cup on the coaster. 'Thanks for getting hold of Reg.'

'All those times when you refused to talk to him and I spoke to him came in handy. Did he help?'

'Yes, and all for the price of breakfast and a cup of tea.'

'He seems a good sort of bloke – very down-to-earth.'

She nodded and stretched out her legs under the glass-topped table. 'Do you think I should tell the police about Rick?'

'You still got the hots for him?'

'Oh yes.'

'Do you think in not telling them you're putting Mark at risk?'

'If I thought that for an instant, I'd do it without a qualm but I really don't think so.'

'He is an actor, isn't he?'

'So what?'

'Actors act and not always just on a stage.'

'I know . . .'

'If they're good actors you can't tell if they're doing it or not.'

'I'm not sure he's that good and why would he be involved in the sort of work he is, if he was also into kidnapping and torture. It doesn't make any sense.'

'I agree, it doesn't, but sometimes people don't make any sense. We're all different shades of light and dark. I know when I was in the force I didn't want to know what my brothers were up to. I didn't ask. They didn't tell me. Didn't mean I didn't occasionally hear things from their wives and girlfriends. But it didn't mean I was going to go off and tell anyone about it. They're my brothers, aren't they? That's the tribal bit for me. You don't ask and you don't go looking. Maybe it's the same for Rick.'

'But he came up with that list of names and he knew I was going to give it to the police.'

'Maybe he's got a score to settle with those people. He gives the appearance of helping you and he gets you on his side and then you're willing to help him out.'

Sam stood up and stretched. 'I should be going.'

'Do you want me to come back with you?'

'No, it's all right.'

'Are you sure?'

She nodded.

'You're not going to do anything stupid again, are you?' He gently took hold of her bandaged hand.

Sam shook her head. As she flexed the hand she felt the cuts sting in protest. At the door Alan hugged her. 'Good luck.'

Sam pressed for the lift but then couldn't be bothered to wait. She ran down the stairs, running faster and faster, trying not to think of the forthcoming call, of what would happen when she said she didn't have her father there and trying above all else not to think about Mark, maimed and trapped and almost certainly dying.

CHAPTER NINETEEN

Sam sat staring at the surface of the table. They were all here again in her front room – Phil, Fiona, the techno guy. Here we go again. Waiting for the call. Sam had heard nothing more from Paula about her father. She was on her own.

She looked at her watch – five minutes to go.

Sam clasped her hands together and rubbed the red swelling on the side of her thumb. She felt eerily calm. There was nothing she could do. Let it come, she thought. I just need to know if he's alive or dead. It's being in limbo I can't endure. She was aware of the muttered conversations taking place behind her, of the rush-hour traffic stop-starting on the New King's Road.

She glanced down at some notes that Fiona had placed in front of her. *Reduce anxiety by avoiding the perception of superiority*. Well, he was holding her brother hostage; he'd tortured him and made her listen. She was hardly going to give the appearance of superiority. *Use positive language adapted to the hostage taker's. Maintain rapport with the hostage taker by reducing emotionality and increasing rationality*. Sam kept reading the last line over and over again. *Reduce emotionality*. And how was one supposed to do that exactly? Cut out one's heart? She sighed and shook her head. She needed to be detached and rational but it was the very thing she couldn't be. The voices behind her were louder now; she dragged her attention away from the piece of paper and back to the people in the room.

She looked at Fiona. 'What is it?'

Fiona tapped her watch. Sam looked at her own – six fifteen. Quarter of an hour *after* the call was due to take place.

'What does it mean if he doesn't call?'

'It could be any number of things. He could have been disturbed. He might be on the move...'

'He could have decided to kill him and dump him.'

'I don't think so. He's gone to a great deal of trouble to kidnap Mark for a purpose. The only thing he's said he wants is your father. He hasn't got that yet. He hasn't even managed to talk to him. This thing isn't over for him until he speaks to him. Why send the finger if not to soften you up for something?'

'That's a comforting thought.'

'I'm sorry, Sam.'

'So, what do we do, now?'

'We wait.'

Sam stood up abruptly. 'I'm going to make some tea and coffee. Who wants what?'

In the kitchen she was filling the kettle when Phil came in.

'If you don't do something about that sink soon it'll fall off the wall of its own accord.'

Sam quietened the screaming tap and put on the kettle. 'You know what I'm like. When things break it never occurs to me that I can get them mended.'

Phil had leaned against the cupboard and folded his arms. 'I suppose that included us.'

Sam leaned against the work surface and mirrored Phil's body language. 'I'm really sorry about the other day. I wasn't thinking straight.'

Phil nodded slightly but didn't say anything.

The kettle had boiled and he turned round and handed her some cups from the cupboard behind his head. He watched as she threw teabags in a pot and coffee grounds in a cafetière.

'Instant will do,' he commented.

'I know, but I haven't got any. Could you pass me the sugar?'

Phil opened a cupboard and grabbed a glass jar with a cork in the top. 'Jesus, Sam, you've got enough coffee in here to keep you going for about ten years.'

Sam shrugged. 'The coffee I like the best is Lavazza but every time I buy it I feel guilty because at the moment they don't produce any that's fair trade so I buy a packet of fair trade at the same time, but then when I run out of the Lavazza I can't bring myself to drink the fair trade because I don't like it as much, so I go back and buy myself another packet of Lavazza and another packet of fair trade.'

Phil laughed. 'Sometimes I forget how complicated you can be.'

'But life is complicated,' Sam said, pushing past him with a cup in each hand.

When she came back into the kitchen, Phil was sitting on a stool, cup in hand. 'I need to talk to you about something.'

Sam stretched across him to grab the remaining cup and assumed the position he had just relinquished against the cupboard.

'The blood we found in Bullingdon Road was Mark's.'

'And the blood on Adrian Hunter's clothes?'

'No, but...'

'What is it?'

'In Bullingdon Road there was a hell of a lot of it. One of the SOCOs said if he'd lost that much blood...'

'I didn't think cutting off a finger wasn't serious, Phil.'

'No, I know, I just think you have to prepare yourself, that's all.'

'How can I? You say that and I don't even know what the words mean.'

At that moment Sam heard her landline begin to ring. Her cup slid from her hands onto the floor, the coffee spilling down the front of her trousers. She swore and, shaking the coffee from her hands, ran out of the kitchen and back into the front room. She sat down at the table and stared at the ringing phone and then at Fiona.

Fiona moved the headphones from around her neck to her ears and nodded.

Sam's heart was hammering as picked up the phone.

'Sam -- what the hell's going on? Paula told me something's happened to Mark.'

'Dad?' The line was dreadful, the background noise a loud roar. 'Where are you? I can barely hear you.'

'The Americans have let us go. We'll be back in the country tomorrow morning...' The line began to break up.

'I can't hear you...'

'Tomorrow morning, Sam, we'll be back then ... I'll phone when we've landed—'

The line went dead.

Sam put down the phone.

'Your father?' Fiona said.

Sam nodded. A flicker of hope sparked in her. She looked at her watch again. It was an hour over the time arranged for the call. 'He's not going to call, is he?'

'It doesn't look like it. You realise we'll need to talk to your father?'

Sam rubbed the end of her nose. 'I wouldn't say he's a big fan of the authorities. He suspects them of leaking the story of him being involved in all those deaths in Northern Ireland to the *Daily Tribune*.'

'I understand that, but if we're to bring this situation to some sort of safe resolution it would be a good idea if you could persuade him to talk to us.'

'I'll do my best,' Sam said but thought that the likelihood of her father talking to the police was less than zero. Neither Max nor her father could be described as team players. She had been so focused on the need to get hold of her father she had not considered what would happen next. She had to have him because that's what the hostage taker wanted. For the first time the thought crossed her mind that her father could be a dangerous liability. For the first time she thought, What the hell's going to happen now? *Reduce emotionality*? That was hardly his modus operandi either.

She'd arranged to meet Rick McGann the following morning in her office.

To keep herself occupied while she waited for him she decided to look for the most recent letter from the Inland Revenue. It was a stupid decision, however, because she was not in the best frame of mind for paperwork. She'd got as far as spreading her papers out on the floor but her mind kept blanking what it was she was looking for. She was sitting on her haunches staring into space when there was a knock on the door and it swung open and she looked up to see Rick standing there.

This time he was wearing blue jeans, a white T-shirt and the same black jacket. He took off his sunglasses and tucked them into his top pocket.

'Looks impressively organised.'

'Don't mock the afflicted,' Sam said. 'I don't know why I even started this. If you give me a minute I'll clear it up and there'll be room for you to sit down.'

She didn't move to greet him physically, allowing the sea of papers to be the excuse, and began clearing the floor.

Rick stood in the doorway as she criss-crossed the various different piles of papers and slapped them down in a heap on her desk. Safely behind the desk she gestured for him to take a seat.

He sat down and dropped his rucksack on the floor next to his chair. 'Did you have any luck with those names I gave you?'

'I haven't heard. I gave them to the police. They were very keen to know who you were.'

He nodded. 'And did you tell them?'

'You'd done me a favour. I didn't think that was fair.'

He grunted. 'Don't worry about me and the police. I'm well used to it, you know. Spent half my twenties being pulled in by them. Being a young Irishman in London in the eighties wasn't a bed of roses, I can tell you. It's why my accent's so toned down. Kieran had an even worse time than me. He lost count of the number of times they questioned him.'

'I can imagine.'

He shook his head. 'No, I don't think you can. I know I wouldn't be able to if it hadn't happened to me.'

'Do you want some coffee?' Sam offered.

'No, I'm fine, thanks.'

She dug a folder out from under the piles of paper and handed it to him. 'This is all of it. My father's statement, the maps, the names of the people he remembers killing.'

'Right.'

His hands were shaking as he opened the file and began to read. Sam pretended to busy herself with stuff on her desk but every page she picked up to read could have been blank for all the information that transmitted from the paper to her brain. A few minutes went past and then he began to read out loud from the papers in front of him: *'My aim in making this information known is that the bodies of the dead may be recovered and given the dignity of a proper burial. The graves need to be excavated by experts but for that to happen the British government has to admit to what they were authorising in Northern Ireland.'*

He stopped reading and looked up at Sam. He looked even paler, if that were possible. For one terrible moment his face began to crumple and she thought he was going to cry. Reg's voice floated into her mind. *Try staying next time.* She closed her eyes. When she opened them again she was relieved to see that his face had returned to normal.

'Your father's looking to get this sorted out.'

'I just don't know. I don't know him well enough to judge. He was in the process of selling his story to the paper when it was leaked. So it was not an entirely unmercenary attitude that he had.'

'But he says here that money's not his motive.' He began quoting again: '*I want to set the record straight. I want the bodies properly buried.* He's looking for resolution.'

'It's possible that he is,' Sam conceded.

'You don't think so?'

'He disappeared when I was four. He did horrible things to my family and then I didn't see him again until last year. Given what I've discovered about him recently, it's difficult for me to believe he has entirely honourable motives.'

Rick nodded. 'Difficult to forgive him.'

Nothing made Sam feel more furious than people telling her that she should forgive her father. Obviously it showed because Rick hastily added, 'Not that I'm suggesting you should, you know. I mean, God, I know nothing about what happened to you, do I?'

Sam didn't say anything. She was waiting for the storm of rage that had been about to break on Rick's head to dissipate. Meanwhile, Rick had taken out the maps on which Geoffrey Falconer had marked the mass graves. He was looking at them intently.

'I wonder if your father would remember mine. Dad's name's not listed here but he says these are only the ones he can remember.'

'You've got pictures of him?'

He nodded.

'Was he involved with the IRA?'

'Ask a direct question, why don't you?'

'If he was it doesn't mean I think he deserved to be shot dead by an SAS assassination squad.'

'Look, Sam, some of my earliest memories are of the British army and the RUC breaking down our front door and turning the house over. They'd descend on the whole estate, searching for weapons. They'd turn us out of our beds and rip up carpets and floorboards. They'd wreck everything; hold us in a room until they'd done all the houses and only then let us go. I remember kicking a British soldier in the leg as hard as I could, throwing pint bottles filled with paint at the Saracens because they'd made my mother cry and were trashing our house. I wanted to grow up as soon as possible and help get rid of the soldiers and stop them doing what they did.'

'You've already told me that. And you haven't answered my question.'

'If you'd listen to me you'd realise I have. You can have no idea what it was like to be a Catholic living in west Belfast in the seventies.'

'No I haven't but—'

'I was seventeen years old when Bobby Sands died in 1981. I woke up in the early hours and everyone was out on the streets, banging dustbin lids and honking horns. Then they started tearing up paving stones and siphoning fuel out of the cars to make petrol bombs. They got hold of JCBs and buses and brought them onto the estate to make a barricade to keep the army out. Do you see what I'm saying here?'

Sam nodded. 'I see what you're saying and what you're not saying.'

'It takes a lot to shake yourself free of that kind of upbringing, Sam. Some people manage to and others don't, it defines them, it's who they become. I'm not a part of it any more but that's not to say it hasn't affected who I am.'

'I wasn't going to let the police know who you were.'

He nodded. Suddenly he looked exhausted as if all the anger and defensiveness had blown up in him and left him depleted and drained. 'Jesus,' he said. 'You know I think I've moved on and then all the feelings of rage and exasperation and just the plain unfairness of it all come crashing back. The trouble is you can feel so bloody justified.'

'I'm sorry I asked,' Sam said. 'It's none of my business.'

He shook his head. 'That's not true either, Sam. I came to you asking for help. You don't know if I'm OK or not. Your brother's missing. You're trying to suss out if I can be trusted. You're still not sure, are you?'

'All of that is true, but the fact of your father being a member of the IRA or not isn't really going to help with that because it's not him I'm dealing with, it's you.'

Rick stood up. 'You know this is the last bit of it for me – burying my father. If I can do that I feel I'll be able to get on with my life. Maybe do something completely different. Start all over again.' He laughed. 'How many more clichés could I get in there?'

'Clean sheet?' Sam suggested. 'Wipe the slate clean? New beginnings? Forward not back.'

Rick grinned. 'Yup, all of those.' He looked down at the papers spread on Sam's desk. 'Can I take a copy of the maps?'

She nodded, walked over to a scanner in the corner of the room and ran off two copies. 'What are you going to do?'

He shrugged. 'I don't really know. Without talking to your father I don't know if he killed him, do I? And then there are two sites, so if your father could remember him it would depend if he could remember where the body was dumped. Do you think he'd be willing to talk to me about it?'

'I don't know and immediately there are other concerns more pressing for his attention.'

'Your brother?'

'Yes.'

'Have you tracked down your father?'

Sam nodded. 'He'll be back in the country soon.'

'Well, at least you know he's safe.'

'It sounds brutal but I don't really care about him,' Sam said. 'He's the means to saving my brother's life. That's all.'

Rick frowned. 'He must mean something more to you than that.'

She just stared at him.

'Will he help you?'

'I don't know, but at the moment he's the only hope I've got.'

He had picked up his rucksack and put his sunglasses back on. Sam saw herself reflected in their blank black surface.

'When the time's right will you ask him about this?' He tapped the maps in his hand.

'Yes, I will.'

'Thanks.'

Last time they had parted he had kissed her on the cheek but then they'd both had a lot to drink. Stone-cold sober she stood awkwardly, tapping a pencil against her thumb, trying to make herself as unapproachable as possible, keeping the desk between them.

'See you, then,' he said.

Sam nodded and he turned towards the door. Suddenly something occurred to her.

'Hold on a minute,' she said. 'Could I show you a photo? See if you recognise someone.'

He turned back to face her. She took the photofit of Brendan out of her bag and handed it to him, wondering why she hadn't done this before. She'd had the photo with her when she was in the Quod Bar. Why hadn't she shown it to him then? He held it in his hands a moment before looking up.

'No, sorry. Who is he?'

'We think he's called Brendan McNally.'

'This is a police photofit, isn't it?'

'Yes.'

'What's he done?'

'We think he might have taken Mark.'

He shrugged. 'Sorry.'

Sam looked at him intently and wondered if he was telling the truth. Something about the way he said 'Who is he?' seemed somehow too casual, too studied, but then maybe she was just being paranoid. She remembered Alan: *Actors act and not always just on a stage*. And she couldn't see his eyes. She wanted to reach over and take off his dark glasses but it would have been too intimate a gesture.

'Well, I'll be seeing you,' he said and walked out of her office.

Sam sat down at her desk and put her head in her hands. She needed to decide one way or the other about Rick. At the moment she was telling him some things and then shutting down about others. She couldn't decide to trust him completely. That wasn't particularly surprising. He'd as good as told her that his father and himself were involved in the IRA. He'd said he no longer was, but Sam doubted it was as simple as that. She knew from her experience of dons in St Cuthbert's and things that her stepfather Peter had said that once you were involved in the secret services they viewed you as theirs for life. Surely the same thing would apply to something like membership of the IRA – once a member always a member. And had Rick really shed his past as he claimed? She thought back to the performance in the King's Head, to the things he had said there. *There was a time when I was filled with hatred but I didn't even know who to hate.* Well, now he did know who to hate, didn't he? If Geoffrey Falconer had killed his father, he'd know exactly who to hate. Had he really thrown all that out? She couldn't believe it. Surely you couldn't just shed all your sectarian loyalties? Surely it was a lot more complicated than that? Was he playing games with her, flirting with her, keeping her off balance and all the time edging closer to what he wanted, relying on her attraction to him to protect himself, always keeping one step ahead?

She checked her mobile was still switched on. Since the call had failed to come in she'd been expecting it at any time. As she was looking at its screen, the phone rang, making her jump.

'Hello?'

'Sam, it's Paula. They're back in the country and they're coming to the office. They should be here in a couple of hours' time. Can you get over here?'

Sam looked at her watch. 'I'll be there. Are they all right?'

'They're alive at any rate.'

CHAPTER TWENTY

Geoffrey Falconer was sitting forwards on the sofa, his forearms resting on his knees, when Sam and Paula entered Max's office. He levered himself upright with some difficulty and stood up. A tough, wiry-looking man in his late fifties, he was wearing a faded blue sweatshirt, green camouflage trousers and black army boots; several days' stubble covered his cheeks.

Sam looked at him and then at Max, standing next to him, and despite the ambiguity of her feelings towards her father and her worry about what he and Max would do, her predominant feeling, looking at the two men, was one of overwhelming relief.

'Christ,' she said. 'Look what the cat dragged in.'

Her father took a step towards her but Sam immediately moved away from him. She skirted the room, stepping round a couple of large black zip-up bags, and walked over to the window, where she stood with her arms folded and her back to the view. He turned and sat back down, flinching as he did so. It occurred to Sam that this is what she'd done with Rick: made sure that there was a large piece of furniture between him and her.

From this position she took the time to look at the two men more thoroughly. Max's arm was in a plaster cast and his face was a mass of small cuts, some of which had been stitched, others taped shut. Her father's head was bandaged and he seemed fatter in his torso than she had remembered, he also had abrasions on his face and a black eye.

'God, aren't you both too old for this kind of thing? Shouldn't you leave it to the younger blokes?'

'It was two young blokes who got killed,' Max said, his voice flat with exhaustion. 'I wanted to get the bodies back – for the families. If it hadn't been for that we wouldn't have gone.'

'Did you find them?'

'No, we got blown up and then had the enjoyable experience of being the guests of the American military. They at least had the good manners to deport us. It's why we got back here so quickly.'

Her father hadn't spoken yet. Underneath the cuts and bruises, his face was the colour of putty.

'Are you all right?' Sam asked him.

He grimaced and half closed his eyes. He dug in the pocket of his trousers and pulled out some pills. He gestured to the water jug and glasses on the table next to the door. 'Could someone get me a glass of water?'

Paula, who'd been leaning against the door since they came in, poured a glass of water and handed it to him. He cracked a couple of pills out of their casing and swallowed them. Sam walked back round to where the two men were sitting and sat down in a chair opposite them. She raised her eyebrows at Max as she tipped her head in her father's direction.

'Geoff took the brunt of the explosion on his back. The bomb blew all the windows in and splintered the wooden front of the bar we were in. It was a while before he got any medical attention.'

'Has he been seen to now?'

'Yes, they think they've taken out all the pieces of glass and they've wrapped him up like a mummy and shot him full of antibiotics, but he didn't have an easy flight because he couldn't sit back in his seat.'

Sam looked across at her father. He was leaning forwards as before, his head hanging between his shoulders. One of his elbows slipped down between his knees and he jolted upright, his face contorted in pain. She'd been worried that he and Max would take things into their own hands but the pair of them were so bashed about they looked as if they could barely stand, let alone do anything more active.

Sam addressed herself to her father. 'The Americans gave you a hard time?'

'Some stupid sod of a sergeant enjoyed himself a little too much at my expense but it wasn't anything worse than I experienced at selection. They lost four men in the explosion. Reverse the situation and we wouldn't have let the medics see them that quickly either.'

'You need to get some sleep,' she said.

'I'll be fine.'

'No, you won't, mate,' Max said. 'You can get some rest next door – there's a bed. Sam can update me and then we can talk once you've slept.'

This time he didn't protest. He got up stiffly and made for the door behind Sam.

Sam dug in her bag and brought out the picture of Brendan. 'Hold on a minute, could you look at this first? His name's Brendan McNally and we think he's the man who's taken Mark.'

He turned slowly and took hold of the photofit. He stared at it silently for some time then handed it back and shook his head. 'Maybe after I've slept . . . '

'The name doesn't mean anything to you?'

'No.'

He went into the room and closed the door behind him.

'What about you?' Sam said to Max.

'I'm fine. Like I said, your dad took the force of the explosion. Protected me from the worst of it. He'll be all right. It's just he couldn't sleep at all on the flight, he was in too much pain. Now tell me what's been going on.'

Geoffrey Falconer untied the laces of his boots, kicked them off and carefully lay down, front first, on the single bed. The photofit tickled at his memory like an eyelash circling an eyeball. He felt the memory move, then lie still, but he was dead on his feet and the painkillers were beginning to have a sedative effect. He closed his eyes and allowed sleep to claim him.

He's walking in the forest. It's summer. The air is warm and the trees stretch up above his head towards a clear blue sky. Dappled patches of sunlight cover the forest floor. He walks through a cloud of midges, which tickle his face, and he waves his hand in the air in front of him and snorts. He leans back against a tree trunk, enjoying the sun on his face, and closes his eyes.

When he opens them, everything has changed. It's night, so dark he can't see his hand in front of his face and he knows that he is lost, all visual markers that would help him find his way out are lost. Fear fills every cell in him, fixing him to the ground. He knows that if he moves he will die, he feels like a mouse that has just seen the shadow of a kestrel against the sun. He flattens himself against the tree trunk. The forest has him and isn't going to let him go. And now he knows exactly where he is. This place under his feet, under the moss, is the grave of all those men he has killed. He is walking over their bones and they know he is here. He moves away from the tree and a twig cracks under his foot. And now he can hear their groans, coming from the earth under his feet, the groans of the men he murdered coming to claim him.

Terrified, he begins to run, crashing into trees, stumbling and falling over then clambering to his feet and running again as fast as he can. And all the time the earth is opening under his feet, he can feel it moving.

Something grabs hold of his foot.

He thinks it's a bramble but when he reaches down to free his ankle a hand grabs hold of his wrist and holds on tight, a hand rising from the forest floor. He takes out a knife and begins to hack at the hand and then he is free and off running again, his breath coming in gulping sobs, his whole body straining with the effort. At last he crashes out of the forest into the open, collapsing onto his hands and knees, gasping for breath. Two feet appear in front of him. He looks up and sees a man holding a 9mm, which is pointed at his head.

'But,' he begins. 'You? I don't...'

Then he sees the finger tighten on the trigger of the gun...

And all he feels is relief.

Sam looked down at her father shouting and twitching in his sleep and considered which bit of him to touch to wake him. Usually she would have prodded his back but because of his injuries it was out of bounds. She grabbed his big toe and twisted.

'Dad, wake up.'

It had the desired effect. He groaned and sat up on the side of the bed, his face bathed in sweat.

'Have you got a temperature?'

He shook his head. 'Bad dreams.'

He got slowly to his feet and followed Sam back into the office. 'How long have I been sleeping?'

'Half an hour or so.'

'I'll look at the photo again.'

He sat down carefully on the sofa next to Max, picking up the photofit as he did so. Sam watched his face closely as he looked at it.

For a moment he said nothing. Sam and Max exchanged a glance. He looked up at Sam. 'Brendan McNally, you said?'

'Yes.'

Frowning, he looked back at the picture, then back at her, and shook his head. 'I'm sorry ... I thought ... but it's not anyone I know.'

Paula put a cup of coffee down in front of him. Using both hands he brought it slowly to his lips, blew on the surface and sipped.

'I've had to go to the police,' Sam said.

He looked at her but said nothing.

'I had to. When I couldn't get hold of you there was nothing else I could do. I've been dealing with DCI Fiona Thompson. She's a trained hostage negotiator. She said she was willing to meet you at a place of your own choosing and alone.'

Geoffrey Falconer glanced at Max and then at Sam.

'I think it will help,' Sam said. 'Please don't go off on your own. I think that'll just increase the risk of something happening to Mark.'

Geoffrey nodded. 'A meeting's a good idea. Can you get hold of her now?'

An hour later Fiona Thompson entered the room. She held out her hand to Geoffrey Falconer and then to Max, who because of the plaster on his right hand had to clasp her hand awkwardly with his left.

'I'm very sorry about this situation with your son,' she said to Geoffrey. 'Sam has told me that you have reasons to be distrustful of the authorities but I can assure you that I am not interested in that part of your affairs. All I'm interested in is getting Mark back safe – that's it and I'd be grateful for any kind of assistance you could give.'

He nodded. 'What have you got?' he asked.

'Not much. Sam's shown you the photofit of Brendan McNally. We've sent his name off to the PSNI. Hopefully they'll be able to help us build up some sort of profile of him.'

He frowned. 'The what?'

'The Police Service of Northern Ireland.'

He grunted in amusement. 'RIP RUC then?'

She nodded.

'You think he's taken Mark back to Northern Ireland?'

She shook her head. 'I think that would be unlikely. It would be an extremely risky thing to do. Usually they're not going to want to move the hostage at all. Each time they do, there's a risk of them being seen or of the hostage escaping. We think it's more likely that Mark's still in England, probably close to where he was taken. He must be holding him somewhere and someone must have seen something.'

'What's your take on the fact he didn't phone when he said he would?'

'Silence is never good. Maybe he was disturbed. Both times he's phoned in on Sam's mobile so I would suggest that you two stay joined at the hip until that call comes in.'

Sam sighed. It was hardly what she wanted to hear. 'You think he will call?'

'Like I said to you before, Sam, this man has gone to enormous lengths to get hold of Geoffrey and he still hasn't managed it.'

Geoffrey nodded. 'It's me he wants.'

'If he's been disturbed or is moving Mark to a new location, he'll phone once that's settled down.'

Sam looked at her watch. It was ten o'clock. The call was sixteen hours overdue.

'I could just take the phone,' Geoffrey suggested, 'easier than us having to stick together.'

Sam didn't say anything. Much as having to stay glued to her father's side repulsed her, there was no way she was going to hand over her phone to him. She knew that if he took the call there was absolutely no guarantee that he would inform her or the police of what had been said or what he was going to do. They'd be left out in the cold and her father and probably Max would be gone.

'No, that's all right,' Sam said to him. Then to Fiona: 'Once he's made contact with Dad what's he going to want then?'

'What do you think?' Fiona said, bouncing the question on to Geoffrey.

Geoffrey Falconer leaned back slowly, wincing as his back touched the seat. 'I think that's pretty obvious to all of us, isn't it? He's going to want to meet me and then he'll want to kill me or kill Mark in front of me.'

'Anyway, hopefully our colleagues in Belfast will be able to come up with some sort of information on McNally and then we'll get a clearer idea of who we're dealing with. One thing I would ask,' Fiona said, turning to Geoffrey Falconer, 'is that you don't go solo on this one. I know your past experiences would lead you to prefer a non-collaborative approach and I see that you have considerable resources at your disposal.' She nodded at Max. 'But I think if you do you'll be putting Mark's life at risk. You must see how important it is for us to keep communicating with each other.'

She might as well be speaking to the pavement, Sam thought, looking at her father and Max, who had listened to Fiona in stony silence and with the slightest of nods.

Fiona continued addressing herself to Geoffrey. 'Is there anything else you could tell me that you think might be helpful?'

He pushed himself away from the back of his chair. 'I appreciate you're trying to help my son . . .'

Fiona stood up.

'I'll see you out,' Sam said.

At the lift, Sam punched the button that would take them to the ground floor. The two women waited in silence, arms folded. The lift came and they got in and the doors closed.

'I realise my little speech there at the end couldn't have fallen on deafer ears,' Fiona said, her green eyes creased in amusement.

'I'm sorry. They're just not team players.'

'Do you think your father's telling the truth?'

'Yes.'

'What happened to him after his service in Northern Ireland?'

'I don't know.'

She looked surprised.

'He's only just come back into my life and the return hasn't been particularly welcome. Look, I'll try and keep tabs on him. That's not going to be too hard while we're waiting for the call to come in but once it has, my feeling is, he'll be gone in response to whatever he hears.'

Fiona nodded. 'We'll just have to do our best to keep track of him.'

Sam let her out into the street and after saying goodbye stood for a moment looking at the lunchtime crowds. In the past she had been of the opinion that nine to five was no way to lead your life. But at this particular moment a regular office job seemed a thoroughly desirable option.

It was mid afternoon by the time Sam and her father got back to her flat. He and Max had had things to sort out and Sam hadn't minded. It was easier to be around her father when other people were there. What she dreaded was being left alone with him. But when he and Max had finished up, she knew she would have to take him home. If they had to be joined at the hip he had to go where she went. He had barely spoken on the journey, only flinching when Sam braked because it pressed him back into his seat.

Now he stood awkwardly in the middle of Sam's living room, scratching at the silver stubble on his cheeks.

'Sit down,' she said.

'I think I'll stand for a bit if you don't mind. My back . . .'

'Coffee or tea?'

'Have you got any food? I'm starving.'

Sam didn't need to look in the fridge to know the answer to that one.

At the local shop she bought bacon, eggs, bread, baked beans, a paper and some cat food for Frank, who she presumed was asleep on Edie's fridge.

When she returned she found Frank spread out on her father's lap, purring like a swarm of bees. He barely glanced at Sam.

'Door opened and he just sauntered in,' her father explained.

'Edie, next door, has got the keys to the flat. She looks after him while I'm away. She probably heard us come in.'

Her father gestured at the carrier bag. 'Why don't you let me do that? I'm good with fry-ups.'

He followed her into the kitchen and fifteen minutes later they were sitting down to eat.

'When did you last have something?' Sam asked.

He rubbed his eyes and yawned. 'Thirty-six? Forty-eight hours? I don't know.'

'What on earth made you agree to go out to Iraq?'

He shrugged. 'Max asked me. It's a good place to disappear.'

'That's all?'

'Oh, I don't know, Sam. It was good money. Maybe I thought it was the quickest way to get myself killed.'

Sam wasn't sure whether he was joking or not. She guessed not, but if he wanted her to feel sorry for him he was going the wrong way about it.

'Look, he's an old mate and I owe him.'

'He says he owes you. He told me you saved him from drowning during SAS selection and it was you who got him through it.'

'He always did exaggerate.'

'So you didn't?'

'No one gets you through selection but yourself. Believe me – you can't do that for another person.'

He yawned again – a real mouth splitter.

'Do you want to get some more sleep?'

He nodded.

'You can use the cushions off the sofa and I'll bring in a couple of pillows and a duvet.'

'OK, thanks.'

'If you pull down the blinds it'll make it easier to sleep.'

Sam came back into the room with the bedding and picked up Frank.

Her father looked disappointed. 'I don't mind him.'

'If you go to sleep on your front, which I assume you're going to do, he'll jump on the small of your back.'

'Oh, I see.'

'And as you may have noticed, he's on the large side.'

She closed the door and dropped Frank onto the ground. Frank turned round immediately, walked back to the door and sniffed at the gap between the floor and the bottom of the door.

'Come on, fatso, I've got food for you,' Sam said, walking down the hall to the kitchen, and Frank pirouetted with the elegance of an elephant in ballet shoes and galloped after her, rounding the corner into the kitchen just in front of her and skidding to attention in front of the cupboard.

When she heard her father stirring, she brought two cups of tea into the front room and sat down on the sofa, next to him.

'I suppose you blame me for what's happened to Mark?' he said.

'Where's that going to get us?'

'But you do.'

'If you hadn't come back. If . . .'

He nodded and leaned back gingerly against the sofa.

'There's something else I need to talk to you about,' Sam said. 'A man called Rick McGann came to my office. He said that after reading the article in the paper about you he thinks your group could have been responsible for killing his father. He went—'

'Wait a minute.' Her father held his hand palm outwards at her. 'When did this happen?'

'It was two days before Mark went missing. He said he wanted my help in finding out first of all if your group did kill him and if so where his father's body was.'

'He comes strolling into your office two days before Mark's kidnapped and both he and the person who's taken Mark just coincidentally want the same thing.'

'What do you mean?'

'Me, Sam. They both want me.'

'I don't think Rick wants *you* exactly. He wants his father's body to bury.'

'Yes, but he thinks he needs me for that.'

'I showed him the maps and your statement. This is not someone who is looking for revenge. He's looking for the same things you claim to be looking for – that the bodies be returned to the families and given the dignity of a proper burial. He read out that bit of your statement. He said he thought you were looking for resolution too.'

'I can't believe a daughter of mine could be so stupid. Are you fucking him or something?'

Sam blushed. 'Listen to me. He's not like that. He's involved with

262

reconciliation work. I think he genuinely wants to find his father's body so that he can get on with his life and move on.'

'You didn't answer me.'

'It's none of your fucking business, but no, I'm not.'

'Well, there's only one way to find out if he's genuine. Let's go and see him.'

'Now?'

'Why not? Sitting around waiting for this call to come in is just going to drive us crazy. He says he wants to meet me, doesn't he?'

CHAPTER TWENTY-ONE

A couple of hours later, Sam and her father were crossing Hungerford Bridge, being buffeted by a strong wind. It was a clear, sunny spring evening and the bridge was busy with people heading for the South Bank. Halfway along a saxophonist was playing 'Baker Street', the music floating down onto the heads of the people in a boat covered in multi-colour dots that was on its way to Tate Modern. Sam dug in her pocket and threw some change into his sax case. The man nodded in acknowledgement but didn't stop playing.

The venue of the Royal Festival Hall had been her father's choice. He'd wanted a public space where there would be a lot of people. If he decides he wants to kill me, there'll be lots of witnesses, he'd said. And Sam hadn't been quite sure whether he was joking or not. The outside of the Royal Festival Hall was a mass of scaffolding and boards but inside it was largely unchanged.

The bar was a couple of people deep and all the tables in front of it were packed with drinkers. Someone was playing jazz clarinet. A table full of Shirley Bassey souvenirs was proof of who was playing the big concert that night.

'Do you want a drink?' Sam asked, nodding at the bar.

He shook his head. 'I'll get myself some coffee from the café.'

Sam pushed herself into the throng at the bar, ordered herself a half of Guinness, and then sat down at a table that gave her a good view of the action at the Shirley Bassey table.

Two large men dressed in enough leather and metal to make them look like extras from a *Mad Max* movie were deep in conversation with an elderly woman whose peach cardigan matched her hair. A pair of immensely high-heeled shoes on enormous feet denoted the stately progress of a turquoise boa-draped drag queen towards the table. The two men and the peach woman fell away as she reached them as if she were Moses and they were playing the part of the Red Sea. A sensible decision, Sam thought.

Her father came back with his coffee. She glanced at her watch and checked her phone was OK. They were early.

'Mum would have loved this,' her father said. 'She had that double LP she played all the time.'

'I've still got it.'

'"I Am What I Am",' Geoffrey said.

'"Breakfast in Bed",' Sam replied.

He smiled and sipped his coffee.

Talking to her father about Shirley Bassey was about as surreal an experience as she could ever wish for.

'Rick's going to bring a photo of his father.'

Geoffrey stared into his coffee cup, picked up a spoon, hovered it over the creamy head and then dropped the spoon into the saucer. 'You don't ever forget them, Sam. At first of course you think you're going to be able to. That if you shove the memory down deep enough it'll stay there or if you drink enough it'll wipe it out but then you find yourself drinking more and more and then the memories start popping to the surface like corks and each one's got the face of a man you killed. And then you know that it's something you're going to have to live with for the rest of your life, those faces bobbing in your mind, and that death's the only thing that's going to end it. And at that point, you know, death doesn't seem like such a bad thing after all. And all of that, of course, is not something that anyone tells you about when they're training you to kill. Because that's all they are doing – training you to kill. They certainly aren't training you to deal with the consequences. That is something you're left to deal with all by yourself in the dark when the nightmares come.'

He picked up the spoon again and this time cut it through the creamy top and began savagely stirring his coffee.

'Do you think that's true for everyone?'

'Unless you're a psychopath, I think it is. I've known a few of those and I tell you they're a different breed altogether.'

'In what way?'

'No feelings. No remorse. No conscience. Excellent killers.'

Sam thought back to her conversation with Phil and Hopkins in the police station. *No conscience. An excellent killer.* It was a pretty accurate description of whoever had cut Dougie Malone's throat and then cut off Mark's finger.

She noticed her father looking over her shoulder and turned round. Rick was walking towards them. He waved at Sam. Sam looked back at her father, trying to gauge his reaction, but his face was blank and gave away no clues.

Rick reached them and looked down at Geoffrey Falconer.

'This is my father,' Sam said.

All the colour had drained from Rick's face. He stared at Geoffrey, saying nothing.

'Do you want to get yourself a chair?' Sam said, pointing to an empty table a couple of feet away.

Rick stared at her. 'Sorry?'

'A chair,' she repeated.

He swallowed and looked back at Geoffrey, who was now looking intently at the scum that had formed on the rim of his cup.

Sam jumped up, grabbed a chair and brought it back to the table, shoving it behind Rick. 'Sit down,' she ordered.

He sat.

'Have you got the photo?' Sam said to him.

He nodded and dug in his bag, then placed the photo on the table. They both looked at her father.

He was running his forefinger over his upper lip, frowning. 'Who are you asking me about?'

Sam glanced at the photo – a man sitting on a sofa, two boys either side of him.

Rick's breathing had speeded up; his hands were tight clenched balls resting on the top of his thighs. 'What do you mean?'

'Who's your father? Who the hell are you asking me about?'

Rick jabbed his finger at the man. 'Him, of course.' He pointed at the man in the middle. 'Do you recognise him?'

Geoffrey pointed to the older boy. 'Who's this?'

'Why? What's that got to do with anything?'

'Who the hell is it?' He grabbed hold of Rick's arm. 'Are you playing games with me?'

'My cousin, Kieran. Why? What's he . . . ?'

Sam wasn't quite sure what happened next. There was nothing verbal to precipitate it but the next thing she knew, she was sent flying over backwards, the table had been turned over and she was looking at Rick and her father locked in each other's arms, rolling around on the ground under the feet of the drag queen, the peach lady and the two extras from *Mad Max*.

She scrambled to her feet. There was still no noise coming from the two men but plenty of noise coming from the onlookers, especially the drag queen, who had managed to break a heel in the mêlée.

Rick and her father were covered in small honey-brown bears, wearing navy blue sweaters saying *Kiss me honey, honey kiss me*. Sam swept the bears away, grabbed the collar of Rick's jacket and pulled, but at that moment the two men rolled over and her father's back was uppermost. Sam applied a strangle to her father and tightened it until he choked and let go of Rick. She dragged him away and dumped him at the feet of the drag queen.

Rick lay on his back, breathing heavily, a red mark forming high up on his right cheekbone. The drag queen was protesting vehemently about her broken heel.

Sam righted the table and chairs and walked over to where Rick was beginning to pick himself off the floor.

'Are you completely insane?' she shouted. 'He's ex-SAS. What the hell do you think you're doing? Don't be such a fucking idiot.'

'He went for me.'

He pressed his hand against his face and winced. Sam picked up an armful of bears and took them back to the stand.

'Sorry about that,' she said as she handed them back. 'There was a bit of a misunderstanding. Look, I'll have one of these.' She pointed out the bears.

The drag queen collared Sam. 'Honey, have you the faintest idea how much it costs to have these kind of shoes made in size ten?'

Sam handed over money for the bear and confessed she didn't and was then saved from a further harangue by the bell going off for the start of the concert. The drag queen turned and, trailing turquoise feathers from her boa, began limping towards the auditorium. Sam took her bear and walked back to the table where Rick and her father were standing, eyeing each other and two security guards.

'It was a misunderstanding,' Sam said to the guards. 'Sorry about the trouble. We'll just tidy this up.' She gestured at the mess around them. 'And then we'll leave.' She bent down and picked up the cup and saucer and her half-pint glass and put them on the table. 'Come on,' she said to her father and Rick.

Outside Geoffrey grabbed hold of the front of Rick's jacket. 'What do you want with me? Where the hell's my son?'

Rick shook himself free. 'Did you kill my father?'

'I had nothing to do with your father. I don't know anything about him. I don't recognise that man.'

'But you do recognise Kieran?' Sam said.

'Yes. Where is he?'

Sam had an image of his face as he sat next to her in the King's Head, it had been completely immobile other than for the muscle twitching in his jaw.

Rick shook his head. 'I don't know.'

'Come on,' Sam said. 'I saw him only a fortnight ago.'

'He was due to come to Oxford with us and help set up at the Playhouse and he didn't turn up. I tried to get hold of him but I haven't seen him since that night in the King's Head.'

'What happened with Kieran?' Sam said to Geoffrey. 'What makes you think it's him? It was years ago. How come you remember him?'

'Because he was the one that brought the whole thing to an end. It was after him I quit.'

'What happened?' Sam repeated.

'I need a drink,' Geoffrey said and set off in the direction of the National Theatre with Rick and Sam trailing behind him.

They walked in silence, weaving their way between the trestle tables covered in second-hand books outside the National Film Theatre. The South Bank was busy, thronging with people seeking to enjoy the first warm evening in May. Beyond Gabriel's Wharf they stopped at a riverside pub. They got themselves drinks and sat outside at a table that looked down onto the Thames.

'You're probably not going to believe me but what I did was save his life. I'd reached the end of the road in Northern Ireland. I couldn't kill another person. He was the one I stopped at. He was just this skinny kid. He was the youngest I'd come across, much too young. I told the others I'd do this one by myself. Walking across the field I kept saying to him, "Don't worry. I'm not going to do anything to you." I kept saying it. It's what we said to them anyway. You wanted them to walk to their own graves, otherwise you had to carry them and that was heavy work over a rain-sodden field in the middle of the night. So I just kept saying I was going to let him go and by the time I reached the edge of the trees I realised that's exactly what I was going to do. He was just this skinny kid . . .'

'Did the others agree to it?' Sam asked.

'They never knew.'

'How come?'

'I told him to get in the trench and I fired some shots. As far as they knew I'd killed him. In fact, I did shoot him but not dead.'

'You shot him?'

'He begged me to. He said no one would believe he'd been taken by us and then come back without a scratch on him. He said they'd think he was a grass and he was terrified of what they'd do to him. He begged me to shoot him. He said if he was wounded at least he could say that he was shot while running away.'

'But if you saved his life what does he want with you now? What's he doing with Mark? None of it makes sense.' Sam turned to Rick. 'I need everything you can tell us. I need to tell the police straight away.'

'No,' Rick's voice had enough of an edge to make the people on the table behind them fall silent and turn their heads. 'Give me some time to see if I can find him myself. Don't tell the police. Let me try and resolve this privately.'

'And how are you going to do that? Kieran's the first direct link we've been able to establish to my father. He knew about me and Mark through the newspaper and through you. He spoke to me at the King's Head and he's missing. We've got to get his name and description out to the police immediately.'

'You're jumping to conclusions. His mother's been very ill recently; he could have gone back to Belfast.'

'But you said the IRA wouldn't let him back in the country.'

'He could have risked it anyway. Give me some time. I'm a better bet than the police. I've been trying to get hold of his girlfriend.'

'No,' Sam said.

'Hold on a minute, Sam,' her father said. 'Why don't we see what he can do?'

'So this is your version of keeping the police informed, is it?'

'He's his cousin. Who do you think has a better chance of tracking him down? Rick or the police?'

'What would you do first?' Sam asked.

'Try his girlfriend, Nuala, again.'

'Do it,' Sam said. 'And arrange for us to meet her.'

'One thing though,' Geoffrey Falconer said. 'We're not going to let you out of our sight.'

Rick took out his mobile and made a call. After a short conversation he closed up his phone and looked at his watch. 'She'll be coming off her shift at ten. That'll give us about enough time.'

'Where do we need to get to?'

'Oxford – she's a nurse at the Churchill.'

Sam grabbed hold of his arm. 'What are you talking about? That's where Brendan McNally was working.'

'Brendan's her brother,' Rick said.

'Why didn't you tell me that when I showed you the photofit this morning? What are you playing at, Rick? Are you working with him? Trying to keep a foot in both camps? Trying not to upset anyone?'

'I was going to tell you. I just needed some time. I've been trying to get hold of Nuala all day . . .'

Sam shook her head. 'So tribal loyalties are just as strong as ever, aren't they? I was a fool to trust you.'

'You can think what you like,' Rick said. 'We need to get going if we're going to be in Oxford in time.'

They went back to Sam's and picked up her car and an hour later were heading out of London. Rick turned round in the front passenger seat and addressed Geoffrey Falconer. 'Did you mean what you said in your statement about wanting to set the record straight, about wanting the bodies properly buried?'

'Yes, I did.'

'Would you be willing to come to Northern Ireland and meet with the families of those you killed?'

'Would you be able to guarantee my safety?'

Rick didn't reply to that.

'Would you come to Northern Ireland and do your best to show me exactly where the bodies were buried?'

'Sam gave you copies of the maps, didn't she?'

'Yes.'

'Well, that's where they are.'

'But I've no idea what we might find there. It was thirty years ago. They could have flattened the forest and built a housing estate, for all I know. I mean, it could look very different.'

'I can give you very precise directions but for me to go back to Northern Ireland would put my life at risk and I haven't been back since . . .'

'Maybe it would help you.'

'Help me get killed perhaps. Like I said before – could you guarantee my safety?'

'No, I couldn't, but you've just been in Iraq – that must be one of the most dangerous places on earth at the moment.'

'With my background Northern Ireland's much more dangerous for me than Iraq.'

Rick looked defeated.

'If the instructions are accurate enough surely you'll be able to identify the place,' Sam said.

He shrugged. 'Not necessarily. Anything could have happened.'

'You won't find your father there,' Geoffrey said.

'I wasn't thinking of myself. I was thinking of the other families.'

The rest of the journey followed in silence. When they arrived at the Churchill Sam parked in the car park and Rick went off to find Nuala.

'Do you think we can trust him?' Sam said.

Her father shrugged. 'One way or another we're going to find that out soon enough.'

A couple of minutes later Rick appeared by the side of the car with a woman. She was petite and pale with light blue eyes, her brown curly hair was tied back from her face. She was wearing a black raincoat and flat black shoes. It was beginning to drizzle and Rick got into the front passenger seat and Nuala got into the back next to Geoffrey Falconer. As she unbuttoned her raincoat, Sam saw that she was wearing a white nylon nurse's uniform with a name badge attached to it.

'When did you last see Kieran?' Sam asked.

'He came down for the weekend three weeks ago. We went to Blenheim.'

Geoffrey lit a cigarette. 'Where is he now?'

She shook her head. 'How should I know?'

'You know we suspect he's taken my brother,' Sam said. 'That he's asking for my father.'

Nuala looked at Geoffrey. 'That's you then, is it?'

Geoffrey opened the window and knocked his ash out. 'Do you know what he wants with me?'

'You may have let him go but you shot him, didn't you?'

'He told me to shoot him. He said if he turned up back in Ballymurphy without a scratch on him they'd think he was a grass. He told me people had seen us snatching him. He said I had to.'

'Well, you shot him in the wrong place.'

He frowned.

'Where *did* you shoot him?' Sam asked.

'Right shoulder – why, what happened?'

'He was a boxer. My uncle ran a boxing club on the estate to try to keep the kids out of trouble. He reckoned if you exhausted them in the gym they wouldn't have the energy to siphon petrol out of cars and throw stones at the soldiers. Kieran was a natural. He won everything he could as a kid and they had big hopes for him. But he never came back from the shooting. There was too much damage to the muscles in his shoulder. He lost the full rotation and the strength, and his right was his knock-out hand. He tried to change sides but he was never as good again. And it didn't work anyway, you know. The IRA was suspicious of him even though you'd shot him. They didn't believe you could be picked up by the SAS and escape. They made him prove how loyal he was and the way they did that was to get him to kill people. When he'd had enough they ordered him out of Northern Ireland.'

Geoffrey sighed. 'I should have killed him.'

Nuala slapped him. His cigarette flew out of his mouth and onto the floor. 'You bastard. What were you doing with him in the first place? He was only a kid trying to keep his nose clean. All you did was shove him straight into their arms. You turned him into a killer. You destroyed any hope he had of escape.'

Geoffrey Falconer reached down for the cigarette butt and threw it out of the window. The colour had drained from his face. 'We were never told why, only who, and I'd reached the end of the road with it all. Kieran was the end of the road for me. He was just too young. I didn't care what he was supposed to have done. I realised as soon as we picked him up. I just didn't have the heart for it any more.'

Nuala was composed now, hands folded neatly in her lap, as if she were sitting on a church pew not in the back of a car. 'You created a killer.'

No one said anything. The words hung in the confined space of the car.

'And you've no idea where he might be?' Sam said.

Nuala shook her head.

'You've not heard from him or seen him in the last fortnight?'

'No.'

'Weren't you worried about him?' Sam asked.

'His mother's been ill. He wasn't handling it well. He told me he needed some space . . . I stopped being worried about Kieran a long time ago. You know you have no control over what's going to happen. That's been the story of his life.' She pointed at Geoffrey. 'You thought you were doing him a favour – well, you weren't, were you? You pushed him straight into their arms, and he never managed to get out.'

'What do you mean?' Sam asked. 'Was he still working for them on the mainland?'

Nuala didn't reply. She looked at her watch and pushed open the door.

Sam joined her outside the car. The wind was picking up and the security lights in the car park cast a brutal orange glare. 'Look, my brother's finger was cut off – please, is there anything you could tell us that might help? My brother's done nothing wrong. He's an innocent in all this.'

'Innocent!' Nuala shook her head. 'You people – and how many innocents do you think have been killed in Northern Ireland in the last thirty years. Kieran was sixteen years old when your dad shot him. You think innocence should protect you? Don't be so bloody naïve.'

Her conversation with Fiona Thompson just before the second call came in flashed into Sam's mind.

'*I don't give a shit about him. All I want is for him to let go of my brother.*'

'*Listen to me, Sam. If you start to give a shit about him that's much more likely to happen.*'

'Please,' Sam said. 'You must be worried about him. And what about Brendan? Is he involved in the kidnapping? Mark's blood was found in Bullingdon Road. Are Kieran and Brendan working together? Is there really nothing else you can tell us?'

'Brendan wouldn't harm a fly. He's not a violent man.'

'What about Kieran?'

'Hope died for Kieran the day that bullet entered his shoulder. It was when it all went wrong for him.'

Nuala's arms were folded around her body, hugging herself. She seemed entirely unreachable.

'I'm very sorry for what my father did to Kieran,' Sam said. 'But please, is there any other information you might have about where Mark might be?'

'I have nothing to say to you and you have no evidence that Kieran's got anything to do with this. You're just pissing in the wind.'

Sam dug in her pocket and brought out her card. 'In case you change your mind.'

Nuala shook her head but she did take the card. She pulled the collar of her coat up round her neck and walked briskly back in the direction of the hospital.

Sam walked away from the car and put a call in to Phil. 'I've got another name,' she said. 'Kieran McGann. He should be in your records. He was picked up a lot in the eighties during the bombing campaigns. My father identified him and he has a motive for wanting revenge against him.'

'Is he the one who gave you that list of names?'

'No.'

'PSNI say they're no good, so I don't think whoever gave it to you was giving you anything useful, Sam. Maybe they just wanted to give that impression.'

Sam sighed and looked over at the car. Rick had lied to her about

Brendan but she wasn't going to tell Phil about him. Not yet, anyway.

'Find Kieran McGann, Phil.'

She got back into the car and slammed the door. No one said anything. She looked at her phone. It was over twenty-four hours since the last call was supposed to have come in. And there was nothing golden about this silence, the longer it went on the more ominous it became. She glanced in her rear-view mirror. Her father's eyes were closed, his face drawn and grey. She was tired and starving hungry. She couldn't go back to Park Town, not with her father.

'Hand me my bag,' she said to Rick and he leaned forwards and grabbed it off the floor between his legs.

After a short search she came up with what she was looking for: the keys to Mark's rooms. They could bunk down there for the night.

She parked in St Giles and they walked from there to the High where they picked up some kebabs.

'You can now say that you've taken part in an important Oxford tradition,' she said. 'The High Street kebab van, the last culinary refuge of many a drunken undergraduate.'

In Mark's rooms her father went straight off to sleep in the bedroom. She and Rick sat finishing off their food.

Sam looked across to where he sat with his feet up on the table and wondered what was going through his mind. He looked gaunt and exhausted. Ever since she'd first introduced him to her father in the Royal Festival Hall, he'd barely spoken to her. Now he's got what he wants there's no longer any reason to turn on the charm. Suddenly she was relieved she hadn't slept with him. Once you'd done that it was so much easier to be hurt, to be let down and disappointed by someone. It's over, she thought, he was seducing me to get what he wanted; now he's got it, he'll drift away and my feelings for him will do the same. The fantasy will pop like a burst balloon. He probably lied about his wife anyway, his ridiculously beautiful wife, that was all probably part of the seduction. Anyway a man who had a wife like that wouldn't be interested in someone like her. He obviously wanted the whole high-heel, spray-on-dress thing, not some scruffy short-arse with enough baggage to fill a jumbo jet. And then, of course, there was the fact that he'd lied to her about recognising Brendan. If her father hadn't recognised Kieran would he ever have told her about that?

Rick took his feet off the table, scrunched the paper he'd been eating out of into a ball, got up and threw it into the bin. He came and sat down next to her on the sofa. He sat close to her, the side of his arm and his leg touching hers. He didn't say anything. Sam felt the warmth of his thigh against hers.

'No easy answers, are there?' he said.

'Not usually.'

'How are you?'

She shook her head.

'Your father was my last hope of finding out what happened. I was so certain he was involved. The timing fitted and my father knew some of the men who were killed. But now I'm going to have to let it go, aren't I? Enough is enough. I'm going to have to accept that I'm never going to know.'

His face crumpled. This time tears slid down his cheeks. He brushed them away but they continued to fall.

Reg's voice came into Sam's head again: *Try staying next time*.

Rick looked at her. 'I suppose I'm just going to have to accept that I'm never going to know.' He reached out and took her hand.

It was ice cold and clammy. 'Jesus, woman, are you all right?'

'Fine,' Sam said. 'It's a circulation thing.'

He put the back of his hand against her cheek. 'You're burning up. I think you have a fever starting.'

'Don't worry about me,' Sam said. 'You're the one who's upset.' She squeezed his hand awkwardly and gently extracted her own from his and wiped it on her trousers. 'Back in a minute,' she said and headed for the bathroom.

She stood leaning over the basin staring at her reflection in the mirror.

Sure, Reg, it's as easy as that. How long had she lasted? About thirty seconds.

She soaked a flannel in cold water and held it to the back of her neck.

When she cried she preferred to do it alone with a jug of margaritas. She'd once had a Lassie moment and experimented with sobbing into Frank's fur but he'd reciprocated with a Mike Tyson moment and savaged her ear. After that, she'd decided that tequila was definitely the best and safest companion for tears.

She thought she was going to be abandoned by Rick, so she left. Well, it seemed perfectly reasonable to her.

When she came back into the room she was relieved to find him asleep, stretched out on the sofa. She sat down in the chair opposite him and enjoyed the freedom of staring at him when he wasn't looking back. Surely he would have known about Kieran's connection to her father. Surely they'd have discussed it. He was like an older brother to him, Rick had said. He was bound to want to protect him. After a few minutes she got up and turned off the light. This wasn't going to get her anywhere. Everyone looked innocent when they slept.

CHAPTER TWENTY-TWO

Sam got up early before her father or Rick had stirred and went out to get some things for breakfast. It was a chilly but bright morning and the walk to the covered market and back revived her. As she was approaching the staircase to Mark's rooms she bumped into Vera Smith, who she knew from the time she had first looked after Mark when he came to the college as an undergraduate twenty years ago.

'All right, love?' Vera said.

'Have you heard about the things that have been going on in the college?' Sam asked.

Vera nodded. 'Everyone's talking about it, but it'll sort itself out. These things usually do.'

'Could you tell me how the college staff felt about what happened to Kenneth Adams?'

'Professor Adams was well liked. A lot of us were very upset at what they did with him.'

'Why was he so popular?'

'He always had time to talk. Very generous with his tips at Christmas and he was good at remembering birthdays. He always asked about people's families. It doesn't take much in life to make yourself pleasant but the thing with Professor Adams was that he was genuine about it. You can tell when they're genuine.'

Sam tried to match this picture of Adams with her own experience of him and failed. 'Was there anyone in particular who might have been upset by his eviction?'

'Look, love, we've all got jobs to lose, haven't we? You shouldn't be looking among the staff. No one would do that to Alex's lawns, not when they're at their loveliest, not when a May Ball is due to take place. It's got to be an outsider.'

Sam nodded. 'How long have you been here now, Vera?'

'This is my fortieth year. I started when I was twenty.'

'A few more years left in you yet?'

Vera shook her head. 'No, dear. They told me a few weeks ago, the same day that boy died. They don't want me to stay on. I'll be gone at the end of the summer. I'll stay for the conferences and that'll be it.'

'They'll miss you.'

'I don't think so. They've been trying to edge me out for years. Places like this have very short memories. If you're not here they'll forget you quick enough. They're keen to get rid of me.'

'I hope they give you a good send-off.'

'I'm not holding my breath.'

A tall young man with a mop of ginger hair stopped and smiled at Vera. 'All right, Aunty?'

'This is Bernie, my Eileen's boy. He's here on work experience.'

'Are you enjoying yourself?' Sam asked.

The boy shrugged noncommittally.

'You're making yourself useful around the place, aren't you? Better than being at the butcher's like your brother.'

He laughed nervously, eyes flickering towards Sam and back to Vera.

'I need to get on,' Vera said. 'Is there any news on Professor Falconer?'

Sam shook her head.

'I'm sure he'll turn up. Maybe he was just upset about that boy dying and needed to get away for a bit.'

Sam smiled. If only, she thought.

Her father was waiting for her when she got back to Mark's rooms.

'Rick's not with you?' he said.

'Isn't he here?'

He shook his head. 'He wasn't here when I woke up.'

'Shit.'

She put papers, two cartons of orange juice and a selection of pastries and croissants on the table and switched on the kettle. Her father seemed depressed and sullen. Sam put coffee and mugs on the table with a carton of milk and a packet of sugar and told him to get on with it. She swallowed her own coffee, waited for the caffeine to take effect.

There was still no phone call and now Rick had disappeared.

'You still convinced he's not involved?'

Sam shook her head. 'I don't know any more. Why did he lie to me about knowing Brendan? If you hadn't recognised Kieran would he ever have told me he knew him?'

'He likes to give the impression of doing something when in fact he's not coming across with anything at all.'

It was exactly what Phil had said last night.

'He came across with Nuala,' Sam said.

'But she didn't have much to say, did she? All that stuff about Kieran. Surely Rick could have told us that before. He's his cousin, for God's sake.'

Sam's phone rang.

Geoffrey put his cup down on the table. It was Nuala.

'There was something I wanted to tell you. When Brendan moved out of Bullingdon Road he said he'd be dossing in a van for a while. Apparently one of the people in the house had one and had told him he could use it. It was a sort of hippy thing, you know, to go travelling in. He made a joke about that.'

'Did he give you any other details about it? What sort of van – the colour?'

'It was a mobile library.'

'Sorry?'

'Robbie, the man he got the room from in Bullingdon Road, he'd bought it from the council. They auction them off from time to time. They're popular with travellers, well built. He was going to use it to live in when he came back from Brussels. Then they had to get out of the house and because he was in Brussels he told Brendan he could use it until he came back.'

'Why didn't Brendan come and stay with you?'

'I wouldn't have him. He'd been with me before Bullingdon Road. I kicked him out. He knew he couldn't come and live with me.' She didn't offer any explanation.

'Did you kick him out because you knew he was stealing from the hospital? Did Kieran know that Brendan was stealing drugs from the hospital?'

There was no answer from Nuala.

'Did he blackmail him into helping him? Is that what happened, Nuala?'

'Brendan's not a violent man,' Nuala said.

'That's what you said last night.'

There was silence on the end of the line.

'Why are you telling me this?'

Sam heard a sigh. 'I'm worried about Brendan. I want to know he's all right.'

'And Kieran?'

For a moment there was silence. 'Kieran's a lost man,' she said eventually and then the line went dead.

Sam filled her father in on the conversation and then immediately phoned Phil and told him what Nuala had said.

'Robbie's the only one of the tenants we haven't been able to get hold of. I'll try him again and see if we can get the registration number of the mobile library off one of the other people who lived in Bullingdon Road.'

Sam closed up her phone and looked at her father. All they could do now was wait. The idea of spending the rest of the day in this room with him waiting for a call to come in made her feel mad. Her conversation with Vera had triggered something in her brain. It would involve another trip to see Barry. Her father would just have to tag along.

They left Mark's rooms and walked towards the main entrance to the college.

'You're comfortable in all this, aren't you?' His glance and the wave of his hand took in the college as a whole. 'You feel at home.'

'I'm used to it, that's all. It doesn't bother me because I don't take it too seriously.'

As they stepped out into the Turl he exhaled heavily as if he'd been holding his breath.

At the butcher's Sam introduced her father as a work colleague; it seemed the simplest thing to do.

'The boy who sold the head,' she said to Barry. 'Is he linked in any way to St Barnabas's College?'

'His aunt's worked there for years. His brother's doing work experience there I think. Why?'

'Vera Smith is his aunt?'

He nodded. 'Is there a problem? He'll be back in on Monday if you want to talk to him.'

'No,' Sam said. 'No problem.'

As they were walking away Geoffrey said, 'Are you going to tell me what this is all about?'

She shook her head. 'A little local difficulty is how the Provost described it.'

Back in the college they found Vera in a room halfway up staircase five, emptying a green metal bin into a black plastic bag. The room looked as if a bomb had hit it.

Geoffrey looked round the room in disgust. 'Could do with a stint in the army,' he muttered.

'Anything the matter, dear?' Vera said, putting the bin back under the desk and straightening up.

'Is Bernie upset by the fact you're going at the end of the summer?'

'Bernie? Why?'

'Has he said anything to you about how he feels about it?'

'Well . . .'

'Do you think he could have been angry enough to do these things?'

'Bernie?'

'Perhaps with his brother's help.'

'No. I've worked here all my life. I don't think he'd do anything like that.'

'But he hasn't got a job to lose, has he?'

Vera didn't say anything.

'Will you talk to him, Vera? I don't want to go to Mrs Prendergast with this, but if there's another incident I'm not going to have much choice.'

'I don't believe this for a minute.'

'I think his brother lied to me. He told me he'd sold the head to a schoolboy for an art class to put me off the trail, and he succeeded, but I think he gave that head to his brother and someone saw him so he had to come up with a story about it.'

'Why do you automatically blame the staff?'

'I didn't, Vera. I automatically blamed everyone else: Mrs Prendergast, Professor Petheridge, Kenneth Adams and his nephew. I didn't think the staff were involved.'

'Professor Adams's nephew!' Vera laughed. 'He doesn't have it in him. Bernie told me a few tales about him when he was helping pack up Professor Adams's rooms.'

'So Bernie knew what he did for a living?'

'Yes, but you've got no proof about the boys, have you?'

'Is there a connection between your nephews and Queen's?'

Vera didn't say anything.

'Is there?'

'They both picked up a bit of work here and there. My brother-in-law works in the kitchens there.'

'Talk to them, Vera, or it'll be out of my hands.'

'Why don't you go straight to Mrs Prendergast if you're so certain?'

'Because I don't want to land them in trouble. The note and the pig's head were relatively harmless pranks, but digging up the lawn is criminal damage. Also, Vera, if they feel upset with the way you've been treated maybe I feel a degree of sympathy with them.'

A young man appeared in the doorway of the room.

'Oh,' he said and blushed.

'It's all right, love. I'm done here,' Vera said.

They all moved out onto the staircase. 'So you'll talk to them,' Sam said.

Vera nodded.

Back in Mark's rooms a couple of hours later her father pushed open the bathroom door and said, 'Could you give me a hand?'

'What is it?'

'I can't get the dressings off my back. Could you do it?'

'Is that a good idea?'

'I should let some air get to it.'

He turned round so his back was towards her. Blood had seeped through, creating hardened black patches against the white material of the dressings.

'I'm not sure how to do this,' she said, picking cautiously at some plaster.

'Tear it.'

She began to tug carefully at the edge of the dressing.

He turned round, his face weary. 'No, seriously, Sam, tear it off. It'll hurt less in the long run.'

So she did.

He swore under his breath and bent over the bath. Sam was presented with something that looked like hamburger mince.

'I'm not sure that was such a good idea,' she said, grabbing a towel and stuffing it into the waistband of her father's trousers as the blood began to trickle down his spine.

He straightened up and dug in a black wash bag and took out a bottle of clear liquid. He handed it to Sam. 'Could you pour this over it?'

Sam looked at the label. 'Are you mad? This'll hurt like hell.'

'I don't want to go to a doctor and I don't want it to get infected. I'd do it myself but I can't reach. I'd make a right mess of it.'

'OK, lean back over the bath or it's going to go all over the floor.'

He placed his hands on the furthest side of the bath and Sam opened the bottle and poured. The fluid ran all over his back, diluting the colour of the blood from red to a frothy pink and dripping off his sides into the bath. Sam grabbed some cotton wool and mopped at the mess as best she could.

He straightened up slowly and sat on the edge of the bath. 'Thanks.'

He shifted his weight and closed his eyes. Sam looked at his back and wondered if she had torn the bandages off too fast. Had she intended to hurt him?

She left him sitting on the side of the bath and sought refuge in the main room.

A couple of minutes later he joined her, wearing a white T-shirt under a blue denim shirt.

'Do you blame me?' he asked.

Sam felt wrong-footed. There were so many things she could blame him for. Where could she start?

'For what?' seemed a safe reply.

'What's happened to Mark.'

Sam sighed. 'Blame isn't going to get us anywhere. Anyway, you said you saved this man's life.'

'You could blame me for not shooting him.'

'Why would I do that? You said he was only a boy.'

He perched on a chair. 'What if it doesn't turn out so well?'

'What do you mean?'

'If something happens to Mark will you feel the same way then?'

'Nothing's going to happen to Mark. But what I don't understand is why you decided to come back now. Why did you decide to make contact? You'd been away twenty-eight years.'

'I thought you had the right to know that your father was still alive.'

'Sure, but I'd had that right for twenty-eight years, hadn't I? It didn't worry you before, did it?'

He had been looking at the floor, his elbows resting on his knees. 'As you get older you realise that you don't have all the time in the world. I thought about the things that I needed to settle. I was curious about what kind of people you and Mark had become.'

'And what did you find?'

'I discovered that I had good reason to be proud of you both.'

Sam turned away from her father and looked out of the window.

'Look, Sam, there's something I've been meaning to say to you—'

Sam's phone rang. She pulled it out of the pocket of her trousers and took the call.

'Give me your father to talk to.'

Adrenaline prickled the palms of her hands.

'We know who you are, Kieran. We spoke to Nuala and we know what happened. She's very worried about you and Brendan. She wants—'

'Shut the fuck up,' the voice screamed. 'Put your father on the line.'

Sam handed the phone to her father and was forced to listen to only one side of the conversation.

'Yes ... yes, I do ... what makes you think I give a fuck about him? Well, you're barking up the wrong tree there, mate. If you've got him there you can check for yourself. Look at his forehead. Ask him who did that to him. So I don't give a shit what you do to him. Go right ahead.' He took the phone away from his ear and cut the call.

Sam grabbed hold of the front of his shirt. 'What the fuck do you think you're doing?'

Her father held one hand out to push her away and looked at the phone he was holding in the other. 'I have to make him think I don't care about Mark. Don't you see? If he knows he can get at me through him and his aim is to hurt me he'll use it. Don't worry – he'll phone again.'

'But what if he doesn't?' Sam shouted. 'What if he goes straight off and kills him?'

'He won't, Sam. He wants me and I've just concentrated his mind on that.'

The phone rang again.

Her father hit the call button. 'No, you shut up and listen to me. You want me, don't you? Well, here I am. Tell me where and when and I'll be there alone. Just you and me. Just how it was before. Now put Mark on the phone.'

Geoffrey fell silent, listening for a short while longer and then cut the call.

'Well?' Sam said.

Her father was holding the phone in his hand staring at the screen. He stood up. 'Come on, we need to get going.'

'Where to?'

'I'll tell you when we're on the road. Where are your keys?'

'They're in my pocket,' Sam said, picking her coat off the back of the chair she'd been sitting on.

'Is he alive?'

'Yes.'

'How did he sound?'

'I'll get my coat.'

Sam stood at the door keys in hand. 'How did he—'

Her hand was on the lock when she felt his thumb against the side of her neck. She knew at once what he was doing. She knew that if she didn't get the pressure off her neck she'd pass out. She began to turn round but found herself pinned fast by him. She tried to stamp on his instep but he was too quick for her. Everything she tried, he countered carefully and with the minimum of force.

'I'm sorry, Sam,' she heard him say. 'Big Boys' Rules.' And then she saw spots dancing in front of her eyes and everything went dark.

She came to with her hands and feet tied. Well, at least he hadn't gagged her. What a fucking fool she'd been! She'd said it to the police, hadn't she? He's not a team player. He's a loner. Of course he was and now he'd ditched her and set off to find the man who had taken Mark. By himself. Mind you, he probably wasn't that worried about how long she was unconscious. All he needed was enough time to get to the car and drive away. She rolled over to the sofa and edged herself onto the seat and then stood upright and hopped to Mark's desk. Turning her back to the phone, she knocked the receiver off its cradle and then, looking over her shoulder, dialled the lodge, then turned round and placed her ear to the receiver.

'Bill, I'm in Mark's rooms, could you come over?'

Ten minutes later she was standing in the middle of the room, rubbing her wrists and thanking the porter. When he had gone back to the lodge Sam looked around for her phone. Had he handed it back to her? She checked in her jacket. He'd taken it. Of course he had, it was his only contact with whoever had Mark. She phoned her mobile. It rang and rang until her voicemail kicked in. She didn't leave a message. She thought back to what she'd heard of his side of the conversation. What exactly had he said? And more to the point, where had he gone?

She tried to ring Max's mobile and again got no reply, then she tried Paula who told her he'd been in the office that morning but had then left at lunchtime and had not come back or said what he'd be doing. Surely he would have phoned Max, Sam thought, he'd need the hardware Max could provide.

She walked into the bathroom and looked down at the blood-stained towel. *What makes you think I give a fuck about him?* Had her father really said that? Was it artificial or was that exactly how he felt? Jesus, what had he been thinking of? *Reduce emotionality.* Well, he'd hardly done that, had he? More like increase it a thousand fold. He'd thrown Mark into a glass cabinet when he was twelve and scarred him for life. Was the man who had done that really going to help save him? Or was he just intent on getting himself killed?

She'd tried her father and Max and got nowhere. Now what should she do?

She phoned Phil and told him about the call her father had taken.

'He didn't tell you where he was going?'

'No, but he's taken my car.'

'Give me the number plate.'

She told him. 'He was goading him, Phil, telling him he didn't care what happened to Mark.'

'He was trying to deflect attention away from Mark onto himself.'

'Well, that's what he said. But is that actually how it works?'

'He wants your father. It's all been a means to that end.'

And the end, Sam thought, how on earth is this all going to end?

'I'm really worried, Phil. What's he going to do with Mark? What on earth is he going to do?'

'Your father gave you absolutely no idea where he was going.'

'None.'

'One thing I should tell you, Sam. We've found Brendan.'

'Where?'

'He's dead, Sam. Some council workers cutting back the hedges found his body in a ditch on the A44 heading towards Woodstock.'

'How did he die?'

'Same MO as Dougie Malone – his throat was cut.'

Sam felt a chill run through her. Kieran was killing everyone who got in his way. The only two left now were her father and Mark. Nuala had said that Brendan wasn't a violent man. At the back of her mind she realised she had been hanging onto the hope that Brendan might act as some sort of moderating influence on Kieran. But now there was no one, no one to stop him. She hadn't had much time for Brendan; after all he was a drug dealer who had contributed to Adrian Hunter's death and most likely set Mark up, but she did feel sorry for Nuala and at the same time guiltily relieved it wasn't Mark who had died.

'Kieran visited Blenheim with Nuala about a week before Mark went missing.'

'There's nothing you can do now, Sam. He needed the contact with you to deliver your father. You've done that, so you're out of the loop. Let's hope Mark is as well.'

'Be careful,' Sam said. 'My father'll probably be armed. He won't go without some sort of back-up.'

But as she put down the phone, the thought slid into her mind: Unless this has nothing to do with saving Mark and everything to do with him getting himself killed.

*

Mark felt the bottle placed to his lips; he sucked greedily at the water but he was only allowed the smallest of sips. Just enough, the voice said, to keep you alive. I haven't decided whether to kill you or not.

And you know what your father said? That he didn't give a toss about you. He'd hurt you himself, he said, so go ahead do what you want. He doesn't think you're worth saving. I'm undecided. How does that make you feel?

The voice continued to drone on in the background but now it was like walking past a parked car that had the radio on but the windows closed. Mark could hear a noise but nothing distinct. Is this what it would be like to die, he thought, this fading in and out, the loss of the frequency? He drifted off. The only thing he could feel was the thumping pain pulsing through his body; there was no refuge from it.

Mark was dragged into consciousness by the scream of metal. But no one spoke to him. There was just the noise followed by silence. Then he felt it, something he hadn't felt for days – fresh air. Fear seized him. He was going to kill him and dump him. He didn't move a muscle. He lay completely still, feeling the fresh air on his face, listening as acutely as he could. Then there were hands on his blindfold and he jerked away from them. The blindfold was pulled off and he opened his eyes, then screwed them shut again, groaning as light blazed against his light-starved retinas. Now the tape was torn from his mouth and someone was cutting free his feet and hands. He tried opening his eyes again and this time saw a uniform.

'Are you all right, sir? Are you hurt anywhere?'

'Water,' he croaked. 'Please get me some water.' His voice was a hoarse croak, a rasp; he tried to get some spit into his mouth but failed.

'We'll get you some.'

'My name . . .' Mark began.

'It's all right, sir, we know who you are. Tell me where you're hurt.'

Someone tried to press a bottle into his damaged hand and he cried out. Then the bottle was held to his mouth and water, God the blessed relief of it, gurgled down his throat. He drank and drank, desperate for every last drop of it. When he'd finished he tried again.

'My name's Mark Falconer please ... tell my sister you've found me.'

'We will. The paramedics will be here soon and then we'll be able to move you.'

He tried to open his eyes again but the images in front of him were blurring. In the distance he heard the sound of an ambulance. The pain in his damaged hand was a steady, grinding throb. He cradled his hand against his chest then felt himself slipping sideways. Someone placed something soft under his head.

'It's all right, mate, hold on, they'll be here soon.'

A hand on his face. 'Stay with me, Mark.'

But he couldn't hold on any more. He allowed his consciousness to drift away past the two men crouched over him, out of the van and into the light beyond.

Sam was at her parents' when the call came through.

'It's Phil – we've found Mark.'

Sam tried to say something but the words wouldn't come out.

'He's suffering from shock and dehydration, Sam. He's in the Radcliffe.'

'How is he?'

'That's the thing, Sam – he hasn't said anything yet. He hasn't regained consciousness.'

'What?'

'He's not come round yet.'

'Phil?'

'He's in a coma, Sam.'

'He's going to come out of it, right?'

'They think it's the shock – the mind closes down in order to recuperate.'

Sam's brain was whirring. She knew he was going to be all right. He had to be. She had to get there. Then another thought cut across her mind.

'What about my father?'

'We haven't picked him up yet.'

'We have to tell him Mark's been found. He doesn't have to continue with the meeting. He doesn't have to put himself in danger.

I'll phone him and leave a message – maybe he'll pick it up. It's over, isn't it?'

'We still haven't found him, Sam. I doubt your father will think it's over. If Kieran McGann's still at large he could do this all over again.'

Sam put down the phone.

Her mother was standing beside her. 'Have they found him?' she asked.

Sam nodded. She tried to speak but a feeling of utter anguish made her double over, her face buried in her hands.

CHAPTER TWENTY-THREE

It was early evening of the same day. Sam sat by the side of Mark's hospital bed, staring at the bleeping monitors and then back at her brother. His right hand was heavily bandaged and his arm was covered in red blotches and horribly swollen. Her mother and Peter were off getting themselves some coffee. He had septicaemia, they weren't sure they were going to be able to save his arm; he hadn't come round since being admitted to hospital. Hearing is the last sense to go, her mother told Sam. What do you mean – last? Sam said. He's not going to die, is he? Talk to him, the nurse said.

Sam cleared her throat. 'I'm here,' she said and then stopped, feeling foolish, not knowing how to continue. She considered a few alternative sentences. Don't go dying on me because I'll never forgive you. I won't be able to live without you. And rejected them both on the grounds of being either inappropriately flippant or overly melodramatic.

She took hold of his uninjured hand and laced her fingers through his, looked at the red welt on his wrist where he'd been tied. He wasn't going to die. He mustn't. She sipped some water from a white plastic beaker and tried again.

'Do you remember when I was being teased at school about my thumb? How the other children wouldn't hold hands with me in the crocodile because they said I had a wart on my thumb? Do you remember you said it was a great thing, a unique thing to have been born with? You said it was something that bonded us together because we both had it – you the extra finger, me the extra thumb and that that was something to be proud of – our link to each other. How we'd always have that, whatever happened. Do you remember, Mark?

You said, tell them you're proud of it. You said it was proof I was going to be a great fighter because I fought back from it being infected when it was amputated. Well, you were right, Mark, and now it's you and you're going to fight back from this as well and you're going to be OK. I know you are because . . .'

Because life is unimaginable without you . . . Because we're bone and marrow and we can't be separated. What's bone without marrow? Marrow without bone?

She held the back of his hand against her forehead and began to bargain with whatever was out there, with a God she didn't even believe in. But she didn't care, she'd bargain with anything – little green men with bulgy eyes, the devil, the void, whatever, as long as the end result was her brother's life.

She felt a slight pressure from his hand, as if he'd tried to squeeze hers. She looked at his face. Nothing had changed. The monitors continued to bleep, his chest continued to rise and fall. His eyes were still closed. But the squeeze had been enough to give her hope. She kissed the back of his hand and placed it back on the bed.

'Everything's going to be all right,' she said. 'You just need to rest. You need to recover your strength. You're going to be fine, Mark. Everything's going to be all right. It's just you're not ready for the world yet. Stay there and rest.'

She heard the quaver of doubt in her voice. That has to go, she thought, from this time on she couldn't afford to doubt. She settled herself back in the chair and folded her arms, her eyes locked onto his face. He was alive. At least he was alive.

Alfie Green, the parking attendant in the car park at Blenheim Palace, Woodstock, looked at the only car left and sighed. It was half an hour past closing time and the last stragglers were still making their way slowly out of the park – it had been the first really hot day of summer, a day for skirts and sandals and shorts, and the park had had its busiest day of the year. A little boy baked pink by the sun and screaming his lungs out was being dragged along by his equally puce-faced mother. Alfie shook his head. Would they never learn?

He walked over to the blue car and peered through the window. It was grubby outside and inside. He kicked one of the tyres; they needed some air. Some stupid sod was still in the park.

The trouble was he remembered the man: a tough-looking bugger, moving stiffly as if he had some sort of problem with his back. He'd stood out – first because he was alone. No wife or kids and no dog. And he didn't look like the kind of man who would take himself off for a walk for the pure pleasure of it. Then there were his clothes. Amongst the shorts-and-sandals brigade his donkey jacket had marked him out. Why was he wearing that on a day that had reached the mid-seventies?

Yes, that was it, too many clothes and no dog and now it was closing time and he hadn't come out, unless he'd exited out of the upper gate and was walking his way back to his car through the village.

Alfie Green was an ex-copper and it was his ex-copper's instinct that made him pick up the phone and contact his brother-in-law, a DS in the Thames Valley Police. The fact that he'd heard that George had a car for sale and he fancied knowing the price might also have had something to do with him making the call. After arranging to meet up for a drink with him the following week, Alfie gave him the registration number of the car and hung up.

It was almost dark now but Geoffrey Falconer had no intention of coming out of the park. He had spent the afternoon familiarising himself with the place. He had paid no attention whatsoever to the beauty of his surroundings, to the lake built by Capability Brown, to the heavy grandeur of the palace itself. Although it had occurred to him in passing that there was a time when the nation really rewarded its soldiers. He had picked up the message from Sam, telling him that Mark had been found, but still he had come. The man had wanted him. He had to be stopped otherwise what was going to prevent him coming after Mark again or Sam or the rest of his family? If he wants me he can have me, Geoffrey thought. He found himself a place in the woods that ran down to the side of the lake.

Midnight at the monument, the voice had said.

Geoffrey looked at his watch, tried and failed to get himself into a comfortable position, then settled down to wait.

Sam felt a hand on her shoulder and looked round, expecting to see her mother and Peter but it was a nurse.

'Are you Sam Falconer?'

'Yes.'

'We've got a call for you.'

Sam followed the nurse to a desk and picked up the phone.

'Sam, it's Phil. Your car's been found in Woodstock at the car park at Blenheim Palace.'

'When?'

'There was a bit of a fuck-up. The call came in at eight but it was only passed on to us now.'

'Blenheim?'

She remembered her conversation with Kieran in the King's Head.

Sam looked at her watch. She'd lost all track of time. It was eleven o'clock at night.

'Can you get someone to pick me up and take me over?'

'Sam, there's nothing you can do.'

Sam struggled to think of a good reason for Phil to do what she'd asked, couldn't and so resorted to begging. 'Please, Phil. You know I'll go there anyway. If you get me picked up at least you'll know I'm not going to go off like a loose cannon.'

She heard him sigh. 'OK, be outside in fifteen minutes. I'll pick you up myself.'

Sam went to find her mother and Peter and tell them what was happening and fifteen minutes later she was in a police car, speeding towards Woodstock.

'What are you going to do?' she asked Phil.

'We've got armed units searching the grounds.'

It was completely dark now in the woods. Geoffrey looked at his watch. Time to get going. He stood up and began to make his way through the trees. He had only taken a couple of steps when he felt a rope slip round his neck and tighten. A memory of going hunting with his father flashed into his mind, of a rabbit trapped by a water butt, the spade pressing down on its neck, its frantic dying screams and the noise of bones breaking bringing the relief of silence. He'd been five years old, and it was the first time he'd ever seen anything killed.

'Stay still,' he heard whispered in his ear, 'or I'll snap your neck.'

Hands pulled his coat down over his arms and searched him. Suddenly the pressure came off his neck and he felt himself pushed violently forwards. He fell against a tree then righted himself and turned round. He looked into the face of the man he had saved thirty years ago, the face of Kieran McGann, who was standing a few feet away from him, gun trained steadily at the centre of his body.

'So, here we are,' McGann said. 'Back in the woods.'

'What now?'

'We go for a walk.'

'But we're already in the woods.'

'That way,' McGann said and nodded in the direction of the monument.

Geoffrey turned and began to walk towards the column.

'Don't you want to know where your son is?'

'I know where he is.'

'Then why did you come?'

'Would you have given up looking for me?'

The two men walked on in silence. It was a mild night. Over to the right of them Blenheim Palace was lit up in majestic splendour and the faint sound of music could be heard floating across the lake. They came out from the cover of the woods and now they were out in the open with the column ahead of them. When he reached the base Geoffrey Falconer stopped and turned round.

'Do you wish I'd killed you?'

'This has nothing to do with what happened then. The IRA want you dead.'

'And you?'

'It's not personal.'

'Fucking bollocks it isn't. You cut off my son's finger. That's as personal as it gets.'

'Why did you pick me up in the first place?'

'We were never told why. We were just given the names.'

'Even with the bullet they didn't believe me.'

He shrugged. 'I did my best.'

'Why me anyway? Why did you decide to save me?'

'I just couldn't kill another person. I'd had it with that. You reach a point and you don't want another dead man on your conscience.'

'Even an IRA man.'

'I didn't care who you were or what you'd done. It was over for me.'

'Why stop with me though?'

'You were so young. We'd not had someone as young as you before.'

'Just my age?'

'It was a big part of it.'

They were silent for a few seconds.

'What happens now?'

'Kneel down.'

'No,' Geoffrey said. 'If you're going to shoot me you can shoot me standing.'

'You'll kneel down now or—'

'No, I won't.'

McGann walked over to him and kicked his legs out from under him. He fell heavily onto his side. He lay still, looking up at the star-studded sky. He thought of the quotation written on the clock tower at SAS headquarters in Hereford:

We are the pilgrims, master.
We shall go always a little further;
It may be beyond the last blue mountain
Barred with snow, across the angry or that glimmering sea...

Would they carve his name there now? He looked into the barrel of McGann's gun and waited.

'I have to do this,' McGann said.

Am I just going to lie here and let him kill me or am I going to do something about it? But even as he thought that he knew the answer, his heels were digging into the earth trying to get some purchase and he was wondering where the first bullet would be aimed. Straight to the head? Or would he aim for the heart?

McGann was moving the gun over his body, as if deciding.

'I saved you,' Geoffrey said. 'It's not my fault your life turned out the way it did.'

McGann's mouth opened. 'It's not about—'

Then he heard the shot and began to twist his body sideways away from the path of the bullet.

*

Sam was walking over the bridge with Phil when she heard the gun go off. Phil's hand clamped onto her arm but she pulled herself free of him and began to hare towards where the noise had come from, towards where the column stood, looming in front of them.

Geoffrey Falconer opened his eyes and stared into the eyes of the man who had been about to kill him. He smelled blood and felt the last spasms of life leave McGann's body. He scrabbled out backwards from under the blood and the brains and the pieces of skull and then the police were there pulling him even further away and turning him flat onto the ground, the grass tickling his cheek and then the smell of blood was replaced with earth and the green tang of spring. He was alive and didn't know whether to laugh or cry.

A young, burly constable stopped Sam before she got to the monument and that gave Phil enough time to catch up with her.

'Come on, you've got to let me go,' she remonstrated.

'Wait,' he said. 'I'll go and find out.'

'Watch her,' he said to the constable. 'She never does what she's told.'

Dead or alive? Alive or dead? She wasn't sure which one would upset her more.

'How are you involved?' the constable asked.

'It's my father.'

My father. The words seemed to hum in every cell of her body. My father. Bone and marrow as much as Mark. Mark was in a coma in hospital. As long as Mark is OK you can have Dad, she thought, and then felt ashamed of herself.

'He's OK.' Phil was standing next to her.

So that's it, she thought, Mark's going to die. The gods must be out to claim one or other of them. They must be. You can't have him, she thought, I won't let you. He's coming back from the dead. You don't get my brother, not at the age of forty, you don't.

'Can I see him?'

He nodded and she followed him up to the base of the monument, where her father stood shivering. Underneath the blood trickling down his face, his skin was grey. It began to rain, light, warm spring rain, light but persistent. Phil left them and walked over to where a group of police officers stood around the body.

Geoffrey's teeth were chattering. 'Sorry,' he said. 'I didn't think you'd take no for an answer. I didn't want you along.'

'You could at least have taken Max with you.'

'It's not his battle, is it?'

'Iraq wasn't yours but you still went and got yourself blown up.'

'I didn't have anything better to do at the time.'

'Did you even have a gun?'

He shook his head.

'You went unarmed and unprotected to meet a man who wanted to kill you?'

He said nothing, staring at her through a mask of blood.

Suddenly she was furious with him. 'You fucking fool.'

Phil had walked back over to them. Geoffrey grabbed his arm. 'Could you point out to me the one who took the shot?'

Phil pointed to a man standing slightly to the side of the group of officers. 'Jimmy's the best shot in the unit.'

Sam watched as her father walked over to him, touched his arm and held out his hand. Jimmy looked down at the hand and then took it. A few moments later he walked back to Sam. The rain had created streaks through the blood on his face. The wheel had turned full circle and here they were again. But this time he wasn't crying and she wasn't screaming. Not yet anyway.

'How's Mark?'

'He's in a coma. He's got blood poisoning. He was very dehydrated and weak. They're saying he's got very little strength to fight the infection.'

He brought his hand up to his face. When he brought it back down it was covered with blood and he looked at the palm of his hand, puzzled.

Phil came back over. 'We need to take you to the station and get a statement.'

'I want to see my son.'

'Mum and Peter are there at the moment,' Sam said. 'That's not such a good idea.'

'We can drive you over to the hospital afterwards.'

'Where's my car?' Sam asked.

'In the car park.' He reached into his pockets and took out the keys and then handed her back the phone.

Sam picked up her car and drove back to the hospital. Her mother and Peter were still there. She sent them home to get some rest. She sat down next to Mark and picked up his hand. 'It's over now,' she said. 'You're quite safe. Everything can go back to normal – everything's going to be fine, Mark.'

But it wasn't. Day followed day. In the blink of an eye, a week had passed and still Mark hadn't woken up. Sam stayed at her parents' and visited every day. She contacted everyone she could think of and set up rotas of people to visit him. She didn't want him left alone, not even for a moment. She phoned and organised and the people poured past his bedside – Valerie, his students, people he'd known at school, the Provost, old lovers, irritating exes, Phil. Sam didn't really care who they were as long as they were people who knew him, as long as they were willing to come and sit and talk to him. As is often the way with these things, people she would never have thought of as being in any way helpful turned out to be gems and people she thought she could rely on faded into the middle distance with lame excuses.

Mrs Prendergast was one of the gems, coming every day without fail after work for half an hour, sitting next to him and gossiping about what was going on in the college. Sam thought it was probably ideal for her – talking to someone who couldn't answer back.

Adams also came with his nephew and they bickered by Mark's bedside. When they weren't bickering Adams read to him from Gibbon's *Decline and Fall of the Roman Empire*. It wasn't exactly a barrel of laughs. They had argued about the merits of its prose, he said.

'Maybe he'll wake up just to get me to stop.'

Vera Smith came as well. 'I talked to them,' she said. 'That should be the end of it. You won't tell, will you?'

Sam shook her head. 'No, I won't.'

After all, what was it in the end? A note, a pig's head, a bit of tearing up the turf. As Valerie had said, schoolboy pranks, a harmless enough revenge for what was happening to their aunty.

'It's difficult, you see,' Vera said. 'They see the young people in the colleges having so much. It's difficult for them not to feel . . .'

'How big the gap is?' Sam said.

'Yes.

Town and gown, an age-old resentment, was as active in many ways now as it had ever been. How could it not be with the estates of Barton and Blackbird Leys only a few miles from the cloisters and the quadrangles of the university?

'They were upset for you, Vera.'

'I knew what to expect,' Vera said. 'I'd worked here forty years but they're younger, they take these things harder . . .'

'The unfairness of it,' Sam said.

'Yes, love, I suppose so. For me, the inequality is just the way it is.'

Sam didn't care what people who visited Mark did as long as they talked to him, as long as they treated him as a living, sentient being. She spent an afternoon in his rooms and put together a tape of music: Culture Club – 'Karma Chameleon', Bronski Beat – 'Small Town Boy', Marc Almond – 'Tainted Love', Abba – 'Waterloo', Fine Young Cannibals – 'She Drives Me Crazy', Paul Simon – 'You Can Call Me Al'. Alan Price singing 'Simon Smith and his Amazing Dancing Bear', Paul Weller and Style Council bringing down the walls of Jericho, Madness and 'Baggy Trousers'.

Mark's tastes were cheesy, ridiculously upbeat, happy, the kind of stuff to get your feet tapping. He'd never been a Leonard Cohen sort of a bloke. The nurses liked the tape, especially the older ones. One of them asked for a copy.

'I thought it'd be all classical music, given what he did for a living,' she said.

'Does,' Sam said. 'He probably would have stuck some on there, to be honest, but I wouldn't know what to choose. This is all the stuff I remember him playing when I was little.'

The nurses, of course, had no idea what he was like, so Sam told them what he liked, what he disliked, what his passions were, on and on she told them.

And with Mark himself she was remorseless, plundering childhood memories and especially ones of the theatre, which Mark loved: 'Do you remember,' she said. 'Do you remember going to see Tom Conti in *Whose Life is it Anyway*? Do you remember Derek Jacobi in *Hamlet* and Bob Hoskins as Touchstone in *As You Like It*? And Ian McDiarmid in *Mephisto*? Do you remember *Kiss Me Kate*? What was the song you loved, "Brush Up Your Shakespeare"? Do you remember, Mark? Derek Jacobi's back on-stage in *Don Carlos* in London and I'm going to get tickets. We'll go and see it together. You have to get better for that.'

When she phoned up to book the tickets the woman asked her what date she wanted.

'How long is the run?'

'Four months.'

She paused.

'Hello?'

'Closing night,' she said. 'Middle of the stalls.'

Every day she woke she said to herself, this is the day he is going to wake up. Today it will happen. It was late May. North Oxford looked beautiful, laburnum, cherry and wisteria were all in flower – the colours took the breath away. There was new life and new growth everywhere. Birds were building their nests and still Mark lay unconscious in the hospital – getting neither better nor worse. Stable. But no one seemed to know if the horse had bolted.

Her father phoned frequently. He said he couldn't visit because he might be in danger and his son's bedside was an obvious place to find him. If, that is, there were others looking for him, and he had no reason to think there weren't.

The days went past and then obviously he changed his mind because when Sam went in a nurse asked her about a short, blond man who had come late one night and she had confirmed yes it sounded like her father, and yes, it was OK for him to be there.

And then one day Sam woke up feeling the worst that she had ever felt, as if the bottom had fallen out of her world. She woke with such a strong feeling of dread and hopelessness that she thought: I can't go to the hospital. I can't face it. I can't play that tape one more fucking time. I can't talk to him as if he's there when he isn't.

She phoned Reg and sobbed down the phone. 'I can't go on any more. It's too much. I don't know what to do any more. Who am I kidding? I'm deluding myself and everyone else. I can't go there today. I can't go near the hospital. I just can't go on.'

'You're exhausted,' he said. 'When was the last time you took a break from it?'

'I haven't. I go every day.'

'Take the day off . . .'

'But . . .'

'You can go in the evening if you want to but today go for a walk, do something different. Otherwise you won't be able to carry on. Take a break, Sam. If you break down it won't do anyone any good, least of all Mark. Give yourself the option not to go at all. You've got other people lined up to see him, haven't you?'

'Yes – lots of people will be there today.'

'Well then . . . but, Sam, get someone to go with you. Don't be alone with it all when you don't have to be.'

Sam phoned Phil and spent the day with him. They went for a walk in the Botanical Gardens and then went to the Trout. They sat in the sun outside the pub eating their lunch. It was the first time Sam had had a chance to ask Phil to fill in some gaps.

'What have you found out?' she asked.

'Nuala said the whole thing was triggered by Kieran's mother being seriously ill. Kieran put out some feelers to see if he could safely go back to Belfast to see her and the message came back loud and clear: you set foot in Northern Ireland and you'll be killed. He was frantic. Then they told him that they'd let him back into the country but the deal was he had to kill your father. The article had come out in the *Daily Tribune* and everyone knew what your father had done and there was information about you and your family. He'd known Brendan through Nuala for years and knew what he was up to with the drugs and the dealing in Oxford. He blackmailed Brendan into making contact with Mark. Brendan already had contacts with St Barnabas's through Adrian, so it wasn't that hard for him to arrange to meet Mark. At first she thinks he was trying to find out through conversation with Mark and you where your father was, but when that didn't work he pursued a more extreme path. The phone that we found on Brendan's body was the one used to make the last call to Mark before he went missing. So presumably Brendan was involved in setting Mark up to be kidnapped. Kieran knew from Brendan that Bullingdon Road was deserted and he also knew about the mobile library. His mother's health was deteriorating rapidly and he was becoming desperate.'

'Did he kill Brendan?'

Phil nodded. 'We found a knife on Kieran's body and there's DNA on there that matches both Dougie Malone's and Brendan's. Nuala's adamant that her brother wouldn't have condoned Mark's finger being cut off. Maybe he and Kieran argued over that, but we'll never know.'

'And his mother?'

'She died on the same day he did.'

Sam tried to tackle a piece of beef and then gave up and pushed it to the side of her plate. Since Mark had been in hospital she'd lost her appetite completely. She was eating in the same way she put petrol in the car, because she knew if she didn't she wouldn't be able to function.

'Presumably the person who hit me over the head in Mark's rooms was either Kieran or Brendan looking for information as to the whereabouts of my father.'

'That looks like the most likely explanation. They would have had his keys. One other thing, Sam. We pulled in Kieran's cousin, Richard.'

'Oh.'

'Was he the one who came up with that list of names? The one who came to your office?'

'What does it matter now, Phil?'

'The reason we called him in was because there were calls between Kieran's phone and his.'

'So – he's his cousin. He got him work with the theatre production he was putting on. Kieran was supposed to come to Oxford to help him set up but he couldn't get hold of him. Of course there were phone calls between them. Also if Kieran's mother was ill—'

'When we pulled him in, Sam, he wouldn't say a word to us. He just turned his face to the wall. You know what they said about the people they tried to interview after the McCartney murder. Well, that's exactly what he did. That's not the behaviour of a man who's looking for reconciliation, it's the behaviour of a man who's got something to hide.'

'He told me he spent half his twenties being pulled in by the police, so he's had lots of practice. Why should he help you? A police marksman just shot dead his cousin and his aunt died on the same day.'

Phil shook his head in disbelief. 'Have it your own way, Sam. But perhaps you should consider that when it comes to this man, Richard McGann, you may have a serious blind spot.'

'There's no proof that he was involved.'

'Just because there isn't any proof doesn't mean anything, Sam, and you know that.'

As they were walking past Worcester on the way back to Phil's house they saw a long queue snaking out of the main entrance to the college and along the street. It could only be one thing, Sam thought.

'Shall we go?' she asked Phil.

But once she'd explained what was involved his response was a resounding 'no'. 'I'll do many things for you, Sam, but sitting through a play in Greek isn't one of them.'

She kissed him goodbye and walked to the front of the queue. 'I'm a friend of Professor Petheridge's. He's expecting me,' she lied.

Seating had been put up facing the lake and was filling up rapidly. The Crazy Frog tune was thumping from loud speakers and three lime-green pontoons in the shape of lily pads floated on the water. In the distance a donkey was braying. She found Professor Petheridge standing by the front row of reserved seating.

He seized her hands and looked earnestly into her eyes. 'How is he?'

'No change,' Sam said. She gestured at the pontoons. 'How's it been going here?'

'Very well, very well. Better than I could possibly have imagined.'

'I queue-jumped. I was wondering if . . .' She gestured at the reserved seating. 'I thought it might keep my mind off things.'

Petheridge swiped a reserved notice off the wooden bench. 'Sit,' he said. 'Next to me.'

Off in the distance the donkey brayed again. Petheridge chewed on the side of his fingernail. 'I do hope she behaves tonight. She's been something of a handful. Our donkey wrangler isn't up to much.'

'What's the plot?' Sam asked.

Petheridge pressed a programme into her hands. 'I recommend the introduction. It's excellent. I wrote it.'

Sam read the first line: *Aristophanes was the original bad boy rapper of the ancient world, the Eminem of his times . . .* she scanned a bit further. *Aristophanes is as relevant today as he was two thousand years ago. What are the frogs if not a parody of the stupidity of persons afflicted by their own preoccupations – the sort of puffed-up personalities we see all around us in today's celebrity culture? Aristophanes used bawdy tasteless humour to make a satirical point. Could he have seen the* Carry On *films or* Little Britain *without wanting to recruit the participants on the spot for his next comedy?*

She was trying to digest this rather startling proposition when two men and a donkey with particularly lush ears walked onto the stage.

Sam had sat through many plays performed in Oxford gardens. The obvious – *As You Like It, Alice in Wonderland, The Importance of Being Earnest* – the obscure – so obscure she'd forgotten the names – that left you wondering if the director had some kind of financial death wish. And then there were the magical ones – *Private Lives, The Rivals, A Man for All Seasons*, the ones in which everything came together, the setting, the play and crucially the weather.

The performance of *The Frogs* that evening slid effortlessly into the latter category. Even the rain made its entrance at the right time, just when the frogs had landed on their lily pads, and it had the good manners to stop shortly thereafter. After the interval, fairy lights strung from the trees round the lake came on, the lights reflecting in the still waters of the lake. Even though she couldn't understand a word that was spoken, there was something about the whole thing that was entrancing and strangely soothing. At the end the cast received a standing ovation. Petheridge invited her to stay for the cast party and because she dreaded visiting Mark she did.

Charlie Stroud looked slightly less pasty now. Maybe the hopping around in the sun had been good for his health or maybe he'd drunk too much Pimm's too quickly.

'Well done,' Sam said. 'A triumph. No casualties.'

He smiled. 'Could I have a word?' He gestured towards the water. The fairy lights were still on, moving slightly in the breeze. They walked away from the rest of the party to the edge of the lake.

'I need to talk to someone about what happened to Adrian.'

Even though the evening was warm, Sam realised that he was shivering.

Charlie was staring out at the lake. 'I was with him the evening he died.'

Sam didn't say anything. As far as she was concerned her investigation was over.

'He came round to my room. He—'

'Hold on, Charlie. Before you say anything, let me just say this: we know he'd been in a fight the night before he died. He went back to his rooms, took a mixture of pills and drank the large part of a bottle of whisky. He passed out, was sick and died because he breathed in his own vomit. There's not enough evidence to suggest that the fight was responsible for killing him. It seems the alcohol and drugs did that. The most likely outcome of the inquest is death by misadventure. Now you can go ahead and tell me what you were going to or we can go back over there and join the others.'

Charlie opened his mouth and then shut it again. She touched his arm. 'Come on,' she said but he didn't move.

'I was in love with him,' he burst out. 'I had been all through school, and he knew it. I thought ... after he told his mother ... I don't think he was ever interested in me but he confided in me and I suppose it gave me hope ... but that evening he was just so cruel, so dismissive. I was very upset ... he said you're the kind of person who makes me wish I wasn't gay. He said he could – never, ever ... we fought. He hit his head. It was an accident. I begged him to go to the hospital but he just laughed it off. He said he was OK ... but then the following morning I heard ...'

Poor man, Sam thought. What a mess.

'The fight didn't kill him,' she said. 'There was no bruising of the brain, no fracture of the skull. The drugs and the drink did that.'

'I think I should go to the police.'

'Well, I don't think his family would thank you for it. His father is very anxious to keep anything about his son's sexuality out of the press.'

'You don't think I should tell them?'

'It's up to you, but I wouldn't. So the scrapes and bruises weren't from the pontoons?'

He blushed. 'No.'

'Fooled by a frog,' Sam said.

She looked down at the water's edge as a large green frog hopped out onto the bank. 'What do you think?' she said. 'It seems quite friendly.'

Charlie bent down and scooped it into his hands. 'I'll go and show Professor Petheridge.'

After the party she went to the hospital and sat by Mark's bed in silence. It was late and she was tired. For the first time since he'd been admitted she was lost for words. It was silent in the room and also in the hospital. What to say? What to do? Something else – something she hadn't tried before. She opened her bag, looking for inspiration and found the book of Shakespeare's sonnets she'd been carrying around since she'd looked round his room. She opened the book up and began to read them out loud from the beginning. She read and she read. She was doing OK until she hit number thirty-nine. She began well enough.

> *O! how thy worth with manners may I sing,*
> *When thou art all the better part of me?*
> *What can mine own praise to mine own self bring?*
> *And what is't but my own when I praise thee?*

Sam ground to a halt.

> *Even for this let us divided live.*

She put the book to one side and put her head in her hands. He *was* the better part of her. What would become of her without him? She'd be left with all the bad bits with nothing to temper them. She'd lose half her memory without him. She'd—

Then she felt his hand move against hers. At first she thought she'd imagined it, but then she looked at his face and saw his eyelids flutter and then open. Then she heard a cough and then she was punching the alarm that linked to the nurses' station. She was punching it and punching it and laughing and crying at the same time and kissing the book of sonnets and thanking Shakespeare and God and whoever was listening. As she turned to see if a nurse was coming she saw her father standing in the doorway.

'He's going to be all right,' she said, but before he could reply a couple of nurses pushed past him and Sam was telling them what she had seen, what she had felt; she was hugging them and dancing round the bed. A couple of minutes later when she looked for him he was gone.

But she didn't care. Mark was going to be all right.

He was on his way back.

EPILOGUE

A week later, back in her flat, Sam woke one Sunday morning to a knock on her door. She didn't move to open it. It was midday but she'd been sound asleep. She'd been sleeping a lot recently, utterly exhausted by what had happened. Back in Oxford Mark was making slow but steady progress. The inquest on Adrian Hunter's death had come and gone and recorded an open verdict. As far as she knew Charlie hadn't gone to the police. There had been no more incidents at St Barnabas's, so she presumed Vera's talk with her nephews had worked. She'd heard nothing from Rick since he left Mark's rooms early that morning but presumed he must have gone back to Ireland for the funerals. This time the letterbox opened and she heard Edie's low flat whistle. When she opened the door, Edie grabbed her arm and began to drag her down to the main entrance to the block.

'Come on, babes. You've got to see this.'

Sam stood squinting in the sun at the New King's Road.

There wasn't a car or a number twenty-two to be seen, only a thronging mass of people. The road was a solid blaze of blue. There were groups of men drinking from one can and holding another, family groups, a young father with a tiny baby asleep in a pouch on his front, an elderly couple and a lone man waving a blue and chequered flag. All of them were swathed in blue shirts and scarves, waving blue and white chequered flags. A little boy walked past wearing a jester's hat of white and blue checks with silver bells on the points. Another man wore a Russian hat. A bit odd for late May.

Sam turned to Edie. 'What's going on?'

'Where you been, babes? It's Chelsea. They won the title. First time in fifty years. They were all up at Parson's Green. I just saw their bus go past.'

A car trying to turn right out of Foskett Road into New King's Road was confronted with the huge crowd of people blocking the road and went into reverse, seeking an easier route.

'Isn't it bloody marvellous?' Edie said.

And Sam had to agree it really was. Someone stopped in front of them. He was remarkable for wearing no blue clothing whatsoever. He was wearing sunglasses and his clothes were predominantly black. Sam became suddenly conscious of her frayed pyjamas and torn sweatshirt, her disreputable sheepskin slippers.

'What are you doing here?' Sam said. 'Are you a Chelsea fan?'

'Isn't this fucking crazy?' Rick said. 'I had no idea this was going on.'

'You haven't come for the party?'

He shook his head. 'I phoned Alan last week and he told me you'd be back in town this weekend.'

'Oh, right.'

Edie was giving Rick the eye.

'Come inside,' Sam said.

'I wondered if you fancied some lunch or something,' Rick said when they were standing in Sam's hall. 'It's a beautiful day.'

'Oh right,' Sam said without enthusiasm.

I deserve sex, she thought.

'It seems too nice a day to stay inside.'

'Mmm, you think?'

I was thinking of staying in the bedroom for the foreseeable future, she thought.

'There's something I need to tell you.'

'No,' Sam said, somewhat louder than she'd intended.

'Sorry?'

'Please don't. Do you mind? Not right at this minute.'

'But . . .'

'I'm sure it can wait.'

She took hold of his hand and felt his long flat fingers. She turned his hand over and kissed the palm. Then she reached up and ran a finger along the deep lines that bracketed his mouth.

Rick was about to say something but at that moment he became distracted by something behind Sam. 'My God,' he said.

She turned round. Frank was sitting in the doorway to the front room with the light streaming in behind him. He looked like an enormous glowing hairy orange.

'Is she pregnant?' he asked.

Sam hoisted Frank into her arms. '*She* is not pregnant. *He* is very fat.'

She carried Frank down the hall and locked him in the kitchen.

'I don't mind cats,' Rick said.

'I don't care,' Sam said. This was not a time she would allow herself to be upstaged by Fat Frank.

She reached up and kissed Rick, she dug her fingers in the back of his neck and began to undo the buttons of his shirt. Rick dropped his bag on the ground and began to kiss her back, his hand slid onto her breast ... An image of the boy on the waltzer flooded her head, the music of 'Upside Down'. It was OK, even if this was a one-off and she never saw him again, even if Phil was right and she did have a blind spot when it came to him. All she could think of was how much she wanted him right now.

At last, Sam thought, as they fell on the bed.

And as the men, women and children in blue nylon shirts passed by on the New King's Road in a blaze of static, Sam and Rick set about generating some electricity of their own, to the background noise of Frank hurling himself repeatedly and furiously at the closed kitchen door.